RAT RUN

'The master of the modern adventure story' – *The Times*

'A master of his craft' – *Sunday Telegraph*

'On every possible count, Seymour is the master' – *The Sunday Times*

'One of the best plotters in the business' – *Time Out*

HAVE YOU READ . . . ?

A LINE IN THE SAND

A decade before, Frank Perry spied for the government on Iran. The information he provided damaged the Iranians' killing capacity for years. Now Iran will have its revenge, and has despatched its most lethal assassin to fulfil the task. Code-named the Anvil, he will move with stealth and deadly commitment towards his objective, unless Perry's protectors can reach him and stop him first. There seems little chance that the past will not have its day once more . . .

IN HONOUR BOUND

Barney Crispin, a Captain in the SAS, is as tough as they come. He is sent on an urgent mission to the Afghanistan border: to destroy one of the Soviet Mi-24 helicopters, a highly sophisticated and virtually invulnerable piece of military equipment, and retrieve the hardware. In order to do so, he needs the help of the Mujahidin resistance and must first train them in the ways of stealth and sabotage.

TIMEBOMB

In 1992, after being fired from a top secret nuclear facility, a top KGB man buried a nuclear suitcase. Sixteen years later he has found a buyer for it. Travelling with the buyer is an undercover policeman, working for MI6. But as their shadowy journey across Europe begins, it becomes clear that their man may be suffering from Stockholm Syndrome and the whole operation is very likely to be thrown into jeopardy . . .

TRAITOR'S KISS

Officially the Cold War is over. Between former enemies, the hand of friendship is exchanged in public. In private, though, the intelligence war goes on. An English trawler strays into Russian waters. When it returns, the captain has a package to deliver to British intelligence. For the next four years a high-ranking Russian naval officer, Viktor Archenko, passes valuable information to MI6. The time has come to get him out.

ABOUT THE AUTHOR

Gerald Seymour spent fifteen years as an international television news reporter with ITN, covering Vietnam and the Middle East, and specialising in the subject of terrorism across the world. Seymour was on the streets of Londonderry on the afternoon of Bloody Sunday, and was a witness to the massacre of Israeli athletes at the Munich Olympics.

Gerald Seymour is now a full time writer, and six of his novels have been filmed for television in the UK and US. RAT RUN is his twenty-third novel.

For more information about Gerald Seymour and his books,
visit his Facebook page at
www.facebook.com/GeraldSeymourAuthor

Also by Gerald Seymour

Harry's Game
The Glory Boys
Kingfisher
Red Fox
The Contract
Archangel
In Honour Bound
Field of Blood
A Song in the Morning
At Close Quarters
Home Run
Condition Black
The Journeyman Tailor
The Fighting Man
The Heart of Danger
Killing Ground
The Waiting Time
A Line in the Sand
Holding the Zero
The Untouchable
Traitor's Kiss
The Unknown Soldier
Rat Run
The Walking Dead
Timebomb
The Collaborator
The Dealer and the Dead
A Deniable Death
The Outsiders
The Corporal's Wife
Vagabond

Rat Run

Gerald Seymour

HODDER

First published in Great Britain in 2005 by Bantam
Press, a division of Transworld Publishers

This paperback edition first published in 2014

1

A CIP catalogue record for this title is available from the British Library.

Book ISBN 978 1 444 76045 3
eBook ISBN 978 1 444 76046 0

Printed and bound by Clays Ltd, St Ives plc

Hodder & Stoughton policy is to use papers that are natural, renewable
and recyclable products and made from wood grown in sustainable
forests. The logging and manufacturing processes are expected to
conform to the environmental regulations of the country of origin.

Hodder & Stoughton Ltd
338 Euston Road
London NW1 3BH

www.hodder.co.uk

For Jacqui

PROLOGUE

The life of Malachy Kitchen moved on, and he neither knew in what direction nor cared.

He sat bolt upright in the passenger seat, rigid. The radio played a pirate station, the driver's choice of music, but the voice boomed in his ear and could not be escaped.

'It was your shoes. I reckoned them as a toff's shoes. Don't get the wrong idea. I'm not a man who draws lines under people, those that should get the bestest treatment. What your shoes did, they sort of interested me. I get to see all sorts, and some tickle me and some don't.'

Malachy had slept the last night in a dossers' hostel behind the great canopy of Waterloo station, not well because of the coughing, moaning and snoring in the dormitory. Home for that week had been the rows of close-packed beds, the smell of the disinfectant and the stink of the fried food in the canteen, the stench of the bodies, the sound of fights and yelled arguments. Each morning he and the others had been turned out on to the street after breakfast, and the rest had shuffled off up the pavements towards the river. He had sat on the steps between the pavement and the shut door and had waited all day for the scrape of the lock being turned, the bolt drawn down and the creak of the hinges as the door swung open.

'Lighten up, that's what I'm telling you. I saw you, found you, and the shoes hit my eyes, and I thought you were worth giving a lift up to. I see derelicts, vagrants, addicts of alcohol and narcotics, see them all the time, and I have an opinion and I make a judgement. A few times, not often, I get the feeling in my water that a man is worth a few hours of my day. You want to know what gets worst up my nose? Well, I shall take the liberty of telling you. When I make the effort, and the customer does not, that sticks in my nose and it itches bad.

I

Are you hearing me? God, man, what does it take you to talk? Don't you understand when you're being helped? Did you fall that far?'

Before the hostel, he had been at the cardboard city in the underpasses of the Elephant and Castle junction. His own space had been a carton in which a twenty-eight-inch widescreen colour television had been packaged, and another that had held a stand-up fridge/freezer. He had begged during the day and drunk at night before sleeping, wrapped in the blanket of a man who had not woken one morning, had been dead when the first commuters had tripped past. Malachy had fallen that far. He had queued for soup; he had shied away from the young policemen who patrolled at night; he had stayed clear of the junkies. Some days he had walked on the bridge beyond the station and had looked down into the muddy swirl of the river, but had not had the courage to lever himself up on to the wall. If he had, and his thin, fleshless fingers had not been able to take the weight, it would have ended.

'When I saw those shoes, stuck out from under your blanket, half covered over with the cardboard, I said, "Sure as God walks this earth, Ivanhoe Manners, this man can be given a hand up." With me, my friend, you get one chance, one chance alone. You fuck that chance and you don't see me back. Plenty of others to spend my time on. You live under the cardboard, you beg and you drink, and your future is an ambulance in the morning and a space left in an underpass. You want that, you can have it, but the warden told me that since you went into the hostel, there was no smell of drink on you – but it's still one chance with me, one chance alone. I can't do it for you.'

What he possessed were the empty olive-green rucksack, which had been filled with old newspapers to make a pillow in the underpass, the fibre dog-tags that listed his name, number, religion and blood group, the clothes on his back, and the shoes. They were all from time gone by, yet he had clung to them. The rucksack had the grime of the streets on it, tears in the front pouches, and two of the fastening buckles were broken. The dog-tags were from Basic Training, always hidden by his fist when he was in the hostel showers, because they were the proof of who and what he had been before. The clothes, almost unrecognizable now, were those of a

2

civilian who dressed well. The trousers had rips at the knees and were coated with dirt, and the jacket was frayed at the cuffs and elbows. It was held across his chest with string. His pullover had unravelled. His shirt collar was part disintegrated. His socks were holed at the toes and heels and were damp from last night's scrub in the hostel's washhouse. His shoes were brogues. Smart when his mother had bought them for him before he had gone away on the last posting, before he had fallen. When he had been dropped off at wherever this journey was taking him, he thought that the grossly large West Indian social worker would take a stiff brush, a bucket of soapy water and an aerosol spray to the car to clean it. The smell, not commented on, curled the man's nostrils.

'If you don't care to communicate, that's your problem. See if I give a damn. It's in your hands, whether you want to climb out of the shit or whether you want to drop back into it. Folk can feel sorry for themselves and reckon the world's done them wrong, or they can pick themselves up. Doesn't mean I'm confident about you. Satisfaction in my job doesn't come frequent – but I just don't know whether you're crap, useless, or not.'

The car edged out of the traffic flow into a tight gap and parked. He knew the road and had begged in it. The driver hoisted his rucksack and walked across the pavement.

Malachy followed him into the charity shop. He stood inside the door, nervous and clutching his hands together. He was ignored, except when estimates were made of his chest size, waist measurement and inner leg. He was not asked what he wanted and the banter between the staff and the social worker did not include him. The clothes were from house clearances, or from the dead. They were chosen for warmth, because autumn was closing in and the air carried a spit of rain. Two pairs of trousers, three shirts, underclothes, socks, a brown-flecked overcoat that a stooping old man might have worn, an anorak, a sports jacket and a pair of bulging trainers were piled on the counter, paid for, then forced into the mouth of the rucksack.

They stopped at a supermarket. Milk, bread, margarine, a jar of coffee, a packet of teabags and a pile of chilled meals for one person were dropped into the basket. He had nothing to decide: the food

3

was chosen for him, and the dusters, the toothpaste, the disposable razor blades and the shoe polish.

He was driven on.

He saw the wide smile, the flash of the teeth.

'Oh, don't thank me, don't bother to. Don't think of thanking me because you don't know yet where I'm taking you . . . There's a cop I know at Walworth Road who says, where I'm taking you, it's best not to go there unless you're inside a battle tank. It's what he says.'

Behind them was the street market that he was told was a den for pickpockets, and the little corner shop that had been robbed twelve times in the last twenty-four months, and then the estate loomed.

'Welcome to the Amersham. The contract architect came back five years after it was finished, walked round and saw what he had created. Then he drove home and topped himself, that's what they say. Welcome to the Amersham estate.'

A concrete edifice, his guide remarked, that was home to eleven thousand souls, and now him, towered through the windscreen on which the wipers worked hard. He could have asked his driver to stop, could have pushed himself up out of the car, taken the rucksack and emptied it out on to the back seat, could have walked away into the thickening rain. They came into the forest of the blocks from which high walkways branched. On the begging pitches, in the underpass and the dormitory of the hostel, there had been a clinging sense of camaraderie, and he knew that if he came on to the estate he would be without that comfort.

Little clusters of youths watched. An old woman hurried past them as they left the car in front of the entrance to the bunker that was the housing allocation office. A man, as sparse built as a scarecrow, gazed at them and dragged on a needle-thin cigarette. A woman screamed at a clutch of children. They went inside the bunker and he was told it had once been a car-parking area, but was given up by residents as unsafe from vehicle thieves and vandals. Walls had been put in, the conversion made to office space. He thought of the command and control posts he had known, long ago, barricaded and reinforced against incoming hostiles and dark, and there was the gleam of light from computer screens.

4

He was led to a desk. He could not hear what the social worker said to the housing-allocation officer, then her voice rapped at him.

What was his name? 'Malachy David Kitchen.'

Date of birth? 'Twenty-fifth of May, 1973.'

Occupation? He hesitated, then spat it: 'None.'

Had he never had an occupation? He clamped his lips.

What was the name and address of his next of kin? He paused, then shook his head, and saw the grim smile of the housing-allocation officer and knew she thought him one more wretch running from the world.

Social security or national insurance numbers? He shrugged.

He was given two keys and barely heard the trilled 'And good luck to you, Mr Kitchen.'

They went up the staircase of block nine because the lift had an out-of-order sign slung across the door, and tramped to level three. He stepped over discarded syringes and scorched concrete where fires had been lit. He kept his eyes down so that he saw the least. In the low light of the afternoon on level three, the rain cut over the wall and splattered on his face but he did not feel it. The majority of the entrances, two out of three, had closed grille gates on the entrances, as if it were valuable to have the further protection of the barricades. The plastic numbers of flat thirteen were askew on the door. He waited for it to be opened but was told it was his, his place, and he could goddamn do it himself. He went into the one-bedroom unit, his home, his refuge. For a moment, like sun on his face, he felt the relief as if, through the door, he would be safe from the sneers and the jibes, the fraudulent compassion . . . There was a living room, a bathroom, a bedroom and a kitchen, and a door that could be closed against the world. His ruck-sack and the plastic bags from the supermarket were on the floor.

'Well, that's it. That's what you get from Ivanhoe Manners, something or nothing. Depends on your opinion. I say it again – it's your choice. You can blow it or you can make it work. If I hadn't seen you then you were dead, finished, a heap of rubbish . . . but I did see you, and knew you were worth helping, and I saw your shoes . . . and I needed the bed at the hostel.'

There was no handshake. He was given a brown envelope, felt the coins and the folded banknotes in it and was told it would tide him over until he was back in the system. Ivanhoe Manners was gone out through the door, didn't bother to close it behind him.

He looked around the room, seemed to see nothing but the bulk of the big West Indian striding away down level three, and the tears ran down his face.

The voice ripped into him: 'Just a few words, friend, so we get off to the right start and understand each other . . . Heh, I'm speaking to you.'

Behind him, by the door to flat fourteen, was a short, pudgy man, mid-forties, in a tight suit, shirt collar straining round a reddened neck and a tie that had slipped. He swiped away the tears and blinked to clear them. Half hidden, masked by the shoulder, he saw a sparrow of a woman, seventy at least, might have been older.

'When I talk to you, you damn well listen. Listening? That's good. This is my aunt. Mildred Johnson – Mrs Johnson to you. Anyone who lives alongside her, I find out who they are. If I don't like what I learn then you're out on your neck. You look after that lady. If you don't, you mess with her, I'll break your fucking back. That's pretty simple, isn't it? I'm a good friend, but a lousy enemy . . . Watch out for her.'

He stared back at the man and saw the veins swell in the neck.

'I'll see you, Millie, you take care.'

He watched the man stamp away. Long after he'd gone, and the grille gate had been locked, he stood at the edge of the level three balcony. He heard the TV start up in flat fourteen. The mist sat over the flat roofs of the towers and darkened the concrete. He rubbed hard at the stubble on his cheeks. The light was failing and he saw below him the way that people hurried to be back inside their homes before the dusk closed on them, and the groups of kids grew in size. He sensed the fear around him. Slinking towards the youths were the shadows of vagrants, dressed like him, dressed rough. Another hour he stood there, and he heard the first of the joy-riders' cars, and saw the first trading-done in fast, furtive contacts, and the first fire lit in a stairwell across the plaza and . . .

A key turned.

Her voice was brisk and reed-sharp. 'You'll catch your death out there. Do you have a name?'

'I'm Malachy.'

6

'He's all bark and no bite, my nephew. Don't worry about him. He's police . . . Do you drink tea, Malachy?'

'Thank you, I always like a cup of tea.'

It was brought to him. A mug with painted flowers and a chip at the rim was passed through the grille gate, then the door was locked again. He cradled the mug and the heat from it seeped into his hands.

Later, a woman screamed and the noise was like a rabbit with a cat at its throat, and echoed between the blocks. It frightened him, unsettled him, and he swallowed the last of the tea, put the mug down behind her grille gate and went inside flat thirteen, his place, locked the door and pushed up the bolt.

That night he slept on the floor, dressed, hungry, his shoes still laced on his feet. He did not know where his journey took him, or care. He had fallen so far. The sleep was deep, from exhaustion, and his mind was black, blank, and he did not dream – small mercy – of whom he had been and where he had once walked and what had been said of him. On the worn, stained carpet that was pocked with cigarette burns he slept away the night, and he did not know of the road that now stretched in front of him.

Malachy Kitchen lived behind the locked and bolted door.

The autumn days had come and gone from the Amersham. The winter weeks had visited the estate, freezing the rainwater pools on the level three walk-way, with chilled winds funnelled up the stairs, and round the flaking concrete corners of the blocks. Spring beckoned and in the window-boxes of a few ground-floor units daffodils bloomed, and where there had once been gardens, now used as short-cut paths, there were a few battered crocuses. The seasons had changed but the torment in his mind had not calmed.

For all the hours, days, weeks and months he could, Malachy stayed inside the cell that was flat thirteen on level three in block nine. The doctors from his past, and the psychiatrist, had had trite names for his condition and explanations; they had not allayed his feeling of disgust for himself and the shame that had come with his actions – all a long way back. Inside the flat, behind the locked door and with the bolt pushed home, he felt secure. Everything that had gone before – childhood in married quarters, boarding-school, the teenage home in a Devon village, the inevitability of following his father's career – was erased from his thoughts in waking hours, but came stabbing at him during the night so that he would wake and find the perspiration dripping from him and not know whether, in the last moments of sleep, he had screamed at the darkened walls.

He existed. Through the autumn his salvation had been the heavy, thudded knock of the big West Indian's fist on his door. Less often in the winter. Now he never came, as if Ivanhoe Manners's life had gone on, as if he had found new destitutes to throw his time at. Through Manners he had learned of the estate's pulsebeat. He could stand now at the back window of the unit and look down on the square below, where the kids' playground apparatus was broken, where the grass was worn away, where many windows had plywood hammered over them, where graffiti were spray-painted on the walls, and watch the rule of the youth gangs. Some days he would unlock the door, draw down the bolt and go out on to the walkway to stare across the estate's inner roads, but only when he knew the door behind him was open and there for fast retreat, the key in the door for turning.

In the early days of life on the Amersham, Manners had come, thrown the charity-shop overcoat at him and made him walk, had bullied him as if that were the therapy he required.

So, Malachy knew where the crack-houses were on the estate; ground-floor units with heavy bars on the windows and steel plates on the inside of the doors where rocks of cocaine were sold and consumed.

'Fortresses, man. They seem to know when the police are coming and can spot the surveillance. They have a nose for the raid that's on its way, and nothing's ever found.'

He knew where the vagrants lived, in which disused garages they slept. He recognized some from the pitches where they begged in the underpass at the Elephant and Castle.

'You'll know this yourself, Malachy. You're in the underpass and we'll say that four hundred people pass you in an hour, four thousand in a ten-hour begging shift, and fifty people drop a pound coin in your cap in the ten hours and think it's for dog food, or for your cup of tea. Fifty pounds in a day, that's good work, and good people have massaged their consciences as they hurry by. And you'll know that dossers empty the cap so often because it's bad for trade if people see what's actually given them. It's all for drugs, and the dog goes hungry.'

Ivanhoe Manners had walked him round the worst dark corners of the estate, where he was safe only because he had the massive prize-fighter build of the social worker with him, where the ceiling lights of the inner tunnels were smashed, where the one-time shopping arcades were wrecked, scorched – where the vagrants hunted.

'They need wraps of "brown". They have to jack up at least every twenty-four hours. You know that, you've seen it when you were under the cardboard. They're scum when they're on heroin. The brown destroys them. They'll steal from their only friend to get the hit, think nothing of stealing from family. They inject, and they chuck the syringes away even when there's a council-provided needle exchange – and kids find them. They got hepatitis A or B or C. They got tuberculosis, they're going to get thrombosis. They thieve – anything they can sell on, but best is a purse or a wallet. The cops all wear stab-proof vests because a used needle is a weapon for the vagrants. They are dangerous, and don't ever forget it, and you go carefully when it's dark on the Amersham.'

Back in the autumn, Ivanhoe Manners had walked him by the shoebox-shaped flat-roofed public toilets.

'They had to close them, the council did. A pensioner, male, goes inside, and a girl follows him. She's offering a blow for fifty pence. He's in the cubicle, panting, gasping, she's doing it. What else is she doing? Doesn't need her hands for a blow, her hands are on his wallet, inside his coat. She's got it, she's off and running, and his trousers and his pants are down round his ankles. He's too embarrassed, poor sod, to come charging out and chase her – if he could. The council closed the toilets.'

And after they'd done their walking, Ivanhoe Manners would come back with him to flat thirteen on level three and they'd use the chess set that the social worker had given him. And with the chess games came the monologues that Malachy seldom interrupted.

'This is where the real war is, a war worth fighting. I never been to Afghanistan and I'm not going to Iraq. But they don't seem to me as places that matter, not to me. Maybe, just possible, we can win a war in Afghanistan or in Iraq, but sure as hell we're losing the war at our doorstep. You go up to the top of block nine and look all around you. From that roof, you'll see wealth and power and Parliament, you'll see where all the big people make their money. You'll see the City – banks and insurance, you'll see the ministries, fat cats running your life – but if you look down by your feet, you'll see where the war is. The Amersham is a dump ground for dysfunctionals. You shouldn't be here, Malachy. No, you shouldn't.'

It was seven weeks now since Ivanhoe Manners had last called by.

Days slipped away in which Malachy went nowhere, spoke to no one. What drove him from flat thirteen most often was that the fridge was empty – no bread, no milk, no coffee, no meals for one. But every fourteen days, regular, the first and third Thursday of each month, he was invited next door for tea.

That Thursday morning, Malachy Kitchen dressed in the best of the clothes bought for him at the charity shop seven months earlier, kicked off the trainers and wiped the brogues with a cloth so that their old brightness returned. He would while away the hours, lost in thoughts and pitying himself, till he heard the faint knock on the common wall. He had little else to live for.

He washed himself. In the shower, piping-hot water cascaded down on him. Ricky Capel always had the lever turned high in the hot sector when he sluiced his body, always washed well, and the suds of liquid soap rolled from his face and chest and down his groin. His short dark hair plastered his scalp. Joanne never had the shower water turned that high: it scalded his skin, reddened it, but he had no fear of pain. Each time he took a shower, it was as if he needed to test his ability to withstand pain . . . That morning he had seen pain, another man's, and it mattered little to him. Above the shower's hiss, he heard Joanne's shout: when was he going to be ready? He did not answer. He would be ready when he cared to be ready.

The overalls he had worn that morning, and Davey's, had gone into the petrol drum at the back of the warehouse, where the fire was lit so that no trace of his visit to the cavernous, derelict unit remained. But he always washed afterwards, and so thoroughly, because he knew of the skills of the forensic experts. With a towel loose round him and water dripping down, he stood in front of the full-length mirror beside the cubicle. He glowed and that brought a smirk to his rounded, child-like face. No one, not any of them in his circle, would have dared to suggest it was a baby's face, but it was untouched by lines of worry, anxiety, stress. Self-respect was everything to Ricky Capel, and respect was what he demanded. He had burned his overalls because a man had denied him respect. The man who had made that mistake was now on the road south of the capital and heading for the coast.

He was thirty-four years old, though his complexion put him younger. He had married Joanne in 1996, and had the one child – Wayne. One of the few decisions he had allowed her was to give him that name. The boy was now seven and an overfed lump, without his father's sleek stomach line. The man who'd denied him respect was the eighth to have died under the supervision of Ricky Capel. At that young age, he controlled an area of the capital running from Bermondsey and Woolwich in the north, Eltham in the east, Catford in the south and Lambeth in the west. Inside that box he had authority over all matters of business he chased after. But, on Benji's advice, he had gone into the City of London at the start of the year. Across the river big money was to be made from the kids who worked in front of the banks' computers, who traded the high numbers and who snorted 'white' to keep themselves alive, alert and awake.

The man who was now bumping in the back of a van and going south towards the cliffs had done the trade in the City, had taken the white, and had pleaded a cash-flow crisis. He had promised that last week an outstanding payment would be made. The promise was not kept. Cocaine to a street value of five hundred and sixty thousand pounds had been given over on trust, and had not been paid for. That was a denial of respect for Ricky Capel. Go soft on one, and word would spread, like the smell of old shit.

Every last trace of the warehouse was gone by the time he was dressed, and little memory of it remained in his mind. The man had been blindfolded when he was brought to the warehouse, still in his pyjamas, and he'd been alternately blustering protests at this 'fucking liberty' and whimpering certainties of finding what was owed by that night, 'on my mum's life, I swear it'. Too late, friend, too bloody late. The bluster and the whimper had gone on right through the moments that the man had been tied down on to a chair, with wide sheets of plastic under it.

'Right, boys, get on with it,' Ricky had said. He needn't have spoken, needn't have declared he was there and, lounging against a rusted pillar, need not have identified his presence. He had spoken so that the man would know who had had him brought to the warehouse, and his voice would have been recognized. In those seconds the man would have realized he was condemned. Suddenly, there was a stain on the pyjamas and the stink of him, because he knew he was dead. Ricky's life was all about sending messages. It would go clear through the rumour mill that a big boss had been cheated, and the message of the penalty for that would run crystal sharp to others who did business with him.

The Merks, that was what Benji called the guys with the pickaxe handles. They were small, muscled, swarthy, had the faces of gypsies, and were hard little bastards. They'd brought cheap sports bags with them so that afterwards they'd have clean clothes to change into. They wore plastic gloves, like a butcher would use, and stockings over their faces so that the drops of blood couldn't mark them. The man had kicked with his tied feet and the chair had toppled. He'd tried to heave himself away, frantic, his bare feet slithering on the plastic sheets, and then he'd screamed. The first blow from a pickaxe handle had battered across his lower face. Blood and teeth had spewed out. The blows broke his legs, arms and ribs, then fractured his skull. He was hit until he died and then some more.

Afterwards, while Ricky watched the man's body trussed up in the plastic sheeting, Davey lit the fire for the clothing. Charlie checked the floor, went down on his hands and knees to be certain that nothing remained.

Ricky Capel liked to keep business inside the family. He had three cousins: Davey was the enforcer and did security, Benji did thinking and what he liked to call 'strategy', and Charlie had the books, the organized mind and knew how to move money. He'd have trusted each of them with his life. The Merks were no problem, good as gold, reliable as the watch on Ricky's wrist. Charlie drove him back from the warehouse to Bevin Close and dropped him off for his shower. It had all gone well, and he would not be late for lunch.

He put on a clean white shirt, well ironed by Joanne, and a sober tie. It was right to dress smart for a birthday celebration.

While he dressed, and selected well-polished shoes, the body was in a plain white van, driven by Davey who had Benji with him. They'd get near to the coast, park up till it was dark, then drive on to Beachy Head. From the cliffs there, which fell 530 feet to the seashore, they would tip the body over. The tide, Benji had said, would carry it out to sea, but in a couple of days or a week, the plastic-wrapped bundle would be washed up on the rocks, as intended, the police would be called, statements made, and then the rumours would eddy round the pubs and clubs that a man who supplied cocaine in the City had been mercilessly, brutally, viciously put to death. It would be assumed he had failed to make a payment and that this was retribution. The name of Ricky Capel might figure in the rumours – loud enough to make certain that no other bastard was late with payments.

Scented with talc and aftershave, Ricky led Joanne and Wayne, who carried the present, next door to celebrate his grandfather's birthday, the eighty-second.

Bevin Close was where he had spent his whole life.

In early 1945, a V2 flying bomb had destroyed the lower end of a Lewisham street, between Loampit Vale and Ladywell Road. After the war, the gap had been filled with a cul-de-sac of council-built houses. Grandfather Percy lived with his son and daughter-in-law, Mikey and Sharon, in number eight, while Ricky, Joanne and Wayne were next door in number nine. Eighteen years back, Mikey had bought his council house, freehold, and been able – after a choice day's work with a wages delivery truck – to buy the property alongside it. Ricky liked Bevin Close. He could have bought the whole cul-de-sac, or a penthouse overlooking the river, or a bloody manor house down in Kent, but Bevin Close suited him. Only what Ricky called the 'fucking idiots' went for penthouses and manor houses. Everything about him was discreet.

Rumour would spread, but rumour was not evidence.

He breezed in next door. Wayne ran past him with Grandfather Percy's present.

He called, 'Happy birthday, Granddad . . . How you doing, Dad? Hi, Mum, what we got?'

The voice came from the kitchen: 'Your favourite, what else? Lamb and three veg, and then the lemon gateau . . . Oh, Harry's missus rang – he can't make it.'

'Expect he's out pulling cod up – what a way to earn a living. Poor old Harry.'

He would never let on to his mum, Sharon, that her brother was important to him. Uncle Harry was integral to his network of power and wealth.

*　　*　　*

14

They were making good time, more than eight knots. Against them was a gathering south-westerly, but they would be in an hour after dusk and before the swell came up.

March always brought unpredictable weather and poor fishing, but on board the *Annaliese Royal* was a good catch, as good as it ever was.

Harry Rogers was in the wheel-house of the beam trawler, and about as far from his mind as it could get, wiped to extinction, was the thought that he had missed the birthday lunch of his sister's father-in-law. The family that Sharon had married into was, in his opinion – and he would never have said it to her – a snake's nest . . . but they owned him. Ricky Capel had him by the balls: any moment he wanted, Ricky Capel could squeeze and twist, and Harry would dance.

Ahead, the cloud line settled on a darker seam, the division between sky and sea. The deeper grey strip was the Norfolk coast, and the town of Lowestoft where the Ness marked Britain's most easterly point in the North Sea. The *Annaliese Royal* was listed as coming from Dartmouth, on the south Devon coast, but she worked the North Sea. She could have fished in the Western Approaches of the Channel or in the Irish Sea or around Rockall off Ulster's coast, and had the navigation equipment to go up off Scandinavia or towards Scotland's waters, or the Faroe Islands – but the catches for which he was a prisoner were in the north, off the German port of Cuxhaven and the island of Helgoland. He had no choice.

He had been a freelance skipper, sometimes out of Brixham, more often out of Penzance, in truth out of anywhere that he could find a desperate owner with a mortgage on a boat and a regular skipper laid low with illness. He would work a deep-sea trawler heading for the Atlantic, a beam trawler in the North Sea, even a crabber off the south Devon coast. The sea was in his mind, body and heritage – but it was damn hard to get employment from it. Then had come the offer . . . He'd talked often to Sharon on the phone, kept in touch even when she had married into that family, and had stayed in contact when the husband, Mikey, was 'away': she always called his time – three years, five, a maximum of eight – 'away', didn't seem able to say down the telephone that her man had been sent to gaol.

It was the summer of '98, and if there had been work on a construction site in Plymouth, and his boy Billy worked on one, installing central-heating systems, then he would have chucked in the sea as a life, closed it down as a profession and learned to be a labourer. He'd poured it out to Sharon. In an hour on the phone, he had told her more about the dark moods than he would have spoken of to his own Annie, and also that the dream of his retirement was wrecked. Got it off his chest, like a man had to and could do best on a telephone. Two days later, his phone had rung.

He couldn't have said, back then, that he knew much of Sharon's son, Ricky. What little he did know made bad listening. Now, the girls were grand and they'd gone as soon as they were old enough to quit, but what he knew of Ricky was poison.

Ricky on the phone. All sweetness. 'I think I might be able to help you, Uncle Harry. Always best to keep money in the family. I've been lucky with business, and I'd like to share that luck. What I understand from Mum is that you're short of a boat. I've this cousin, Charlie – you probably don't know him because he's Dad's side of the family. Well, Charlie did some work on it – would it be a beam trawler you need? There's one for sale in Jersey. Doesn't seem a bad price, a hundred and fifty tons, eight years old, and they're looking for a cash sale. I think we can do that for you. Don't go worrying about the finance, just get yourself over there next week and meet up with Charlie. That going to be all right, Uncle Harry?' Charlie had called him and they'd arranged to fly to the Channel Islands. At £275,000, the boat was dirt cheap and when he'd met Charlie at the airport, the cousin had been lugging a suitcase . . . and he didn't need that many clothes for a twenty-four-hour stopover.

He'd named her, with Annie's input and her blushes, the *Anneliese Royal*, and she was best quality from a renowned Dutch yard. His dream of life after retirement was reborn. Billy, his boy, came off the building sites and with his knowledge of central-heating systems was able to learn the engineering. His grandson, Paul, left school, and had started eighteen months back to sail with them. He had a year of happiness and dumb innocence. Then . . .

'Hello, Uncle Harry, it's Ricky here. I'd like to come down and see *your* boat. When do you suggest? Like, tomorrow.'

One sailing in three, he would receive a short, coded note. Where, when, a GPS number, and the port he was to return to with the catch. Sometimes he had a hold full of plaice and sole to bring ashore, and sometimes the hold was bloody near empty. The big catch, from one sailing in three, was off the north German coast. He'd be guided on to a buoy by a GPS reference and, attached to the buoy's anchoring chain, the package would be wrapped in tight oilskin. This one, which he was now bringing towards the fishing harbour of Lowestoft, had weighed real heavy. Billy and he had struggled to drag it up over the gunwale on the port side. He reckoned it twenty-five kilos in weight. Harry read the papers, and could do sums. At street value, he'd read that heroin sold at sixty thousand pounds a kilo. Arithmetic told him that down below, stashed in the fish hold, he had a package valued at £1.5 million, give or take.

He was brought his mug of tea, and snapped at his grandson, who fled below.

Always a foul temper when they came into port, because that was where he'd see the police wagon or the Customs Land-Rover parked and waiting. They used five of the North Sea ports, varied it, never regular enough for the law and the harbour masters to know too much about them, never infrequent enough for them to stand out and attract suspicion. In two years he would retire, he had Ricky Capel's promise, and then he could live his dream . . . but not yet.

He didn't talk about it to Billy, just gave him his cut and turned away. He thought he might be destroying the life of Paul, his grandson, but there had never been a right time to jump off the treadmill.

In the middle afternoon, as the wind force grew, the shoreline came clearer.

Billy would have finished gutting, would be breaking up the package and dividing it between rubbish sacks and their own kitbags. They would take it onshore, then in his car he would reassemble the twenty-five kilos and drive it, alone, to the drop-off point. Afterwards Harry would take himself to the Long Bar in town, drink till he staggered off to the B-and-B where he had a front-door key. By midnight, Ricky's cousin would have done the collection and Harry would be snoring drunk and asleep.

He was ashamed that he had shouted at his grandson, but the tension was always bad when they were within sight of shore and had a package on board.

The trail started in the foothills of northern Afghanistan.

Far into remote mountains, in little irrigated fields, farmers grew the poppies and were the first to take the cut; it was subsistence farming, and without the poppy crop they would have starved. For the farmers, the recent American-led invasion of their country had been a gift from God: their previous rulers had reduced, on pain of death, the growing and harvesting of the poppies, but now no government writ reached them.

It was a slow-moving trail. Eighteen months from start to end. At first the journey took the poppy seeds to market for haggling and argument, then buying. As opium, the product travelled in caravans of lorries, camel trains or in pouches on mules, north out of Afghanistan. It reached the old Spice Route, half a millennium old, and in Dushanbe, Samarkand or Bokhara Customs men, warlords and politicians took more cuts. The price was beginning to ratchet.

Then, on to Turkey, the nexus point of the trade, where the laboratories waited to render opium into raw heroin. Ten kilograms of opium made one kilogram of heroin. More cuts, more profits to be taken from the farmers' labour. Turkey was only a staging point, not a place of consumption.

Europe was the target. Each year, the craving for and addiction of Europeans to heroin demanded a supply of an estimated eighty tonnes. Turkish gangs took it on. Across the Bosphorus or by ferry over the Black Sea and a landing in mainland Europe. Up into the war-ravaged Balkans and more division of the product made in Belgrade or Sarajevo, and the price kept climbing as more men took their share of the profits. When wads of dollar bills were passed, the lorries drove unsearched through international boundaries. On into the Netherlands and Germany. The trail led to the United Kingdom, the biggest consumer of heroin inside the European Union.

Expenses soared. Wealth was being made that the humble, illiterate farmer in Afghanistan could not comprehend – but the men bringing the trail to its end had made evaluations of risk against

18

profit. The risk was a prison sentence of twenty-five years' in a maximum-security gaol, but the profit was huge. Only a few had the skill to stay ahead of the ever more sophisticated techniques of law enforcement set against them. By ferry, tunnel, car or coach in the bags of pensioner tourists who saw no wrong in making easy money, inside the cargoes of lorries, and by boat to unsuspected landing points where vigilance had slipped, the freight landed.

A man had paid up and housed what he had bought in a warehouse or a lock-up garage. He was a baron and remote from the process of the street. He sold split portions of what he had purchased to a network of regular suppliers; he was hands-off, crucial to the process but distancing himself as far as he could from risk, while retaining as much as he could of the profit.

The supplier further diluted the purity of the heroin with flour, chalk or washing powder, made more divisions and traded with dealers, the street gangs who controlled a small area of territory in a country town, a provincial city or in the capital. The supplier took his share.

The dealers sold on the street, but only after further dilution. They were the last in line and their cash rewards were as meagre as those of the mountain farmers. The dealers had the addicts begging them for wraps – tonnage reduced down to a single gram, enough for a day's hit. No cash, no sale. Without money the addict was shut out as a customer. Thieving, begging, mugging, stealing were the only ways the addict could feed the need.

On a housing estate in south-east London, the trail marked out for one little share of Afghanistan's poppy harvest came to an end.

Malachy knew her life story, and more. He had been led into each cranny of her existence. He sat opposite Mrs Mildred Johnson and drank tea poured through a strainer that caught most of the leaves, a present from a distant relative on her wedding day. He ate ham and cucumber sandwiches, her late husband's favourite filling for his lunch when he'd driven a double-decker bus in London.

Not expected to talk, only to listen, he occasionally nodded and tried to be attentive. He knew her life story because the same mixture of anecdote and memory was served up each fortnight, but he never

19

showed signs of boredom or irritation at the repetition. He would be there for two hours. She had a small carriage clock with a tinkling chime – a present from her nephew, Tony – and at four o'clock on the first and third Thursday in the month the knock would come on the wall, and at six o'clock, without ceremony, and always the refusal that he should wash up the cups, saucers and plates, when the hour was struck, he would be told that it was time for her to dress to go out to bingo. He was then dismissed.

He knew she was seventy-four. She had been widowed twelve years back after thirty-nine years of marriage. Her husband, Phil, had left no money and she survived on the state's meagre generosity. Her elder brother, Graham, and her sister-in-law, Hettie, were dead. Her only living relative was her nephew, Graham and Hettie's son, Tony – something 'important in the police', and she'd snort.

He thought she must spend the first three hours of each day scrubbing, cleaning, dusting her one-bedroomed flat. It was spotless. If a crumb from a sandwich fell from his mouth, Malachy was always careful, immediately, to pick it off his trousers so that it should not fall to the carpet.

Her first married home, when she was a school-dinner lady, had been in a terrace that had been demolished to make way for the Amersham. She, Phil and the budgerigar had moved into the first block to be completed thirty-two years ago. After his death she had been transferred to block nine, level three, flat fourteen. However bad it became, she said each fortnight, she was not leaving the Amersham. She had stayed on, refusing to cut and run, while all her friends and long-time neighbours had either died or left.

The nephew, Tony – and she did a good imitation of the whip of his voice – had alternately nagged and pleaded with her to quit, even to come and live with his family. She had refused . . . She liked to tell that story. Tony had paid for the grille gate: three hundred pounds, even though the fire people at the council had warned that a locked grille gate made a potential death-trap for the elderly. She was staying on.

To entertain Malachy to tea, and he reckoned it one of the

reasons he was asked on those two Thursdays a month, she wore every item of jewellery she possessed. Her fingers were ablaze with rings, her wrists with bracelets, her throat with chains and a Christian cross, and he thought that if she had been able to plug into the lobes more than a single pair of earrings she would have. He assumed they were kept in a box under her bed for just these occasions. She would not have worn them outside because she was street-wise. She had told him: she never took money with her that she did not need to spend when she went to the outdoor market stalls. She only went to the bingo on a Thursday night with Dawn, from flat fifteen. She read the weekly paper, and sometimes over tea with Malachy she would recite the reporting on the most violent crime on the Amersham. He had been listening again to the story of the last coach outing of the Pensioners' Association to Brighton, four months ago, when she changed her tack abruptly: 'You want to know what Tony says you are?'

'I don't think it's important.' He shrugged but he could feel the cold at his back and his hand shook. The last tepid tea slopped on to his lap.

'Tony says you're a loser. He's cruel, Tony is. What Tony says is that you're a loser, Malachy, and a failure.'

'I expect in his job he has to make evaluations – probably the right judgement most of the time,' Malachy said quietly, simply. He had not spoken to Tony, the nephew, since the first day. He had kept his distance, had stayed behind his locked door.

'What happened in your life to bring you down here? Must have been something awful. You don't belong with us. Something awful, worse, an earthquake.' She seemed to struggle for the words, and the abrasive independence that was her hallmark wavered. 'Tony says you're a waste of space and I'm not to spend time with you . . . Was it something I couldn't understand, like a catastrophe?'

He said, 'It's nobody's business but mine. I . . .'

The clock chimed. He did not wait for the final stroke of six. He was up, out of his chair, and scurrying for the door. He didn't thank her for the tea or the sandwiches. He thought he would be dissected with Dawn that evening at the bingo – and when the next knock came on the common wall, on a Thursday, he would ignore it. He

21

closed her front door behind him, fastened the gate and ran next door to his own refuge.

With the lock turned, the chain across and the bolt up, he sat on the floor and the darkness blanketed him. He did not know that, outside on the walkways and in the alleys, shadows gathered and searched for the price of a wrap of brown to feed a needle.

'I can't come, Millie. I got the flu, pain where I didn't know pain was. I'm sorry.'

Dawn was tall, would once have been beautiful. She had the ebony skin of wet coal, was from Nigeria, and cleaned Whitehall offices. Perhaps her generosity was used, or perhaps Mildred Johnson truly regarded her as a friend – but never as an equal. Her one son was in the merchant marine, a deck-hand for a Panamanian-registered company, and he never came home. Dawn minded her neighbour, and was occasionally thanked for it.

She was in her dressing gown. 'I tell you, just to come from my bed, get myself to the door and your door, that was agony. I mean it.'

They went to the Tenants' Association evenings and on the Pensioners' Association outings and sat beside each other at the Senior Citizens' Christmas Lunch. They were together on shopping trips and at the East Street stall market. She was with Millie on one Sunday a month when they went on the bus to the cemetery where Phil's ashes were buried. Together, once a week at the Cypriot café, they splashed out on pie and chips and milky tea. Dawn was always there if Millie was ill, and cared for her. She had been told that every-thing in the box under Millie's bed was left in the will to her, not the nephew's stuck-up woman. She saw annoyance spread on the slight face below her own.

'Well, that's it, then.'

Dawn croaked, 'I'm sorry, Millie, but I'm really sick. I'm going back to bed. I can't help it.'

'I didn't say you could.'

'Get the man, him . . .' Dawn gestured feebly to the next door on the level three walkway. 'Get him to walk you – or don't go.'

The door was closed on her, and the grille gate. She staggered back into flat fifteen, slumped back on to her bed and the pains surged.

12 January 2004

The sign on the lightweight door said: KNOCK – THEN WAIT TO BE ADMITTED. *But every room in Battalion Headquarters was part of the fiefdom of Fergal. As adjutant he had free run. He pushed open the door. There was no electricity from the main supply that day because 'bad guys' had dropped a pylon, and the stand-by generators were barely able to match HQ's requirements. No air-conditioning was permitted and the wall of heat hit him. Inside, he could detect the scent used sparingly by the sergeant, pretty little plump Cherie, and, stronger, the body smell of the new man.*

'Morning, Cherie – and morning to you, Mal. How's things in Spooksville?' *Fergal had a drawl to his voice, knew it made him sound as if he was perpetually taking the piss – and didn't care, because an adjutant cared damn all for anything other than the welfare of his colonel, codeword Sunray.* 'Not too bombarded, I hope, with this GFH's problems. Sorry, Mal, I was forgetting you were new with us – GFH, God Forsaken Hole.'

He leered at the sergeant. In the officers' mess, there was a sweepstake on when she would first get herself shagged; it was held by a lieutenant who ran the battalion's transport and he'd decreed that her probably outsize knickers, as a minimum, would be required as proof – the prize now stood at thirty-nine pounds sterling. The way she looked, with the glow on her cheeks and the sweat stains on her tunic blouse, Fergal didn't think it would be long before there was a claimant . . . A girl always looked good with a damn great Browning 9mm hanging in a holster on her hips. But his business was with the captain, her companion, who was not that new – had been with them for four months.

'Yes, Mal, Sunray would like you up at Bravo.'

'If you didn't know it, I've actually a fair bit to be getting on with right here.'

'Are you not hearing me too well?' *He heard Cherie's snigger.* 'I said that Sunray wanted you up at Bravo. It's not for discussion, it's what he'd like.'

The battalion in which Fergal was adjutant recruited other ranks from the tenements of Glasgow and the housing estates of Cumbernauld. The fathers or uncles of many had served two decades earlier. The

23

officers, those with good prospects of advancement, came from the landed estates of the west Highlands. They were a family, a brotherhood. The feeling of being part of a clan, with a regimental history of skirmishes, bloody defences, heroic advances and battles, stretched back for three centuries. Their museum was packed with trophies from the campaigns of Marlborough, the epic of Waterloo, colonial garrisoning, the foothills between Jalalabad and Peshawar on the North West Frontier, the kops of South Africa, the fields of Passchendaele and the hedgerows of Normandy, then Palestine, Malaya, Kenya, the Aden Protectorate, and endless dreary little towns in Northern Ireland. Soon, when the booty had been crated up, museum space would have to be found for souvenirs of the Iraqi desert. The battalion had heritage and tradition, and its family strength recognized the danger of allowing strangers to infiltrate its ranks. Outsiders were not wanted.

'If you're not too busy, Mal . . .' the sneer was rich in Fergal's voice '. . . Sunray would like you up at Bravo tomorrow.'

Alongside the battalion's headquarters building, separated by its sandbag blast walls and its coils of razor wire, was the Portakabin occupied by the Intelligence Corps personnel assigned to them – the sergeant, Cherie, and the captain, Mal, as he was called in the mess. Put bluntly, and it was Fergal's right as adjutant to be direct, the Intelligence Corps captain was a cuckoo. He didn't fit, was not part of the family or a member of the brotherhood. The battalion had its own intelligence officer, Rory, a good man. They did not need the stranger, who knew nothing of the history, tradition, heritage that would see them through – if God was kind – the six-month posting to Iraq. The man didn't mix well, didn't share their culture.

'We've a resupply convoy going up at oh-six hundred hours local tomorrow. You can go with them. What have you got on your plate at the moment?'

The answer was crisply put, as if the captain, Mal, accepted the unconcealed hostility shown to an intruder. There was a rattle of information on pipeline sabotage, clusters of incidents where the crude-oil supply from the wells was disrupted on routes through the battalion's area of responsibility, profiles of suspected 'bad guys', and the man never looked up from his screen as he spoke.

'What does that add up to?'

24

'That we don't have the resources to guard the pipes, that they can be blown up virtually at will, that the oil supply is persistently vulnerable, that we're charging around and getting nowhere. I have to have more time because I haven't yet sorted a pattern of attacks – who's doing it? Identities, safe-houses. Whether they're Iraqis or from over the Iran border, I don't know . . . That's what's on my plate. My opinion, at the moment, we're wasting our time.'

Two nights before, in Sunray's office, the same statement had been made, and not appreciated. After the captain, Mal, had gone, Sunray had told his adjutant, 'I won't have that defeatist crap. Christ, I'm under enough pressure from Brigade on these damn pipes . . . I want answers from him, not just excuses for ignorance. Aren't answers what we have the right to expect from the Intelligence Corps? If he can't do better then perhaps we should get him doing something useful, away from that wretched little screen. Work on it, Fergal.' He had: something useful was at Bravo Company, eighty miles up the road, and Sunray had concurred. What the battalion could do without, when Brigade was breathing hard on them, was to be told they were wasting their time. It was probably true, but it shouldn't have been said by an interloper.

'Up at Bravo, an elder was murdered, drive-by shooting.'

'I know.'

'He was a good friend of ours and—'

'Shot because he was a good friend. We like to peddle this hearts-and-minds stuff, delude ourselves the majority love us and are grateful for liberation, that the opposition is only a minority and mostly from over the border. He was killed because of his association with us – that's a death sentence.'

Icily: 'If you don't mind allowing me to finish, Mal . . . Thank you. We're going to show the flag up there, have an arrest sweep. We have to react. You're a local-language speaker so you'll do the initial screening and interrogation, see who should be passed down the line.'

'Be happy to – if your Jocks haven't beaten them all half insensible.'

'That is fucking outrageous, an insult.'

'Please yourself.'

The adjutant was at the door. He knew the answer to what he'd say, knew what training the Intelligence Corps people had – pretty

25

little plump Cherie couldn't hit a main battle tank at twenty-five yards with her Browning 9mm, and the quartermaster who took her on shooting practice wedged his knee between her thighs to keep her steady and held her arms out rigid, but she still missed the biggest target they could knock up. He put the question: 'You're trained on combat weapons and patrol procedures? You should be if you're going up to Buffalo Bill territory, Bravo's ground . . . Of course you are.'

He knew she was not back yet, and it made him fidget. Malachy was aware of all of the night sounds of the Amersham, every noise from the plaza at the back. He should first have heard the clatter of Dawn's flat shoes and the shuffle of Mildred Johnson's feet, then the screech of the grille gate, the front door opening and shutting, the blast of the TV through the common wall.

She had disrupted what little peace he owned. He could not have told her how much he appreciated the two sessions a month of tea and sandwiches and listening to her talk, and now he sensed the relationship was broken, past repair. He still sat on the floor, wrapped by the darkness that was barely reached by the plaza's lights. Her prying had brought back the pain of memory, not to be escaped from.

He could see it: a child lost in his imagination, succouring fantasies, playing solitary games around the married quarters at Tidworth, Catterick, Larkhall or Colchester . . . Father was the Northern Ireland expert and always there; mother, a deserter from a nursing career, full-time unpaid organizer of other ranks' wives clubs and counsellor of teenage brides on credit-card debt and trying to keep together a hopeless partnership. Walter and Araminta Kitchen had been too consumed with the job and the good deeds to notice that their lone child was isolated. He remembered coming into the kitchen with homework, arithmetic that he couldn't do, unaware that his father had learned that afternoon he was not sailing with the Task Force to the South Atlantic, and getting a volley of abuse over a gin glass for thinking homework counted in the scale of things, and running. Sent to boarding-school in Somerset. Short visits from his mother, and an aloof one from his father to see the school play. Worst day ever at school was his father's visit a year after his retirement as brigadier, with full dress and medals, to inspect the Combined Cadet Force. Not an unhappy childhood, compared to what some at the school put up with, but remote from love. Of course he would join the army: his small act of rebellion, and it had taken bottle, was to decide – himself – when and where. And then the puce-faced, spluttering reaction of his father when he announced that he'd enlisted, that afternoon, and been passed through by a Birmingham recruitment office, to be a private soldier and bottom of the heap. 'Silly little bugger,' Walter had called him, and Araminta had said quietly to her husband, 'Not to worry, darling. It never lasts when middle-class boys go slumming it.'

All the sounds, that evening, of the estate had wafted up to his room: music and screams, the wail of the sirens, then the intermittent flashes of blue emergency lights.

The memories came round as if in a loop, as they always did. He was in childhood, father away and mother out. Too awake to sleep. No escape possible. He heard the stampede of feet, the thud of them, then the hammering on his door.

Malachy felt the fear catch his body. He crawled away across the floor towards the far wall. The beating on the door was ever more insistent, and there was the cry of Dawn's voice.

It came in a torrent when he finally opened the door. If he had interrupted, it would not have halted her. She was in her night clothes. No slippers on her feet. Incoherent and with tears welling.

'It's Millie . . . What happened to Millie? Do you not know? The bingo. She went. I got flu. I can't go to the bingo. I tell her. I say to get you to walk her, or not go. Did she get you? She went on her own. I told her not to. Nobody ever goes to bingo alone and comes back alone. She did. They got her, the vagrants got her. She's mugged. You know what she has in her bag? She never has more than five pounds, that is before the bingo starts. They went for her bag. After the bingo and a cup of tea there would be two pounds only. She didn't give it. She hung on to it for two pounds. They dragged her. She fell. She is an old lady. She hit her head, and then they took her bag.'

He rocked, felt himself cringe. He did not say what her nephew's opinion of him was: a loser and a failure. Malachy could not tell her that Mildred Johnson would not have asked him to walk her to and from bingo because he had said that a story of a catastrophe was nobody's business but his, that he was the last man from whom the proud, obstinate little lady would have begged a favour.

'She's in the hospital. The police had found her bag, without two pounds. In the bag is my name and my flat number. In my bag is her name and her number. I cried when the police told me . . . Why, Mr Malachy, did she not call you to take her and to bring her back? Why? You were her friend. Why did she not ask you?'

2

'How is she?'

The nurse looked up. She had been hovering over the bed. 'Are you a relative?'

'No – no, I'm not. Just a friend.' Malachy held the flowers beside his leg and the water off them ran down his trousers.

'How close a friend?'

'I live next door to Mrs Johnson.' He was supposed to have been, once, an expert in interrogation. With the tables turned, now, the questioning unsettled him. He shuffled his feet. The nurse's body blocked his view of Millie. It was the furthest he had been away from the Amersham since he had come to live there the previous autumn. It had been a big journey for him to get to the sprawled complex of St Thomas's Hospital. That morning, Dawn had come again to his door. She must have been on her way home after the early cleaning shift in Whitehall. He had thought of Millie, and the guilt had seared him.

'I suppose that'll do ...' The nurse had a freckled face and bags under her eyes, seemed half asleep with tiredness and spoke with an accent that was west of Ireland. 'She was knocked out. We thought about Intensive Care but there wasn't a bed. She got the best we could give her, but it wasn't IC, with pulse, blood pressure and pupils checks every half-hour, and we didn't think there was inter-cranial bleeding ... That's why she's in General Medical. So, it's serious bruising to the head and a broken arm – not a complicated break. Always the same with the old folk – they hang on and don't let the bag go. Silly, but that's them for you.'

The nurse moved, started to smooth down the bed. Millie, to him, looked so small. She was half sat up against a pile of pillows. She wore a loose-fitting smock, several sizes too large for her. Her face, usually proud, independent and haughty, was a coloured mass of bruises, and the right side of her grey hair had been shaved away above the ear. He could see the two-inch-long gash with the stitches in it. Her right arm was across her small chest, enveloped in a sling. She seemed to stare at him, baleful and defensive. He did not know whether he was recognized, if that was the stare she gave to anyone approaching her bed. The nurse slipped a thermometer into her mouth, which was puffed, with distorted lips.

'She'll be in two or three days, because she lives alone and there's no one to look after her. Problem is that we might ship her out today, and if she starts vomiting or goes to sleep, we've an inquiry to worry about. When the swelling's down on the arm it'll be pinned or plated – and she'll have to manage. That's the way it is, these days.'

'There's a friend next door to her, a good lady. She'll be there.'

'And you said you were a neighbour.' The nurse put down the thermometer, then fixed Malachy with her eye. 'I expect you'll give her a hand – or do you go to work?'

'I'll do what I can,' he murmured. 'I don't suppose you have a vase?'

He had gone to the East Street market. He had considered how much he could spend. The benefit he was entitled to, after deductions, left him with eighty pounds to last for two weeks. Divided up that gave him spending money of five pounds and seventy-one pence each day. He had asked the woman on the flower stall for the best she could do with five pounds. It was a good display of bright chrysanthemums that he had brought to the hospital.

The nurse reached to the bottom cupboard of the cabinet beside the bed and took out a man's urine-sample bottle, grinned, filled it with water from the basin, and took the flowers from Malachy. As if she'd made the judgement that he wasn't capable of flower-arranging, she did it for him and settled the stems in the bottle. 'The vases all get nicked,' she said. 'It's the best I can manage. Don't stay too long. You shouldn't tire her.' She left him.

Malachy sat on the end of the bed beside the little bump her feet made. He did not know what to say, or whether it was right to say anything. He tried to smile encouragement. She had turned her battered head enough to see the flowers. He felt his inadequacy.

When he was with the dossers, sleeping in the underpass on and under cardboard, drinking with what he had made from begging, and knowing he could not fall further, he had not felt this low. The silence nagged between them.

Maybe an hour passed. She slept and he sat dead still so as not to wake her.

The question cracked in his ear. Brusque. 'What's a piece of shit like you doing here?'

The nephew was behind him. He carried a large, varied bouquet in one hand and a clear plastic bag in the other, packed with apples, pears, bananas, peaches, a pineapple and grapes.

'Why are you here?'

He was shivering. His whisper was a chatter in his teeth: 'I came to see if I could help.'

'Oh, that's good, "help". Didn't "help" enough to walk her there and back – no, no.'

Malachy stammered, 'She didn't ask me. If she'd asked me . . .'

'No fool, Aunt Millie. Wouldn't have reckoned you up to it, walking her there and back.'

'She didn't ask.'

'You came down from a great height – right? Hit the bottom – right? I know who you were and what you did. I know what they called you. Fancy phrases from the medics, but the truth from the Jocks. I know.'

His head drooped into his hands. He sensed the nephew go past him and he heard the kiss placed on Millie's forehead, would have been where the bruises were. More sounds. The splash of water, then the thud in the tin waste-bin, the crackle of the Cellophane wrapping on the bouquet.

He kept his hands tight on his face, could feel the stubble on his palms.

'What I don't know, my friend, my little piece of shit, is where you're going. Are you going to go on failing? That's easy, isn't it? I don't know if the only road you're comfortable with, my friend, is the easy one . . . Take your bloody hands off your face. Look at her! Does that take guts, looking at an old lady who's been done over for her purse? Look at her and remember her.'

31

He did. He saw the slightness of her and the bruises in their mass of colours, the thin upper arm in its sling. And he saw the stems of his flowers upside down in the bin, and the glory of the bouquet on the cabinet. He pushed himself up from the bed and turned for the aisle that ran through the ward.

'There's an easy road and a hard one – most, when they've fallen like you have, take the easy one.'

Out of the hospital, he walked on the embankment. The river seemed sour and dirtied. Rain ran down his face, was not wiped away. He walked on and did not know where, walked until a massive cream and green building – an architect's dream – blocked his path. Then, he turned, retraced his steps and headed back to the Amersham where he could hide behind a door that was locked and bolted.

Had Frederick Gaunt looked out through his fifth-floor window, reinforced and chemically treated glass that could withstand bomb blast and electronic eaves-dropping, he would have seen a man walk on the Albert Embankment towards the wall that blocked further progress to the building where he worked, then loiter and drift away. But there was more on Gaunt's mind that lunchtime than the aimless advance and retreat of another of the capital's work-shy low-life – that would have been his description if he had seen the loafer. His sandwiches were untouched and his bottle of mineral water unopened.

Gaunt's room in Vauxhall Bridge Cross, the monolith occupied by the Secret Intelligence Service, was in an isolated corner of the building. Nominally, eight per cent of the Service's budget was devoted to the investigation of organized crime, but the resources made available to this section of the fifth floor's open-plan areas, cubicles and rooms had been pared down to meet the demands of Iraq and the burgeoning al-Qaeda desks. Gaunt did Albania. On another man's back it would have been a hairshirt, an irritation that required continued scratching without relief, but he knew the way the system worked and would have reckoned bloody-minded sulking to be vulgar.

The lunch was uneaten and the water undrunk. Little that normally landed on his desk, dumped without ceremony by Gloria, required more than dutiful attention. Albania's organized crime was the trafficking of narcotics, firearms and people. His CX reports were carefully crafted, always readable, and painted a clear picture of a society wedded with enthusiasm to criminality. Most could have been drafted when he was half asleep – not the one that now turned in his mind.

'You haven't touched them – you have to eat.' Gloria put down a further file on his desk, already crowded with seven paper heaps. 'No breakfast, no lunch, and I'll wager nothing proper last night.'

He grimaced. She scolded because she cared about him. The first of the files had arrived the previous morning and the heap had built through the day. Most of the pages now referred to telephone traces sucked down by the farm of dishes on the Yorkshire moors. Once he had been on the cusp of the Service's investigations – before he was moved aside: a victim of the Service's need to produce scapegoats after its greatest ever, and most humiliating, intelligence failure. Now he was again at the centre. Little, irrelevant, corrupt, fourth-world Albania was top of the tree. He chortled to himself. He had been at his desk till ten o'clock last night, back in at a few minutes after five that morning, and would be there that evening long after the day shifts had finished.

'I really do insist that you eat.'

It had been the day when al-Qaeda came to Albania: what he had lived and dreamed for. He thought they must have almost forgotten, down on the AQ desks, that Frederick Gaunt still inhabited a little corner of their space. A link was made – and he'd have admitted it was a tortuous one – between the kings of the terrorist war and the barons of European criminality. Happy days, happy times.

'*Please*, Mr Gaunt – please, eat something.'

'What never ceases to amaze me, Gloria, is that they still use the old telephone. God, will they never learn?'

One file listed an address in the city of Quetta in west-central Pakistan, in the foothills of the mountains that straddled the Afghan border – probably close to where the venerable Osama was holed up in a damp cave – with an estimated population of 200,000, and among them was Farida, wife of Muhammad Iyad: listed occupation, bodyguard. She lived there with the kids, but he was long gone.

33

The second file was of the life and times of Muhammad Iyad: more important, whom he guarded, all choice items.

The third file comprised a security report from Islamabad of a surveillance team's witnessing of a gift-wrapped parcel being hand-delivered to the house. Included were black-and-white still-frame images of her showing her mother a gold chain necklace. Anyone close to her would have passed the gift to her in person. Who other than a husband in hiding somewhere would have sent a married woman an expensive present? Records, attached, showed it to have been her wedding anniversary when she received the gift.

The fourth file listed a telephone call made on the landline from the house to a number in Dubai, in the Gulf. The transcript of the brief call listed, no names, her 'love, gratitude and always my prayers'.

The fifth file was slim. The only overseas call made from the Dubai number – no transcript provided – was to a satellite phone in southern Lebanon.

The sixth file, again a single sheet of flimsy paper and again no transcript, recorded a call from the satellite phone located inland from the city of Sidon to a number in Prague, capital of the Czech Republic.

The seventh file, courtesy of the BIS in the city, identified a message received in Prague on a number that was tapped. The transcript was one line: '*Gift received. Love, gratitude and always my prayers.*' The number in Prague to which the message had been sent was monitored because it was used by an Albanian national, believed involved in the organized-crime racket of moving Romanian, Ukrainian and Bulgarian girls to northern Europe for prostitution. The warmth of his smile spread because Wilco's signature was on the cover note.

In front of him now, brought to him by his faithful PA – and he'd have sworn she had the same caring eyes as her spaniel – was Wilco's latest message. The Albanian was a café owner and prosperous. Records showed he also owned a third-floor apartment in the Old Quarter of Prague, and the unpronounceable name of a street was listed. He began to wolf his sandwich, gulping it down, then swilling his mouth with the water. 'Satisfied?'

'It's only you I'm thinking of, Mr Gaunt.'

34

She could have called him Frederick or Freddie – she had been with the Service for twenty years, fifteen of them running his desk at home and abroad – but she was never familiar. Without her, his professional life as a senior intelligence officer would have been so much the poorer. He said, 'I'm going off to see the ADD, dear Gilbert, to tell him I want to run with this. Meantime, message Wilco that I'm controlling it, and all signals come to me, please.'

He was up and scraping sandwich detritus from his shirt, then buttoning his waistcoat, reaching for his suit jacket from the hanger.

'Shouldn't I wait till you've received the Assistant Deputy Director's confirmation?' She seemed to tease.

'Take it as read. They're all callow youths and girls on AQ (Central Europe). He'll be glad to give it to someone who knows his butt from his arm. Oh, and say something nice to Wilco.'

He strode away, noisy on steel-heeled shoes. Terrorists in bed with criminals made for formidable copulation.

He walked up the street with a plastic bag dangling heavy from his hand. It was the last time that Muhammad Iyad, the bodyguard, would need to collect food from the *halal* butcher in the market behind the Old Town Square, salad vegetables and bread. By the following evening they would have started on another stage of the journey.

Because this was his work and why he was respected, he tried to be as clear-headed and alert as his reputation demanded. Among the few who knew him, it was said that he was the most suspicious, most cunning of all the men given the task of minding the precious and highly valued operatives of the Organization. Coming back to the apartment on the top floor of the building in the narrow alley behind Kostecna, Muhammad Iyad used all the techniques that had long become second nature to him. Three times between the Old Town Square and Kostecna, he had broken the slow ambling pace of his walk, had darted round corners, then stood back flush to the doors at the entrance of old buildings and waited the necessary minute to see whether a tail would come after him. Twice he had stopped in front of women's clothes shops and positioned himself so that the reflection showed the street and both pavements behind him. Once, on Dlouha, at the entrance to the pizzeria, he had abruptly turned on his heel and gone back a hundred metres, a fast stride that would have confused men who followed him, and they would have ducked away, would have shown themselves to him, the expert. From the doorways and shop fronts and by the pizzeria, he had seen only a fog wall of tourists' bodies, local kids, striding office workers and meandering women. But that day, his mind was clouded.

He knew the man he guarded as Abu Khaled . . . but his thoughts were not on him and his security. On pain of death, or on the worse pain of disgrace, he would not have told the man of what he had done while they had travelled and of the reward it had won him. The man did not know that a necklace had been purchased in the gold market of Riyadh. The money to buy it had been from the banker who handled transactions for the Organization. He himself, Muhammad Iyad, had chosen the necklace of thick, high-quality links, and the banker had promised that it would be delivered by courier to the address in Quetta – not by mail because that would have been unreliable and would have endangered his safety. If it had been known what he had done, he would never again have been entrusted with taking a man of importance towards his target. The message had come back to him two days before. '*Gift received. Love, gratitude and always my prayers*.' He had rejoiced. The image of her, and the little children, had filled every cranny of his mind. He could see her, touch her, hear her. It had been wrong of him to make the gift – it was against every law laid down by the Organization – but the weakness had come from long years of separation. His love of the Organization was shared with his love for his family, for the woman who had borne his children. He did not know when, if ever, he would see her again. The net around the Organization was tighter, more constricting. It seemed at times – worst when he tried to sleep – to suffocate him . . . so, walking towards the alley behind Kostecna, between narrow streets and old buildings of brick and timber, he attempted to maintain his habitual alertness, but the picture of her, with the necklace he had chosen, competed.

He was certain of it. He would have sworn to it on the Book. There was no tail.

36

Fully focused, as he was not, Muhammad Iyad might have noticed that the no-parking sign at the end of the alley, on Kostecna – which had not been obscured when he had passed it at the start of his shopping trip – was now covered with old sacking bound tight with twine.

He had been two months with Abu Khaled, moving and minding and watching over him. He had collected him in secrecy from a lodging-house in the Yemen's capital, Sana'a. They had travelled overland, north into Saudi Arabia – the home of the swine who danced to the tune of the Great Satan's whistle – had skirted the desert and gone up the Red Sea coast, then cut back towards the desert interior and into Jordan. All of the Organization's planning had been, as always, without flaw. From Jordan into Syria, then Turkey. At each stage safe-houses, transport and documentation had met them. Then across the sea by ferry and to Bulgaria . . . and the change that had first unsettled Muhammad Iyad.

They were in the hands of Albanians. The common language was broken English or halting Italian; they were Muslims but without the dedication to the Faith that was his and Abu Khaled's, but those were the arrangements made by the Organization. He could not, and he had tried to, fault them – but he did not trust them. From Bulgaria, via Plovdiv and Sofia, to Romania. Overnight stops in Romania at Brasov and Satu Mare, then into Hungary. More documentation and new cars waited for them at Szeged and Gyor before they had slipped over the frontier and into Slovakia.

If they had used airports his face and that of Abu Khaled would have been caught on the overhead cameras, and their papers would have been copied and stored; the cameras were dangerous because they could recognize a man's features. Whether he wore spectacles or a beard the computers could identify him. The borders they had crossed were always remote, not the main routes where the Customs men had been trained in techniques by the Crusaders. They had come, after sleeping two nights at Prievidza, out of Slovakia and into the Czech Republic and had been taken to a café in Prague, then driven to the safehouse, an apartment high in an old building. The word given him, and he could not doubt it, was that with each step towards the destination greater care was required.

They had been five nights in Prague while the detail of the final stages was finalized. In each car or lorry they had been moved in, under the back wheel in the trunk or stowed behind the seats in the cab, was the black canvas bag that he was never without. Against his body, at each border crossing in Yemen and Saudi Arabia, Jordan, Syria and Turkey, a snub-nosed pistol, loaded and in a lightweight plastic holster, had gouged into the soft inner flesh of his right thigh. At every stop point his hand had hovered on his lap and his belt had been loosened so that he could reach down for it and shoot. He would never be taken, and it was his duty to ensure that a prized man such as Abu Khaled was not captured alive – too many had been; too many had talked to their interrogators. The first bullets would be for those who questioned them at a border crossing, the last two would be for Abu Khaled and himself.

Nor did he take note of the green-painted delivery van, cab empty, without side windows, that was parked where every other day it was forbidden to stop by the sign that was now covered.

The following night they would cross the frontier into Germany, in the hands of the Albanians . . . The pistol was now in his waistband, at the back, under his jacket and the coat he wore against the cold. At the street door, he swung round, gazed back up the alley. No one followed him. No man or woman turned away quickly, or ducked their face to light a cigarette, or snatched a newspaper from a pocket and opened it. Cars, without slowing, sped past the green van on Kostecna.

He went in, closed the door behind him. The next evening they would start the last leg of the journey. It would end far away on a northern coastline, and there he would hug his man, kiss his cheeks and pray that God walked with him . . . He began to climb the stairs. The plaster had flaked from the walls with damp and the light of the alley had been extinguished by the shut street door, but he thought only of his wife . . . The Organization had ordered that he should leave his man, his work done, on that seashore.

He lived in paradise but it brought him little comfort.

All his waking hours, worry squirmed perpetually in Oskar.

As the light failed, the rain off the sea thickened and the wind whipped the white caps behind him, Oskar Netzer sat on the bench in the low watch-tower among the island's dunes. At his back, four or five hundred metres behind the tower's wooden plank wall, was the North Sea. What he studied through the tower's hatch window was a lagoon, a bog of rank water and marsh, reeds and the eiders.

The island was at the centre of what would have seemed, if seen from a high aircraft, the long-cleaned vertebrae of a great mammal but one that, in the moment of death, had tucked its legs into its body. The islands formed an archipelago a few kilometres north of the Frisland coast of Germany. The head of this fallen beast was Borkum island, the base of the skull was Memmert, and Juist was the neck. The shoulders, the largest of the islands, was Norderney. Then came a bump on the spine: Baltrum. Baltrum was the jewel. The long backbone continued, broken by a channel between Langeoog and Spiekeroog. The creature's drooped tail was Wangerooge, the tip Minsener Oog. Together they acted as a sea wall that protected the mainland from the worst of the winter storms blowing in off the North Sea. The islands had been created over centuries by the tides and currents pushing together displaced mounds of seabed sand. They had shifted continuously, their basic shapes surviving only when the seeds of the tough dune grass had taken root and bound the sand grains together. They had no soil that could be cultivated and the greenery that had sprouted was only the coarse grass, thick low scrub and occasional weather-bent trees. The upper point of all the individual islands was never more than twenty-four metres over the high-tide sea level. The smallest and the most beautiful, Baltrum, was five thousand metres long and a maximum at low water of fifteen hundred wide. Baltrum was Oskar Netzer's home.

He was sixty-nine, and five years ago he had watched his wife's coffin lowered into the sand of the small cemetery in Ost Dorp, overlooking the low-tide mudflats and the mainland, after forty-one years of marriage. He loved no other human being and was himself unloved by all of the five hundred permanent residents on Baltrum. He was unloved because he struggled, every day and with every breath, to block the march forward that he was told was necessary if the island's community was to survive. He was wiry, without a trace of fat on his stomach. His cheeks, always seeming to carry three days' bristle, were mahogany-coloured from sun, rain and wind. He wore that day – as all days whether the sun baked or the chill wind cut – a pair of faded blue fishermen's overalls and stout walking boots, with the cap, half rotted, of a Frislander on his silver hair.

A third of his island, his home, was now covered with the little red-brick homes of those who came only in the summer and of those residents who let rooms for the wasp swarms of summer visitors. It was argued by the island's mayor, and the elected council, that visitors needed facilities. Oskar fought each one with passion. The latest, which he would fight that evening at a public meeting, was an application to expand the floor space of an existing Italian-owned fast-food pasta and pizza outlet.

From the tower, he watched the eider ducks feed in the lagoon, preen and sleep on its banks. They were elegant, peaceable and so vulnerable. Each development, he believed, eroded their place on the island. His anger at development burned in him as he sat on the bench and muttered the arguments – not so loud as to disturb the eiders below him – that he would use later against the intrusion of more strangers. The season for visitors would not start till Easter week; there was still a month before they came. The quiet was around him, and the rumble of the sea far behind him. He would fight because without him the island's calm was shorn of defence and he did not care whose march he blocked.

The note was on the floor just inside the outer door.

Malachy had been in the kitchen cooking sausages and chips. Without the TV's noise through the common wall – and his own was not switched on – it had been deathly quiet in flat thirteen with only the whir of the microwave and the bleep of its bell, but he had heard nothing, no footsteps padding along level three's walkway and no rustle of paper as it was inserted between the bottom of the door and the carpet. He had brought in the plate, with the sausages and chips, and put it on the table. As he had pulled out his chair he had seen the note.

He went to it and bent to pick it up; it was folded in half. His first thought was that it was from Dawn, a report on Mildred Johnson's progress . . . No, she would have knocked on the door. He lifted it, opened it.

40

Once, handwriting was something he had known about. In the first days at Chicksands, years back, they had spent half a day learning the points to be recognized from handwriting: ill-educated writing, intelligent writing, disguised writing. The hand of this note had formed large, clumsy characters in ballpoint on a sheet from a notepad. The pressure of the point and the size of the letters told Malachy that a right-handed person had written with their left hand:

> *Your phone will ring three times, then stop. A minute*
> *later it rings three more times then stops. After 30*
> *minutes be in the parking area under Block 9, bay 286.*

He shivered. Far out over the estate he could hear music played loud and shouts of argument, but around him was silence. He crumpled the paper, then let it drop. He turned to go to the table where the food waited for him, then hesitated and retrieved the note. This time he ripped it into fragments, carried them to the toilet and flushed them – as if that might help him forget the demand made of him.

An intruder had broken into his world.

He sat at the table and ate his meal. The telephone was on a low table of stained wood. The room's furnishing was basic, battered: a table and two upright chairs, of which only one would safely take his weight, a two-seater settee whose coarse covering was worn on the arms by age and previous tenants, a bookcase with empty shelves. A single picture hung on one wall, a fading print of flowers beside a river; the glass was cracked at the upper left corner. A light with a plastic shade hung from the centre of the ceiling. And there was the low table with the telephone. It was the same as the day on which Ivanhoe Manners had brought him to the Amersham. He had done nothing in those months to stamp his character on the room. In fact, it mirrored Malachy Kitchen. It was as if he had determined to show nothing of himself, as if he were frightened to display himself. What there was he kept clean, but did not add to it.

As the hours passed, Malachy sensed his life had changed again, but he did not know whose hand controlled him. Maybe he should pack his clothes into a black bin-bag, go out through the door, close it behind him and walk away. Go down the stairs from level three, turn his back on block nine and head off into the night . . . But he sat on the carpet where he could see the telephone. The demons came again, and what had been said to him and of him, the squirming sense of shame. There was no one he could have turned to.

Ricky felt the excitement, always the same when he took delivery.

He wore plastic gloves. He counted out the packages, in the light thrown by a battery lamp, and the contents of each weighed one kilo. With a knife he had slit one open, had seen the dark powder and sniffed it. He would not open any of the other twenty-four tightly bound packets of brown – no need to, not where they had come from. The last divisions of the load coming to him had been made in Germany and he would have trusted that source with his life. Ricky was in a derelict factory on the north side of the Peckham Road. Once, it had produced cheap leather coats but that market had now gone to Turkey, and he rented the premises. He had realized long ago that it was a waste of his money and dangerous to own the property where the twenty-five-kilo or fifty-kilo parcels were split. Around him, but with cut-offs for security, was a loose network of experts and facilitators. He wanted a driver for a shipment: he hired one. He wanted enforcers, such as the Merks: he went outside for them. He wanted premises: he rented them. He wanted information: he bought it. He wanted a chemist: he went into the market-place . . . It was his way of operating, and he believed it to be the safest.

Security was everything with Ricky Capel.

Little details missed sent men down for the big bird stretches. The men in the A Category gaol wings had all missed little details, and would do fifteen years for the mistake. He despised them.

Each packet was checked, after the one that had been opened, to be certain that the sealing had survived the immersion in the North Sea – but he wore gloves and out in the yard, between the building and the high wall, a brazier was already lit. He wore gloves so that fingerprints would not be on the oilskin wrappings or the taping, but his sweat would line the interior of the gloves, and DNA traces could be taken from a plastic glove. The gloves would be burned, and where he and Charlie had walked on the factory floor would be hosed down as they left so that their footprints were washed away.

42

The checking in the factory was the only time that Ricky Capel would be hands-on with the packages. Charlie had driven the parcel up from the east coast – still with the smell of the sea on it and the stink of fish. Davey and Benji would move the single-kilo parcels on to the drop-offs: more labyrinthine arrangements and more gloves for burning. Of course there were risks – everything about life was risks – but they were kept minimal. His success in achieving this was why Ricky was not in Category A, why he created fear, why he was worth – so Charlie told him – more than eighty-five million pounds. Yeah, yeah, not bad for a young 'un still short of his thirty-fifth birthday. And the factory was always swept for bugs, camera and audio the day before a package was brought for splitting.

Ricky dragged off his gloves. Charlie had the parcels: he was splashing them with water from the hose, washing away the smell of fish and the sea, then walking them to the doorway. Outside, Davey and Benji were in the wheels, a jobbing builder's van and a pick-up with a sign on it for garden clearance. He never moved the stuff in a Mercedes, or in a Beemer, not in anything that would be noticed.

The van and the pick-up drove away. He dropped his gloves into the fire, then heard the hose water on the floor behind him. He knew all the stories, because Benji told him, of the mistakes men had made and the details that had been missed. The latest in Benji's list: the guy who did cocaine, and was bringing in 160 kilos when he was lifted. He ran racehorses and had called one of the nags by the name of the top 'tec who'd done the Krays, which was just pathetic and shouted from the roofs for attention. He'd got fourteen years. Another guy stole a dog, a bull mastiff, off a kid, kept it as his own and let it ride in his car, then killed a punter he was in dispute with, put the body in the car to dump it and there were dog hairs on the body that were matched to the dog he'd nicked, and it was life with at least twenty-one years. His granddad didn't do details and had been third rate. His dad had missed the obvious and was fourth rate. Not the boy, not Ricky Capel.

Charlie's gloves went into the fire.

'You OK, Ricky?'

'Never been better.'

He watched the gloves disintegrate. Later that night, fifteen suppliers would have the twenty-five packets – and would have paid for them. Where they went after that, cut down, divided and sliced up across south-east London, was not his concern. The trade on estates, in back-street pubs and from unlit corners was beneath Ricky Capel's interest.

'I'm feeling good.'

The room was a mess of shadows. When it rang, the telephone was faintly lit by the street-lights below the window, filtering inside. At first, Malachy started to crawl forward to pick it up, but before he had reached it, the bell had gone three times and then the silence startled him. He did not know who played with him. His hand dropped and he slumped. He could have reached out and lifted the receiver, then let it hang from its cable and drop to the carpet; had he done so, the telephone's bell could not have pealed again. Instead, he cringed, left it in its cradle. The bell screamed for him, seemed to shatter the room's quiet.

Half an hour later, Malachy closed the outer door behind him and padded down the walkway. It was near to midnight. Over the railing, he could see the little clusters of figures, where they would have been when Mildred Johnson came back from the bingo. On the last flight of the stairs he had to scrape himself against the graffiti to get past two vagrants hunched down: one had the sleeve of his coat rolled up and a syringe poised above the skin; the other was probing with his fingers for a vein in the back of his leg, contorting himself and cursing at the effort. He could smell them. They seemed not to notice him. He thought the first would use the syringe and then, if the other had found a vein, it would be used again. When he was past them he stumbled down the last flights of the steps, then leaned against the street wall and panted. To go on or turn back? If he turned back he would have to retrace the route past the vagrants with the needle.

It had been the intention of the architect responsible for the Amersham's design that residents should park their cars and vans under the blocks, but for the last fifteen years, no man or woman had dared to leave a vehicle in the garage spaces: smashed windows, stolen radios and tyres, vandalized paintwork had cleared the cavern areas. Interior lights, set in the support pillars, were broken and only the street-lights reached under the low concrete ceilings. The residents who had cars left them out on the street now, under the high lights: they could come out from their barricaded front doors, peer down from the walkways above and check them.

Between distant pillars, a small fire guttered. Shadows flitted round it and he heard low voices. Above him was a sign, paint flaking, detailing the numbers of the parking bays. He looked for the number he had been given, then breathed hard and stepped into the interior. He had on the rubber-soled trainers from the charity shop, but however lightly he attempted to walk, his tread seemed to shout his advance. Sometimes his feet crunched on broken glass, and once he stepped and slid in fresh faeces. He could just see some of the numbers on the pillars, enough to guide him towards the far wall. The outline of a car loomed in front of him. He felt the weakness in his gut and at his knees, then the hiss of a window being electrically lowered. He tried to see inside and could make out a head in a balaclava.

The voice was muffled through the wool. 'Is that you?'

'It is me.'

'Wanted to hear your voice, know it was you.'

He knew the voice. *'What's a piece of shit like you doing here?'* and *'You look after that lady . . . Watch out for her.'* He said curtly, 'I know your voice and we do not need, for whatever your purpose, this crap in the middle of the night.'

'Fighting talk from a big brave boy. Understand me, I am not here, I was never here. Ever get the idea that I was here and shout about it, and it'll be your word against mine – and your medical history against the busload of people who will stand up and swear on the Bible, good and firm, that I was elsewhere. Forget it. Those are the rules. I am not here and you never met me here. You got hold of the rules?'

'If you say so.'

'I say it. I said that I'd find out about you—'

'You did.'

'Don't interrupt me, doesn't make me happy.' A pencil torch flashed on in the car, and the beam shone down on a file of papers. 'You are Malachy Walter Kitchen?'

'I am.'

'Son of Walter and Araminta Kitchen, born 1973?'

'Yes.'

'On leaving school, a year's teaching in Krakow, Poland?'

'I cannot see that that is relevant to anything.'

'Everything of you, to me, is relevant.' The papers on the lap were turned. 'You joined the army. Your father was a senior officer, now retired. You were recruited into the ranks. Basic Training, then Germany, Logistics Corps. I suppose it was a gesture – a poor one, and it did not last. Right?'

'I'd have thought you had better things to do with your time than pry into my past.'

'Easy, Malachy, easy, there's a good fellow.' There was a stifled chuckle. 'You were pulled out. There's a letter in the files from your father. A request was made to friends to give you a hand up.'

He ground his teeth. 'I didn't know. If I had I wouldn't have accepted the offer.'

'That's convenient – always good to keep the pride. So, you went to Sandhurst, to the Royal Military Academy, to be made into an officer. Not much of one, only "fair" ratings for team work. Described as a "loner" – but they're down on numbers, these days, and they pass through what they've got.'

'My academic work was graded "above average". I was good enough for what I wanted to do.'

'Absolutely right. You were accepted into the Intelligence Corps in '96. Dad couldn't complain about that – it was respectable. You were at the corps' base at Chicksands for three years. Your assessments give no indication of what will happen. It is said of you that you show aptitude for working under pressure on your own. You were one of those solitary people who makes a virtue of not needing company. Where I am we have a few. They've slipped through the net, and they're arrogant, opinionated, not good work colleagues. Once we've spotted them they're out. Do you recognize yourself?'

'I recognize nothing. It's your game.'

'You married Roz in '98. Wasn't clever but you did. Daughter of a warrant-officer instructor at Sandhurst. You set up home in married quarters at Chicksands. But that's not my business.'

46

'That is not your bloody business.'

'Not my business except when I can see I'm pouring salt on to a raw wound. Trekking on, you're then posted to Rome to be on the military attaché's staff. That must have been nice, bit of a doddle, I'd have thought. Cocktail parties, NATO exercises and updating the Italian army. Heavy stuff.'

'I did what was asked of me.'

'Back to Chicksands. Working to Major Brian Arnold. Rarefied long-range guessing on the agenda. What do we know about the Iraqi order of battle? How mobile is a Republican Guard armoured division? Who are the personalities in command of Iraqi units? Where have they been trained? What is the quality of Iraqi logistics and support arms? War is getting closer, work hours longer – earlier away from the little woman and later back. Immersed in work, head never above the parapet . . . Am I getting it right?'

'If you want to believe it, you can believe it.'

'Don't get shirty with me, Malachy. I'm the one with a home and family to go back to. You've neither. The war starts. All those clever papers you've written, they're all proven crap. The Yanks slice through the defences, which was not in your predictions. No, you hadn't got that right. Hardly time to blink and the fighting war's over, and it's peace. You are one of many, suddenly sitting on your hands and looking at the sun shining down on Chicksands. Your trouble, though – and it's the same trouble for all the work-obsessed geeks – is that you don't do hobbies. Nothing to fill your days, and nights. Not going well with the lovely Roz, eh? Then Major Arnold drops his bombshell. You're off to Iraq.'

He understood. It was as if a rope had tightened round his throat. He said hoarsely, 'There was work, worthwhile work, to be done there.'

'That's better. Now we're singing from the same hymn sheet – excellent. And the excreta's in the fan. Supposed to be mission accomplished, but it's not. The time for rose petals chucked under the tracks of tanks is a memory. It's about terrorism and about improvised explosive devices and law-and-order breakdown and the assassination of collaborators, and a dream that's as sour as old milk. First you get to Brigade in Basra. I expect they get the message – another

47

junkie from Intelligence, boasting brain power over brawn and telling the brigadier where he's doing it wrong – short-cut to getting popular, eh?'

'I was coming with a different viewpoint.'

'Soon as they could get rid of you, Brigade did the business and packed you off to a battalion of Jocks, somewhere out in the sand. That must have been a thrill. They're real soldiers, getting their arses shot at, and now on their territory is a guy from outside their ranks. I expect you didn't hesitate – with the full weight of your Intelligence Corps expertise – to point out to the commanding officer where they were going wrong. I read a little note from someone at the HQ: a gathering in the officers' mess and everyone's yapping about what should be done, but the I Corps officer reckons they're talking shit and can't keep his mouth shut, says, "My opinion, anyone who thinks he knows the short-fix answer to southern Iraq's problems is ill informed." I'll bet that went down as well as if you'd pulled the pin and dropped a hand grenade. So, they sent you—'

'All I did was tell them what I thought.'

'Back to the old self-opinionated stubbornness – couldn't let it go then and can't now. They sent you up to a company base, codename Bravo. I'd hazard that there were a fair few at Brigade, Battalion and Company who'd have raised a cheer if they'd known you were going to fall on your face. You went out on patrol—'

'That's enough.'

'Not good listening, eh? Getting sensitive, is it?'

'It wasn't like anyone said.'

'What did they call you, Malachy, after the patrol?'

'I don't have to listen.' He was shouting.

'What was their description of you, Malachy?'

'Go fuck yourself.'

'A bit of spirit, Malachy – that's what I want to hear. I think we're progressing. You don't want me to say what they called you, all right, how they described you, all right, you haven't forgotten. It's hung round your neck. I said you were a failure – a man can live with that. But a man can't live with what they called you. Am I right, Malachy?'

'Cannot.'

48

'Anyone stand your corner, speak for you? I don't think so. Think of topping yourself, Malachy, ending it?'

'Thought of it.'

'And you fell – no work, no wife, no family, no friend. Collapse, booze, mind broken . . . You were lucky you ended here.'

The fire beyond the pillars flared and there was a shriek of laughter that echoed through the car park, across the empty bays.

'What did you lose, Malachy?' The voice had softened. 'What replaced personal pride, self-esteem, respect? Shall I answer? Would it be shame?'

Malachy whispered it: 'Disgust.'

'What's it like? I don't know.'

'It's demons. It's always with you. It's a torture chamber. There's no time in the day or the night that it's not with you.'

'Let me tell you a story, Malachy, and listen well. I'm a young copper. I'm with a mate and it's the middle of a balls-freezing night and we get this call in Hackney. Intruder on the roof of a warehouse. My mate goes up on the roof, and I'm tracking along on the ground. My mate goes through the roof. I saw him in Stoke Mandeville when he hadn't been there – the spinal injuries unit – more than two days. He was weeping his eyes out, couldn't have been consoled because he was diagnosed as near quadriplegic. I made a big effort, because it had cut me right up, saw him again in a month, and when I went into the ward I could hear his laughter. It was food time and he was learning to eat and it was all over his front and his face, just like everyone else had it. He said to me, quiet, "What you learn in here, there's always someone worse off than yourself." A good sob story, yes? Last I heard of him he was doing a job, from a wheelchair, in police communications. Being called a cripple – that's not as bad as what they called you, but it's down that road. He was thought of as useless. Are you useless, Malachy?'

'I don't know,' he said simply.

'Do you want to find out?'

A ripple of panic caught him. He sensed that everything was choreographed. 'What if there's no road back?' he blurted.

'Always is, you have to believe that – otherwise stop fucking about and living like a goddamn recluse. Walk on to the bridge and bloody well jump. But you have to believe it. Malachy, get something in your mind.'

'Tell me.'

'You saw her. Bruises, broken arm, violated like they'd raped her.'

'I saw her.'

'There's a road back, Malachy.'

Through the open window a slip of paper was passed to him by a hand gloved in black leather. He saw the glint of the eyes through the balaclava's slit as the man reached across. There was no light to read what was written on the paper and he pocketed it.

'What do I have to do?'

'Don't *have* to do anything, Malachy. The vagrants steal to buy the wraps. With the money they steal, from an old lady's purse, they buy. The dealers sell to them. You do what you *want* to do, Malachy. You do what you think is right, and maybe that'll make a ladder for you. Goodnight, keep safe.'

The window was raised, and the engine was gunned to life. Without headlights, the car reversed sharply and swung, squealed tyres, between the pillars and out into the lit street. Malachy stood rooted, his mind pounding confusion.

3

He woke. It was already past eleven o'clock.

The banging on his door drummed into his head. If it had not been for the sound Malachy would have slept on. He dragged himself off the bed.

It had been a sleep he had not known for months, for a year. No dreams and no nightmares. No images squirming in his mind.

The banging persisted. He shouted out that he was coming, but his voice was faint from a dried-out throat and the banging did not stop. He pulled on his trousers that he had dumped last night on the carpet when he had fallen, collapsed, on to the bed.

'Yes, I'm coming. For God's sake, I'm coming!'

Out of the bedroom, he walked past the table. There was the mat on which he put his plate, the little plastic containers for salt and pepper, a mug he'd left there from which he'd drunk instant coffee – and the sheet of paper. He snatched it up and buried it in his pocket.

He went towards the door.

Last night, back from the parking bays under the block, he had read, again and again, what had been passed to him through the car's window. He had sipped the coffee and told himself he would sleep on it, not decide anything till the morning. He would not commit himself till the morning; he did not have to . . . his decision. It had been the best night's sleep he could remember. But nobody owned him.

'I'm coming.'

He unlocked the door and dragged down the bolt. He paused, seemed to suck air down into his body. He could not remember when last his door had been banged on but, then, he could barely remember when he had last slept a whole long night and been free of the demons.

Dawn was there.

'I went to see her,' she said.

'Yes.'

'Are you not concerned for her?'

'Of course I'm concerned for her.'

'You want to know how she is?'

'I'd like to.'

'I thought you would be there. I thought you would have visited her. She had Tony early before he went to work, then me when I have finished. I thought you would be there . . . but I look at you, and I see you were asleep.'

'I thought I'd go later on,' he said weakly.

'She does not sleep. She has the pain in her head and the pain in her arm, both are severe. Worst is the pain in her soul. Do you understand me?'

His voice was limp. 'Please, explain to me.'

'A policeman came yesterday afternoon and gave her a victim number. He asked her if she could describe her attackers. It was dark so she could not. The policeman said there was a camera covering the stairwell, but it did not have film in it. There are many cameras for show, but few with film in them. It hurts her that no one will be punished. I am sorry that you did not travel to see her.'

'I slept in late, didn't mean to.'

He thought his excuses demeaned him to the tall African woman, elderly, but still cleaning ministry offices and staircases, and thought she regarded him with contempt. Probably working through her mind were the snippets of his history that she knew. Had once been a gentleman, like the men with individual offices that she rose early to clean. Had been disgraced and had collapsed. Had been a vagrant living rough, like the vagrants who had stolen from her Millie.

'Don't you go tiring yourself, Mr Malachy. You go back to bed. Not good for a young man to exhaust himself. In three days she will be coming out, when they have done the pin in her arm. I apologize, Mr Malachy, for disturbing you.'

She was gone, away with her dignity.

He closed the door.

He pulled the piece of paper out of his pocket. Three names. Not the names of vagrants but of members of the High Fly Boys who strutted the Amersham. He studied them, then took a pencil stub and began to write down, hesitantly at first, then feverishly, what he would need to buy.

13 January 2004

Baz was the section's star. Had to be one, and it was him. The way he was going he was close to being the platoon's star. The company commander always noticed him and he'd heard he was listed for his first stripe, and he'd get it within the next fortnight. Baz was the best shot in the platoon, and when other Jocks in the section couldn't reassemble an SM80 or a GPMG after cleaning, it was to Baz they turned. Back at the depot, east of Inverness, Baz played right central stopper in the battalion soccer team. As a member of HQ platoon of the company, Iraq suited Baz as well as a good glove fitted a hand.

He listened to the briefing. Baz didn't rate the corporal. He himself could have done the job better, blindfolded and with an arm behind his back. Because he didn't rate him, he hardly listened as the corporal, reading off notes, told them what route they would take, on foot, out of Bravo. Two and a half hours of showing the presence. Baz, like every other Jock at the police station, knew a lift was coming the following morning, and that the patrol was going out that afternoon to give the impression that everything was normal, quiet, routine; a break in the patrolling pattern might sound a warning to those in the identified buildings who were to be lifted.

Baz always liked to speak up, to show he was alert. 'Excuse, Corp, aren't we short of an interpreter?'

'Behind you. Mr Kitchen's coming with us.'

He turned. Baz hadn't seen the officer, must have reached the briefing when the gats and the gimpy were being checked and armed. The officer was standing with Sergeant McQueen. He'd seen him arrive when the resupply convoy had come in from Battalion in the morning. Talk round the HQ platoon was that he was a desk driver, from Intelligence, and it had been overheard in the mess by a Jock doing officers' breakfasts that he was an Eternal Flame – 'never went out'. Though he was alongside old Queenie, Baz was struck by his aloneness, like he didn't fit and knew it, seemed remote from them. A good-sized man, but his uniform was clean as if it was straight out of the dhobi line, his boots hadn't dirt on them, and his webbing was looser than it should have been. His flak jacket was not fastened across his chest, he had no cam-cream on his cheeks and forehead, and he held an SM80 as if it wasn't part of him.

'*Does he do worm-speak, Corporal?*'

'*He reads Arabic writing and speaks Arabic lingo. He'll do any interpreting we need – and you'll watch his back, Baz.*'

'*Be a pleasure, Corporal. Don't like his face, though.*' *Baz spat into his cupped hands, then crouched, scooped sand into his palms, then went the two strides to the officer.* '*Don't mind me, sir, but you've no cam-cream. This'll do.*'

He wiped the mess, spittle and sand on to the officer's cheeks, forehead and chin, smeared it good and hard right up to the rim of his helmet, which was askew, like he wasn't used to wearing one. He could sense the nervousness, like this was a new experience for a Rupert . . . All young officers were Ruperts, all Ruperts were fair game. There was a little wave of laughter behind him from the section, then old Queenie slapped his hand down.

'*Just trying to help – that's much better, sir.*'

They didn't have to be told what they might face when they were out in the village: it might be a scrum of cheerful, screaming kids, offers of God-awful sweet coffee from the stalls, an RPG round or a burst of automatic – might be a welcome or might be a full-blown ambush. Not knowing was what made it good for Baz.

'*Right, let's move.*' *The corporal was on his way. Baz was not surprised that the company commander and the platoon commander hadn't come out to hear the briefing and see them go. They'd have been working on the planning of the morning lift, heads down over the maps of the locations and where the block forces would be to stop the bastards legging it.*

At the weapons pit, a square metre of sand between three walls of sandbags, they armed the rifles and the gimpy, the machine-gun. He didn't hear the scrape of the mechanism behind him. Baz could always muster a nice smile. Didn't have to say anything. He smiled well as he took the officer's rifle, worked the bullet into the breech, checked the

54

safety was on, murmured that they always had one up the spout when on patrol. He saw the blush on the officer's face – bloody Rupert, useless Rupert. The blush showed up through the smears of sand and spittle. All of the section's faces, everyone at Bravo's, was sunburned or tanned dark, but this man drove a desk and never went out. There was a whisper of thanks, barely heard, and Baz's smile was sweeter: he was in control, like he always wanted to be.

There was banter among them, a few cracks as they tracked along the embankment towards the village. Then joke time finished. They looked for freshly moved sand at the side of the road, where a bomb might be buried, and they looked for control wires. Baz was back-marker and in front of him the officer's shoulders heaved up and then sagged, like he was breathing hard. In Iraq, nothing frightened Baz – he was a star. Now, coming to the village's first buildings, he knew the officer was not battle-trained, and it amused him.

Nine in the section, plus the officer. Two sticks of five on each side of the one street and far up in front of them was the square.

He sensed it, and the corporal would have done. All of them would have sensed that that afternoon the place was bad. No grins or little waves from the shop-keepers, the bin-liners – the women head to toe in black – were scurrying to get clear of their approach, and there weren't kids mobbing them for sweets. Most days, in the village, the atmosphere was good; a few days it was bad. If it was bad, he would get to shoot; if he fired he would slot. Baz was the best shot in the headquarters platoon, but the place not to be, in action, was back-marker. He ran forward, loped half a dozen strides. He was at the officer's shoulder, saw the way the rifle was held with white knuckles.

'Do Tail-end Charlie. Watch me, do as I do. Keep my arse safe. Don't lose me.'

He was past the officer. The section was strung out on either side of the street and had started to make the short, fast surges that the sergeants who had done Belfast taught them. He watched for the corporal's hand signals, when to move and when to be in a doorway.

A steel shutter slammed down. The last stretch of the street, into the square, emptied. Baz knew it: the shutter going down was the sign.

Two shots. None of the Jocks down. A single shot. All of the Jocks sprinting. The instructors called it 'doing hard targets'. Run, take cover, search for enemy, run again, making it hard for the bastards to get a target. He saw, just before the forward Jocks of the section reached the square, the corporal's hand signal jagging to the left where a street came in at right angles to the main drag. They were all sprinting. More than half of the Jocks were already gone into the street off to the left. He would have looked behind him, checked for the officer, but he saw the bad guy, saw him clean, clear – bearded, in a robe, ammunition pouches on webbing on his chest, AK in his hand. Baz had the rifle up, was controlling his breathing, trying to find the bastard in his magnifying sight – and he could smell behind him, filtered through the shutters, the scent of fresh-baked bread.

There was a thunderclap of noise behind him. He recognized it. Rocket-propelled grenade. He looked up fast, high, saw the impact point a dozen feet over him, between two windows, and glass came down. He didn't look for the officer but shouted for him to move himself. He had the bad guy again in the sight. One shot, aimed. Ice cool. Like it was the practice range. Breath controlled, the trigger squeezed. Baz saw the white robe lift up and the AK rifle seemed to be thrown aside. Then the target was lost behind the mass of deserted stalls.

'I slotted him. I got a hit,' Baz yelled. He felt the pride. Then he was charging for the street corner. Two more single shots came. In and out of doorways, the section stampeded along the street, spread far apart. He was back-marker. Tail-end Charlie was his place. Baz was always last man in the section on patrol because he was the best . . . He thought, for a brief moment, of the officer. Would have got past him, running, when Baz was aiming and preparing to fire – a hell of a shot, two hundred yards, definite no less – and he forgot him. All sprinting, until they had doubled round the back of the mosque and had reached the school gates. They were crouched against the wall of the school and the corporal darted back to him. No more gunfire, but a siren sounded urgently, back in the square's area.

The corporal reached him. 'You all right, Baz?'

'I'm all right – he isn't. Hear the feckin' ambulance? I slotted one.'

'Where's the Rupert?'

'I slotted him well, saw him go down, had an AK, confirmed kill – up ahead.'

'He's not. Holy cow . . . Jesus. Where's the Rupert?'

'Definite, he wasn't hit. There was an incoming RPG, but way high – by the bread shop – but no small arms incoming. All the small arms was forward.'

'So where the hell's the Rupert? All I bloody need.'

'I'm not his bloody nanny. I wasn't pushing him in a goddam pram. I got a kill. He's not hurt, the Rupert, because there were no shots that could have hit him. I tell you what I got. I got a marksman and dropped him . . . How do I feckin' know where he is?'

Baz heard the corporal on the radio, and the staccato response that the section should work their way back, use the route they'd taken. There was a shortage of manpower at HQ, but they were trying to put together a response, and at the end: 'For God's sake, how have you lost him?' They left the school and came back round the rear of the mosque, then along the narrow street they'd used to get clear of the ambush and on to the main route into the square. The ambulance came past them, the back door flapping open to show the feet on the stretcher. Baz caught a glimpse of the blood staining the robe. They checked doorways and alleys, behind and under cars. Then the lead Jock yelled out and crouched in a gutter beside a dropped helmet.

A hundred yards on the flak jacket was lying in a heap of goat shit.

When they saw him, he was on the embankment.

He was shambling back towards Bravo's HQ and behind him was a gang of small children. The jeering laughter of the kids came back to them, and Baz saw that some, the boldest, ran to within a few yards of him and threw stones at him, trying to hit his bare head, but missed. And Baz saw the hands, hanging loose, not holding a personal weapon. He heard the corporal mutter, 'The idiot, he's lost his gat.' They ran to him, heaving for breath, and the feckin' sun beat down on them. Baz's mind worked hard, where he had been and what he had said. He would have died for his section, gone to his Maker for his platoon – not for an outsider. They reached him as a personnel carrier came in a dust storm from the gates of Bravo. He seemed to stare straight ahead and there was no recognition in his eyes for those who gathered round him, and no response to the corporal's repeated and ever more frantic questioning. Was he OK? What had happened to him? Where was his weapon? He just walked on.

57

Baz took the moment. 'He couldn't feckin' hack it, Corporal. He ran. He dumped us and ran. He chucked his helmet and his jacket, and his gat. That's yellow, Corporal. He's a feckin' coward. Couldn't do the business. He legged it. Look, there's not a mark on him . . . A feckin' piece of wet shit – what he is, look at him, is a lurker or a skiver. A bloody coward, that's what he is.'

If it had been the same van, still the green one, Muhammad Iyad would not have noticed it. They had eaten bread, salad and goat's cheese, and later he would pack, in good time for them to be ready to move as soon as the car pulled up at the street door. Before that he would sleep, so that for the journey through the night he would be alert, his senses sharpened by rest. It was not the same van.

It was smaller, black-painted and newer. When he stood at the far side of the window, under the eaves of the building, he could just see the top of the no-parking sign covered with sacking held by twine. His mind turned on the problem . . . Kostecna, in the oldest part of the city, churned with traffic. It was forbidden to park on Kostecna. Permission might have been given for one vehicle, perhaps, to park while urgent work was done in a building. There was no sign of work. No artisans came with equipment to and from the van. Muhammad Iyad had a mind that bred suspicion. The position of the van was perfect: the view, except that it had no windows, from the centre of its side, gave direct access to a watcher down the alley. He heard a belch behind him, then a murmured question: what did he see?

Not taking his eyes from the window, Muhammad Iyad asked to be passed his binoculars, a pocket pair, from his black bag. He held out his hand behind him, and when the binoculars touched his fingers he snatched them. With them at his eyes, whipping at the focus he began minutely, inch by inch, to examine the sleek, shiny side of the van. For a moment he was not aware, as he strained to find what he searched for, that the man, Abu Khaled, was behind him and had wriggled against the wall to look over his shoulder, see what he saw. Suspicion had kept him alive. In Sana'a, Riyadh, Amman or Damascus, if it were not believed he could be captured he would have been shot on sight. He would not be captured, never would be. A little hiss of anger slipped his lips because the traffic on

Kostecna had log-jammed and a high lorry obscured his view. His eyeline had been on the indentation in the van's side where plate sheeting could have been removed to make way for windows. There was rare sunlight that afternoon in Prague and it fell on the van, highlighting the indent. He squirmed to better his position.

The lorry moved on. His gaze moved over the paintwork, then slipped back to the indentation. The breath of the man was in his ear. He would have sighed his satisfaction. He saw the machine-worked hole, the size of a single Yemeni riyal coin or one Syrian lira, drilled but not punched in the way a .45-calibre bullet would have done. He had found it. With almost savage strength, Muhammad Iyad propelled the man away from him. He heard Abu Khaled stumble back, trip, fall to the floor, and then his oath.

He stepped back from the window, saw the man he guarded lying on his back and scrabbling with his hands and feet to stand. Sweat was clinging to him. In all the days and nights they had been in Prague, Abu Khaled had never been out of the third-floor apartment. It had been his cell. The mark of his importance was that he should never leave the building, for fear of being identified by a camera or a security official. Five nights and most of six days he had been shut away from sight – now the alley and the street door were watched. Sweat clung to the bodyguard because he remembered her words, passed to him: '*Gift received. Love, gratitude and always my prayers.*'

Quietly, matter of fact – because panic was never his – Muhammad Iyad said, 'We are watched. They have observation on us.'

'Did you get it?'

'I did.'

She had heard the rattle of the camera's shutter. He eased the camera down from the aperture. It was on his lap and she strained forward to see the screen. The images flickered.

'What do you think happened up there?' Polly asked.

'First he was looking down the street, then he had binoculars. I think he was studying us. Then another man came – look, there is the second man, difficult to identify. Then movement, and both are gone.'

59

'It's a bastard, isn't it?'

'Any show-out, Polly, is a bastard.'

'I think, Ludvik, that we should back off.'

He raised his eyebrows high. 'Because you want to piss, or you do not like Czech cigarettes, or because we have shown out?'

She punched his arm. Polly Wilkins shared the interior of the black van with Ludvik, who was middle-ranking, mid-thirties, middle ambition and opinions, in the Bezpecostni-Informacni Sluzba. He fancied her. No way was she going to get herself involved in a relationship, on the rebound, with a Czech counter-intelligence officer, even if she had been dumped by email. And this was not a place for a relationship to flourish. She was desperate to pee but there was no bucket in the van. No bucket, but a mountain of squashed-out cigarette butts between their feet. Relationships had not been on her mind since she had received Dominic's new year email.

'I think we should get out. Leave them undecided, not sure.'

'You are the boss, the representative of the expert in such procedures.' He seemed to laugh at her.

As well he might. Polly Wilkins was big on Iraq, could have bored to gold-medal standard on weapons-of-mass-destruction evaluation, but was now on a fast learning curve on the Czech Republic, people-trafficking across porous borders, Albanian criminality and al-Qaeda movement. There weren't enough hours in the day, or the night, to satisfy the steepness of the curve – which was good, meant Dominic's bloody email, the hurtful bastard, from Buenos Aires was getting to be history. She reckoned Ludvik laughed at her because he thought she was wet behind the ears and knew precious little of nothing about stake-outs and surveillance, and what would happen next.

'And I want the pix printed up.'

He wriggled into the front. She looked back a last time, through the hole, at the upper window and a dishcloth now hung from it, as if to dry – but there was rain in the wind. He drove away fast, leaving her to fall about in the back and cling to the camera. She told him about the dishcloth and he swore. Down Kostecna he was shouting into the microphone of his headset.

God! Did the daft, dumb, sweet boy never look at the traffic in front of him? He had turned to her, teeth shining as he grinned.

'That'll be the signal. People who would never, pain of death, use a phone. A signal that they are threatened. We have the squad readied, we'll go tonight. You want to watch, Polly, want to be there?'

'Thank you.'

More than rubbernecking on a storm squad going in, watching from long distance, she wanted to get her hands on the prints off the digital camera, wanted them on the airwaves to Gaunt. She'd had his signal that he was taking charge. He was, almost, a parent to her. At the end of Kostecna, half on the pavement, were two more closed vans, like the green one they had used and the black one, and she assumed that that was where the storm squad waited. It would be a coup, a triumph for him.

She had time to get a download of the pictures, get to the embassy and secure communications, send the signals, then be back to grand-stand the storm squad. She giggled. She thought of Gloria bringing in her signal, with the good close-up photograph of the man with the shopping, and the long-lens image of two men at the window. She could imagine old Gaunt's shoes jerking off his table as he hunched to read what she had sent.

'Why do you laugh?' Ludvik called from the front.

'Classified,' she said, mock-haughtily. 'UK Eyes Only.'

The shoes, brightly burnished, swung from his desk and tipped a file on to the floor. Gaunt leaned forward and peered down at the photographs. Little gasps of pleasure slipped from his lips. He had a magnifying-glass out of the drawer by his knees, and bent lower so that his head was close to the top pictures, black and white, blown up to plate size. Without ceremony, Gloria retrieved the file from the carpet. He asked her, not looking up, if she would be so kind as to cancel dinner that night with the deputy director general – a merciful relief but the excuse was cast iron – and to ring Roman Archaeology (Fourth Century) at the British Museum and post-pone with apologies his lunch date for the next day. The second set of photographs was more problematic: a face at the end of a tele-photo image, grained and difficult, and the same face half masked by a pair of pocket binoculars, then a second face behind it but in shadow and indistinct.

Almost with reluctance, as if it were a distraction, he reached for his telephone. He dialled internally, was connected to the assistant deputy director's aide and asked – steel in his voice, not for negotiation – for an appointment, soonest, like in five minutes. Gloria hovered. Would she, please, signal Wilco with his congratulations and thanks.

Tie straightened, waistcoat fastened, jacket on, files scooped up and tucked under his arm, he headed for the top floor and the ADD's eyrie.

The assistant deputy director was Gilbert. His office was at the start of the corridor leading from the lift. Promotion, for which Gilbert strove, would take him further down the corridor and ultimately to the double doors and the suite of rooms at the end.

Gilbert had survived the earthquake that had destroyed careers in Weapons of Mass Destruction. He had presided over the dismantling of the desk and the shuffling away to side eddies of the victims. He was always guiltily awkward in Frederick Gaunt's company. Yet Gaunt's approach to him was one of magnanimity and scrupulous deference, with the intention of exacerbating the guilt.

'It is Muhammad Iyad, that is confirmed. Muhammad Iyad is a bodyguard, a minder. He watches the backs of principals and moves them in safety. That he set up this flawed chain of messages to get a gift to his wife, and then to hear back from her of its safe arrival is – and with your experience you'll know this better than me – quite extraordinary. In the past he has escorted high-value targets into and out of Afghanistan, into and out of Saudi Arabia, et cetera, et cetera . . . You know all that, of course you do. Now – and it is a present from heaven to us – we have him in Prague. I venture, and I'd appreciate your opinion on this, that he is currently bringing an HVT into western Europe. I would hazard that such a high-value target, an individual of such importance that Muhammad Iyad has been given responsibility for him, would be a co-ordinator, not a foot-soldier or a bomb-layer, not even a recruiter. What I think we're looking at – and I hope you'll feel able to confirm my thought – is an Albanian-organized rat run for al-Qaeda. Isn't that the phrase all the suburbanites bitch about? Use of side-streets, alleys, lanes for the school run. In this case, the rat run avoids all but the remotest border crossings, only goes where there is least scrutiny. Anyone being brought through, with that degree of effort, can only be an HVT. I guess that we're looking at a co-ordinator. There's a face here . . .'

He shuffled the photographs on the ADD's desk, then laid on top of them the sequence showing the minder with the binoculars and the blurred, indistinct image of the partially hidden face behind.

'I suggest that there is our co-ordinator, and – if you agree – I'd like to run it through the boffins. This evening, our friendly Czech sisters will arrest Iyad and this unidentified man, and Polly Wilkins will be on hand to fight our corner. They're bottled up – the BIS are only waiting for darkness. It should be quite a coup, Gilbert. You'll smell – deservedly – of roses. You'll be toasted in Langley – the Americans are outside the loop at the moment – when we care to announce it, with trumpets.'

He was going out carrying his files, was at the door.

'May I say, Freddie, that I much admire your attitude – you know, to life, so very professional.'

'Thank you. Kind words are always appreciated.'

A blurt. 'I was very sad at what happened to you. I moved mountains to block it but was overruled from on high. It wasn't me . . .'

'Never thought it was, Gilbert. I'm grateful for your friendship. A co-ordinator will be a good catch, and he'll be all yours.'

He strode off down the corridor towards the lift. It was said throughout the lower floors of Vauxhall Bridge Cross that the assistant deputy director had saved himself only by an excess of brown-nosed diligence – but it made Frederick Gaunt happier to hear the cretin squirm. But true happiness would be the capture of a co-ordinator and the breaking of a rat run.

He stood naked in front of the wardrobe and sang to himself a song of the mountains, a fighting man's song. His fingers ran over the material of the suit jackets hanging in front of him. His voice reached a crescendo as he made his choice. There were ten suits from which Timo Rahman could select the one he would wear, and twenty ironed and folded shirts were in the wardrobe drawers; on the rail inside the left door were forty ties. At his father's knee he had first learned the words of the song and the lilt of its tune.

The suit he took from its hanger was expensive but not ostentatiously priced in the shop overlooking the waters and the needle fountain of the Inner Alster. The shirt had been bought for him by Alicia in the Monckebergstrasse, where she liked to go, where the Bear accompanied her. The tie had been a present from the girls for his last birthday, his fifty-third. What he would wear that evening had quiet class, he thought, but would not have cost as much as what would be worn by any of the three men who would entertain him for the concert and then for business over a late dinner. They were bankers: they could show the finery and demonstrate the wealth of their profession . . . Timo Rahman, and it was the basic rule of his life, 'never courted attention. The mirror, on the right door of the wardrobe, as his song died from its peak, reflected his body. In the flesh at the side of his chest was a puckered, still angry scar, the width of a pencil, the result of a .22-calibre bullet. On his muscled belly, near his navel, was a second scar, five centimetres in length, where a knife had slashed but had not penetrated the stomach wall. That evening the bankers would see neither the bullet nor the knife wound. They were from many years back. It was eighteen years since Timo Rahman had left his father, left the mountains north of Lake Shkodra, and had been one more Albanian making the trek to the German city of Hamburg in search of success. He had found it. The evidence of it was that he would be the guest of three bankers for a concert at the City Hall and would be taken to the Fischerhaus, a private room, for dinner, where they would scrabble for his investment cash. The days when he had fought were long past. Success was his.

Timo Rahman was the *pate* of Hamburg. At police headquarters, far out to the north of the city at Bruno-Georges-Platz 1, they would refuse to accept the presence of a godfather in the city. But he ruled it: the city was his.

As he dressed, the girls came to him, brought by their mother. They chattered to him of their day at school, in Blankenese, and what they would be doing the next day. They could have walked to school from the villa, but that argument was long over. They did not walk the five hundred metres to the school with their friends: they were driven by the Bear. It was his rule, and beyond dispute. Their mother, Alicia, knew it but the girls did not. A man of Timo Rahman's prominence in the world of organized crime had many enemies. They drove to school, and the Bear was always armed – and the pistol, listed as being for target practice, was legally held.

The girls had holidayed in Albania, his country and Alicia's, but they would grow up as Germans and would know nothing of the source of their loving father's wealth. They chattered about school outings, sports events and music lessons. He was straightening his tie, listening to them and indulging them, and he turned.

Both the girls had their backs to the picture on the dressing-room wall.

They never noticed it now, had not spoken of it since they were small.

He looked past them, listening to them but without attention. Timo Rahman could have bought any painting in any gallery in the city of Hamburg. Financially, no work of art, oils or watercolour, was beyond him. On the wall behind the girls, in his dressing room, was the picture of which he was most proud. Once black and white, now sepia-tinted, with little tears at the sides and a line across it diagonally where it had once been crudely folded, it had written on it in faded writing in the English language: 'For Mehmet Rahman, A worthy comrade in arms and a most loyal friend, Affectionately, Hugo Anstruther. (Lake Shkodra, April 1945)'. It showed a hillside and a cave and in the foreground was a smoking fire with a cooking tin on it. Three men sat cross-legged near the fire. Anstruther was the tallest, head and shoulders above Mehmet, Timo's father, and the squat, cheerful little man who was Percy Capel. Behind, nearer to the cave's entrance, were five of his father's followers, all draped with ammunition belts and proudly displaying the weapons dropped for them. On the day of his father's burial, near to that cave, his mother had given Timo Rahman the picture from his father's bedroom. It was still in the plastic frame, bought in Shkodra fifty years before. It was an icon for him, and his daughters never spoke of it, as if the privilege of youth in Blankenese, in the villa up the dead-end private road, in Hamburg, had erased any interest in it.

Each time he sang that song he thought of his father and gazed at the valued photograph. And the link lived on . . . but he had no time that evening to reflect on it.

Timo Rahman kissed the girls, told Alicia – not that it was her business – he would be late back.

The Bear, who would have died for him, drove him into the city.

'No, no, don't turn your back on me. I want to know. How did you twist him?'

She was Tony Johnson's wife. Every senior officer at the National Crime Squad said she had had a better future than him, would at least have made inspector and might have gone as high as commander. But she'd jacked it in and now worked in an antiques shop and said it had taken years off her, getting out.

'Come on, come on. Spit it out.'

When he had come back last night she had been asleep, and had still been asleep when he had gone to work that morning. He'd done the day, then a crash conference had been called without notice in the evening on his specialist work area, organized-immigration crime. He hadn't had the car with him, and a points failure had held up the trains. They were in bed and he was desperate for sleep . . . No way he could treat her as Need To Know; if she hadn't packed it in he'd have been calling her 'ma'am' by now. She knew everything he did about the life and times of Malachy Kitchen. He told her what he'd said in the parking area.

'You never had a mate who fell through a roof and did his spine.'

He shrugged.

'You've never told me you'd been to Stoke Mandeville hospital – have you?'

He shook his head.

'You invented the whole bloody thing – right?'

He nodded.

'Is he up for it? They're vicious little creatures. What is it they're called? Yes, right scumbags and you told me – the High Fly Boys. They'll be fine for a start. Can he do the business?'

He kissed her, reached over and switched off the light on her side, then swung himself away from her.

'All right, I haven't seen Millie and you have. But this is heavy stuff. I only hope you're comfortable with it . . .'

★   ★   ★

66

The High Fly Boys ruled that corner of the estate. Their territory was blocks eight, nine, ten and eleven. The Rough Track Boys had different ground, over towards the Old Kent Road, and the Young Walworth Boys had the blocks on the west side of the Amersham. The High Fly Boys kept to their own patch, which had fair pickings, and if there were no sales they could smash in a car window for its radio, or run keys down its side, then demand cash for its future protection, or break any sheet of glass that was not reinforced with mesh, or jostle a mother with her pram. The police never caught them. No one on the estate ever dared to inform on them. They ran free.

They pushed wraps of brown. They bought from the Amersham's main dealer, sold on to the vagrants, took their share and strutted the streets, alleys and walkways of the part of the estate that was theirs. Their uniform, shoplifted or gained by threats from a store manager who didn't need hassle, was a sleek leisure suit, Adidas or Nike trainers that were top of the range, gold chains, and they talked a code patois that coppers couldn't crack. Each, in the High Fly Boys, had his own tag.

Danny Morris's was Cisco. He was mixed race, from a one-night stand between a white American USAF technician and his West Indian mother. He led the High Fly Boys. He rode a £550 mountain bike, stolen. If there was war he had access to a pistol, hired by the twenty-four hours. If it was normal he carried a switchblade knife. He had no fear of what police or the courts could do to him. He could barely read, but knew the telephone number of a solicitor, and understood enough arithmetic to work out his cut from what he sold. He knew by heart all of the regulations governing stop-and-search by police officers, all of the custody legislation. A probation officer had once told him he was 'arrogant and in denial of your unacceptable behaviour', and he had spat in the man's face. He was eighteen years old and had no comprehension of the next week's horizon. He took a pitch, each evening, near the door of the Pensioners' Association and waited for instructions from the dealer on the night's trading.

Already there, his bike against the wall, was Leroy Gates. Leroy's tag was Younger Cisco. His ethnic mix was Italian father, whereabouts

67

unknown, and West Indian mother. He was sixteen, could neither read nor write, and stammered when stressed. Excluded from mainstream education at fourteen, after four suspensions, he was classified in a confidential social-services report as 'effectively outside parental and institutional control and . . . locked in a culture of despair, he refuses to believe that worthwhile opportunities other than petty criminality are open to him'. His angelic face and sad eyes were hidden by a ski mask when he thieved. He was the hard one of the gang.

Last to the corner by the Pensioners' Association doorway, shuttered and locked, was Wilbur Sansom, aged fifteen, with the tag Younger Younger Cisco in the identifying style of the gangs roaming the estate. It was probable, from the colour of his skin and the structure of his face bones, that he was of north African and Arabic origin; it was not known. At a few weeks old, he had been dumped in a telephone box in Deptford, then fostered. For the courts, and in the past for school registers, he had the family name of the proxy parents, Sansom; his first name had been allocated to him by a nurse at the hospital he had been brought to from the telephone box. He was a disappointment to teachers, foster-parents, police and social workers. Younger Younger Cisco – he would not answer to anything else – could read well and write with a strong hand. A child psychiatrist had rated him as having above average intelligence. He was slight in build, and seemingly unthreatening, so the Sansoms had given him a mobile phone for his fourteenth birthday, so that he would feel more secure when he was crossing the estate to and from school or the youth club.

The Rough Track Boys had beaten him more than was necessary to steal his phone. It had been replaced by his foster-parents, but within a week he had come home, mouth bleeding, without the second phone, courtesy of the Young Walworth Boys. He had offered himself to Cisco's gang for protection. As a visible member of the High Fly Boys he was no longer a target for violence. He never went to school, was known to the police, had collected four court cautions and was threatened next with an Antisocial Behaviour Order. He cared nothing. With his gang he was safe. His value to Cisco and Younger Cisco was simple. He could read the

68

instructions written on cigarette paper by the dealer for pick-ups and drop-offs; he was their eyes.

Later, as the night closed down on the Amersham, they would move to a black hole in a fence behind which block eight's big rubbish containers were stored, and shadowy figures would flit towards them – the vagrants they despised, clutching money and ready to buy. Everyone who wanted wraps and craved brown knew where to find them. For the three teenagers it was a night the same as any other, and cold rain spattered the shoulders of their leisure suits as they waited for the early buyers.

It was like the first steps on an ice-covered pond. Malachy laid out in front of him what he had bought: rope from the hardware shop on Walworth Road and a penknife to cut it, parcel-binding tape from the stationer's in the side-street off the market, and a plastic toy from a stall. He also had the clothes from the bin-liner that had been under the bed.

He checked the purchases and the clothing, as he had before. It might have been kit and weapons for an exercise on Salisbury Plain, the Northumbrian moors or a patrol in a sprawling Iraqi village. He went through each stage of the plan that had fastened in his mind.

He could rely on what he had seen done.

He had been at the depot for recruits, a week short of the end of fifty-six days' Basic Training. Before he had left home, his father had told him, 'You're pig stupid to have gone this route. I wash my hands of you. All I can say is, remember that a lion pride rejects a weak cub. Drop short of your platoon's standards and the rest of them will be merciless. The private soldier turns into a ruthless thug when punished collectively for the failure of one of their number . . . but it's your choice.' He'd gone. No letters from the retired brigadier, and none written to him or to Malachy's mother. One recruit was useless – should have gone for premature voluntary release – but hadn't quit. That recruit had been half dragged and half carried, in full kit, on the half-mile road run. He had been covered-for when he had lost his beret. His final act had been the making of his barrack-room bed: wrinkles in the hospital corners of the blanket. An officer doing the inspection with the platoon sergeant had commented on it snidely. After escorting the officer out of the barracks room, the sergeant had come back and gone nose to nose with that recruit and had bollocked him with a spittle-dense volley of obscenities, then barked the punishment: the sergeant had been shown up in front of the officer and had gone for the top-heavy punishment, collective. The platoon was 'confined to barracks' for five days, with extra duties and doubled inspections. Malachy had stood at the back, not spoken, not intervened and had not taken part when the platoon took its revenge on that recruit. In flat thirteen, on block nine of the Amersham, he remembered the revenge of the platoon.

It was what he would replicate, but he did not know whether it was for Millie Johnson's bruised face and broken arm or for himself.

When he had checked each item he would take with him for the third or fourth time, the rope had been cut into lengths and the plastic toy was out of its packaging, Malachy stripped off the clothes that had been bought for him at the charity shop. The trousers in the bin-liner stank, as did the shirt and socks. He dressed in the vagrant's clothes he had worn in the underpass at Elephant and Castle when he had begged, drunk, and slept. He put on his head the rolled-up woollen hat that had been pulled down over his face, with eye slits and a mouth hole, on the nights when it was cold enough for a pond to freeze.

Last out of the sack were the old shoes, and he slipped them on.

He locked the door behind him and went off along the walkway, paused for a moment at the top of the stairs, ground his nails into his palms, as if that would strengthen him, and joined the night's shadows moving on the Amersham.

4

On another morning, the sirens would have woken Malachy.

Dawn was breaking over the estate. He slept until full daylight. There was no reason for him to rouse himself, get up and wash, decide whether to shave with the blunt blade and dress in the charity-shop clothes. He had not been asleep when the sirens started, vague and distant at first, then clearer as they came closer. He had not slept because he had waited for the sirens, had lain in his bed, ears keen, through the long hours of darkness. When the sirens approached, coming up the Old Kent Road, then swinging into the Amersham, he could have pushed himself off the bed, gone to the window and looked out over the plaza towards the flat roof of block eleven, but he did not. He knew what the ambulance-men, the fire brigade and the police would find.

It had rained in the night but with the dawn came a low sunshine that spilled through the window. He had not drawn the curtains. If he had slipped off the bed and looked out on to the far side of the plaza, the sun's weak light would have fastened on his work. He had no need to see it.

The clothes from his work were now back in the bin-liner, with his shoes, the penknife, the remaining tape on the roll and the plastic toy. He did not know yet whether he felt satisfaction at what he had done. He rubbed his cheek, and could feel the thin scratches from fingernails that had penetrated the woollen hat. There was a bruise on his right shin where one had kicked him but it was only with a trainer and the bruise was little more than an irritant; nothing in comparison to those on the face of Millie Johnson.

He rolled over, turned his face to the wall and his eyes were locked shut. Others would come to stand and gawp, but Malachy had no need to.

* * *

A crowd gathered on the worn grass beside the kids' swings and roundabouts in the plaza.

That morning, Dawn would be late for the ministry. It was too good to miss: her supervisor always said that a watch could be set on Dawn's punctuality at work – even when she had had the flu she had been there with the mop and bucket and the vacuum cleaner. Not that early morning. She positioned herself at the edge of the crowd, did not reckon to use her bony elbows to force a way to the front. At the back she was closer to the parked fire engines, the two ambulances, the police cars and wagon. It was the best show she had seen in many years on the estate, better than any of the Christmas cabarets at the Pensioners' Association or at the annual parties for the Tenants' Association. Two of them had been hoisted up on to the flat roof of block eleven and one still hung suspended from the rope. Where she was, Dawn could hear the conversations among the firemen, the ambulance teams and police officers, and it was good listening.

A fireman said to his senior, who had just reached the plaza, 'Never known anything like it, Chief, not on the Amersham. I suppose it's a feud between the low-lifes, what the army would call "blue on blue". Done a proper job, though. They're all taped up, ankles together and wrists behind their backs and they've gags in their mouths. Then rope was tied round the ankles and they were hung out over the edge of the roof with the rope fastened to the block's communal TV aerial. Been there half the night and they couldn't shout because of the gags in their mouths, and they wouldn't have wriggled around, would they? Bloody sure I wouldn't, not with more than a sixty-foot drop under me and my life depending on whether the rope's knot held. I'd have done what they did, stayed damn still. The word is that they're the kingpins of the local horror story, call themselves the High Fly Boys. Tell you what, Chief, they were that. They were high and they were flying, except for the rope. Must have been there for hours, and nobody saw them till the light came up. What I'm getting, they're right nasty scallys. They're the gang that push the class-A stuff round the estate. Last night, if you'd asked me, I'd have said – and sworn on it – that they were frightened of nothing. Different story now. Don't quote me, Chief, but this call-out's been a real pleasure.'

In front of Dawn the crowd parted. Few of the residents who lived in the flats overlooking the plaza dared to look direct into the faces of the two youths who were escorted by the ambulance crew and police officers through the opening that the residents made. Dawn recognized Leroy Gates and Wilbur Sansom – everybody on that part of the Amersham knew them. They sold; the vagrants bought. It went through her mind fast: because they sold and the vagrants bought, her best friend, the closest, was in hospital with an operation scheduled for that evening – the swelling would be down enough – to pin or plate a broken arm, and her face was a bright mass of bruises. The thought of Leroy Gates and Wilbur Sansom swinging upside down through half the night, and no help coming, was sufficient to bring a smile to Dawn's face, the first time she had allowed herself that little luxury since the call had come and she had rushed out – no night buses – to tramp all the way to the hospital by the river. She did what none of the others in the split crowd did: she fastened her eye on them. But they didn't meet her gaze: they shivered. If the ambulance crew had not held them up by the arms, they would have collapsed. She spat in front of them – had never done anything as crude in her life before. They came past her and she looked away from them and up towards the roof of block eleven. The third was being pulled up by firemen towards the angled edge of the flat roof. She heard what was said.

An ambulance girl spoke to her boss: 'First signs are, and it's extraordinary, there's not a mark on them. They were traumatized when the fire guys lifted them up on to the roof, but we did quick checks on their bodies and we didn't find anything. They weren't beaten, nothing like that. They can't speak, in a state of terror. I've been here before, when there's been war between the High Fly Boys and the Rough Track Boys, and there's been blood. Not this time. I hope they've put them on plastic, because they've wet themselves and shat themselves – God, do they stink! My opinion, they should go to hospital for a check-over, maybe stay for a day's observation, but it's not medical help they need. They're in shock. I doubt anything in their charming little lives has been like this. Don't know how I'd be if I'd been hung out to dry like a bloody piece of washing – makes you think, doesn't it? – and wondering whether the rope

73

would hold. Different, isn't it? Not that I'm complaining, but it's not what usually happens when these dysfunctional creatures scrap. Just different.'

The last group came through the crowd and headed for the cluster of vehicles. Dawn saw Danny Morris. His face was pale grey and she could see where tears had streamed from his eyes and had run up by the bridge of his nose and over his forehead. He was carried. His Nike suit had been pure white but the crotch was stained and the fabric over his buttocks. She rejoiced. The barricades on doors such as Millie had, the fear of old people about going out into the night, the need to clasp at a handbag and try to keep it safe from being snatched were because of the likes of Danny Morris. If it had been the day before, if she had seen him and the others walking on the pavement towards her, she would have backed away into a recess and hoped she wasn't noticed. She did not look into his eyes but, with purpose, stared at the groin stain, and hoped he would see. It was a pity if it was what the fireman had called 'blue on blue': it would have been better if those on the Amersham had set aside their fear and struck back . . . Not possible. If the Rough Track Boys had done this there was still cause to rejoice. Behind Danny Morris, a policewoman carried the plastic evidence bags: small ones contained wraps, the larger ones lengths of rope and cut sections of heavy masking tape. Dawn saw that Danny Morris, who was hardly capable of walking and whose arms were held, was handcuffed.

A policeman briefed his sergeant: 'It's bizarre and it leaves me confused. Doesn't seem right for us to put this down to the other gangs. Any sort of fight and there would be blood, mayhem, noise, chaos. None of that. Not a word, not a call. And not a sound . . . Somehow somebody got them up on the roof having broken down the entry door up there, trussed them like bloody chickens, fastened the ropes to the TV aerial stanchion, lowered them over the edge and walked away. That's not the Rough Track Boys or the Young Walworth Boys. They haven't the wit for it. For them it would have been knives and, perhaps, a shooter, if there was that much aggravation between them. It's sort of vigilante stuff, but we've never had that all the time I've been on the Amersham. There aren't the sort of people here who're up for it . . . I just don't understand. Looking on the bright side, and there's reason for that, they each had a wrap – and I guarantee it'll be a wrap of heroin – in their pocket. At the least we can do them for possession of a class-A drug. If the sun shines on us we can probably add "intention to trade". They were so scared . . . That little rat Morris, he clung to my legs when we got him up and safe, like I was his guardian angel. It's made my day. Only one cloud. If the High Fly Boys are out of business, lost too much face, and there's a hole, then more scumbags'll be lining up to fill it. Still, someone did the business and did it well, if you know what I mean.'

The ambulances drove away, then the fire engines and the police numbers scaled down. As the crowd thinned, Dawn glanced down at her watch and started to run. She needed to be lucky and get a bus quick on the Walworth Road. As she puffed out of the estate, she thought of the excuses to be concocted for her supervisor, and what she would tell Millie later. She would be at the hospital straight after work, be there when they took Millie down to theatre and be in the ward for when she came back from the operation. She ran well, happy.

They should have gone at midnight, but the assault had been delayed till five in the morning. Then more delay.

It was now past eight and Polly saw Ludvik stride along the pavement towards her. He was grinning, hand lifted, thumb raised. About damn time too. Behind him, at the end of the alley, the storm squad, backs flat against the wall, edged towards the outer door – big men, black overalls, helmeted, and enough fire power in their fists to start a war. The first postponement had been about the other occupants on the staircase leading to the top-floor apartment under the roof: should they be moved to safety, and how much noise would that make – how much warning would it give? There had been a debate, and at two in the morning, as she had shivered under her coat, a minister had come to add his opinion, and Justin Braithwaite – her station chief – had pitched up to add his pennyworth, but by five o'clock it had been agreed that the other occupants would be left to their beauty sleep. Then the second postponement: did they need a probe, audio or visual, drilled up from the floor underneath into the apartment, and how much noise would that make and how would they get into that apartment without waking the dead throughout the building? With his second pennyworth, Braithwaite had been succinct: 'For fuck's sake, just get on with it.' Then there had been interference on the radio links between the storm squad and their control. Braithwaite had gone back to his bed, a second minister had come and there was the question of what would happen to the building – historic, part of the city's heritage, dating back to the fifteenth-century rule of Wenceslas the Fourth – when the top-floor apartment was stormed. They had waited for more fire-tenders to reach Kostecna. Then other occupants had started to leave for work and had had to be grabbed and silenced at gunpoint – more arguments.

Now they were going.

Polly Wilkins had once spent a day with what Frederick Gaunt irreverently called 'The Hereford Gun Club'. She had been with three other recent Service incomers to the special forces on the edge of a country market town. There, she had stood under an old clock tower and read the inscription:

> *We are the pilgrims, Master, we shall go*
> *Always a little further. It may be*
> *Beyond that last blue mountain buried with snow,*
> *Across that angry or glimmering sea.*

She'd thought it naff and self-indulgent, until she'd watched a training session in their Killing Room: she had been deafened and almost frightened to death by the explosions and ricocheting rounds, the smoke and the shouting, and she'd crept back to London in awe of the pace and ruthlessness of the simulated attack. Now men from the Prague police were going into a Killing Room, doing it for real. She wondered how good they were . . . from Hereford she remembered overwhelming power and speed. Were these men, young Czechs, good enough?

Time to find out. Ludvik strode close to her.

She recalled the last signal from Gaunt: 'Good on you, Wilco. From this distant end we anticipate the capture of a full-blown co-ordinator. We are all ears, Gaunt.' She had always been Wilco to Frederick Gaunt, his little joke. Old RAF slang for 'Will Comply' was 'Wilco'. It was a name that indicated his admiration for her – Polly Wilkins did as she was asked and, more, had the dedication. Other women at Vauxhall Bridge Cross thought it patronizing. She did not, and wore the name like a badge, with pride.

Ludvik said, 'We are going now. As your Mr Braithwaite remarked, "For fuck's sake, just get on with it." We are, at last, to get on with it. Perhaps it will be spectacular. You have a seat in the best row of the theatre and—'

'Please, Ludvik, shut up.'

It was not meant to wound his enthusiasm. But Polly Wilkins thought it almost obscene that a storm – gun against gun, body against body, faith against commitment – should be treated as theatre by those who would not be a part of it. In the Killing Room at Hereford, as they had come in, she had sensed naked terror and had realized the acute danger created by the assault. The squad was out of her sight, had disappeared through the outer door. She imagined them creeping, soft-footed, up the worn stone steps of the staircase. Behind her, beyond the police cordon, the fire engines revved their engines and made ready, and the ambulances had the doors open and . . . the attack started.

From the upper window, under the old roof tiles where the dishcloth still hung, came the sound of battering, fast, desperate blows, the strike against the apartment door's lock. Then the shooting. At first, one weapon recognizable by its sharp clatter on automatic. Then answering gunshots. A scream, shouting, competed with the firing.

She knew, instinctively, that it had already failed.

Half a minute after the first blows on the door high in the building, with a sledgehammer, Polly Wilkins knew it was screwed. By now, if the storm squad had succeeded, there should have been the thunderclap of the flash grenades in the room and the curl of the immobilizing gas swirling from the window. She thought that the bodyguard and the man reckoned by Gaunt to be a co-ordinator, had been ready for them and waiting. More volleys of shots, but not the flash grenades and not the gas canisters.

Ludvik said, 'I think they will be inside very soon.'

'Accept it.' Her voice was cold. 'They're not inside. Because of the bloody heritage you waited too long. It failed.'

77

'You cannot call it failure, which is insulting. You cannot, yet, call it failure. They are closed in. They have nowhere to go.'

She said, as if tiredness swept over her, 'What my boss would say. Dead they're hunks of meat, alive they're an intelligence dream. We wanted to talk to them.'

He bridled. 'I suppose you will report we are incompetent.'

'I will report that the heritage of the Old City dictated more fire engines were ordered up, that you had many fire engines but no explosives to blow the door off.'

'They are inside, that is what is important.' He faced her, intense. 'Trapped. I tell you, Polly, I believe you give these people too great an admiration. They will shoot, and they will think. When they have thought of their position they will surrender. They are going nowhere. Give an enemy too much importance and he will dominate you.'

She blinked as the pain of exhaustion caught her. She looked up the alley. Two casualties were brought out. The one with the face wound had rich red blood dribbling from the mouth in his balaclava and she could hear the choke in his throat. The other was carried by two colleagues and his hands were across his lower stomach, down from the bottom edge of his bulletproof vest, and he howled as they struggled to run with him. She felt small, alone, so inadequate. And Ludvik, alerted by the beat of the boots and the howl, watched with her.

Polly said quietly, 'I don't give them too much importance.'

They went back to a café behind the cordon.

He crawled across the floor towards the half-open window. It was slow going and the pain came in rivers. It was a big effort for him to crawl, and a bigger one for him to locate the grenade's pin and work his finger into it. He gasped, dragged out the pin, then propped himself up on an elbow and tossed it through the window. For a moment it seemed to bounce on the sill and he wondered if it would roll back and drop down beside him, but it did not. Far below he heard it bounce, men's yells, panic, and the explosion.

Muhammad Iyad bought time. Not much time left to him, but time for the man he protected.

78

The door was barricaded with the cooker and the refrigerator, and with the mattresses from the beds, all wedged between the door and the wall opposite by the table, chairs and the wardrobe from the bedroom. If they came close on the landing above the staircase, he fired sprays of bullets on automatic above the barricade, then slithered back to a corner where the answering shots could not find him. He was down now to his last grenade and to his last three magazines of bullets.

He lay in a pool of his own blood. It was smeared across the carpet from each time he had manoeuvred himself to the firing position. It came from a chest wound and from his shattered knee. To kill the pain, he had only his faith in God and the image of his wife, and the thought that the man would use well the time given him. It was an hour, more than an hour, since they had last approached the door when he had expended a whole magazine from the machine pistol, and a handful of minutes since he had thrown a fourth grenade through the slit of the open window. Of course he would die in the little room on the top floor in a city far from his home and the family he loved. He had no fear of death. The only uncertainty in the mind of Muhammad Iyad was that he had not given the man the time that was needed.

Before they had come – in the night – before he had heaved the barricade into place, he had cleaned the apartment. With water and soap, he had scrubbed down every surface where the man's fingers might have rested, plates he had eaten off and cups or glasses he had drunk from. The bedding in which he had slept, the clothes from the man's bag, his tooth-brush, razor, and spare trainer shoes were piled in a loose heap in the room's centre. They were there because Muhammad Iyad was one of the few in the Organization who understood the power of the enemy. The skill of their fingerprint experts and the quality of their ability to examine for microscopic particles of DNA were known to him. No trace of his man was to remain when the ability to fight – not the will for it – had seeped from Muhammad Iyad's body.

There were new sounds beyond the barricade – scraping noises, as rats might make, and he thought they chipped away stones from the dividing wall under the roof tiles and sought to come at him from above.

79

He knew about the grenades with the thunder noise that deafened and the flash that blinded, and about the gas that choked. Too long – if he waited for them to come, waited too long, and he was unable to light the fire . . . . but every second he delayed, each minute, every hour he bought, gave the man more time. They were closer, more urgent in their work.

Muhammad Iyad hoped that prayers would be said for him. He trusted that in his village, in the far-away mountains of Yemen, men would speak well of him. There was a story of the dying moments of the great prince Saladin, who had defeated the Crusaders on the hill of Kurn-Hattin. He had been told the story, as a child, by the imam of the village: when Saladin lay dying he called for his stand-ard-bearer and ordered him to ride round the limits of the city of Damascus with a torn-off rag from Saladin's shroud on the tip of the standard-bearer's spear, and to shout out that Saladin had gone with no more of his possessions to his grave than his shroud. It was fitting to be so humble, and Muhammad Iyad hoped to ape the great prince. Nothing would go to his unmarked grave, the body buried in the dead of night, but his faith in God, his love for his family and his sense of duty to his brothers and friends. He fired an angled burst into the ceiling, towards where the scraping had been, and heard the rats squirm back. An oath was muffled by the stone-work and the ceiling's plaster cascaded down to whiten him and make a film over the blood in which he lay, like the snow of the Afghan mountains. He reloaded, tossed away the empty magazine and called instructions, as if he was ordering another man where to be and when to fire.

He felt the weakness growing – knew that God and Paradise beck-oned. If he delayed, if the weakness overwhelmed him, the DNA would not be destroyed. He took the last grenade from the black bag and the last magazines, and a box of matches. He laid the grenade on the whitened floor, put the magazines on top of the heap of bedding and clothes, then made a little burrowed space at their base. He tore up scraps of paper from the bag, the coded instructions for each move forward in the journey. He struck the first match, and the paper lit.

Then he struck a second match, lit the paper better, and a

third, and blew lightly on the fire; blood from the chest wound was at his lips.

When he saw the flames climb and spread, Muhammad Iyad pulled the pin from the grenade and slid it under his stomach, his gut held down the lever. If he moved, or was moved, the lever would fly free and seven seconds later the grenade would detonate.

The smoke gathered in the room and the wind from the open window fanned the fire.

When the bedding and clothing under the magazine caught and the heat reached furnace point, the bullets would explode and career round the room and into the walls and the ceiling, which would win more minutes; if he shifted away from the fire the grenade would explode.

He did not think he could have done more to win the man time to get clear and resume the journey to the north German coastline.

He had something that day to tell his wife.

The wind came in low off the sea and caught the wires that divided the gardens of the properties in Westdorf. The homes, the few that were occupied all year and the many that were opened and aired only when the tourist season started, were now packed close together. When Oskar and Gertrud had come to the island of Baltrum, in their flight from his family's past, it had been a perfect refuge. Now every hand-kerchief of open ground in Westdorf, and in the twin community of Ostdorf, was packed solid with buildings. He, the complainant each time there was a whisper of new foundations going in, was now over-looked each summer and swamped by visitors; he hated them. If Oskar had not been so old, and the arthritis in his knees had been less acute, he told himself he would have moved to the neighbouring island of Langeoog, or even to the more deserted Spiekeroog, but it was a fantasy. Gertrud was at Ostdorf, and he would never leave her.

Oskar Netzer lived in an old house in the heart of Westdorf. Homes on the island did not have names but were identified by numbers. The lower the number, the older the house. A hundred years before, his would have been the home of a fisherman. Its number was 23A, but around him and prying into his life were 248,

212, 179 and 336. All were empty, locked and shuttered, and would stay that way till Easter week; he loathed Easter, when the hordes returned.

No one visited Oskar at house number 23A. No guests were invited in. Anyone who called could state their business at the door even if the rain lashed on them. In the years since Gertrud's death, not a single person had seen the inside of his living room or gone up the stairs and witnessed the state of the bedroom or been led into the kitchen for a welcoming mug of coffee. The house was enveloped with grime. His living room was littered, table, chairs and floor, with planning applications for development. He rotated the sheets on his bed every three or four weeks, and hung out the dirty ones in summer or winter to be washed by the rain; the winds took away their smell. In the kitchen, pots, plates and pans were encrusted with fat. It was – and his neighbours were loud in their complaints when they arrived for their summer vacations, from Bremen or Hamburg, Cologne or Düsseldorf – a pig-sty. Their opinions did not concern him, and the filth of his home had little effect on his health. The resident doctor on the island had opined that Oskar Netzer was not mentally unstable, merely *eccentric*. The secret of his past, the shame he carried through blood, was known only to him and had been shared only with Gertrud, who was dead now.

In a month, there would be a mass of wild flowers that he could pick from his overgrown garden lawn, which was never mown, and take to the cemetery. That day there were daffodils for cutting. The wind snatched at his overalls and heavy coat, ripped at his old Frislander's cap and rifled against his face.

He left his front door flapping open.

A councillor came out of the supermarket. Oskar had opposed the building of the second supermarket, had succeeded in delaying it for two years before permission was given. Behind the supermarket were the high floodlights of the public tennis courts. Oskar had fought them, and their building had been post-poned for twenty-eight months, until his objections were overruled. To the mainland side of the tennis courts was the monstrosity of the Fitness Studio, his greatest defeat. But for every failure there had been successes: a block of holiday apartments, permission reluctantly refused by the council, an all-weather football pitch and eight new homes – and now the extension to the pasta and pizza outlet.

The councillor with his trolley was in front of him.

'What a charming sight – the dutiful widower with flowers, a devoted man for whom a stranger might feel sympathy.'

'Your way, the island would be concreted from north to south,' Oskar growled. 'From east to west.'

'But the stranger would be ignorant. The stranger would not have known of the poison an old fool can spurt.'

'I do what's right for Baltrum.'

'Flatulent arrogance. Can't keep your nose out, can you? Have to interfere. The island survives on the money it makes in the season – and only a senile idiot fails to see that fact.'

'Step aside.'

'When I've finished,' the councillor spat back. 'All of us, in a competitive world, strive for the future of the island. Each year thousands of euros, which could be better spent on our community, are wasted by the required legal investigations to your objections. You, one man, bleed us dry. Prying and interfering, Herr Netzer, is all you are good for . . . I say this, and I am not proud of it, she is better where she is than listening to the drivel you manufacture.'

'Would you have made money from the extension to the pasta and pizza place?'

'I offer you the future. One day you will interfere once too often, pry into a hole, find a wasps' nest and be stung. Who then will help you?'

'I go my own way. I know what is right.'

The trolley was pushed out of his path. The wind fluttered the councillor's hair. The short spat had no effect on Oskar. He thought that the price he paid for his vigilance was the rudeness of those who did not comprehend his concern for the island of Baltrum. He would not change, he would fight until death took him – as it had taken Gertrud. He strode away and his fist was tight on the stems of the daffodils. To his right was the grass strip for light aircraft to land; he had opposed it and said that the noise of the planes would disturb the island's wildlife. Further to his right was the little lake that was fed only by rainwater and the field converted to a children's play area; he had opposed that and said it was too adjacent to the *Westheller*, the marshland, a summer haven for wading birds. Before he reached Ostdorf, the smaller of the two villages at the western end of the island, a horse-drawn cart had veered by him because he would not give way. All building work was done in autumn, winter and spring, and the materials were brought in by the ferry, then loaded on to horse-drawn carts to be taken to the site. This one was to change a two-bedroom house into a five-bedroom eyesore, the extra rooms for visitors – and that fight, too, after a year of conflict, he had lost.

He came to the cemetery at the limit of Ostdorf's development. The flowerbeds in the garden of house number 23A, which she had tended, were overgrown and beyond recognition, but the daffodils she had planted still flourished for him to pick. The garden in front of her grave was meticulously tended. Not a weed in the sandy soil. He bent awkwardly, lowered himself to kneel and laid the flowers in front of the stone. They had a cleanness and purity about them, which should have been the island's virtues.

On Baltrum, Gertrud – dead five years – had been the only soul who knew of his past, and the torture it had brought him. She had sat beside him, and his mother, in the Hamburg lawyer's office when his uncle's will was read and when the letter of confession – with a dying man's shake in the handwriting – had been produced. First the letter had been read in the lawyer's clipped tone; its second reading had been in his mother's halting, shocked voice. The confession had driven him from his work as a construction foreman in the Blohm & Voss shipyard: he had resigned the day after the visit to the lawyer's room in the humid summer of 1975. He had sold their property, a three-room apartment in Hamburg-Rothenburgsort, cheaply for speed. They had gone to Baltrum, bought the house and he had believed himself safe from the intrusion of the outside world.

As a child, Oskar Netzer had come through the *Feuersturm* bombing in August 1943. As an adult he should have been stronger when confronted with the letter of confession; he had not. It had made of him the self-centred recluse kneeling in front of the weathered stone. He was alone with her, the only company – other than the beloved eider ducks – that he sought.

84

'I showed them, my sweetheart, that they could not ignore me. They loathe me but I do not care. I thought they would burst blood vessels. Now, coming here, I am accosted by a councillor – you will remember him, Schulz, with the face of a goat. He accuses me of interference, prying, putting my nose where it has no business. The idiot thinks he offends me. I am proud of his description. More important, my sweetheart, is that the eider are back . . .'

The rain came on harder, soaking his shoulders and the back of the coat, and dribbling on his face; it crushed the blooms of the daffodils and ran on to the stone.

In truth, not much more than interference, prying and putting his nose into other persons' business remained in the life of Oskar Netzer. It was his spine.

The Bear drove Timo Rahman away from the house in Blankenese. As they approached the electrically operated gates, Timo lowered the window, extended his arm and waved. He looked back and for a moment glimpsed the wan face of Alicia in an upstairs window, but she did not wave to him. They pulled out into a quiet street, and he had the window up again.

To neighbours, there was little remarkable about the Albanian who had come to live among them in. Blankenese, a *speckgurtel* district of Hamburg. Blankenese was one of the affluent 'bacon-belt' areas of the city, where the well-fed had their homes. Those neighbours knew little of the man who kept himself to himself, whose wife they rarely saw, whose children were taken by car to school and driven home. His name was not in the newspapers, he did not entertain locally, and offers of drinks or summer barbecues were always politely refused – 'We are already committed on that evening/weekend/lunchtime, and so are unable to accept your kind invitation.' It was the way of the *pate* that the least should be known about him.

He had come far in his life from the village north of Shkodra in the Albanian mountains close to the border with Montenegro.

A VW Passat had been parked on the main road, backed into a driveway so that its occupants could see up the dead-end street and respond easily to whichever way his car turned on the main road: north towards the Blankenese station for the S-Bahn line, or south and the Elbchaussee. Timo leaned across the Bear's shoulder and peered into the mirror. A woman was driving the Passat with a man as her front-seat passenger. Sometimes the surveillance on him was covert, and needed his instinct – and the Bear's – to spot. Sometimes the police of the Organisierte Kriminalität section put a car on his tail in the full knowledge that it would be instantly identified. It was a gesture, covert or obvious, and one to be ignored. Lesser men than Timo Rahman were in the maximum-security wing of the gaol at Fuhlsbüttel. Other than to visit a blood relation eleven years back he had never been there, and such visits were now inappropriate and beneath his stature.

He did not remark on the Passat, two cars back in the traffic behind them, neither did the Bear.

It was the assumption of Timo Rahman that every remark he made – in his bedroom, his kitchen, his car, at a business meeting – was overheard by audio devices. He had been told that the police of the Organisierte Kriminalität boasted to favoured politicians that the equipment available to them was the best in Europe. Nothing that incriminated him ever passed his lips and those he dealt with were schooled at the same desk. He discussed with the Bear, as the VW Passat followed them, the weather forecast for that day in northern Germany, as any of his neighbours would have.

Inside the speed limit, the Bear drove down Elbchaussee. Set back from the wide road, which wound down from the high ground above the river, were the great mansions where the élite of the city's commerce and banking had made their homes, with views across the estuary to the Airbus factory. He could have lived there, could have moved Alicia and the girls into an Elbchaussee home, but it would have drawn attention to him. Timo lived in Blankenese, without the views, among the chief executives and principal department heads, and did not draw comment. But his financial empire, always moving on a steady path to greater legitimacy, based on stocks and bonds, property holdings and aircraft leasings, could have bought him the best.

Fewer than a dozen men – and the woman whose face had been at the upper window of his home – could have brought down the empire of the *pate*, could have consigned Timo Rahman to the

Fuhlsbüttel gaol by their testimony. He had no fear of them. Alicia, watched by her aunt in all her waking hours at the villa, was incapable of action. The Bear could have sent him to the prison they called 'Santa-Fu', but the idea was ludicrous. The net of loyalty around Timo – of which the Bear was part – was the same in Hamburg as it was in the mountains of Albania. It was based on the centuries-old diktats laid out in the *Canun* of Lek Dukagjen, was based on the *besa*, which was a man's word of honour – and violation created an inevitable *hakmarrje*, the blood feud. As his father had in Albania, Timo Rahman sat at the head of a clan, a *fis*, in Hamburg. He had brought with him the disciplines of the *Canun* from the village north of Shkodra to the richest of German cities, and with his baggage had been the impenetrable strength of the *fis*.

The route the Bear took him that day was past the old fish market, where he had been shot by a Russian in the right side of his upper chest. It was when the Russians had come, refugees, into the city, sensed the wealth of the pickings – narcotics, weapons, girls – and sought to muscle aside the power in place. Some of the Russian groups had been 'persuaded' at gun-point to go elsewhere; some had laughed at the advice and had fought for territory. Timo's way had sent the message five times. Russians dead, packed like herrings into ice boxes, then dumped in the boots of cars, which were pushed off the quay of the fish market car park into the waters of the Elbe. The man who had shot him, spitting through his gag, struggling to break the rope on his elbows, had gone into the boot of his Mercedes and he – Timo – had slammed down the lid. All the way to the quay's edge there had been kicking inside the boot . . . and he had helped to push the car over the edge. He had had no more difficulties with Russians. Three or four of the men who had helped him in those days, twelve years before, could have put him with their testimony into a cell at the Santa-Fu, but they were all the *gjak*, blood relations, who would not have contemplated betrayal.

The Passat remained behind them, and took the same turn away from the fish market. Political friends, men bought with money, told him of the director of the unit that dealt with what they designated organized crime. The pinnacle of the director's police career would be the conviction of Timo Rahman, but he would never reach it.

The Bear headed for the Reeperbahn. It was where Timo had begun, where he had been knifed. He took the narrow cut through and they were held up behind a tourist bus that paused for photographs of the street with the high wall at its end and the gap through which only pedestrians could go to the brothels. At the police station, high and brickbuilt on the corner of the Reeperbahn, where the detectives had always failed to link him to ownership and 'immoral earnings', the Bear swung right and into the wide street. Young, fresh from Albania, he had dismissed the Germans who ran the Reeperbahn, fought them and overwhelmed them. Three or four of those who had been at his side in that little war of guns and knives, all Albanians from the northern mountains, could have sworn evidence and imprisoned him, but they were *miqs*, relatives by marriage, and would have died rather than be accused of treachery against him.

Now, increasingly, he was clean. His business activities were distant from the wars on which he had built his empire. The Bear brought him to Schauenburgstrasse and the premises of one of the oldest and most respected legal companies in Hamburg. A fellow guest, but arriving by a different doorway off the street, would be a city politician against whom no stigma of corruption existed. In a private room, over lunch, there would be discussion on the development funds necessary for the building of high-quality offices on one of the few bombsites remaining from the *Feuersturm*; minor investment and major profit in return for development permission being nodded through Planning. Neither the politician nor the lawyer who would chair the discussion, knew of the *Canun* or of the *fis*, had little comprehension of the reach of a blood feud and the vicious reprisals that could be brought down on them and their families, but they understood the threat of public disgrace that an appearance in court would bring them and those they loved, and they would not have lasted a sentence of imprisonment in the Fuhlsbüttel gaol. He was safe from them.

For Timo Rahman the meeting was routine. A matter of greater complexity was nagging in his mind as he took the lift to the upper floor where the lawyer practised hospitality. That matter, the rewards for which were great and the challenge huge, would take him to the western coastline. It excited him because the ground to be covered and the cargo to be delivered were new to him, and the risk to his security was devastating. He shook the lawyer's hand and was ushered inside. What nagged at him was his feeling of certainty that the man he must rely on was a foreigner with no understanding of the loyalties of Timo's people, the grandson of his father's comrade in war, Ricky Capel. The coded name Timo had given him, spoken with contempt, was 'Mouseboy'.

Rubbish day, and from the window Sharon Capel, matriarch certainly of number eight and probably of all Bevin Close, saw the bin lorry edge into the top of the cul-de-sac. Her own wheelie was outside her front gate, on the pavement, but her daughter-in-law next door received better treatment because the boys came down the side of that house to collect her wheelie, then put it back by the kitchen door. Joanne had that small luxury because nothing that concerned her husband, Ricky, was too much trouble for the bin-boys.

Sharon had lost track of time. If she had realized how late it was in the morning she would not have been dusting in the front room. She kept the house spotlessly clean because there was little else for her to do. It hadn't always been that way. She had been in Men's Underwear at British Home Stores for most of Ricky's childhood, and spent evenings washing up in a café, all the years that Mikey was 'away' doing bird and his share of what had not been retrieved by the Old Bill was running down. Mikey had been in Brixton, Wandsworth and Pentonville too long and too often ... and when he was out she had kept up the jobs because the big one that he was going to retire on always fucked up. Mikey had been between release and rearrest on a day when the bin lorry had come into Bevin Close. That same day, Ricky had been a month past his twelfth birthday – and from that day his sisters, Therese and Rachel, had detested him. Small wonder that Therese now lived in Australia and didn't write, and Rachel was in Canada and didn't ring. They should have beaten him that day, made a line and queued up to thrash the little sod – but none of them had. He had stood by the door with his fists clenched and no one had dared face him down when the bin lorry had come along Bevin Close.

It was the day she had realized the nature of her son.

The cat was a coal-black neutered tom and the family called it Soot. It was worshipped by the girls and however many bloody years Mikey had been inside it always greeted him when he came out, like he was Soot's favourite. The cat was old and could be 'caught short'. That morning, wheelie-bin day, Soot had been shut inside little Ricky's room – probably an open window downstairs had slammed the door. Ricky had gone to his room and found that it had crapped right in the middle of his bed. He'd brought the cat down, holding it helpless by the neck, and before any of them could intervene, he had wrung the cat's neck, then smiled, like it was nothing, and taken it outside the front, where the wheelie was waiting for the bin lorry. He had lifted the lid, dropped the cat inside, then gone straight back upstairs, brought down his bedding and dumped that in the wheelie too. He'd come back in, had stood by the door and had dared them, his grandad and his nan, his mum, dad and sisters, to do something. If he had screamed abuse at them, they would have done 'something'. Not like that . . . calm as anything, a little smile at the side of his mouth and no creases on his face. His eyes – Christ, his eyes – had been so bloody cold that they'd terrified her. Not just her: Mikey, who had been a quality get-away driver for wages snatches, and Percy, who had been a one-man crime wave in burglary after his demob. All of them frightened by a boy of twelve because of what was in his eyes.

She went on with the dusting and cleaning. Because of the money her son gave Mikey, she didn't have to work, didn't have to do anything but keep the house clean and cook his favourite meals, and she doubted he even remembered killing the cat.

That day there was a harsher atmosphere on the Amersham. Malachy sensed it.

Not a new dawn, but more a day clouded with uncertainty. He walked.

Old ladies did not linger to gossip with friends as they would usually have done during the daylight hours, kids were not on the soccer spaces, young mothers stampeded with their prams, and the vagrants had disappeared, as if they were fearful of taking the blame for what had happened.

He went right round the perimeter of the area that had been, until the early hours of that morning, the territory of the High Fly Boys. He passed doorways of flats that had been deserted since they'd been torched in disputes, past windows that were boarded up because residents had fled, and along the walkways until he reached the steel barricades erected by police to prevent the pushers having free run. He walked by the empty shopfronts and the closed-down daycare centre. Ivanhoe Manners had told him, months before, that more than fifty million pounds for the New Deal for the Community programme had been swallowed by the estate. He could see no evidence of its value. He strode past the never-used garage with parking bay 286. Fear of the unknown blanketed the estate, and it was because of him.

He did his circuit and when he came back to the main entrance of the stairwell of block nine, he stopped, turned and leaned against the concrete.

Had he concern for the estate? Did he care about Millie Johnson? Was he now self-obsessed? No answers. The estate was in shock because the order of its life was altered. Millie Johnson, waiting for the anaesthetist, wouldn't have cared, not a damn. Just self-centred crap to make him, Malachy Kitchen, feel better, think he was taking a worthwhile step on the ladder.

Nothing achieved, nothing changed for the better.

As self-centred, as self-indulgent as when he had been asked to screen suspects from a lift operation and he had remarked to the battalion's adjutant: 'Be happy to – if your Jocks haven't beaten them all half insensible.' Hadn't told the adjutant, or Cherie who shared the Portakabin with him, of the email that had come in that morning. Not from Roz – he hadn't heard from her for three weeks. The email was from Major Arnold – decent Brian Arnold who might have qualified for the title of kindest old guy at Chicksands. Hoped he was well, hoped his work was interesting, hoped he'd fitted in, hoped he would note 'There's a lot of bicycling these days round Alamein Drive. One cycle is most popular. Cheers and good wishes from all of us deskbound warriors, Brian.' It meant, in code, that Roz was the base bicycle: the Chicksands honey-pot was his home, halfway down the left-hand side of Alamein Drive. So self-centred that he had snapped the sarcasm at the adjutant, and so self-indulgent that his mind had been a country away from the village street when the ambush had been sprung and the RPG round had come in close.

5

Feverishly, Malachy polished.

Back from his walk, the door locked and bolted behind him, he had gone to his bed, knelt and taken the shoes from the black sack.

They were his most valuable possession. His mother had said, 'I know it's all sand and donkey poo down in Basra, dear, but there'll be times when you need to be smart. Your father found that in Aden when he was a sprog subaltern and you were just a star in my eye. You should never be short of a good pair of shoes. I always say that a man's character is judged by his shoes.' Roz hadn't gone with him to Devon for that last lunch before he'd flown from Lyneham to Iraq. She wouldn't have gone if elephants had been dragging her – not after his father had refused to attend his son's wedding to a girl who wasn't 'suitable'. Over sherry before lunch his mother had produced the gift-wrapped parcel with a ribbon round it. When he'd opened the box, the shoes had gleamed at him, and they'd fitted to perfection. He'd gone back with them that night to Alamein Drive and had not shown them to Roz, but he'd worn them on the flight down, and all the days that he was in Brigade before his transfer to the Scottish-based battalion . . . and he'd worn them when they had flown him out.

Roz had hovered above him in the bedroom at the quarters. He had packed a rucksack and a suitcase, everything he would need except the helmet, the flak-jacket and the Browning 9mm, which would be issued to him the next evening when he landed. The evening sun had lit the bed. She had stood over him while he had transferred the neat piles of clothing into the rucksack and the case, and had not helped him. He had sensed the attack was coming and had not known what would trigger it. The shoes had. The strings of the sack were fastened. The photograph of her that he loved

93

most – he had taken it at the Colosseum in Rome, the light bright on her hair and on the walls behind her, happiness on her face – in a silver frame that her parents had given them went into the suitcase and he zipped it shut. He had laid out the starched uniform he would wear on the aircraft, and then he had gone to the wardrobe and taken out the box and the shoes. The attack had gone through sarcasm to anger then on to a sneer when she had seen his mother's note and the crosses for kisses. 'Oh, that's nice. Only the best good enough. What did they cost – two fifty? Where did you find two fifty to spend on a pair of shoes? Isn't there anything *here* that needs two hundred and fifty quid spending on it? Sorry, sorry, a present from Mum. How touching. Be sure to send her a postcard from sunny Basra and tell her you're wearing Mummy's shoes and keeping them nice and shiny.' Her father had retired as a warrant officer (Instructor) at the Royal Military Academy; his father had retired with the rank of brigadier – he'd thought it didn't matter, and had been wrong.

He polished hard – as hard as he had worked on the boots issued him for Basic Training before his father had pulled strings and opened the gates of Sandhurst for him. Malachy sweated as he rubbed the cloth over the toes and was frenzied at his work.

When he had left Chicksands, when he had tried to find work as a civilian, he had worn those shoes. His mother had never seen them on him; his mother and father had declined to meet him. And he had worn the shoes when he had taken the train to London, when he had laid out his money on the counter of the off-licence opposite Marylebone station and had bought the two four-packs of Special Brew, then found a bench and had started, for the first time, to drink away the demons. Midnight, with nowhere to go, and he'd ended up with the derelicts – without a blanket and without cardboard – and he'd seen the eyes covet his shoes. He never took them off. If he had taken them off, that night or in the nights of the weeks that followed, they would have gone. In the hostel he had slept with them under his pillow. His watch had gone, a twenty-first birthday present from a godfather, and his wallet, and his money from begging, which had been in a cheap little purse on a bootlace round his neck, with his tags, but his shoes had stayed on his feet.

Now it was as if Malachy tried to polish away the scars, on the shoes, of his life. With ferocity he burnished the toecaps. They shone – he could see his face in the brogue patterns. More polish. He gripped the left shoe and worked the cloth over it.

He heard the knock at his door and Dawn's voice called to him.

He turned the lock and drew down the bolt. She did not look at his face but stared at the shoe. She said distantly, eyes never off the shoe, 'I am going to the hospital. I want to be there when they take Millie to theatre, and then I will stay till she is awake again. It will be late when I come back. I am going to have to walk from Walworth Road, from the bus. Would you, please, meet me from the bus? I would like that.'

'Of course I will.'

'There is a café by the bus stop. Can we say at eleven o'clock?'

'Yes.'

'Am I silly to be frightened of walking in the Amersham that late, even after what happened to the boys?'

'I don't think so. I'll be at the café by the bus stop at eleven o'clock.'

The siege was over. The firemen's tenders blocked Kostecna, and a lacework of hoses ran down the alley that was too narrow for them to pass. Ladders were thrown up against the building's walls and water dripped. Wisps of smoke filtered up between the tiles where, hours before, there had been flames and billowing black clouds. No more gunfire from under the roof, and the last grenade explosion was a distant memory. It had a finality about it. Hard for Polly Wilkins to recall the excitement of being in the different vans that had kept the street entrance under surveillance, and the frustration of being held back while the storm squad had gone in, and the emotion of seeing the bloodied casualties brought out.

She was at the alley's entrance, where it joined the street, and from there she could smell the charred roof timbers on which the hoses played. Every five minutes, sometimes less, she demanded of Ludvik when she would be permitted to climb the stairs and see the scene for herself; each time she was offered only a shrug. Of course Ludvik did not know. What had been dramatic in its unpredictability now had a dreary certainty. Polly understood why her station chief,

Braithwaite, had gone back to his office and had stayed there. She shivered as the evening's cold settled on her – not that it mattered, but that night there might be one of the year's final frosts. The last time she had phoned Braithwaite to complain about the slowness of the fire crews and the further delays in her getting up the stairs to see where they had made their stand, he had said to her, with annoying plausibility, 'You can put a kettle on the stove, turn on the gas and light it, but shouting at the kettle won't make it boil faster.' She detested that sort of banal logic.

All around her, she heard the cursed protests of residents whose apartments were unaffected by the fire but who were still prevented from returning to their homes. They seemed unable, unwilling, to comprehend the scale of the threat that had settled among them in the top-floor apartment. Bombs, killing, mayhem, catastrophe – the face of al-Qaeda. Two men of al-Qaeda were dead – not an arm or a hand or fist of the Organization, little more than the tip of a fingernail.

She swore aloud and Ludvik turned sharply to look at her.

Polly wouldn't explain. So few did. Dominic had not understood. He was Foreign and Commonwealth Office, had a future, and had bought her an engagement ring with a double diamond twist; the wedding had been talked of vaguely for 'some time next year' and they'd lived together at his Battersea flat, not her Wandsworth pad. He had been posted to Buenos Aires. 'You'll like it there, darling, fascinating culture. You don't want to hang around that place where they kicked you.' What about him chucking in the FCO and coming out to Prague? 'You're not serious, darling, are you? What? Throw up my career?' Was the work of the Secret Intelligence Service of less importance than tramping a cocktail circuit in Argentina? Two months after she'd arrived in Prague and a month after he'd bedded down in Buenos Aires, the email had come: 'Don't think this is going to work. Sorry about that but you made the bed and you'll have to lie on it. Please send the ring, at your convenience, to my parents and they'll know what to do with it. No hard feelings but better to cut and run. I wish you well, Dominic.' The end of the great affair of Polly Wilkins's life . . . because he didn't understand. Only Frederick Gaunt understood. Al-Qaeda, and what it could do – the importance of a co-ordinator – dominated her life, left no room for love . . . damn it.

She waited, with Ludvik, to be called forward, and wondered how it had been for the two men in the top-floor apartment during the last moments of their lives.

Flush against the road, bright as a temple of light, was the gaol wall. They cruised down Artillery Lane.

Ricky Capel did not know how many hundreds of men were held in HMP Wormwood Scrubs. Truth was, he knew little about the prison. He knew about HMP Brixton, about Pentonville and Wandsworth because – as a kid, with his sisters – his mother had dragged him to them and in through the big gates to see his father. What he could remember was that he had screamed and fought and she had held his arm, vice-like, and each time he had seen his father brought through a far door into the visits area, with the screws pressed round him, he had gone quiet and buried his head in his mother's shoulder. He had never looked into his father's face, had never spoken. Out of the big gates, each time, he had run like the wind to the bus stop and not looked back at the walls. But he didn't know Wormwood Scrubs because his father had never done time there . . . He thought his grandfather had, but that was before he was born.

'Go right,' Ricky said, from the back seat.

His cousin Davey drove, and his cousin Benji was beside him. His cousin Charlie was next to Ricky in the back. They turned into Ducane Road. Davey was a harder enforcer than Ricky, didn't care a fuck about the blood he drew and the pain he inflicted. Benji was a clearer thinker than Ricky, scratched at an idea till there was a plan to execute it. Charlie had more comprehension of money and how to move it than Ricky, how to wash and rinse and scrub it clean. But the decision-taking was Ricky's, and he brought together their differing talents. When Ricky, the youngest of them by five clear years, said what would happen there was no disagreement. His leadership was accepted.

The gaol, brilliant under the high arc-lights, fascinated Ricky. He had never been in prison. Few secrets existed between Ricky and the cousins; but his fear of prison was one of them. It was not something he would confide to them, to Joanne, his parents or his grandfather. He kept the secret close, but it lurked in his mind as he peered up at the height of the walls. Only the top floor of the nearest wing was visible, lights behind small barred windows, some of which had washing draped outside. Inside the car, even with the window down and straining to listen, he heard nothing. However many hundreds of men were there, and staff, and however many barred gates there were to slam shut, no sounds came from the place.

'Go right again.'

'There's cameras on us,' Benji murmured.

'I said, go right again.'

'Sure thing, Ricky.' Davey eased the wheel, took them into Wulfstan Street, and past the quarters for prison staff. A curl of contempt licked at the side of Ricky's mouth. Two screws were walking on the pavement, anoraks over their uniform shirts, each carrying a plastic supermarket bag with the possessions they took home from their shift.

'Then right again – isn't this the place, Benji, what you were talking about?'

'Braybrook Street, spot on, Ricky.'

'Tell me about it, like you did.'

They left behind the north-west corner of the prison's perimeter and Davey slowed to a crawl. Behind them were the walls, the lights, the wire and hundreds of men – Ricky twisted a last time to see – then, to the right, was a great open mass of darkness, football pitches, open parkland and the floodlights of a running stadium. On the left, behind a line of parked cars, were semi-detached homes like the one where Ricky lived with Joanne and Wayne.

'It's Braybrook Street, late sixties, sixty-six or '-seven. There's three guys in a car and they've got shooters and they're parked up and killing time before a job's ready. A police car, three blokes in it, comes by and doesn't like them sitting there. They're going to do a check on the vehicle.'

'Like it will be if we don't keep moving. Go on, Benji.' It was as if Ricky were an addict, needed the fix of hearing the story again now that he was here, a gawper in the shadows between the street's lights and half hidden by the parked cars.

'One of them in the vehicle's Roberts, Harry Roberts. The first copper leans through the window and starts with his questions. Roberts shoots him, then gets out, shoots the second copper in the street. I think that's the story, and the third one's shot in the police wheels. Two of them's gone, but Roberts is still inside, or was last time I read about him. Thirty-something years he's done.'

'Mad, wasn't he?'

'It was just after they'd finished with the rope. A few months earlier and they'd all have hanged. Roberts didn't get hanged but he's done thirty-eight years and—'

'OK, OK, I heard you.' Ricky didn't need the story any more. 'Wasn't smart, was it?' In unison, the cousins nodded agreement. 'Right, let's get on back – what's the business?'

They drove away from the gaol.

Charlie said, 'The big new growth area is behind that wall and behind that wire. Class-A stuff is what they want when they're banged up. They want brown and they want coke, and I reckon it's Es as well. What I hear, eight out of ten who go down are showing traces of class-A stuff when they have the check on arrival. That's a heavy market, which is not tapped into. There's no organization for regular supply and that presents an opportunity too good to miss out on. The key thing is "regular", and there's no exploitation of the market yet. There's useful money to be had and it's where we should be.'

Ricky sniggered. 'What you'd call a captive market . . .'

The cousins all laughed, always did at Ricky's humour.

'How do we get it in?'

Benji said, 'Three ways I've identified. First, quite simply, you chuck it over the wall. The price is going down, the street price is depressed because of supply and demand – supply's terrific – and you get some joker with a good arm and he lobs the packets over, and you accept the screws'll find two out of every three, but if you time it for exercise hours the chance is that you'll win with thirty-three and a third per cent. Tennis balls are good, split open, stuff inside, then taped up, and they're fine for chucking. They do that up

99

in Manchester I've heard. Second, you use visitors. Do all the orifices, know what I mean? If there were proper detailed searches on visits there'd be uproar, a mutiny, and not half the people would get inside to see the people. But that's getting harder because there are more dogs and more scanners that sniff the class-A stuff. It's also dispersal of effort. To get good quantities in you have to use too many mules who're swallowing and stuffing – and clogging up the visitors' toilets. Third, you find a screw with a problem – debt, sick kiddie, girlfriend who likes the good life. One screw for one gaol, and he goes in once a week and he has one distributor on the inside. The screw's not going to turn himself in, and the distributor doesn't have to know where it's coming from – so there's a cut-out.'

'How do you get the payback?'

Davey said, 'That's the distributor's problem whichever way you go, Ricky. It's for him to organize. Every taker he sells to has to make the arrangements for payment outside, and the distributor's responsible for getting the cash together. If he's messing you, Ricky, then he's walking a fine line. Bad things can happen to him inside. And bad things can happen to his family outside, and he knows that.'

He had the outline for the enterprise from his cousins. His decision. None of them would have presumed to tell him what that decision should be. They were in the late-evening traffic on the Harrow Road, heading for London's central streets.

'We'll set up the Scrubs first, and if that works we'll go for Wandsworth – I'm not touching Pentonville or Brixton. We'll create a weekly guaranteed supply to one distributor. We find a screw, or a workshops-supervisor guy to take it in. That's how it's going to be.'

Davey grunted assent.

'Good thinking, Ricky,' Charlie said.

A little irritant anxiety broke in Ricky Capel. Would they ever tell him he was wrong? Then a mirthless chuckle came into his throat and a smile cracked the smoothness of his face. He was never wrong. His father had been, not Ricky, and his grandfather had made enough mistakes to get himself inside more than he was out. Davey would drive them across London and they'd pick up the old man, who'd have had a gut full, and bring him home.

* * *

In a corner far from the bar, Percy Capel sat with his cronies. The British Legion, its members former servicemen, was home from home. He was a legend there and he bathed in the glory of the story, which was enhanced by his refusal to talk detail.

Inside the Legion building, tucked away from the bar – to which he seldom went for drinks but allowed others to fill his glass – it was well known that he had been behind enemy lines in the Second World War for months, and should have had a medal for it.

At those November ceremonies in front of rainswept memorials – as the retired squadron leader, their chairman, intoned his address – he and the others present, at awkward attention, wore the medals given them. Percy Capel should have had the Military Medal for his service in Albania: Major Anstruther had been given the Military Cross. What they all knew in the Legion bar was that Percy had been flown back to Alexandria, and the medal citation had gone up to the Gods for ratification – and that Percy had then been nicked by the Redcaps for stealing the petty cash out of a staff officer's bedroom while the bugger slept there. The way he told it, Percy had the cash off the dressing-table and was on his way out when the bedroom rug had gone walkabout under his weight, slid on the polished marble floor, and he'd gone arse over tit and wrecked his ankle. He'd scarpered down a drainpipe and been lifted while he was limping back to barracks. Two years in the glass-house at Shepton Mallet after repatriation in close arrest. When he told that story and the refills of his glass came thick and fast – 'Oh, don't mind if I do' – laughter bellowed the length and width of the bar. But he never talked, for a pint or a laugh, about Albania.

Some tried and failed.

His reply was always the same: 'Saw things done there, my friend, that would make your hair stand—not things for talking of in company.'

Could have talked about the major, the greatest man he'd ever known. Major Hugo Anstruther, who was lined up to inherit thousands of Highland acres, and a titled wife, had taught Percy Capel – his batman, handyman and donkey-minder – everything a man needed to know in the arts of safe-blowing and burglary, and everything a man did not need to know, except in Albania, about how to slit a sentry's throat silently and plant explosives on a bridge that would be detonated under a convoy, sending men, screaming, to death. On the flight out, after the Huns' surrender, Major Anstruther had said to him, 'I think, Percy, you'd be wise to forget most of what you learned with me or at best you'll spend most of the rest of your life locked up and at worst you'll go to the gallows.' He'd seen the death notice for the major, nine years ago, in a newspaper. That night he'd gone on the overnight sleeper to Fort William, taken a bus, then walked four miles and reached a little stone church as they were lifting the major's coffin from the hearse. He'd stood at the back. Anstruther had had the full works: medals on the coffin, piper to play him out, estate workers in their best clothes and enough children and grandchildren to fill a charabanc. Nobody had spoken to Percy. They'd just walked by him like he was a dog turd. Rain coming down heavy, and him in his one suit that he'd wear next at Winifred's funeral, and then at his own.

When they'd all left, just the gravedigger left to smack his spade into the lumps of sodden clay and fill the pit, he'd gone close. The gravedigger had been young and a self-rolled fag hung on his lip. Percy, drenched, had said that he had fought with the major in Albania. 'Where's that?' Water streaming down his face and through his suit jacket, Percy had said he and the major had been comrades in arms. 'When was that?' He'd walked back four miles, had waited two hours for a bus, and caught the night sleeper to London. He had a week in bed with the shivers from his soaking.

They didn't need to know, in the Legion bar, about Major Anstruther and the gang in the cave led by Mehmet Rahman.

Percy Capel didn't buy drinks. Could have done. He had his war pension and his old-age pension, and he lived for free with his son and daughter-in-law and wanted for nothing, and he had the hundred a week in cash that Ricky gave him. Ricky knew about Albania and Mehmet Rahman, and had traded on his grandfather's war. Percy hated his grandson but still took his money.

He was in full flight. 'I was doing this job, a real big property down in Esher – that's a bit off my beat but I'd read in the paper who these folk were – and I'm upstairs and pocketing the stuff and a bloody dog, sounding like a wolf, is up and roaring at the closed door. I'm doing a double-fast runner, down the drain-pipe, when . . .'

Ricky stood at the far end of the bar. Hand up, finger beckoning.

'Sorry, guys. Got to go. My round next time. Doesn't like to be kept waiting.'

He shuffled towards the door, leaving the laughter stifled and his drink unfinished. The talk at home, over the years, about Major Hugo Anstruther and Mehmet Rahman, the little case of mementoes under his bed, had launched the little piece of vermin. He was responsible in part for the empire of his grandson . . . God, it weighed on him.

'Coming, Ricky. Good of you to collect me.'

Everyone danced to Ricky, just as Percy Capel did.

Harry, who was Sharon Capel's brother, danced any way that Ricky wanted him to dance. By dancing, he kept the dream alive.

He was in the wheel-house and rocked gently in the skipper's seat as the *Anneliese Royal* swayed at its mooring ropes. She was ready to sail, except for the ice. Before dawn they would be gone. In an hour Billy and young Paul would drive up to the quay, the ice would be loaded, they would slip the ropes and be gone into the night. Billy had monitored the forecast and told him that for this week weather conditions were predicted as good, not the week after.

He read and he dreamed, and the dream was his sole escape from Ricky Capel.

The dream was of finding a Brixham-built trawler, a boat from the south Devon yards of eighty years ago. It might be up a creek in the south-west, or tied up and forgotten on the Hamble, or left to rot on the mudflats outside a port in Scotland or on the Isle of Man. If after all those years of inactivity – because the diesel engine had taken over from sail power by the late 1940s, which had dictated the dumping of the old trawler fleet – he could discover a trawler with a sound hull and a good keel, Harry's dream would be launched. In his retirement, free of Ricky Capel, he would potter on the carcass of the boat and hope that, before his death, he would have resurrected it, placed in it a new mast, scrubbed the decks and varnished them till they shone, and could put to sea, move across the water at a crisp seven or eight knots in a south-westerly with the full red sails that were the colour of Devon earth – and be in heaven.

He had an hour to read before they brought the ice on board.

But dreams needed paying for. Without Ricky's money, the dream would die.

The book – reminiscences and anecdotes of life on the old powered trawlers – was faded, frayed and had stains on the pages from fingers that had dripped with the fluid of fish stomachs.

When he finished a favourite passage, he locked away the book and waited for the pickup's headlights to spear across the quay. They would fish for five days – without having to navigate towards a marker buoy off Cuxhaven or the rock outcrop of Helgoland to collect a waterproof package – then come back and moor in harbour during the length of the forecast storm, and maybe go to the west and home.

Finally, she had been permitted inside.

Past midnight, and Polly had climbed the stone staircase and had allowed Ludvik's hand to remain on her arm as she stepped over the debris left by the firemen.

A mass of floodlights used by the police and men of the BIS played over the interior. The rain came through the ceiling where the fire had destroyed the roof and pattered on her head. From the doorway, four ladders were laid out over the exposed floor beams because the planks had gone. Two had been placed so that they gave access to either side of the charred heap that had been left untouched by the fire crew.

She shuddered. The smell of the burning, which had been doused by the hoses, then damped by the rain, caught in her nose, but overriding it was a stronger stench, sweet and sickly. She had never been close up to it before, but instinctively she knew it. Quite deliberately, not brooking argument, she pushed Ludvik aside, then sharply tapped the shoulder of a man in front of her and gestured for him to move out of her path. He shifted, and the lights dazzled her through her steel-rimmed, unfashionable spectacles. She shoved her hair out of her face and hitched her skirt high over her knees; if her tights laddered that was of no importance. She slipped plastic gloves over her hands. She had authority because the BIS, the successor to the former Communist regime's StB, had been trained in modern counter-intelligence techniques by agencies from the United Kingdom. She knelt on the ladder to the left of the heap, steeled herself, then reached for a further rung and began to edge out over the open beams.

She was slight but the ladder creaked under her weight, and the cold snatched at her bared legs. She came closer to the source of the stench, and called over her shoulder: 'Has anything here been touched or moved?'

Ludvik answered her: 'Only by the fire, not by us.'

The lights stayed on the heap and the stench drew her forward. She reached out towards the growing clarity of the shapes. Nearest to her was the machine pistol, scorched and lying among burned bedding. At the Fort, above the coast outside Portsmouth, she had done weapons training with the bland instructors who thought all recruits were idiots. Polly had been one of the few who had listened . . . She lifted the barrel, held it pointing to the rainclouds between the beams and passed it behind her, careful that the trigger did not snag. It was taken. She found five blackened magazines and knew from their weight that their bullets had been exhausted. As her hands groped closer to the largest unrecognizable shape in the pile, a sharp, wounding little memory came back to her. She had been driving with Dominic to Scotland for their first week away after they had met. They had been near the border and had stopped to picnic but a cloud had come dark over them from Longtown, made by the funeral pyre of the animals slaughtered to contain the epidemic of foot-and-mouth. They had hurried on but the stench had stayed in the car, even with all the windows open. Dominic was gone, but not the memory of the stench.

She held a hand.

There was a gasp behind her, then nervous titters. The lights were on the gloves she wore and the black bones of a hand in hers. The clothing was gone, and much of the flesh. She thought she might vomit. She put down the hand, detached from the wrist because the muscle had burned. She felt the shape of the arm, then the torso and her fingers flickered up to the skull. A jawbone, an open mouth, eye sockets. It seemed to her that she learned more from the touch than from the glare of the lights on the face. They had called him Muhammad Iyad. She wondered how it had been for him in the final spasms of his life, his mouth wide with agony. Had his faith in God sustained him, or the love of his woman, or had he died in terror – cursing those he served? Her head bobbed, and she shook the thoughts from her mind. Her fingers dismantled the heap and found nothing more.

'Right,' Polly said briskly, to the men behind her. 'That's one of them. Where's the other?'

A murmur of voices behind her, then Ludvik's hang-dog response. 'They have found only one cadaver.'

'You had the building sealed, you told me.'

'Only one body was found.'

It was as if she were a child, and a present in gaudy wrapping was offered her, and when she reached for it the present was snatched away. The prize was gone.

She turned and started to crawl back along the ladder. With the time differential between Prague and London, it would now be 10.35 p.m. at Vauxhall Bridge Cross, and Gaunt would be waiting. With the certainties of night following day, and spring following winter, she knew Gaunt would be at his desk with his shoes up on it, and waiting for her signal.

Polly Wilkins swore obscenely, and came off the ladder.

Frederick Gaunt read the latest epistle from the whey-faced creature who had written the report, now heavily circulated, on the Service's future.

The in-tray left for him by Gloria was empty, its contents either gone to the shredder or dumped on her desk in the outer office for filing. He had done his emails through the evening. Nothing remained for him to read except the report – *The Secret Intelligence Service in 2010* (Confidential) – which made his lips curl in irritation.

It was crap.

In five years the Service would 'understand customer and partner requirements'. What was the Service? A division of the bloody London Underground?

He was old school and regarded 'jargon-mongers' with contempt . . .
Maybe he should have gone when the knife hacked through the
team responsible for the weapons-of-mass-destruction analysis.
Could have gone then, on full pension as a sweetener, and joined
the happy ranks of the Whitehall discards. Could have busied
himself with his great love of Roman archaeology, set out his stall
in a tidy guest-house, like the one at Bradford-on-Avon, and been
within walking distance of the excavation, spent his days chipping
with a light hammer, digging with a hand trowel, brushing at the
mud and stone, letting out little whoops of pleasure as the villa gave
up its secrets.

Walking away, he had realized long ago, took courage: perhaps
more courage than flowed in Frederick Gaunt's veins. No wife: she'd
gone with that hairy-faced beggar to a smallholding in Herefordshire
to live like a Balkan peasant. No children: their mother had poisoned
their minds against him and contact was lost. No friends: an officer
in the Service was adept at avoiding commitment to people outside
his tunnel of work. No prizes to bask in: the war went on, different
enemies but the same endless threat. When he left he would be one
more of the old farts who was unable under the strictures of the
Official Secrets Act to say boldly from a bar stool: 'Do you know
who I used to be?' He would be another senile bore, with Roman
artefacts for company and a guest-house for home.

He stayed on and endured the *crap* of the jargon-mongers. And
he waited . . . And he forced the pages of *The Secret Intelligence
Service 2010* (Confidential) into the teeth of the shredder . . . And
around him the building was hushed. He did not know whether
Wilco would come through on a secure phone line or use the
encrypted teleprinter. He would not nag her. Polly 'Wilco' Wilkins
was the best girl he'd ever supervised, and the most loyal, and the
most unlucky in the twin fall-out of the WMD analysis and love. It
would have been an unspeakable crime to pester her for news. He
knew that the storm squad had gone in, had been halted in its assault,
that fire had ravaged the building and nothing more.

All of it real. He doubted that the author of *The Secret Intelligence
Service 2010* (Confidential) – the purveyor of crap – had the smallest
comprehension of real Service life. Men's lives on the line,

body-to-body fighting, dying in combat as duty for their country or for their faith: real life.

He drank the final splash of coffee and grimaced. He could see a barge progress, west to east, down the Thames and past Parliament. He was wondering if its driver was heavy on 'understanding customer and partner requirements' when the teleprinter against the wall behind him began its shrill chatter.

He read.

> *Gaunt,*
> *Bloody disaster. One, repeat one, body on premises. Body is badly burned but I believe forensics will identify Muhammad Iyad. Your co-ord slipped the net early and MI bought him a start of up to 24 hours. So, no identification of co-ord and all internal DNA traces obliterated by fire (my estimate).*
> *Will be chasing loose ends in the morning. The bastard is that BIS promised me the area had been secured. You told me once: (quote) Life's unfair, always has been and always will be (end quote). Right now, I believe you.*
> *Love,*
> *Wilco*

He had said that to her when she had poured out to him on the phone that Dominic in Buenos Aires had ditched her. A wry, sad smile crossed Gaunt's face. It seemed to matter more to her than losing her fiancé that a potential co-ordinator of al-Qaeda had been mislaid, was loose in Europe with a full day's time bought him. He signalled her.

> *Wilco,*
> *If life were easy, everybody would be doing it. Sleep tight.*
> *Gaunt*

He closed down his desk, switched off the light and left darkness behind him. Frederick Gaunt, bowed by disappointment, went along the silent corridors, down in the elevator, across the hall, where he failed to notice the greetings of Night Security, and home to the loneliness of his flat. He felt himself to be in a maze of uncertainty and did not know where his path would lead or who would walk with him in similar ignorance. But Frederick Gaunt was not a quitter, and the loss of the trace on the co-ordinator would bring him to his desk early and back to the trail.

He whistled to himself as he walked across the bridge.

13 January 2004
Taking charge: that was the talent of Hamish McQueen.

As the company's senior sergeant, he ran Bravo.

'What the hell happened, Corp? What sort of shambles was that?'

The section's corporal told him. A patrol, routine. An ambush, not routine but handled. 'Actually, we did well, Sarge, really well. We had three incoming fire positions and we did good neutralizing on them, and we have at least one confirmed kill. Everything was brilliant. We did good hard target, did it at speed, didn't give the hostiles anything to hit. They took punishment and they broke off. Did you stop the ambulance?'

'We stopped the ambulance. One dead and one likely to corpse. Both males. No women or kids, which means the best fire control. I'm not criticizing the response, which I'd consider entirely appropriate, that's not the shambles. What's the story with him?'

In front of McQueen, the corporal seemed to duck his head away, evasive, as if he did not want to answer. McQueen gestured, thumb raised, to his right, where the officer sat on one of the plastic-seated chairs outside the operations room where men from the bunker took a soft-drink break or a smoke: he was staring forward and his shoulders seemed to tremble. Across the yard, the crews of the Warriors, the quick-reaction team, had been stood down and McQueen saw that men from the patrol were at the centre of little knots, pouring out their tale, and that all eyes were on the officer.

'I'm struggling, Sarge . . . '

'Well, struggle a bit bloody harder. What am I going to report to the major? No one's going to bite you. What's the story?'

'I was up forward – I was trying to handle a bloody fire-fight.'

'Say what you've got to say.'

'We did the hard-target bit at speed, then doubled round the back of the mosque and didn't stop till we were by the school. That was when we realized he wasn't with us.'

McQueen pressed without mercy: 'Spill it. You realized then that Mr Kitchen was not with you. We've got your radio call on that – it's logged. What did you do?'

'Doubled back. Went back the way we'd come ... You know where we found him.'

'You got his helmet and his flak-jacket, not his personal weapon. I am not criticizing you because there's no cause for that. I'd say you did bloody well. You've got to understand there was a right panic here – that is, serious panic. I'm moving on. Who was closest to him?'

'Baz was. Baz says he lost him when we were doing the hard-target stuff.'

'How do you rate that boy?'

'Good kid. A bit lippy, but a good kid. Their chief guy, Baz dropped him, and with him down, the rest quit. We were in shit till Baz slotted their main man. He did well.'

McQueen's gaze raked from the officer, still sitting and still alone like he had some plague affliction, across the yard from where the private soldier, Baz, stood at the heart of a cluster and was holding forth. Hamish McQueen had been with this Scottish regiment for eighteen years, and when the vacancy opened up he stood the best chance of any of the company sergeants to get the nod and promotion to regimental sergeant major. Better than most, he recognized a mine-field. As if he walked among trip wires and pressure plates, he considered where he stood now, and its implications.

For the sergeant there had been enough soft talk. 'Are you telling me, Corporal, that Mr Kitchen did a runner?'

'He was with us, then he wasn't with us – can't say different,' the corporal said evasively. 'We found his helmet and his flak-jacket dumped, didn't find his weapon. There was kids following and jeering at him, but they weren't a threat.'

'For fuck's sake, Corp, did he do a runner?'

'What else? Can you see a mark on him? I can't. What we reckon – yes – he ran. That's what we reckon. Yellow bastard, feckin' quit on us.'

'You talking? Baz talking?'

He saw the section corporal suck in a deep, deep breath. 'All of us talking . . . There's not a mark on him, and his helmet's gone and his flak-jacket and his gat. Where's he going? Back to Bravo. It's all of us bloody talking.'

'But you never saw him turn and run . . . Tell me.'

'For Christ's sake, I was in a firefight, then trying to do extraction. You tell me, Sarge, what else fits? Far as I know, first incoming and he's gone, that's the RPG and it was way high.' The corporal blurted: 'It's not my fault, I'm not to blame if he's a yellow bastard, a Rupert who couldn't hack it.'

'Leave it there, Corp. Go get yourself and your boys a brew. I'll take it on.'

He turned away and strode towards the sandbagged operations room. As he took the few steps, his webbing clanking across his chest, Hamish McQueen reflected that his report in the bunker would be the hardest he had ever made to his company commander. Too damn right . . . He passed the man who still sat on the chair and whose gaze was void of expression. For a company sergeant major, who had ambitions to take on the role of regimental sergeant major, it was high risk to denounce an officer for running from combat. He would play it straight, take the white line down the middle of the road, and report what he had been told. Others, higher up the chain, could play God, but not Hamish McQueen. He would relay only what had been said to him. He didn't look down at the man as he passed him – he could think of no greater disgrace for a man than to be labelled a coward who had done a runner under fire – but hurried inside the bunker.

Deciding on what shirt, what trousers and giving a last shine to his shoes had eaten into the minutes of the schedule that Malachy had set himself. The shirt was not ironed but it was the best that had come from the charity shop, and the collar was not frayed. The trousers were not pressed but had only been worn once since their wash in the launderette. Clean socks on, and the shined shoes. Then Malachy stood in front of the little bathroom mirror, smoothed his hair into shape and used a finger to etch out a parting. The shoes set him off; he looked better than he had since Ivanhoe Manners had brought him to the Amersham.

It was twelve minutes to eleven and, beyond the windows, thick darkness blanketed the estate.

He would have to run down the stairs, sprint through the plazas and jog the length of the streets coming into Walworth Road. He'd cut it fine, but he would be there for eleven o'clock at the bus stop. He thought he had enough money to spare.

Buying rope, packaging tape, the plastic toy and the multi-blade penknife had eaten into his fortnight's benefit money. He had the drawer open and counted out what he could spare: enough for a port or a sherry for Dawn and a Coke for himself – there would be a pub in the road open till late. He slotted the drawer shut, slipped the pound coins into his pocket, and started for the door.

Suddenly he was late. He unfastened the lock and reached for the bolt.

The telephone rang. He had the bolt down and the door open, and the bell cut after its triple ring.

Then the silence clamoured behind him. To get to the bus stop, as he had promised, Malachy Kitchen would now have to push himself. His breathing came hard and his finger rested on the light switch by the door. Breaking a promise or keeping a promise? *You do what you think is right, and maybe that'll make a ladder for you.* To escort an old lady from the bus stop, after a hospital visit, back through the dark shadows of the estate? The minute had gone. The phone rang again. To let her meander alone, clutching her bag, through the alleyways of the Amersham and into the blackened stairwell where a smashed light had not been replaced? The quiet fell round him after the third ring.

6

'I'll bet you were begging for the call. Praying for it.'

The voice and the words, spoken in the shadows of the night, were crystal clear in Malachy's mind. He walked out of the stairwell street entrance of block nine and headed for the exit road from the Amersham.

'You had a taste for it, didn't you? All down to me. I knew you'd come. Don't give me that stuff about "I done my bit". You've done precious little of damn all, and without me that's how it'll stay. You hearing me?'

The sun was over the highest tower, block four, and little cloud puffs scudded around its brilliance, but down on the street he was sheltered from the wind. In the dark, in the parking bay, the wind had funnelled between the pillars, peeled off the car and buffeted him.

He had heard, 'If you think you've "done my bit", go and look at her. I'm telling you very frankly, because I nearly trust you, we push paper round desks but we alter nothing. Enough, that's us, to get little newspaper headlines and "God, aren't we great?" stories on local TV, but we're not affecting the trade – it's the trade that put Millie where she is. You know what happened up north a few months ago? I'll tell you. A big city, with police costing millions a year, had to admit it was so swamped with class A that it had "lost control of crime" in its area. That's direct, what they said. "Lost control". Not Bogotá, not Palermo, not bloody Kiev or Chicago, but a city you can take a train to. Barely surfaced in our papers and TV, because it was a bad-news story. Who wants bad news? But it's where we are. You live in this sink – Christ, I couldn't – and you see what's not on TV and in the papers.'

The sun had brought the baby-mothers out. No thin gold finger-rings, just prams to push and toddlers to traipse towards the play places, or the swings and slides that weren't broken. Twice since he had lived on the Amersham, Malachy had seen children who could barely run, not understand, happily carry syringes picked up from the gutter back to the baby-mothers. Once he had seen a little boy, done up in his best party clothes, kneel in the mud with a syringe and fly it over his head like it was a rocket.

'Up north, that time, they got round to admitting what we all know. We're losing. Not that you ever will, but if you came into my place – where I push my poxy bits of paper around – you'd see that only the arseholes and the career wonks find anything to cheer about. When we do get ourselves wound up, and head off to do the good things, we're tripping over the European Court of Human bleeding Rights and we're flat on our bloody faces. I'm telling you this because I reckon you understand, Malachy Kitchen, about losing. You're a loser big-time – but you came running when you were called.'

He came out past the last of the big blocks and walked a street towards the corner shop that Ivanhoe Manners had pointed out to him. There had been – he knew it because Millie Johnson had told him over tea – two more armed robberies since the twelve the social worker had spoken of. And the *Southwark News* had quoted the Asian shopkeeper as calling himself 'a sitting duck', with no insurance company prepared to quote for him. He couldn't quit because there was no buyer idiot enough to take it on. Guns under his chin, clubs in front of his face, CCTV and the panic button useless.

'My estimate of you is that you're sick, spewing it up, with losing . . . so I've got plans for you. You did well – three kids out of the picture. You did what we cannot. Over the line, of course, sufficient to get you banged up and a charge sheet as long as half your arm. You should look at me as a visiting angel, who pitched up to help you get your life back, and if you make it I'll be on the sidelines cheering you. You got a long, long road. You won't be coming to me with "I've done my bit", will you? You won't disappoint me, will you? That would really upset me, because – whichever way you look at it – I'm helping you.'

Malachy cut through the Green Street market, sidled past the stalls heavy with fruit and vegetables, thin clothing and tacky-bright toys; another plastic pistol was in the place where his had come from, good enough for a ten-year-old in daylight and good enough to scare the shit out of three gang youths at night. He glanced at his watch and quickened his stride. He saw ahead of him the traffic on Walworth Road, and the bus stop.

'Think of it as a pyramid – that's what all the clever buggers at the Home Office do. Right down at the bottom are the vagrants, the addicts, who have to buy and have to thieve and have to ambush Millie Johnson. They're dross, not worth the sweat. Next up from them are the pushers, the High Fly Boys, and you wrecked them, which was well done and got you on the ladder. Keep climbing. Read this name, memorize this address. The dealer feeds the pushers. He is at the next level of the pyramid. If I wanted to crank it up I could say that he has Millie Johnson's blood under his dirty little fingernails. Got it in your memory? Good. I'll have the paper back. Look after yourself, Malachy, because no one else will, and a dealer fights dirtier than kids do.'

He crossed then and looked up Walworth Road. Three buses came, in crocodile formation, towards him. They stopped, disgorged passengers and pulled away. He would wait till she came. More minutes and more buses. He idled. He knew what time she left work, and what time she would get the ride from Whitehall. She came off the bus.

Dawn, the cleaning lady who was his neighbour and who was the friend of Millie Johnson, walked right past him. She saw him, recognized him and anger twitched at her mouth. She ignored him. He had a cavalcade of excuses to offer her – gone to sleep, dozed off – and a litany of apologies to make for leaving her last night to come into the estate alone, but the excuses and apologies went unsaid. As she crossed the road he watched the pride in her walk – she was not dependent on a man whose promise did not count. He followed her, but did not run to catch her; he hung back when she stopped in the market and bought fruit, which he knew she would later take to the hospital.

He had a good life, well organized. Jason Penney, a month past his twenty-eighth birthday, lived in a ground-floor flat. The one-bedroom unit had been allocated by Housing to a pensioner and was suitable for a disabled person. Legally, Penney was disabled, and to prove it he had a doctor's certificate, stating his severe knee-ligament injuries, which had cost him £250 in cash from a Ghanaian medic and entitled him to benefit. But the disability money was chicken-feed to his other earnings. Illegally, he had inserted himself, his partner, his baby and his dog into the pensioner's home. As a base of operations it was ideal.

He sold class-A narcotics on the Amersham. What the customer wanted, the customer had – but only class A: he shunned cannabis and the derivatives as too bulky to handle and with insufficient profit margins. He dealt in heroin, cocaine powder, crack cocaine. Whatever the market demanded, he could get: MDMA tablets, made from a base of amphetamine, ketamine, 2C-B, and ephedrine or methylamphetamine. Where the market took him, he followed. A bad week gave him, clear, a thousand pounds; a good week, two thousand, but in a worst week, if he was arrested and nailed down with evidence, he faced seven years in prison. The money he made, and the risk of going to gaol, led Penney towards a life of exceptional caution.

The caution dictated where he lived.

His live-in partner, Aggie, had had his baby. Aggie had located the pensioner, and later, together and over three weeks, they had watched the block and the pensioner's door for suitability. That was eight months back. She had befriended the old man, a half-reformed alcoholic in his early seventies: meeting him, getting him into conversation at first, later, dropping off six-packs – 'You're my friend, aren't you? No problem'; later, getting inside, close to him on the sofa, cuddling him, touching him up – infatuating him; later, shopping for him – 'Don't thank me, it's for nothing, anything I can do to help'; later, moving in with the baby – 'Just while I sort myself out, and I'm ever so grateful'; later, Jason Penney's at the door, with his dog and his bag – 'He's ever so nice, you won't know he's here, and the dog's lovely. We'll all be company for you.'

In a month, Aggie had given Penney what he most wanted. He had safe premises among the pensioners' units that were about at the bottom of police priority taskings for surveillance. Penney, his partner and the baby had taken the pensioner's bedroom, the dog had the hall, the old man spent his days in the kitchen and slept on the front-room sofa with receding memories of the cuddles and the affection. And how was the old beggar going to get rid of them? No way. Changes were made to the flat, discreetly, and unnoticeable from the outside. Steel sheeting covered the inside of the front and back doors. New locks, bolts and chains were fitted. A trellis of bars reinforced the windows. The pensioner's home, in which he stayed with an ever-open can from a six-pack, had become the fortress of the Amersham's premier dealer. The final touch: Penney had hired a welding torch for twenty-four hours, gone out on a wet November night and worked the flame over the manhole cover in the street in front of the flat, where the sewage went through. If they were serious, first thing the filth did when they raided was get the manhole cover up outside and slot a plastic sack over the pipe outlet into the main system. First thing a dealer did, when the sledge-hammers hit the door, was flush what was in the house down the toilet. Jason Penney reckoned himself ahead of the game.

Aggie collected for him from the supplier. Anything up to a full kilo of brown or white, up to a thousand tablets, was brought back to the estate by the palefaced, unremarkable girl with her baby. Aggie moved the brown, the white and the tablets in the pram under the baby, with shit and piss in the nappy that hid the dull scent of heroin, cocaine or MDMA, from the house to the stash place that was a hollowed-out cavern behind a loose concrete block in a play-area corner where the lights did not reach. Jason Penney, with perfect security around him, was a king on the Amersham.

The men and women in Housing, burdened by workloads and short staffing, had no interest in investigating areas from which no complaints came. The pensioner's neighbours, similarly elderly and cowed, who would have seen Penney's shaven head, his muscled, tattooed body and his Rottweiler, were not daft: they would not call any police hotline even if it claimed confidential response.

He was irritable that day. He'd snapped at Aggie and bawled out the pensioner, had raised his fist to the dog so that it had backed off and crept to its corner. A little tremor of worry itched in him. He dealt with Danny Morris, Leroy Gates and Wilbur Sansom, had done ever since he'd set up in business on the estate, had found them good and reliable. He knew what had happened to them. He believed he felt the pulsebeat of the Amersham, but he could not have said who had left them suspended from a flat roof for most of a night.

He kept her in an apartment at Chelsea Harbour. It had a small balcony that looked down on the river, a small living room, a small kitchen and a small bathroom, a big TV with video and DVD, and a big bed that fitted tightly into the small bedroom.

She grunted hard.

The apartment, across London from Bevin Close, with the girl in residence, was the greatest luxury in Ricky Capel's life. It was leased in her name, two years and renewable, but the girl was more complicated: she had been bought for cash, then the money had been paid back and she was a gift. Maria, twenty years old, from Romania, was smart, clever and long-legged, and had worked out of a brothel in King's Cross.

The thong, suspenders and little lacy brassière that she always wore when he arrived, the high-heeled shoes and the silk robe were scattered in a trail between the front door of the apartment and the bed.

Maria was high luxury to Ricky Capel and high risk.

The times he was able to get away from the cousins, and from Bevin Close, were luxury because then he thought he breathed freedom. He tried to come to Chelsea Harbour once a week, but if his life was complex and business burdened him, it was once a fortnight, which made for expensive luxury – with the lease, her spending money and her presents. It was liberation when he shed his family. Free of Joanne, who did sex only when she reckoned she had to and was always bleating on about the thinness of the wall between their room and Wayne's, and refused straight-up to do anything beyond basic. The girl, Maria, rode him on the bed, and his hands reached up for the hang of her breasts, and she grunted louder as he pushed up into her and her head was back like it was ecstasy for her. Her fingernails, long and painted silver to match her lip gloss, caught in his chest hair and scratched at his skin. He let out sharp, stifled squeals, and her grunts came faster.

But high risk. For Ricky Capel to have set up his girl at Chelsea Harbour opened little cracks in the defence wall built round his wealth and enterprises. He had met her in the hours after his first meeting with Enver, who hummed round King's Cross in a flash Ferrari Spider. Charlie had identified the business opportunity. Albanians ran girls into the country, but they hadn't the cover: Customs and Immigration had peeled eyes for Albanians driving white vans into Dover, Folkestone or Harwich. They were losing too many and too much cash, and they were operating on foreign territory. It was Charlie's proposition. Ricky should get himself up alongside the Albanians and take over the cross-border, cross-Channel runs. He had access to the drivers and to the lorries they brought back from the long overland European hauls. He would be paid up front by the Albanians for the transport, and take a cut from the brothel earnings where the new girls would work. The way Charlie told it, it was pretty straight, and Benji had suggested approaching Enver. He'd heard that Albanians stuck by their word, were professional, made good partners. They'd done the meeting, had shaken hands on a deal, and then there had been food in the club. The girl had stood at the back and her eyes had never been off him. Christ, he'd wanted her, like he'd never wanted anything. Bought her, hadn't he? Bought her for cash, peeled it out of his pocket, and told Enver that there'd be no more bloody customers for her, and he'd collect her when he'd got premises. In a careful life, it was the wildest thing that Ricky Capel had ever done – bought a tart out of a brothel off an Albanian.

The way she grunted on him, the whole of that building at Chelsea Harbour, through concrete floors and concrete walls, would have heard her. Bloody, bloody – God – marvellous, and he clung to her breasts.

In his third or fourth meeting with Enver, long after he'd taken delivery of her, Ricky had told him, sort of casual, that his grandfather had been in Albania in the war. What was his grandfather's name and where had his grandfather been? Percy Capel, up in the north – and he'd struggled to pronounce the place name – with a Major Anstruther. Next time they'd met, him and Enver, Ricky had been given an envelope. In it was what he'd paid for the girl. Enver had giggled and told him why the money had come back. Enver's uncle was in Hamburg, Germany. The uncle's father was Mehmet Rahman, who had fought with Major Hugo Anstruther and Flight

Sergeant Percy Capel against the Fascists in the mountains north of Shkodra. Small world, small bloody world.

She was coming, crouched over him, bellowing, like he was the best shag she'd ever had.

He did not rate the risk she represented. The Albanians, from that distant link between a grandfather and the father of an uncle, were his partners – well, not real partners because he controlled it all. He called the tune, Ricky did. He was never backed into a corner. He bought off them and used Harry's trawler to bring in the packages. He used his network of knowledge for haulage companies to help them get the girls, from Belarus, Ukraine, Bulgaria and Romania, into the country. He hired them – his cousin Benji called them 'the Merks', the mercenaries – for heavy punishment if a man showed him disrespect. He had no cause to sweat on the arrangement: he had not lost control, never would – and the money rolled in for Charlie to wash, rinse, scrub clean.

She came, then him. Ricky sagged on the bed and she rolled off him. She peeled off the condom, and went to make him tea. Always tea, never alcohol. He lay back and gasped. She was his best, his most precious secret.

Mikey Capel always watched little Wayne, Ricky's boy, play football for the under-nine team of the junior school, St Mary's.

He was on the touchline in the park area. There were no trees to break the force of the wind and he was huddled among the young mums and other grandparents. In a mid-week afternoon there were few fathers. He was at ease, liked the gossip among the men of his own age and a quiet flirt with the mothers. He enjoyed those afternoons. Little Wayne wasn't good, only useful, and he was hidden away by the teacher in charge on the left side of midfield where the kid's shortcomings in talent had least effect on the side's efforts; little Wayne was always picked by the teacher because his father, Ricky, had provided the team's shirts, knicks and socks, the same colours as Charlton Athletic, who used the Valley down the road. Maybe 'useful' was putting it strong, but it was fun for Mikey to watch him . . . He knew, that afternoon, where Ricky was and with whom, why he wasn't on the touchline.

Actually, the game against Brendon Road Junior was absorbing enough for him not to notice the powerfully built man, perhaps five years older than himself, with an erect bearing, sidle to his shoulder. The noise around him had reached fever pitch. The ball was with a little black kid, might have been the smallest on the pitch but tricky like a bloody eel, and he was wriggling down his team's right touchline and the St Mary's left side and was coming right up against the faded white markings of the penalty box. The black kid had skill.

'Go on, Wayne, fix him!' Mikey yelled, through his cupped hands.

The little black kid, the ball seeming stuck to his toe, danced round little Wayne.

'Don't let him, Wayne! Block him!'

Oh, Jesus! The ball was gone, and the kid nearly gone, when little Wayne shoved out his right boot – most expensive that Adidas made for that age group – hooked it round the kid's trailing leg and tripped him. Oh, Christ! The Brendon Road mums and grandfathers howled for blood – red-card blood – and the whistle shrieked. Oh, bloody hell. But the referee didn't send him off. He merely wagged his finger at the sour-faced child.

A rich Welsh accent rang in Mikey's ear: 'I suppose his dad's bought the referee. Chip off the old block that one, vicious little sod – proud of him, Mikey? I expect you are.'

He swung. Recognition came. 'It's Mr Marchant, isn't it?'

'And that's Ricky Capel's brat, right?'

'That is my grandson. I thought he tried to play the ball and – and was just a bit late in the tackle.'

'About half an hour bloody late. Like father, like son. I always reckon you can tell them, those that are going to be scum.'

'There's no call for that talk, Mr Marchant.' But there was no fight in Mikey's voice.

His mind clattered through the arithmetic of it. Would have been nineteen years since he had last seen Gethin Marchant, detective sergeant, Flying Squad – a straight-up guy and civilized, never one to make a show. The Squad had come for Mikey, half six in the morning, and the afternoon before they'd done this factory pay-roll and all gone wrong because a delivery lorry had blocked in the get-away wheels and they'd done a run with nothing. Mr Marchant had led the arrest team, nothing fancy, and the door hadn't been sledgehammered off its hinges before Sharon had opened up. Even given him time to get out of his pyjamas and dressed. And allowed him to kiss Sharon in the hall so that the neighbours wouldn't have too much to tittle over, and Ricky had come out of his bedroom and down the stairs, like a bloody cyclone, and thrown himself at the arresting coppers. Barefoot but he'd kicked at shins and kneed balls, and then he'd jumped up more than his full height and head-butted a constable hard enough to split the man's lip, flailing with his fists. It had taken three of them, and his mum, to subdue the thirteen-year-old Ricky, and the girls at the top of the stairs had been weeping their bloody eyes out . . . Proper upsetting it had been.

'Where's Ricky now? Doing his scum bit?' The Welshness lilted, but there was contempt in the hard voice of the retired detective sergeant. 'God, I'd hate to think I'd fathered that sort of creature, and that there was another coming along, same vein. What encourages me, it'll all end in tears because it always does . . . Sorry, sorry. Nice to have met up with you again, Mikey – got to go.'

Mikey saw Gethin Marchant scurry, as best he could at his age, on to the pitch. The little black kid was down, in tears, and the foul had ended his afternoon's football. When the game restarted, while the detective sergeant held the little bundle of the boy on his shoulder on the far touchline, the Brendon Road kids scored, and then the referee blew his whistle for full time.

Little Wayne came to him. 'We was bloody robbed. We—'

'You were shit,' Mikey, the grandfather, snapped back. 'Next time your father can watch you. It won't be me.'

No, Ricky wouldn't be there to watch little Wayne, because Ricky was screwing on those afternoons when St Mary's had matches. He had a good mate, been inside with him and shared a cell with him, who now drove a mini-cab for a company at the bottom end of the King's Road. They drank together some Tuesday nights. The mini-cab driver had been waiting for a fare at Chelsea Harbour when he'd seen Ricky with his bottle-blonde tart, her big boobs and long legs. Mikey had never cheated on Sharon. He remembered, looking down at little Wayne, what the retired detective had said.

He grabbed the sulking child's hand. 'Come on, let's go home.'

What had been said, which he believed: *It'll all end in tears because it always does.* He strode away across the grass and the mud, dragging the kid behind him.

'What's the priority?'

The question came from a line manager, who lived his working life in a complex surrounded by thousands of yards of fencing and razor wire, protected by armed guards, built on moorland in north Yorkshire, west of Scarborough on the coast and north of Malton. At Menwith Hill – officially an outpost of the British listening spies at Cheltenham – the National Security Agency, headquarters at Fort Meade in Maryland, called an American tune. The majority of the budget for the intercept databases on this wind-scarred, remote ground of bracken and heather, was in dollars.

He who pays the piper calls the tune.

At Menwith Hill, great white golfball shapes rise above the moorland, sometimes glittering in sunshine and sometimes misted by low cloud. The balls protect the scanning dishes that suck in millions of phone communications every day. Then computers, operating at speeds of nano-seconds, interpret what has been swallowed into the stomach of the beast. Hundreds of NSA personnel have made this corner of the United Kingdom into a little piece of the Midwest of America. American needs, in the War on Terror, dictate how the computer time is allocated. British technicians must accept the reality, however unwelcome, of being the subordinate partner.

So, the line manager demanded clarification of the priority level of the request from London. 'I'm sure you'll appreciate, Mr Gaunt, that matters related to Pakistan, Egypt, Yemen and the Saudi Kingdom take most of our time – and that's all linked, as you know well, to US requirements. Prague isn't high, no. If you were to tell me that by monitoring all satphone and mobile links out of Prague to wherever in Europe, I would be meeting a category-four priority level – you know, life and death, Mr Gaunt – then I might be able to play with a bit of machine-switching, *might* . . . and I'd have to know, Mr Gaunt, in what language we'd be most likely dealing, and what the trigger words are. I think that if I had your assurance, and I'd need a back-up signal of authorization that this was category-four minimum, then I might, *might*, be able to help. Are you there, Mr Gaunt? . . . Albanian language, that's not easy. Oh, might be Arabic, or a Chechen dialect, oh . . . No trigger words? . . . All I can say, Mr Gaunt, is that I'll do my best – say three or four days. Yes, Mr Gaunt, and we're pushed at this end too . . .'

The screen gave Polly a black-and-white image of the interior of the cell.

Ludvik, at her shoulder, asked her remotely, 'Do you not approve?'

'Not for me to have an opinion,' she murmured. 'I just have to hope that what you're doing is effective. Whether I like it or not is irrelevant.'

Yes, old matters of ethics and morality took a back seat in the new war. She saw a bucket lifted and the water from it was thrown so that it splashed on to the face and head of the man she knew to be a café owner from the east of the Old City, out by the Florenc bus station. The water ran down his cheeks and chest, and blood sluiced off the injuries inflicted on him. She thought, momentarily, that this was a return to days long gone when Stalin's purges had filled these same basement cells, and before that as Gestapo interrogators had gone to work to extract the names of the assassins of Reichs-Protector Heydrich.

'It is necessary.'

'You did not hear me say it was not,' Polly said softly.

The cells, dark little cubicles with high, barred windows of dirty glass that looked out at boot level on to the interior square of the police barracks, were where Communist and Nazi torturers had been. They could similarly have justified the pain and brutality of what they did. Now it was the turn of the *democrats* to use that cell and to beat, slap and kick, deprive a man of sleep, make him scream in agony, and to hide behind the wall of 'It is necessary'. As the water dripped to the floor, the man's head lifted and his bruised face focused again on the ceiling, the work resumed. Short-arm, closed-fist punches to the face, booted kicks to the kidneys and when the café owner's head dropped again, his grey hair was caught and held up so that the target remained accessible. There was no high horse on which Polly Wilkins could have sat and played indifference. Over the last two years men and women from the Service had trooped in and out of interrogation rooms at Bagram in Afghanistan, at Guantanamo Bay and at holding camps in Iraq – her people, her colleagues. No bleat from the Service then about ethics and morality. Of course, her hands and their hands stayed clean because they let surrogates do it and could then claim ignorance. And others were shipped, in the name of the War on Terror, to cell blocks in Damascus or Cairo, and transcripts were sent back – with no bloodstains on them – that drove forward investigations.

'What has he said so far?'

'Nothing of importance.'

'Perhaps that's because you have hit his face so often that he cannot talk any more,' she said drily. 'Do you think he might talk better if you hit his face less often?'

'Do you want information or do you want your conscience to be comfortable?'

'Oh, for fuck's sake . . .' She turned away from the screen. If her mother and father – both teachers in an insignificant country town in Wiltshire, both thrilled that their daughter worked for the Defence of the Realm – had known what their daughter watched on a TV screen they might have vomited. But, far from home, it was the reality of what she did. She looked back at the screen, then blinked and peered harder at it. If they had not held the café owner's grey hair, his head would have fallen on to his soaked chest, but they did, and his hands rose briefly and feebly to protect his face – fingers over his eyes and mouth – before they were ripped away and another punch landed.

'Can you zoom in?'

'No, it is a fixed lens.'

'I want to go in there.'

'Because we do not understand the skill of interrogation? Do we need another lesson from SIS?' The sarcasm hit her. 'Why?'

'Just put me in there, dear friend, because, by your own admission, you have learned nothing. Good enough?'

She was taken down a flight of stone-flagged steps and along a corridor where men lounged on hard chairs, read newspapers without interest, smoked and stripped her with their eyes. Down more stairs and into the basement. She walked boldly and with purpose, wanted only confirmation of what she had seen, in black and white, on the screen. The door was opened for her. Bright light speared from a lamp into the café owner's face. The men turned from their work and stared at her. The head was permitted to fall.

She went close to the chair on which he was propped, then knelt in front of him. Her body masked what she did. She took the café owner's hands. The man's fingers clawed at hers, as if he believed she was his salvation, his release. She was not there for kindness. She examined the hands quickly, then let them drop on to his lap, which was wet with water and urine. She stood, turned her back on him, and walked out of the cell into the corridor.

'What was that for?'

No reply from Polly Wilkins as she swept by Ludvik. She went out into the inner square of the building where Communists and Fascists had been, and felt herself dirtied. She thought of the shower she would take, endless and soapy – and drove away.

Of the many companies owned by Timo Rahman, all doing legitimate business, one shipped furniture to Hamburg from a factory at Ostrava in the extreme east of the Czech Republic. The tables and chairs, side-boards, chests and wardrobes would be inexpensive in Germany and Timo had identified a good market for those made from beech wood. The company's offices, warehouse and showroom were in the Hammerbrook district.

The message was brought from Hammerbrook by a young Albanian boy – a good, clean, intelligent worker – who was the son of a second cousin of Timo. Because the boy was *gjak*, a blood relation, he had been entrusted with the message by the company's manager who was from the *miqs*, a relative by marriage. Nothing had been written down, and the message was in the boy's memory – the telex from the factory at Ostrava was now in slivers, having passed through the company's shredder.

That evening Timo was the guest at a restaurant of a *Rathaus* functionary who dealt with the provision of care homes for the elderly – an area he had decided was promising for expansion. The city's government, near bankrupt and bumping along on empty, needed private capital for investment in the homes to fulfil an election promise. Late in the meal, the Bear came to Timo's shoulder and whispered in his ear. Apologies were made. Timo slipped from the table, out of the restaurant and on to the pavement where the boy waited.

Timo saw the boy's nervousness and confusion. He had heard of him but had never met him – his job in the office was a reward for the cousin's loyalty. He smiled with warmth and hugged the boy to reassure him. Then the message was stammered out against the noise of passing traffic and the music that spilled from a discothèque.

'This is what I am to say, from the shipping section of Home Furnishing. "Regret cargo load 1824 has not been forwarded. Our local agent is indisposed. Also half of the cargo is damaged and cannot be sent, and the remainder, which comprises the more valued items, is missing. We await further information." That is all. The telex was signed by the director at Ostrava. I apologize for disturbing you on such a minor matter, but that is what I was instructed to do.'

If he felt a frisson of anxiety, Timo gave no sign of it. He asked quietly, 'Would you repeat the message?'

He was told it again.

The boy was hugged and sent away into the night. Timo murmured to the Bear that he would need ten minutes to extract himself from the functionary's table, then they would drive.

An hour later, he stood in a car park far out to the west of the city, beyond his home at Blankenese and stared down at the quiet dark flow of the Elbe's estuary. He watched a freighter coming downriver and pondered. Whenever a difficulty obstructed him Timo came to that viewpoint, near the village of Hetlingen, and the Bear stayed in the car. It was where he scratched his mind for solutions when problems reached crisis point. It was indeed a difficulty. The coded message gave him the extent of it. The local agent – the café owner – was a unit leader, a *kryetar*, of a clan, a *fis*, to which Timo was allied, and 'indisposed' was the cover word for 'arrested'. A half of the cargo was 'damaged' and could not be sent: the lesser man of the two was dead. The second half of the cargo, the part that contained the 'more valued items' was missing: the man he had been paid,

127

handsomely, to move on from Hamburg was in flight. He did not know what evidence had been found, what the interrogation of the *kryetar* would throw up, what link could be made between himself and the fugitive. He seemed to see, as he stood in the darkness and watched the river traffic, the walls and roof of the maximum-security wing at the Fuhlsbüttel gaol. The extent of the difficulty – he would never have acknowledged that crisis had hit him – was that, for once, Timo Rahman did not know how to protect himself.

More rain in the late afternoon came with the wind that battered the island. He would not intervene. Oskar Netzer could see a frightening beauty in the shape and lines of the circling marsh harrier, the killer. He knew all of the harriers on Baltrum. Of the three pairs who nested and bred there, two had gone south for winter migration and were not yet back, but one had stayed. He watched the male bird hunting; an hour ago he had seen the hen hover over a reed bed with lichen in her talons for nest-building. Against the darkened clouds, the harrier's upper body feathers and wings made an almost black silhouette. Earlier it had shouted its *kee-yoo* cry, but now it was silent, dangerous and beautiful.

In the lee of a dune of low scrub, sheltered by the base of the viewing platform of weathered timber, he watched the killer quarter the marshland and knew that when its patience was exhausted it would come over the sand, the bushes and the little stagnant lake. Oskar could recognize the beauty of the harrier, which was the enemy of those he loved. Sitting there, with a little rain splattering his back, the swirl of the wind in his hair, and the cold on his face, he could recall the birds of beauty that had come high over him when he had been a child and terrified by the havoc they had brought. The Fortresses during the day, silver specks in front of their vapour trails, the Lancasters and Halifax bombers at night, sometimes caught in the cones of searchlights, had cruised elegantly over the city and had made the *Feuersturm* below them. They had taken the lives of his father and more than forty thousand other citizens of Hamburg. He knew about beauty and about death flying high for a target. He had no right to intervene in the ways of nature, but the pain was in him.

The harrier in front of him had a wingspan of a metre. He knew it would come to kill and feed. The wind strength changed. It swung and slackened. The reeds beyond the little lake where the eiders gathered were no longer bent and flailing. So fast . . . The fate of a duck, one among them, was sealed, but he would not intervene. Earlier the wind had blown the harrier away from the lake with its green weed covering. The bird, of course, could cope with wind speeds to storm level, but now it would be easier for it to circle, select and dive. It was a lottery as to which of the gentle eider ducks would be chosen. It had been the same lottery that had killed his father when the wall of a blazing building had collapsed and other men on the hose had survived.

He spat, but not noisily enough to disturb the quiet around the lessening whistle of the wind and the rain. It was their island: it was home as much for the marsh harriers as for his eiders. As the bombs had, when he was a child, the bird plummeted. One moment, peace – the next, the chaos of panic. He heard the *kok-kok-kok* shriek of a male eider, and half of its brilliant white winter plumage was buried under the killer's weight. The struggle was brief. The harrier began to rip at the chest feathers, where white became black. They floated up in the lighter wind, and red flesh was exposed. Oskar was aware, then, as the harrier feasted, of little calls of excitement.

He looked up.

There were six of them, three couples. They were festooned with binoculars and cameras with jutting lenses, and wore heavy water-proof clothing. They seemed, to Oskar, to rejoice in the images their cameras trapped, and when they were satiated on photography they replaced cameras at their eyes with the binoculars and magnified their view of the slaughter. Then they were bored, and moved on.

The marsh harrier was a third of the weight of its kill. It could not lift the carcass of a male eider and fly with it to where the hen built the nest in the reeds. It would fill its crop, then fly to its partner and regurgitate her food.

The male eider, ravished, was left in the mud among a snowfield of feathers.

He pushed himself up. It was Oskar Netzer's habit to follow visitors who came into the territory of Baltrum's wildlife haven. He could stalk as well and as silently as the hunting harrier. He skirted the lake where, already, the surviving birds returned and clattered into the water. He took the path that the photographers had. He did not look ahead at their receding backs but kept his eyes on the ground beaten down by their walking boots. He followed to find fault – and purge his anger. Grim satisfaction settled at his mouth.

He bent and picked up the Cellophane wrapping of a boiled sweet that rested on the most recent indent in the mud of a walking boot, and a scrap of the shiny paper that had been around a chocolate bar, then three discarded matches. Further along the path, he retrieved the squashed filter tip. He quickened his stride. When he reached them, they were sitting on the crest of a dune and overlooked the sea channel between Baltrum and Langeoog islands. They had a Thermos open and drank coffee from plastic beakers. When he came towards them, they looked away from the white crest waves and smiled a welcome at him through the rain.

He attacked. Oskar opened his palm and allowed to drop close to their feet what he had picked up. A sweet wrapper, a piece of chocolate paper, matches and a filter tip.

'You come here, where you are not wanted, and you desecrate the place. Go away and take your rubbish with you.'

They stared at him in growing amazement.

'Go home. Scatter your filth on your own ground.'

Their faces flushed. He thought, was pleased by it, that he had destroyed their pleasure in photographing and watching the marsh harrier rip apart the duck. He turned and strode away.

Behind him a chorus of voices erupted, which he ignored.

'What a fucking idiot . . . No, just some sad fool . . . Must live here. The isolation's turned his mind . . . Wrong. Not the isolation, has to be something more and something deeper . . . Probably his whole life is seeing what's different each morning. I doubt a flea moves here without him knowing, the fool.'

He heard the laughter but kept walking. He felt better for the spat. He believed it his self-appointed duty to keep the paradise of Baltrum pure. He went back to the lake where he could watch the eiders. The harrier, fed, would not kill again for three or four days but the carcass was there, to be seen and to hurt him.

★ ★ ★

From the shadows of the fenced hedge that surrounded the sheds where the Amersham's maintenance staff kept their tools, Malachy watched the ground-floor door of the pensioners' units. He learned the rhythms of the dealer's evening and night.

He was tucked away, hidden and hunched down, with his back pressed into the thickness of the hedge. Old thoughts and old lessons stirred in him. At Chicksands, he had been a student in surveillance classes. The instructors, hardened and bland from time in the Province, had tried to drill into him and others from the corps what they had practised during months in south Armagh's hedgerows and west Belfast's ghetto streets. Sheep, 'because they're so bloody curious', and dogs, 'always the worst because they have that damn gene of suspicion', were to be avoided. An itch could do for a man because it made movement, and movement in a lie-up sangar was discovery, or a fly up the nose.

The classes had run for a month, two hours every Thursday afternoon for four weeks, and they'd seemed so inappropriate to Malachy as he prepared for his posting to the military attaché's office at the embassy in Rome. He dug deep to remember more of what he had been told on those Thursdays when his mind was clouded with the statistics of the Italian armed forces and NATO strengths. 'If it's a one-man lie-up, and it has to be sometimes, you'll feel isolated. Keep your head clear. Start feeling bloody sorry for yourself and you'll show out. Stay focused. Everything you see in front of you is relevant,' the chief instructor had said, at the end of the last Thursday.

He'd been packing away his clipboard of notes when a young sergeant had raised her hand diffidently. 'Excuse me, I've just one question,' she'd said. 'What do you do if a dog's right up against you, a mean dog?'

The chief instructor had grinned. 'I tell you there's not a dog I can't handle. Get through to them and they're all soft as brushes. Act like you've the right to be there – if you show fear the dog'll recognize it and you're screwed. You want to be on your hands and knees and offering love, tender loving care. Any dog'll fall for it. And don't ever forget that a dog that lives in a home is always put out at night for a sniff round and a crap. Last thing, the dog's going to be out and free to run. When I was based at Bessbrook Mill and we were doing a lie-up near a farm at Newtown Hamilton, there was this big hound, a massive bugger, and . . .' Malachy had slipped away, had felt the need for more time on his Italian files.

There were no sheep on the Amersham, no flies in the darkness to get up his nostrils, but he had seen the dog.

It had come out with the woman an hour earlier. She'd pushed the pram one-handed, and had hung on to the short leash with the other. It had strained and pulled her and its head had been high as it sniffed the air. She'd been gone twenty minutes, in the direction of the kids' play area.

A television was on in the pensioner's unit living room and the brightness flicked at the curtains and lit the bars.

After she'd come back, the man – the target – had brought a plastic bag out through the door and dumped it in the wheelie on the pavement. He thought of all those who had made the demons. They cavorted in his mind: soldiers, officers, medics and Roz, the retired brigadier, who was his father, and the prim, tall woman, who was his mother. The little man who had owned the estate agents had called up the last of the demons . . . . He wondered, crouched in the darkness, whether any of them considered what had happened to him – often, rarely or never – and whether he was a source of amusement or was forgotten.

With him, Malachy had the sticky-backed binding tape, rope, a length of cloth, the plastic toy and half a packet of digestive biscuits. A mini-bus came to the edge of the estate, the road beside the pensioners' block.

He watched. Three youths jumped down from the side door. He had seen them, each face lined with terror, as they had been hoisted up, then lowered jerkily over the rim of the flat roof. They would have blinked at the view, bird's eye, of the spinning pavement below. Freed on police bail, Malachy assumed. There was division among them, sullen argument, as they stopped close to the ground-floor door – where they would have gone before. But this was another night, after unpredicted change. The door opened. The dealer's voice came sharp to Malachy: 'I heard your bloody voices. Don't come here no more. Get the message – you're dead, history. Piss off.'

Malachy felt nothing, as if the demons had cauterized emotion, no sympathy for them and no anger. He saw them drift away and one gave a finger to the closing door. Youths joined them. They were jostled, pushed and one fell. Then they ran. He had no concern for their future.

He had gone feral, did not recognize it and none who had known him would have. He wore the vagrant's clothes, damp and stinking, and the lustre of the shoes was gone, with smeared mud from toe to heel.

It was past midnight. Malachy ached with stiffness as he huddled into the hedge's shadows. A chain was loosened, a bolt drawn, a lock turned. Light flooded the pavement. The dog, off the leash, bounded out, crossed the road and came to the grass in front of the hedge. He saw the man stand in the doorway and there was the flash of a cigarette lighter. The dog came to the hedge, cocked its leg. *If you show fear, the dog'll recognize it and you're screwed.* He saw the smoke, across the road, rise from the man's mouth. He cooed softly, so gently, and in his hand were biscuits. There was a moment when the hackles on its neck were up and the growl was deep in its throat – then the docked tail swung, wagged and against his hand was the warm wet slobber of the mouth. He gave it *love, tender loving care.* He stroked the jowl fur of the dog and murmured at its ear.

The snarled shout came across the road and the grass. 'Come on! Where are you? Just get on with it, you little fucker. Hurry up! Do I have to come and get you?'

133

The sirens had sounded across the estate and there had been a single shot from a low-velocity weapon, muffled and distant. Then Malachy had slept.

He was curled on the living-room floor, his breathing regular. No dreams to toss him. On the carpet, he was a fallen statue. If he had dreamed it would have been of old Cloughie, sixth-form history, the romantic, who broke up the Thirty Years War or the Industrial Revolution or the Rise of Parliament with unconnected poetry. Sometimes Tennyson, more frequently Keats or Shelley. Hunched, as if broken by exhaustion, he lay without a cushion at his head. If old Cloughie had been with him on level three, block nine, his surrogate parent would have found the relevant passage

> Near them on the sand,
> Half sunk, a shattered visage lies, whose frown,
> And wrinkled lip, and sneer of cold command,
> Tell that its sculptor well those passions read,
> Which yet survive, stamped on these lifeless things,

and would have recited in his falsetto tone, shrill with excitement. But he did not dream. The images were gone, lost under the shifting sand – he slept deep.

He was naked.

The vagrant's clothing was back in the bin-liner, under the bed in the next room with what remained of the tape, the rope and the plastic toy. When he had come back he had eaten the few biscuits left in the packet and had put the wrapping into the rubbish can. Then he had begun to clean the shoes. Like a fanatic, fighting off tiredness, he had wiped off the mud that had camouflaged their shine, smeared on the polish and rubbed till they glowed in the dull light. Only that self-given task had kept him awake.

He needed to hear the sirens: they were proof that what he had done was not mere imagination. They had come, finally, before dawn. When the wind had pushed back the curtains and first light had seeped inside, he had heard the shot and had not known what weapon had fired it.

Malachy slept. Far from him, as if briefly he escaped their reach, were the voices that accused. Then . . . Maybe a door slammed on the walkway. Maybe a car below screamed when the gears failed to mesh. Maybe the dream was never far enough away. He twisted and jerked on to his stomach.

He woke.

Rubbed his eyes.

Felt the cold of the air on his body.

Hands on his ears, as if that would shut out the voices that dinned in his mind.

His body shook.

'God,' he cried out. 'What do I have to do? What?'

13 January 2004

'*Where's that wretched man now?*'

'*Outside, sir, sat on a chair.*'

'*Bloody hell, it's all I need.*'

'*On a chair, sir, in the sunshine.*'

The major, commanding Bravo company, paced his operations bunker, made a little trail of bare concrete where the dust was kicked aside. Frustration, not the Iraqi heat, flushed his face.

'*You know, Sergeant McQueen, what I've got on my plate?*'

'*A whole load of shit – excuse my vulgarity – sir.*'

'*Piled up and bloody high with it . . . What's he saying?*'

'*Nothing, sir. Far as I've heard, not said a word.*'

'*And lost his weapon?*'

'*Could say dumped his weapon, sir. The section retrieved his helmet and his jacket, which he apparently abandoned in the street.*'

135

'No explanations?'

'Not that I've heard, sir.'

Around the major were his second-in-command, his signals corporal, the platoon commander of the section involved in the patrol, and his batman, who had brought him a meal-ready-to-eat supper that he had not touched; he did not know when he would get a mouthful down him. Sergeant McQueen was by the sandbagged doorway and, looking past him, the major could see one of the chair's legs and one of the wretch's shins and boots. None of the men in the bunker would offer help or be asked to.

'I can't go on the net on this.'

'No, sir. It wouldn't be wise. Better to put down on paper what you know. Personal to the colonel. Not clever to broadcast it on the radio. You to the colonel.'

'Where do I find the time to do that?'

'Respectfully, sir, you have to find it.'

'Right now I haven't the time.'

'No, sir.'

'I am trying to organize a lift and I have an O Group in an hour, and the chance of getting in at dawn fast and out faster is receding by the bloody minute. I am waiting to hear back from the village elders, who are complaining about the section's response to a full-scale ambush. Christ, what are we supposed to do? Chuck toffees at them when we're taking live rounds? X-ray 12 is reporting barricades going up round the market and they're gathering for the funeral, and . . . And a high-velocity weapon is missing, and I've got an officer I'm told is a coward.'

'That's what the men are saying, sir.'

'A coward. It's about as bad as it gets.'

'The men with him, sir, they're using choicer language.'

'I'll hear it again – warts and all. Makes no difference that he's an officer . . . Wrong, does make a difference because he is not an eighteen-year-old Jock, first time away from his mum with eight weeks' Basic behind him and never out of the UK before. He's a bloody officer, experienced, supposed to lead from the front. Tell it to me, and don't stop if I throw up.'

He was told the story for a second time. He recognized the

canniness of Sergeant McQueen: no opinion of his own offered. As he listened, the major cursed the interruption to his planned lift. He saw the interpreter – a former policeman, not trusted a bloody inch – hovering at the door, and gestured irritably for his second-in-command to field him. He thought his section had done well: the corporal had shown fine leadership, and the Jock who was the marksman had performed in the best traditions of the regiment. In his grandfather's war, the wretch on the chair outside the bunker would have been tied up to a post, blindfolded, given a lit cigarette and shot. In his father's war, there would have been a stamp on the file: 'LMF' – dismissal and disgrace for lack of moral fibre, and a job digging field latrines. The second-in-command handed him a scrawled note: the elders would be at Bravo's main gate in two hours, after the O Group briefing. Then he might get down some of his bloody meal-ready-to-eat, if the flies had left any.

'. . . So, that's it, sir, according to what the section members have said. Do you want me to bring him in, sir?'

'I do not.'

'They're all good men, sir.'

'I think I've heard enough.' He broke the pacing. In his own war, somewhere buried in a filing cabinet, was a paper he had never bothered to read: it was titled Battleshock. *Might as well have been* Bullshit. *He felt no guilt that the paper was unread. He could not have imagined that one of his own men, his Jocks, would ever be labelled a coward.*

'What's to happen, sir?'

'Put him somewhere in isolation where he can't infect anyone else. He can be shipped down to Battalion in the morning with prisoners. We've wasted enough time on him. They can sort him out down there.' The major's voice softened, as if puzzlement caught him. 'It'll run with him for the rest of his life, won't it? I don't know how you'd ever get shot of it, being called a coward. *Can't imagine there's any way back.' He paused. 'Right, the world moves on – without him. I'll do the O Group myself.'*

'I'll find him somewhere to sleep, sir,' Sergeant McQueen said, impassive. 'It's not your worry, sir, what his future is or isn't, and what he does with it or doesn't.'

Her knee nudged the bucket, spilling it. The water flushed out over the floor and the suds went with the flow. The tiled floor of the first storey of the ministry was, momentarily, awash. Dawn's stockings were soaked, as were the hem of her skirt and her dull green regulation apron.

The bucket, on its side, rolled crazily and noisily away from her. Her supervisor came running.

Dawn should have had a look of humble apology on her face, should have ducked her head in shame at her clumsiness. She had been late to work that morning, and in less than twenty minutes the first of the gentlemen and ladies who occupied the ministry's offices would be pouring through the main door to be confronted by a danger zone of slippery tiles. She laughed, and saw a frown pucker her supervisor's forehead.

The response was icy. 'Perhaps you'd care, Dawn, to share the joke with me.'

She pushed herself up, took her weight on the mop's handle, grimaced, righted the bucket, then began to swab the river and shepherd the suds towards her. She didn't care about the frown and the scowl. She had been with the ministry early-morning cleaning team longer than any of the other women, had a reputation for reliability . . . but that morning she had been late to work, then tipped over her bucket. She laughed again and the echo rang down the corridors off the landing.

'Are you well, Dawn? Do you need to go and lie down?'

Her laughter, infectious, wiped the frown and warmed the chilliness of her supervisor. The young woman squatted beside her. 'Well, you'd better tell me.'

She lowered herself, laughter shaking her body, and sat on the top step. 'I was late, Miss.'

'Correct, Dawn, you were late.'

'I was late, Miss, because I just seen the best thing ever.'

An audience had gathered, the rest of the cleaning women, brought by Dawn's laughter.

'You'd better tell us, Dawn, or the place'll be a tip.'

One more convulsion, then she launched: 'The Amersham is tough. The Amersham is a hard place. I know, I have been there

138

twelve years. The Amersham is the toughest and the hardest. Druggies, thieves, muggers, we've all of them – but what we don't have is police officers. Maybe the Amersham is no-go for them. My friend next door, she is in the hospital and they have pinned her arm because the druggies thieved off her. There is no law on the Amersham. Two days ago, three boys of a gang that pushes drugs were attacked and hung upside down from a roof, which was good, but today was better.'

'So, what was the big joke today, Dawn? And do hurry it up if this floor's to be done.'

'Yes, Miss. Of course, Miss. Today would make a dead man laugh, I promise you. On the estate, the dealer is untouchable. Everybody is frightened of him. Jason Penney. We all know his name. The police, who we never see, are alone in not knowing his name. I don't know where he lives but we know his name – don't speak it, I am afraid if I say it, but know the name. This morning I came out of my block to go to the bus – I am not going to be late – and I hear the sirens. The Amersham now is filled with police. I follow the sirens. I see Jason Penney. It is very funny, Miss . . . Jason Penney is tied to a lamp post, tied at his ankles with tape and his arms are behind him and round the lamp post and the wrists are tied. He has this cloth in his mouth and cannot shout and there is more tape over his eyes. It is better, Miss, more funny . . . Also tied to the lamp post, with rope, is his dog. The dog is a brute. The dog strains to attack the policemen who want to come close to free Jason Penney. The dog does not under-stand – it will not allow them to be near. None of the police will approach the dog. They are on their radios. He has been there all night, with his dog, and his woman will not telephone the police because he deals heroin and cocaine, and the neighbours, all old people, will not telephone because that involves them. He wants to be freed, Jason Penney does, because he has been there all night and he needs to pee. But the dog keeps the police back. He has to piss. It's all down his leg, steaming. I promise, you can see the steam because the morning is cold. Everybody there, watching, is laughing at Jason Penney. Nobody before, nobody would laugh at him. We are all laughing. The police bring an officer with a gun. It is the Amersham, not Baghdad. Because of the dog they have a gun, and the dog will have to be shot. I would not have complained but this woman pushed to the front. She works at the Dogs' Home, at Battersea. I clean the offices here, she cleans the pens there. She said the dog must not be shot, must be put to sleep.'

'Tranquillized, Dawn, that's the word – tranquillized.'

'Yes, Miss, put to sleep. Everyone now is shouting at the police that the dog must not be killed. We wait some more. Jason Penney, he cannot wait, he pisses again in his trouser. Another man comes and he shoots at the dog with a dart, but that is not enough. The dog is too powerful for one dart. Another is used. Then we have to stay back until the dog is asleep. Only when it is snoring, like a man with beer, do the police go forward. What I then heard – because Jason Penney is finished, cannot make fear any more and we have laughed at him – a woman who knows took the police to a place in the children's play area where the drugs are stored, and the police took them. It is what I heard. What I know, the police cut the wrist binding and put handcuffs on him. He will never come back. Nor will his woman and his baby. We are rid of them.'

'I have to say, Dawn, that vigilantism can be ugly and is dangerous.'

'No, Miss, you do not live on the Amersham. You do not know how rare it is for us to laugh. I promise you, Miss, if you had seen the steam on his trouser leg then you would have laughed, however wrong it was. I am happy . . .'

She squeezed the last of the water off her mop and it dripped back into the bucket, and from the high windows above the landing the sunlight glistened on the tiles.

'I think it will be dry, Miss, when the gentlemen and the ladies come.'

The trawler rode the light swell, made seven knots, and pulled the net behind it on the North Sea's bed.

The speed Harry made with the *Anneliese Royal* was enough to keep the mouth of the net open. The radar had shown him that fish were there but he could not know till the net was retrieved what he would find in the 'cod end', the pouch where the catch was trapped. Billy was out at the stern watching for the drag on the tackle that would tell them they had snagged an obstruction. He had the boy, Paul, with him in the wheel-house and he talked of what he loved.

'All done by sail by men who knew the sea and had the skills handed down to them. A hundred years ago those men were lucky to make a wage of twenty shillings a week, a pound of our money a week. Brixham men were the finest in all England, could handle the deep hull and the long keel in any weather, brilliant men – and they fought. Fought so bad when they muscled in on the Newlyn fishing port that there were pitched battle riots there and the Royal Navy sent a destroyer to make peace. In 1896, imagine it, a destroyer with four-inch guns sent to break the fighting. Now, look, I've every device science can make to take me where I'm going and show me where the fish are. A hundred years back, under sail with a sloop rig, they had only their experience to guide them. No radar, no GPS. They were fishing right round the waters of the UK – Channel, North Sea, Atlantic, Irish Sea, the Western Approaches – and the skippers knew where they were from a lead line because there were no charts. They'd smear tallow – that's grease from sheep fat – on the lead at the end of the line, and the length of line out would tell the skipper the depth and when the line came in there were scraps of the sea bed stuck in the tallow, and they'd recognize it. They could "taste" the bottom from the tallow and know where they were. They was brilliant men – and the sea was filled with fish, like they were shoulder to shoulder, belly to back. They were the best.'

Harry sat in his swing chair and sipped the coffee the boy had brought him, and the boy lounged back against the chart table. He thought the boy was interested. He heard the clump of boots and saw Billy at the open wheel-house door.

'It was Brixham men, in 1837, who sailed right up the Channel, right out into the North Sea, and they were going for the Dogger Bank between Tynemouth and the Danish coast, and they found the Silver Pits, just south of the Bank. No lie, in one haul of the trawl, one boat brought in two thousand and forty pairs of flatfish, sole . . . They were pioneers, wonderful men.'

'And we're crap. Right, Dad?' Billy chuckled. 'Any chance of some work getting done?'

The boy followed his father away, back to the stern. Soon the trawl would be over and the diesels would turn the capstans to drag the nets in, and they would spill the catch down into the fish room – no bloody way would there be 2040 pairs of sole, not even if the whole of Lowestoft's fleet was out, but it was Harry's dream that he would find an old boat and work it back to seaworthiness and, if he were blessed, the boy would help him sail her . . . if Ricky Capel freed him.

If he were ever freer than the catch, struggling and thrashing, in the cod end of the trawl.

The morning sunlight splashed through the windscreen. Ricky sat in the front passenger seat and was driven over Tower Bridge into the City of London. He looked away from his cousins and down on the river-boats, on the column of barges being towed downstream and the pleasure-craft with tourists on the open deck. There'd come a time, Ricky reckoned, when the cousins outgrew their usefulness to him. Like old shoes, old socks, too holed and too worn. What then? That was his problem: he did not know. In the future, for another day . . . Right now, they headed for the narrow streets of the City. Charlie reckoned the City might be a step too far, but acknowledged the market-place there. Benji had identified the hole, then had seemed to back off and shelve his enthusiasm. Davey hadn't an opinion on it.

Three guys had gone down in the Crown Court in south London. Twelve years, nine years and eight years. 'Dumb,' Ricky had said. 'Bloody mad.' Charlie had murmured that the Assets Recovery Agency was now looking for the profits the trio had made from a trade of seven million a year turnover and that was big bread, and Benji had stated the obvious: cocaine in the City was good money and there was a vacuum in the market-place. 'Fucking idiots,' Ricky had called them. 'Fucking idiots to flash their money.' Davey's job: the car had been swept that morning for bugs, was in a secure garage each night. It was an ordinary saloon that attracted no attention. Inside the car they could talk.

Turning in his seat, smiling the baby grin at Benji, Ricky asked, 'You going to fight me on it?'

'You'll do what's best, Ricky. It's off our territory. What I'm saying . . .'

'Go on, say it.'

'We don't have people here. It's not our place.'

'Big bucks. What's your take on it, Charlie?'

'The wankers want cocaine, can't sit in front of their little screens and press the tits without it. We know that. We know also that they're mega-rich, can't spend it fast enough. But unless they're dosed up, they don't perform and get ditched. Against that, we've no organization up here, we don't know people. We don't know the suppliers and we don't know the dealers – we don't know who to trust.'

'It's just to have a look,' Ricky said softly, and still smiled, but his eyes played the menace they'd recognize. 'Just to get a feel.'

He rarely came into the City. He would have needed Charlie to tell him how many millions he had invested – after laundering – in bonds, shares and trusts that were handled behind the Monument, in Cheapside, Leadenhall Street or Cornhill. His face was pressed against the window. He watched the ones Charlie called the 'wankers', young men striding the pavements, or loitering outside for a cigarette, or carrying sandwiches and coffee beakers from the fast-food counters. Some of them, a few – dosed up on snorted cocaine – might have taken responsibility for seeing those bonds, shares, trusts grow. Other than the apartment in Chelsea Harbour, he had no use for the money Charlie washed for him. To spend it was to flash it, to flash it was to be a 'fucking idiot', to be a fucking idiot was to go down in a Crown Court for a dozen years. What was it for?

It bothered him. Late at night, Joanne's back to him, looking at the bloody ceiling, hearing the goddamn clock chime downstairs, it turned in his mind. What was it for? He was the clever boy who'd never been lifted, never pushed himself up the snouts of the Crime Squad or the Criminal Intelligence Service, lived like a bloody virgin with his legs crossed in Bevin Close. He didn't do yachts down in the South of France, didn't do private jets to the Mediterranean, didn't do big charity bashes with celebrities and camera flashlights . . . and didn't do time. Every move he made was weighed; each place he spoke his mind was swept for bugs. No mates to be with like his grandfather had had, or like Mikey, with his friends from inside . . . Percy had never had power; neither had Mikey. Ricky had power.

They went past banks, the old buildings used by the traders, the new towers for the insurance people, the wine bars they filled during the lunch hour and for binge-drinking after work, the sandwich outlets at which they snatched their lunch, the subways they poured from in the mornings and dived into in the evenings. For an hour they drove. Davey let the traffic hold them, was not impatient when they were blocked by delivery vans. The cousins all kept their peace. Ricky swallowed the sights, absorbed them.

He thought – and it frustrated him, but he did not share it – that risk ruled him . . . just a local boy and happy to do a patch of south London. No flair, no balls. Safe and comfortable. Around him there was a market, bigger than anything he'd ever gone for, of cocaine addiction, and the market was holed because three 'fucking idiots' had gone down. 'Don't try to run till you've learned to walk,' Charlie always said.

They were up by Aldgate and turning into Jewry Street. Davey had taken him on two full City circuits.

Ricky said, 'I've seen enough. God, what a bloody awful place. This is how it'll be. Start at the bottom and test it. I'd say a sandwich bar. Put a new man – better, a new woman – into a sandwich bar, just one of those holes in the wall, and sell out of it. Don't touch any of the dealers or the suppliers who are already there. Set up from scratch. A new man or a new woman who is a cut-out. Get some kid from the north, wherever, someone who's not known or doesn't know us, to act as courier – take the stuff in and bring the cash out. Wrap it round with cut-outs. Let it run for a year, then maybe it's another sandwich bar. There's a hole to be filled and we're going to fill it. You OK, guys?'

Benji said quietly, 'One thing, Ricky. What about the Scrubs? What about gaol delivery? The Scrubs or the City? I mean, you can only take on so much new stuff. Which comes first?'

'Both of them. They both come first.'

They all nodded with enthusiasm.

'Spot on, Ricky,' Benji said.

* * *

144

Polly ducked her head to the policeman. That gesture, and she was a master of it – humble and requiring help – always opened doors for her. Ludvik was supposed to have phoned ahead, had promised he would, and she had told him, with true sincerity creasing her face, that all she wanted was a few minutes' poking time around the café: 'You know, Ludvik, only to get a sense of where we're at. I wouldn't want to waste your time, and I'm better on my own.'

For a moment the policeman hesitated. If the phone call had been made – it probably had not – the officer guarding the café's front door had not been warned to expect her. Her ducked head, a glimpse of her knee below her skirt, her smile and the flash of her diplomatic card were sufficient for him to stand aside. Excellent . . . She had dreaded delay, a radio transmission to a senior officer, a senior officer speaking to a lord high panjandrum, and her left to kick her heels. The Czechs of the BIS could share with her, but she would not reciprocate. The café's door was splintered at the lock where it had been battered open. If she had been delayed, explanations would have been demanded of her, and she had no intention of offering them.

She went inside, and pointedly pulled the door shut behind her. She wanted no witnesses.

In that basement cell, where the café's owner had been beaten, where nothing of value had been recorded on the interrogation tape, only Polly Wilkins had registered the spots of white paint on the man's hands. Had it not been for the black-and-white images of his crumpled body and bruised knuckles, she might not have seen them. In the cell, when she'd held the hands, the spots had been more indistinct, but they were there.

Chaos in the café bar. Every table turned over, most of the chairs broken, a carpet of smashed cups, plates and glasses, and the chrome coffee machines split open. She thought it pure vandalism – and unnecessary, stupid. If a forensics team had followed inside the men who had broken down the door they would have found nothing, everything contaminated. She looked around her. Pictures of mountains hung askew on the walls or had been ripped off their hooks and lay smashed on the floor. Posters for last year's rock concerts in Albania were shredded. Photographs of a football team survived behind the bar counter; she noted them. It was all about detail, not about the most that could be broken, ripped, smashed, shredded. Her flat shoes crunched glass and china as she went through the café bar to the back. Every door of the ovens left open, every pot and every pan dropped, every cupboard searched through and the contents scattered. When she cabled Gaunt, when she had something to signal him, there would be one tetchy paragraph about the need for a new item on the courses for the BIS: search procedures and good housekeeping. The walls in the kitchen were lime green, but dumped out from under the sink was a small tin of paint: white. She moved on. She had seen from the street, before she had used her little-girl-lost eye-flutter on the policeman, that there was a side door beside the café entrance with two bells. Above the café were three floors. Simple to deduce. The floor immediately above was part of the café's premises; the two top floors were separate.

She climbed the stairs, difficult because the carpet had been pulled from its nails. There was a living room, a bathroom and a bedroom. More devastation. From the landing she glanced briefly into the living room, but the walls were pink. Yellow-painted walls in the bedroom, of no interest to her. The bathroom had white walls. A picture of the sequence played in her mind. A dishcloth hung out above an alley behind Kostecna. A man comes, perhaps the café owner himself, and notes it. Inside the café, time racing, a frantic effort to hide evidence. A stash point is made, filled, hidden. She roved over the toilet, the stained old basin, the shower cubicle with the collapsed screen, then saw the fractured mirror, and the smear of new paint at its side.

She put her fingers behind the weakened fastenings of the mirror and heaved. It came away and plaster spattered from the screw holes.

The paint behind the mirror should have been grey-white, but it was pristine. Not so good, not so smart. Everybody told her, when they bent her ear, that the Albanian crime gangs were the most sophisticated in Europe . . . but not with a paintbrush. She ran her fingers over the white patch, felt its slight tackiness, and could smell it. She could not see a join – that, at least, was clever. She made a fist with her hand and hit the patch hard with the heel. Her hand came back and she yelped with pain.

146

Downstairs, in the kitchen, she found a hammer.

Back in the bathroom, Polly swung her arm back and belted the whitened patch where the mirror had been. Hit it again, and again. Paint cracked, a wood screen splintered, a brick was loosened.

With the hammer's claw she prised it out. She grinned: she was Carnarvon in the pharaoh's tomb. She slipped on plastic gloves from her shoulder bag, and made ready a clutch of plastic bags. She reached inside. First, she extracted the money, euros and dollars, maybe five thousand in all-denomination notes and put them into the first bag. Then she lifted out four passports, one from Argentina and one from Lebanon, one from Syria and one from Canada; she flipped the pages of the visa and immigration stamps. Syria and Argentina were a pair; Lebanon and Canada matched them. She could follow the trail of two men. Saudi, Jordanian, Syrian and Turkish stamps in two passports; Bulgarian, Romanian and Hungarian in the Argentine and Canadian documents. No Czech visas. She would have bet on it that one passport was charred and unrecognizable in the debris of the top-floor apartment, and that another was in the inner pocket of the man who had slipped through the cordon's net. She flipped back the pages. In those from Syria and Argentina she found the photograph – easy to match from the files sent by Gaunt – of Muhammad Iyad, dead because of a present to his wife. She stared at the photograph in the passports of Argentina and Canada, and whooped in excitement. They went into another bag. Last out was a cheap stationer's notepad, bound with a wire coil. The writing, she knew it but could not read it, was in Albanian *Tosk*, page after page of scribbled accounts, notes and phone numbers, but before the blank pages, shreds of paper were lodged in the coil as if the last sheet used had been torn out. The notepad went into a third plastic bag. She put all the bags at the bottom of her shoulder bag, then covered them with the makeup sack she never used, her spectacle case, her mobile, her headscarf and, finally, her purse. She replaced the mirror, used her thumbnail – swore when she broke it – to tighten the screws and cover the hole she'd hammered, then kicked the debris on the floor to the far side of the bathroom.

She thought of Gaunt. Poor old Gaunt, who had had his share of slings and arrows, who had had to tramp up to the top floor and tell the weasel, the ADD, that a storm assault had failed to net the prize. She would have him singing. She went down the stairs, steadying herself on the rail so she did not slip on the uprooted carpet, left the hammer in the kitchen. She emerged into the light, but the policeman looked away from her evasively.

Ludvik leaped out of a car parked on the far side of the street. He hurried to her. 'What was your business there?'

'Like I told you, just "to get a sense of where we're at". That's all.'

'Did you find anything?'

'Of course not. Your people had searched with impressive rigour.' Innocence, no sarcasm.

Did she want a lift? No. She thanked him. Trust nobody, Gaunt had told her when she'd gone to work for him. 'Not your best girlfriend, Polly, not the man you sleep with, not your mother. Only trust yourself.' The savaging of the WMD team, Gaunt's fall and her shuffled out of sight – others drifting to shamed retirement – had shown her the truth of it. She went back on the Metro to her office in the embassy, clinging to the strap of her bag.

Gaunt had said on the phone, 'I'm not fucking about, Dennis, don't have time to. I'm the opposition and I'm trying to hurt us – who's the man that's most important to me? Who, above all others, do I protect? I think I know but I want confirmation.'

There were three police at the first checkpoint. A handsome woman, her figure set off by her uniform, fair hair protruding from under the back of her hat, looked at his offered ID, then checked for his name on her list and ticked it flamboyantly. The other two police were dour, with Heckler & Koch rifles slung from straps across their flak-jackets. Gaunt did not queue with the riff-raff, but drove to the head of the next line, was again scrutinized, was again passed through. There were more guns on the approach road, more on the perimeter fencing, and on top of the building ahead he saw the dark uniforms and jutted shapes of marksmen's rifles. Dennis had said he would be at the magistrates' court that morning. If Gaunt wanted advice, counselling – maybe a shoulder to snivel on – this was where he had to come. Behind the court building were the high walls of HMP Belmarsh.

Gaunt had never been here before, far out to the east of London. The drive had taken him an hour and he was late and irritable, but he needed the answer. The prison and the magistrates' court were set on the flat, reclaimed land of Plumstead Marshes. It would take more than sunshine, he thought, to brighten the place.

More checks, and inside the building's hallway he had to pass through a metal detector, empty his pockets on to a tray and put his briefcase through the scanner.

He and Dennis had been at Officer Training School together, then done time as junior cavalry officers – a unit of Lancers – before they reached the rank of major. Both had been washed up, having failed to make the promotion grades, and both had gone the civilian route; the difference was that Gaunt had taken a position in the Secret Intelligence Service, while Dennis had entered the Security Service. In Gaunt's mob, Dennis's crowd was regarded as junior, second best – not that he would show it that morning, whatever the provocation.

Having produced his ID for the fourth time, he was issued with a clip-on card, then led by a clerk to the canteen.

Dennis was there. 'Good to see you, Freddie. Been so long. Tell you the truth, I was quite surprised to get your call. You know, we hear things. I'd assumed, what with the spring-clean in your lot – the WMD people – that you'd have had the chop. So, you managed to avoid the cull. Well done.'

'Just need a spot of your wisdom . . . Never believe what you hear, Dennis. I'm alive and still beavering.'

'The little woman, is she well?'

'I think so. Last I heard she was . . .' He could have made a reference to Dennis's obvious weight increase, could have suggested he might consider going to a consultant about the lump on the left side of the nose, could have asked about the recent leapfrog advancement of younger officers over the man opposite him. He did not. 'It's good of you to make space for me.'

'You're looking a bit peaky, Freddie.'

'Pressure of work.' His smile was affable. 'You're busy, I'm busy. I have a question for you. Who is a jewel? Who, in an AQ operation, is the man who must be protected? You'll understand, of course, if I'm sparse with detail. Who gets a bodyguard? Who is worth dying for to buy time for escape?'

'In our neck of the woods?'

'Not yet – sorry, can't expand on that – in Europe, and he's on the move.'

'Come on.'

Dennis stood, left a tip on the table that was barely decent and led him to a guarded door at the far end of a corridor. They were passed through, and Gaunt was eyed with suspicion. More guns, more flak-jackets. Down a staircase flanked with white-tiled walls, then into the cell block. A food trolley was wheeled noisily in front of the doors and plates of meat, congealed sauce and rice were pushed on to the shelf space set in each door. In turn, Gaunt saw hands come to the shelves and take away the plates. Then the flaps fell.

'They're having early lunch. Some damned delay in the paper-work, so they won't be up till afternoon. I worked on it, and that's why you had to flog yourself down here. There are eight of them on remand. Take a look for yourself.'

Gaunt did. There was a spy-hole in each cell door. The interiors were brightly lit. Some ate, picky and choosy; some had put the plate down beside them on the thin plastic-coated mattress and stared blankly at the food but did not touch it; one wept silently; one sobbed noisily and his shoulders shook. Gaunt estimated their ages at between eighteen and mid-twenties. They were all Asian. He assumed they were of Pakistani ethnic origin. Above his jeans, one wore an Arsenal football top, and another's T-shirt advertised Suzuki motorcycles. Trainers were common to them all. He remembered, now, on the far side of the canteen from where Dennis had sat, the families in the dress of Rawalpindi, Peshawar or Karachi, and the lawyers huddled with them. At the seventh cell door, when the guard stepped aside to allow him to get to the spy-hole, he saw a youth who was different – not by his clothes but by his face. All the others had seemed broken and bowed down, whether they cried or whether they stifled their misery. This was a boy, not yet a man, whose attention lay in the computing magazine he read, who had an alertness the others lacked. He checked the eighth door.

Halfway down the block, Dennis leaned comfortably against a tiled wall. 'Seen enough?'

'I suppose so.'

'They're the haul from Operation Angurvadel – not my idea of a moniker by the way, down to a bright spark on the AQ desk who did Scandinavian studies at Lancaster. It's a sword in Norse mythology that burns bright in war and goes dull in peace. Anti-terrorist and the Branch had a terrible problem with it, and most of us. Anyway, al-Qaeda and the warrior's, Frithiof's, sword came together. We hauled them in. They're foot-soldiers, from east London, west London, Luton and Bedford. Look at them. Do they seem threatening to you? Of course they don't. Some would label them the Enemy Within. I tell you, Freddie, they were all out of their depth. We had taps on them through their mobiles, we had their homes bugged, we had them under surveillance for weeks before the arrests. Actually, they were quite harmless. There was "chatter" among them that was enough to get us interested. They did not have detonators, or commercial or military explosive, but the "chatter" was sufficient to spell out their intention. We have lines into most of the mosques where the hot air's shouted. Put simply, they never had a chance – and they'll probably get ten years each, for being naïve, gullible and subject to the indoctrination of a recruiter. Still with me?'

'So, they're not jewels?'

'None of them has been near an AQ training camp in Afghanistan or Yemen. Nearest they've been to the sharp end is watching videos of atrocities and fire fights in Chechnya, Saudi and Iraq. That doesn't mean they wouldn't have been prepared to detonate a bomb in the centre of London or at Cribbs Causeway or at Glasgow airport, and go up with it. No lack of courage, just a lack of expertise . . . which is what's holding them back and why we are still, most of the time, winning.'

'What are they short of?'

'Please, Freddie, patience. What they have in common: they were all born in the UK, they all come from respectable families, none of them has a police record. We pick them up because when they get faith in a large dose they've headed for a mosque and an imam who is talking *jihad*. They read a manual that details the methodology of "blessed strikes". But that's not sufficient. What if there are foot-soldiers who don't go to a radical mosque and we don't pick up because they're not close to a firebrand imam? What if they're directed by a man who understands the acquisition of explosives, detonators, who understands our capability of electronic surveillance and how we can make mobile phones dance to our tune? Then we're in trouble. That's the nightmare that gets me to my desk before half seven, and I don't leave that desk before ten in the evening – a group of foot-soldiers we've never heard of, a recruiter we haven't identified, and they're controlled by a man whose safety is worth dying for.'

'Who is that man?'

'Don't you know, Freddie? I'd have assumed you did.'

The cell block seemed to close round him. He could smell the food, the toilets, the sweat of the guards in their protective vests. The corridor lights shone down dully on Dennis's face. Suddenly Gaunt was cold and bile rose in his throat. He choked it out. 'That would be a co-ordinator?'

'If you knew, why did you bother to trek over here? He comes in, organizes at a level of quality, then is well gone before the "blessed strike". They accounted for all of the Madrid train crowd, except the co-ordinator. The co-ordinator is your jewel, Freddie. If a co-ordinator had had his hands on that lot . . .' Dennis waved expansively towards the cell doors '. . . they wouldn't be here, and we'd have been shafted – good and proper.'

'Thank you.'

Halfway up the stairs, going towards clean air and clean light, he turned and caught Gaunt's sleeve. 'If you get the whisper that your man's coming near, you'll tell me, won't you? Give me chapter on it and verse – or it's explosion time and fucking catastrophe. You will?'

'If I get the whisper. If . . .'

Outside, Gaunt sat in his car for a full ten minutes. His hands shook and he waited for them to calm. Nothing in his life – Cold War warrior, Iraq war warrior, organized-crime war warrior – had prepared him for what he had seen, young men who were pitiful in defeat and slumped in cells, and for what he had heard. He thought of Dennis, pompous and point-scoring, hurrying to Thames House each morning before the throb of the capital city beat on the masses, and the nightmare that engulfed him.

He drove away through the blocks and past the guns. The image of the co-ordinator, free and running loose, stayed with him all the way to his desk, and the hideous problem: if the Prague trail went cold, where to bloody look for him.

The policeman watched Timo Rahman with the closeness of a hunting fox.

He was Johan Konig. It was the start of the second week of his attachment to the Organized Crime, Division. He had come from Berlin, seconded as assistant deputy commander. On bogus credentials he sat in on the meeting. Probably his presence in the offices of the Special Investigation Unit of the Revenue – and the deception used to put him there – violated Rahman's human rights. He was forty-seven, short and barrel-chested, and his hair had thinned. Inside the close circle of men and women in Berlin with whom he had worked, Konig had achieved a reputation as a detective of stubborn persistence. What had brought him from Berlin to Hamburg was this target: a true prize.

Rahman had not spoken since the meeting had begun. On his side of the wide, shiny table, the Albanian was flanked by three accountants who talked for him. Konig was at the end of a line of four Revenue men. Carafes of water and glasses, not used, stood in front of each team with bundles of files. The meeting had been called, so the notification to Rahman's accountants had stated, to discuss routine general matters. Each question from the Revenue men was directed to Rahman personally, and each answer came back from whichever accountant covered that particular issue.

The man fascinated Konig, who spoke fluent Albanian. He had been on the anti-corruption team of the International Police Task Force sent to Pristina in Kosovo. He had learned there of the ruthless qualities of Kosovar Albanians, their endemic criminality, cruelty, secretiveness and power. His transfer from Berlin to a city where he was unknown was for the express purpose of bringing the *pate* before the courts and convicting him. Konig was intrigued by his target's bearing – for the first half-hour of the meeting he had thought Rahman's demeanour was almost of indifference.

Indifference? Few men, when their investments, property portfolios and interest on deposits ran to millions of euros a year and they were examined by a Revenue team working only on special investigations, displayed indifference.

The man's skill impressed him too. The file Konig had read stated that Rahman spoke good German and read it well. But each time a question was asked him in that language he gave no sign of understanding. That was clever. He looked blankly at his accountants, left them to answer.

Formidable.

Rahman, as Konig knew it, dominated the sex, narcotics and human-trafficking trades in the city. He controlled them. He was the leader of the wealthiest *fis* in western Europe. He had the power to kill, corrupt and intimidate, yet he appeared to be a humble businessman with no ambition other than, through his accountants, to pay his dues in taxes. Konig thought it the performance of a master.

The Revenue men on his side of the table did not know Konig's position. He had been introduced to them as an investigator from Berlin's tax unit; he was there for experience, they had been told, on an exchange visit. He had no need to intervene, was as quiet as the target he watched. Always, if it were possible, Konig wanted to see a target – close up – to watch his hand movements and see if his fingers fidgeted, sense whether he was nervous and note if sweat came to his neck. Did the tongue flick over his lips to moisten them? Did he shift in the chair? Was he too friendly and agreeable, or too hostile? To gaze into the eyes . . . The meeting would soon be over. Konig had not looked long into the eyes.

Had not dared to.

There were Russian gangs in Berlin, Polish *mafiya*, the cold little bastards from Vietnam who ran the cigarette trade, pimps from all over eastern Europe, and Albanians. He would have looked into any of the eyes confronting him across an interview table in the interrogation block and not been fazed. An experienced police officer, twenty-nine years of service behind him, a spell at Wiesbaden with

154

Intelligence, and time in New York on secondment, he had never before failed to look deep into the eyes of a target. Something in the eyes of Timo Rahman – and he could not have explained it – unsettled him. He would have thought himself without fear. He found that each time Rahman glanced along the length of the table and at the men opposite him, he looked away. Never before.

His mind had drifted. Sunlight made zebra stripes on the table from the blinds, sharp lines, formed patterns on Rahman's face. The man scratched his head, then looked down at his watch.

Indifference? Johan Konig understood. Preoccupation. Wants to be somewhere else, handling another situation.

Extraordinary ... Timo Rahman, with his accountants, was having his wealth dissected by a body of the Revenue endowed with sanctions and his mind was elsewhere. What could be more important than the business at the table? Every minute he had sat in the room now seemed to Konig to be justified. A weightier problem exercised the *pate* ... From problems came mistakes. The policeman felt his confidence surge. He looked into the eyes.

Chilled, bright, the eyes met his. He did not look away. He held the Albanian's glance. That was a victory. The meeting broke up. The Revenue men, at the door, shook hands with the accountants in turn, and with Timo Rahman. Konig stayed at the table. A problem he could learn about, a mistake he could exploit. As the door closed on them, he tilted back his chair to gaze at the ceiling and wondered what, or who, would explain it.

As Malachy finished his meal – a meat pie, boiled potatoes and beans – then wiped the plate with bread, he heard them coming along the walkway.

There was a deathly hush on the Amersham that day and the sounds drifted to him clearly.

Wheels squeaking, a heavy footstep, shuffled shoes approached, then passed his door and stopped. He gulped the last of the bread and listened. Keys turned and there was the scrape of the barricade gate opening.

A big voice, familiar. 'Home now, Millie, where you should be. Dawn'll get you to bed and then you rest.'

The next door shut and the gate clanged to. A moment of quiet, then a rap on his own door. 'Heh, Malachy, you there? You there, man?'

He pulled down the bolt and turned the key. The great bulk of Ivanhoe Manners filled the doorway.

'I was by here. Seemed right to call on you. I do driving for the hospital when I have the time – you know, a day off. Brought Millie Johnson home, and her friend. She's in a wheelchair for the moment, but she's strong in spirit. Her guts, they should be an example to those who lock themselves away.' He stared keenly at Malachy. 'Are you going to leave me standing here?'

Malachy stood aside. 'Whatever you want.'

'I want to see how you are. Are you standing on your own feet, or are you leaning, or are you on the floor?'

'I'm managing,' Malachy said softly.

'Are you ready to move on?'

'I don't know.'

'You got work, you looking for work?'

Malachy shook his head, then hung it.

'There's work out there for those who look for it. With work you could pay a proper rent, and free up the unit. Eight months here, right? I've a queue that needs units. You tell me, Malachy, what's happening on the Amersham, what gives?'

He saw the social worker gaze around him. He would not notice anything different from the day he had been brought here – same table, same chairs, same TV and settee, same carpet – would not know that through a door and under the bed, in the bag with the vagrant's clothes, were the last of the tape and the rope and a plastic toy. But Ivanhoe Manners missed little.

'You done well on the shoes. That's good polishing. They're the right shoes to wear if you go for a job. They show purpose, like you're climbing back. I asked, what gives on the Amersham? Police don't know, and we don't know.'

Malachy shrugged, like he avoided events beyond his bolted and locked front door.

'I'm asking, Malachy. Three of the High Fly Boys strung upside down off a roof and their authority finished, that's happening. A

156

class-A dealer roped to a post, that's happening. I have this gigantic and massive confusion, man. Help me.'

'I don't think I can.'

'You please yourself . . . I don't support what happened to the boys or the dealer, no sympathy for it from me. A gesture, but it's the way to anarchy. Where did the spark for it come from?'

'Nothing for me to say that would help you.'

The big man went back to the door, opened it, and his smile beamed white teeth at Malachy. 'Get on the road, man. You done your time here. Get walking in those fancy shoes. You need your life back, and sitting like a cat in a cage won't do it for you. Do it soon. Each day you're here – whatever was in your past – that's a wasted day. I'm offering advice and it's meant kindly. You should feed off that little woman's courage. Get living again.'

'Thank you for calling by – I'll go when I'm ready.'

He closed the door after the social worker, locked it and pushed up the bolt.

8

The train rattled across country on a slow, stopping line.

In a few days the clocks would go forward and the evenings would stay brighter. Dusk hovered over the carriages and the track, and weak pinpricks of light marked remote homes set among the grey of the fields, hedges and woodlands. It was a complicated journey for Malachy, the longest he had made since coming to London: one leg from the Amersham estate to Victoria, by bus, the next on a fast train south to Redhill and the last on the line that stopped everywhere, at Marlpit Hill, Penshurst, Paddock Wood, Mardon and Headcorn. His journey was nearly complete.

The carriages were filled with schoolchildren, their bags and noise, with shop workers and shoppers, with the first of the office commuters to get away from their desks. He wore the old clothes and his shoes were caked with mud from a litter-strewn garden in the play area. He stood in the rocking space between two of the carriages – he smelt and knew it. His woollen hat was low on his head and the collar of his coat was turned up to mask his face. As passengers passed him, to board the train or get off it, they hurried by because of the smell that came from the plastic bag gripped in his fist. He never put the bag down but kept it tight against his leg. Malachy knew that at every station there were cameras, and that cameras were now routinely fitted inside train compartments. An old world returned to him: he recalled lectures from long ago. Care ruled him, and he had regained a long-lost cunning. His ticket, expensive but not wasted money, was for Folkestone, far beyond his destination; it would act as a confusion if his route was traced. The clatter of the train soothed him and the map given him and memorized, then destroyed, was loose in his mind. In a few minutes, as dusk fell, he would reach the stop they had chosen.

There had been money with the map. Without it he would not have been able to buy the ticket and fill the canister in the bag that smelt.

The train had begun to slow and a remote voice announced the approach of the next station, Pluckley. Now the lights, set back among bare trees and behind cut hedges, shone more fiercely.

In his mind, with the map, was the quiet rasp of the voice from the darkened interior of the car, from a face he could not see.

'You've done better than I thought you would, a hell of a sight better. Nothing more is asked of you. All I can do is tell you what's at the next stage upwards of the pyramid. You hit the bottom level, the pushers, but they're just low-life scum. Above them is the dealer and you took him out and he won't be back, but he's only a vile little creature. It's your decision. Who feeds the dealer so that he can sell to the pushers? You may say, and you've the right to, that you went far enough ... Trouble is, what I'm thinking, all you've done is disrupt temporarily the trade on the Amersham, and that may not be enough to help you where you want to be. Up the ladder, right? You want to be able to look in a mirror, see your face and not cringe in disgust – am I there? Are the dealer and the pushers sufficient to get you as high up the ladder as you need to be if the mirror's showing you your face? But, like I say, it's your decision. You can walk away, or you can ask the question and I'll answer it.'

The train jerked, slowed some more, shook as the brakes were applied, began to crawl. He pulled the wool hat lower and lifted the collar-flaps higher. Kids, shoppers and commuters gathered around him, but he turned away his face as their lips curled in disgust at the smell.

'I thought you would. You were right to ask the question – well done. It's an easy one to answer. It would put you right up the ladder, high up it, if that's where you want to be. Me, I can't do it. I work at a desk, I'm ring-fenced with regulations, I'm going through the motions – like the people round me, and the people above me. Yes, we look busy, we're good at that. We pump out the spin about the success of what we do, get it into glossy brochures, and when I go home at night I can honestly say to myself, total honesty, that I have achieved less than nothing. They're cleverer than us, sharper and

159

smarter. When my pension's ticking over nicely, building, why should I care? I saw Millie, got me? My aunt, my blood, and I saw her. You are on her doorstep and you are there and you are available.'

The train lurched to a stop. Others pushed past him and hurried off down the gloomy platform. With the wool hat down and the collar up, Malachy followed them. If a camera found and tracked him, he offered it little for identification.

'A dealer needs a supplier. That's the stage up the pyramid, a supplier. Way over the level of the Amersham. He's big, *big*, and ugly. He lives fat and well. You knock over a supplier and that will send a shockwave – not an earthquake, but a real good tremor. Shakes the room, swings the light, moves the furniture, brings the plaster down. That gets noticed . . . I never met you here. People will swear on a Bible that I was never, late at night, in a parking bay, on the Amersham. We never talked. You are on your own and I will disown you, your word against mine. The word of a man labelled a coward against the word of a police officer with twenty-six years' service and not a blemish on his record. Sorry about that, but it's worth the reminder. How you do it is your business. He's the supplier.'

Malachy came out of the station and down a street, then left the high lights and the memory of the map brought him to darkness and on to lanes hemmed in by hedges; his lustreless shoes splashed in puddles. He stepped out. Occasionally cars swept by him, accelerating and spraying him as if he had no right to be there. The plastic bag, weighed down by the canister, thumped against his thigh. He remembered everything said to him, of him and overheard – what it had done to him, and what had been taken from him. He saw in front of him, clearer than the trees, hedges and homes up long, curving gravel drives, the ladder and the steps on it. He walked for nearly an hour before the twinkling lights of a remote building, set back from the lane, confirmed the map and showed him the supplier's home.

'Come on, girls. Hurry up, for God's sake. You're beautiful enough already. Move it, please.'

Laughter rang through the panelled hall and spilled from two of the bedrooms up the wide sweep of the stairs.

He needed laughter, had been short of it that day. George Wright needed laughter and a good party to get him past the aggravation of the morning. The scumbag, Penney, off the Amersham up in south-east London, was a broken stick – taken out, humiliated on his patch and now in a police cell. The scumbag had just taken delivery and not paid up. Should have paid up that morning, with fifteen thousand in used notes. All about cash-flow. The cash-flow of a dozen dealers, after George Wright had taken his cut, was needed to pay the importer. It was all tight – money in and money out – and when the money coming in was short there'd be a problem with the money out . . . and that was what was owed to the little bastard with the baby face, Ricky Capel.

He had a good coat, Armani, hitched on his shoulder, and the tie of Friends of Kent County Cricket Club loose at his throat, and he was waiting for his 'girls'.

The party was at Fortescue's place. There would be people there from all the villages between Hothfield and Bethersden. Fortescue always threw the best parties – live music, caterers in from Royal Tunbridge Wells, and a cabaret turn down from London – and the cream came from the villages, commerce and the professions. It was the mark of George Wright's acceptance into the community as a respected and admired businessman that he always received the embossed invitation to Fortescue's spring thrash, and the autumn one.

He had a reputation for success. Fortescue, and the others who sent invitations to the Wright family, believed he dealt in quality cars. Bread and butter, so they believed, was in the Mercedes top-of-the-range models or BMWs, and also in Ferraris, Lamborghinis, and Morgans with no waiting time for delivery. The private-clinic consultants, legal senior partners, farmers with a thousand acres of prime land, the chief executive officers and their wives would have gone puce and needed resuscitation if they had known that their neighbour, friend and sometimes guest dealt in the class-A drugs they whinged about at parties. His trade and the source of his wealth were well hidden, tucked away under the floorboards of his office off the living room.

God, would they never come? 'Hurry up, girls, do me a favour, shift it.'

George Wright sweated. Not on the delayed appearance of his 'girls', but on the problem of cash-flow if a dealer defaulted. He took no exercise, was plump to the border of obesity. Sweat pooled at the back of his neck and on his balding forehead. He needed the party, needed it bad. The thought of Ricky Capel made him sweat, even if the shortfall was only fifteen thousand, less his own cut. Last year a dealer in Croydon had done a runner after taking delivery, and not paid up. George Wright had gone to his bank in the centre of Ashford, drawn the necessary cash out of his deposit account and used it to make up what he owed. He'd told Ricky Capel of his problem. 'Glad you did that, Georgie,' Ricky had said, grinning, snake eyes flashing. 'Wouldn't want you, whatever the reason, to see me short, wouldn't want that. Who was it turned you over?' A week later he had read in the evening paper – and found it hard to hold the page steady – that the dealer's body had been located in Ashdown Forest; the police were quoted as saying he had been tortured, then garotted with cheese wire. He hadn't seen Ricky Capel since: communication was by mobile phone, pay as you go, with number changes every two weeks, and drop-offs and pickups. *Wouldn't want you, whatever the reason, to see me short . . .* Hadn't forgotten that.

They came down the stairs. Melanie in a little black dress and Hannah in an off-the-shoulder scarlet number, both a picture.

Melanie knew what he did – knew but did not ask details. Hannah was wrapped up in her pony and her gymkhana rosettes, didn't know, and thought money grew on the orchard's trees.

He was on a treadmill from which there was no exit point. Everything he owned came from supplying class-A narcotics. The house, a mock-Tudor pile with mock-Tudor panelling – worth a million at least, maybe one point two, and no mortgage on it – was from heroin and cocaine. The landscaped gardens, the paddock and the stable block for the pony were from heroin and cocaine. The friendship of the neighbours and party hosts was from a social position based on heroin and cocaine. Without it he had nothing, would be back to door-to-door insurance-selling, where he had been before brown powder and white powder had intruded into his life and he'd snatched at it.

'You're both a bloody treat. Fantastic.'

There was no sharp step off the treadmill – he knew too much about too many. If he grassed he had the certainty that no gaol was safe for him. And no safety for Melanie and Hannah . . . He helped his wife and daughter into their coats, shrugged into his jacket and paused in front of the mirror to lift his tie. He collected his keys.

His own vehicle was a scarlet-bodied vintage Jaguar. His 'girls' followed him out to it and closed the door, mock old timbers, behind them.

He drove away, left lights blazing behind him. He went down the tarmacadam drive, past the post-and-rail fencing of the paddock, flicked the sensor that opened the outer iron gates and turned into the lane. Their chatter was vivid around him – who would be there, what the cabaret turn would be, what they'd eat. The foreboding fled him. In his compartmentalized life, George Wright could usually slip without effort from the world of supplying heroin and cocaine, sold to him by Ricky Capel, into that of one more successful and legitimate businessman resident in the Kent countryside.

Melanie was saying what she'd heard – it was supposed to be a secret worth taking to the grave – about the identity and the act of the cabaret from London.

Hannah shrieked: 'Watch out, Daddy!'

Hadn't seen the man. He swerved to the right side of the lane, then corrected. Only a glimpse. A man, a dosser, vagrant or tinker, stood blinded by the Jaguar's lights, pressed himself into the hedge and averted his face. He was clutching a plastic bag. They were past him. He swung his head, looked back into the darkness beyond the glow of his tail-lights, saw nothing. 'Bloody hell! Never seen him before. Where does he think he's going? You did the alarm?'

'Of course I did,' his wife answered. 'Relax, George. We're going to a party. Forgotten that?'

It was another half-mile down the road to the party's fairy-lights and the thud of music.

They had done an hour at the Fortescues' house of drinks, nibbles and conversations yelled to be heard above the four-man, striped-waistcoat-and-bowler-hat jazz band when his host loomed at George Wright's side. 'You see that?'

'See what?'

'Didn't you hear them?'

'Hear what?'

'God, George, are you deaf or pissed? Two fire engines going up the lane like bats out of hell. What's up past you? Only the Gutheridges' place, but that's two miles, then the Blakes' market garden, then the cottages, but if they were going to any of them I'd have thought; coming from Ashford, they'd have used the Tenterden road . . . know what I mean?'

George Wright broke away, ran up the stairs, headed for the side bedroom where the Fortescues' boy, Giles, slept when he was home from school. He blundered through a room filled with books, hi-fi equipment, hockey sticks and tennis racquets and dragged aside the curtains. He pressed his face against the mullion lead and the glass – real, not mock like the windows of his home – and saw the glow in the sky and sparks climbing like they were fireworks, and fancied he could make out through the screen of trees what seemed to be the licking tongues of flames . . . He sank to his knees and the sweat ran to his stomach bulge and he seemed to hear laughter, like Ricky Capel's, that billowed up the stairs with the music.

'Don't mind my asking, Ricky – where's your necklace?'

'Round my throat. Where else would it be?'

'Not that one, not your mum's. The one I gave you. Why aren't you wearing it?'

His hand went up to his throat. He felt the thin chain – Sharon's present to him for his twenty-first – and touched the crucifix that hung from it. 'Don't know,' he said. 'Don't rightly know. Somewhere.'

She was paring her fingernails, had her head down as she sat in the easy chair and the TV prattled with a game show, worked hard with the file, did it with the same intensity with which she cleaned the house.

'You said you liked it. Why've you taken it off? Cost ever so much.'

Ricky had said he liked the heavy gold chain from a Bond Street store. He had not taken it off. It had cost a little more than three thousand pounds, and that was with the discount for cash – his money. 'It's somewhere.'

'Of course it's somewhere . . .'

She must have been satisfied with her fingers. She kicked off her slippers and started on the toenails, scraping at them like it mattered. 'Have you lost it? Don't tell me you've lost it. Did you?'

He had not known that he wasn't wearing it. She had bought it for him last Christmas and he had worn it every day, every night since then.

'I don't know where it is.'

'You *have* lost it?'

'Maybe I have, maybe I haven't.'

'You got to know whether you lost it or not. You got to know whether you didn't like it and took it off.'

'I don't.' There was a snarl in his voice but with her head bent over her toenails she would not have seen it.

'Well, have you looked for it? Yes? Where have you looked for it?'

'I didn't know it wasn't on.'

'Oh, that's great. I buy you a necklace, big money. You say you like it. You promise me you do. You lose it and you don't even know.'

Her voice had a chisel rasp. Seemed like the beat of a dripping tap, had that rhythm and persistence.

'I'll look for it.'

'I hope you will . . .' Right foot done, she started on the toes of the left. 'I'd say that looking for it is the first thing you should do. That necklace, Ricky, was supposed to be important.'

'I said I'd look for it, all right?'

'Where? Where are you going to look for it?'

'I don't know. If I bloody knew it wouldn't be lost.'

'No call for you to swear at me, Ricky. I just gave it you, I didn't lose it.'

He had been so tired that evening. What he'd wanted was to be quiet at home. She'd cooked him a good spaghetti, with meat sauce, and had not burdened him with talk. He needed, that evening, to think through the implications of the instructions he'd given to the cousins. *Both of them, they both come first.* Getting stuff into the gaols and into the City, two priorities to run together. Maybe Benji should run the gaols and maybe Charlie should aim himself at the City and the tossers there. Maybe he should bring in Enver Rahman and get his people to handle the distribution to a prison employee – whoever Benji could bend to carry the stuff inside – and maybe his people could sit in a sandwich bar in the City and trade stuff there. All to be worked out, all to be turned over in his mind . . . not the loss of a necklace.

'I'll find it.'

She turned to him. Didn't often see it, but there was a stubbornness in her eye. 'You should – what's a better time to start than now?'

'I'm thinking.'

'Thinking about where you lost it? Changed the sheets this morning, it's not there. Did you take it off and pocket it? No, you'd remember. What about the car, Davey's car? Ring him – tell him to look in the car for it.'

'No.' His mind raced.

'Why not?'

'It's too late.' He tried to recall when he had last noticed the necklace.

'Too late? It's not ten o'clock. What else has that idle ape got to do?'

'He's my cousin, and I'm not ringing him.' He thought he knew.

'I'll ring him.'

'You bloody won't.' It had bounced on his chest as he heaved himself up, into her, on the big bed in the Chelsea Harbour apartment, and her nipples had snagged the chain.

'I care about that present, even if you don't. Watch me.'

Joanne was up, going for the hall and the telephone. He surged after her. Ricky caught her in the doorway. For a fraction of time he felt himself threatened: she had the steel nail file still in her fist. With a short-arm punched blow, he hit the side of her face. Had never done it before. He saw the shock in her eyes and mouth, then the flush colouring her cheek.

He could not speak.

If she had cried out, if she had fought him and tried to slash his own face with the pointed file, he would have taken her in his arms and kissed her, told her he loved her, made excuses – pressure, problems, things he was sweating on. She did not. He saw contempt.

Quietly, as if it mattered to her that she did not wake Wayne, she went up the stairs.

* * *

166

The marriage had been thought by their families to forge an alliance. She lay on her back, dressed, in the spare room and stared up at the ceiling, her cheek tingling from the blow.

She had known him from school. She was taller than him then, and taller than him now. They were thrown together at school because the Smyth and the Capel breadwinners were away. Seemed natural for them to be close because their fathers were. In Brixton, the fathers shared a cell. In Wandsworth, the fathers were on the same landing. In Pentonville, the fathers had been in adjacent cells. Her father was a snatch man, his a driver. While the fathers tramped the exercise yard, together, the children were in a school playground.

Lying in the darkness, Joanne felt her cheek and her teeth. Nothing broken but there would be a bruise, big and rich, in the morning.

The first boy she had kissed had been Ricky Capel, tongues in mouths and him with smoother face skin than hers. The first boy she had had sex with had been Ricky Capel, her showing him what to do in her bed when their mothers were gone visiting. They had left school together, not a qualification between them, the only ones in their year who were not encouraged by the teachers to make something of themselves. She hadn't gone out with him when he'd been on the streets for thieving, but he'd talked about it with her and she'd told him where he was wrong and where he was right, and he'd listened. Natural that they'd be married. They were inseparable. Soulmates. His mother and her mother would have liked a church and a white dress. They'd done a register office, and then a reception down at the British Legion. 'I don't want nothing flash,' Ricky had said. 'I don't want nothing that draws attention. Just the Smyths and the Capels and the cousins.' The alliance her father had hankered after had not happened. Ricky had said her family were crap, couldn't keep their mouths shut, were losers. She had moved into Bevin Close, next door to his mum and dad and his grandfather. She was distanced now from her own clan, did not confide in them – would not tell them that he had hit her face.

No tears, only the anger. She heard him pace below. She would not go down the stairs and tell him that the loss of a bloody necklace mattered not a damn to her, and she knew he would not come after her.

She had been told by Sharon about the cat, had been told by Mikey about the arrest and the kicking of the detectives. Nothing surprised her now. She was a woman of intuition and intelligence. Might spend her days under the eye of her mother-in-law, keeping a house clean, cooking meals and not complaining if they were wasted because Ricky was not back when he'd said he would be, looking after her child, but she knew the weakness of her husband. Her own father had explained it years back: 'He'll go away, hazard of the job. He'll be put inside. Nobody stays out, not for ever. You got to put up with it, girl, like your mum did, like his. Actually, it'll be the making of him. A man who's not done bird isn't rounded off. Terrible pressure there is on any man the longer he stays out. Once you've done it, realized you can handle it – well, then it's a cake walk.' She had watched the swell of his irritation, like that pressure built, because he had not been inside . . . They didn't talk about life any more. He didn't bounce ideas at her, tell her what he was thinking, planning. They had nothing.

His grandfather liked to come next door, old Percy did. Old Percy was the only one in the Capel family that Joanne now had time for. Made her laugh. Used to tell his stories and she'd end up fit to bust with her sides in pain from the laughter: how he'd screwed up, how he'd cocked up. But two years back, old Percy had told a different story. No weeping, no sentiment, but told with a cold rancour that didn't sit easily on a grandfather's shoulders. Winnie had died in '93, and she'd gone to the funeral – not married yet to Ricky but regarded as family. A bloody awful day, cold and wet, and a hell of a turn-out for her.

Two years back, on the anniversary, old Percy had called by. He'd have been driven that morning by Mikey to the cemetery and would have laid some flowers and had a quiet moment . . . Mikey had brought him back and old Percy must have made some excuse and come to see her. First he had talked about the girls who had fled abroad. Perhaps she'd encouraged him to talk, reckoned it was a therapy for him. No smiles that day, no laughter, only the story that had chilled her. He had done big bird, had done a war, and could tell a story. She had not known that a story could be so heavy with bitterness brought from a grave. 'You're the best thing that ever happened

168

to him, love, not that he has the brain to know it. Don't know how you live with him. My Winnie couldn't stand the sight of him, reckoned the girls were right to get out – but she missed them. You heard about the cat? Yes? We were all frightened of him, what he might do . . . My Winnie was in hospital and sinking. Ricky and I went to see her. Ricky was all smarms, all comforting. You could see it in her face, she loathed him. He went out to the car park for a fag – or maybe to do a deal on his mobile. She hadn't much strength left. She said to me, "We should have drowned him at birth. That's what we should have done, Percy, drowned the little bugger. Drowned . . ." Last thing she ever said. She turned away, she coughed, she was gone . . . All that hate in her when she moved on – not right, is it? To hate when you're dying. You watch him, love.' Told the story once, and she'd shut it away, had tried to obliterate it . . . But Ricky had hit her.

He could yell, he could scream, but it wouldn't be her hand that reached out to save him. Lying alone in the darkness, in the quiet of Bevin Close, she wondered what, who, could drown him.

'You all right, Polly?'

'Fine, I'm OK, just fine.' She did not look up. She was bent over her desk and light cascaded down in a cone from the lamp and fell on the cheap little notepad with the wire coil binding it.

'The photographs have gone, and your prelim report. Well received. So it bloody well ought to have been. Can't the rest wait till the morning? If not, can I get you a sandwich, some coffee?'

The girls in the office, long gone home, had told her often enough that she allowed Justin Braithwaite, station chief (Prague), to load work on her as if she were a pack-mule. Because she did not confide, entertain them with the soap-opera of her life, they knew so little. After being dumped by email from Buenos Aires, work kept Polly Wilkins sane . . . She realized her rudeness.

'Sorry. I'm grateful you called by. Nothing, thanks. I want to go on hitting it.'

'Just checking. Freddie's at the other end of the line, sleeping in. You can handle it?'

'I can handle it.' A yawn creased her face and she giggled. 'I'll pack in when it's done.'

'Goodnight, Polly.'

He was gone, closing her door softly behind him. She glanced at her watch, and grimaced. Hadn't realized it was deep in the small hours, that the embassy had emptied and the city slept. She heard him move away through the outer office and there was the bang of the grille gate closing on the rooms used by what Consular, Trade and Political called the 'dirty raincoat crowd'. At first, responding to the email, she had joined everything. Within a week she had signed up to art-appreciation courses, walking weekends and clay-court tennis lessons. Within two weeks, nursing a bruised brain, blisters and elbow ache, she had gone into Justin Braithwaite's office, spilled out the story of her broken relationship, had brushed away his offered sympathy and pleaded for work. Work was salvation.

What she respected most about her station chief, he had not offered a homily on the effect of tiredness on the quality of performance; nor would he take personal credit for what she had achieved inside the smashed, ineptly searched café. How many in London, among those who had savaged the desk, would not have claimed a medal and citation for what she had found? Precious bloody few. It was an old work technique. After dumping the passports with the blown-up photographs on Justin Braithwaite's desk, and after writing up her report for encoding and dispatch and leaving it with him, she had gone on a search of every cupboard, drawer and storage box in their offices and in the secure section of the basement they used. She had been among old cobwebs, spiders' territory, and had finally retrieved the graphite powder.

The notebook, of course, should have gone in a pouch to London. A courier should have been sent pell-mell from Heathrow to collect it, bag it, chain it to his wrist, and fly it back for the boffins to handle.

Not Polly Wilkins's way.

Freddie Gaunt would back her and Justin Braithwaite had not overruled her.

If she had not been hurt the way she had, belted, bounced off the walls like she was a rag doll, she would not have had that streak: bloody-minded awkwardness, her signature. She yawned again and felt the ache in her shoulders. A maxim of the Service was 'Find, fix, strike, exploit'. She thought, if she could stay awake, she would have the means to exploit.

The technique, using graphite powder – fine and black – was what they taught at the Fort down on the south coast. Recruits on the induction course, computer literate, grinned and patronized the instructor when he lectured on the use of graphite powder and told stories of how it had been used by old men, long retired, from the Service or the Soviet enemy or the east Germans. She had a double page of the *Prague Post* spread across her desk. On it was the first blank page of the notebook, where top sheets had been torn out. Difficult for her, in exhaustion, to keep her hands steady, but she lifted the sachet of powder and tilted its neck, then let the grains cascade down. God, what a bloody mess.

She lifted the open notebook, hands shaking, shook it and let the powder run on the page, up, down and across. Then she spilled the mess-on to the newspaper.

She saw the writing, could make out the faint outline of the digits. She copied what she read in a wavering hand.

A man had died that another might be given time to flee. A man was tortured and stayed silent that another's flight might be hidden. She saw them both: charred skull, bruised and bloodied features. She had respect for them . . . She would undo them, make the death and pain wasted. That was her work, done better because of respect.

Polly studied the numbers, then her mind glazed and the sheet of newspaper careered up at her, and the powder was in her nose, eyes and mouth. She slept at the desk and the graphite – a weapon of the long-past war – smeared her cheeks.

A hand shook his shoulder.

Gaunt woke, startled. His arm was thrown out from the blanket and scalding tea slopped on to his chest. His eyes opened.

Over him, trying to steady the mug, was Gloria.

'Apologies if I frightened you, Mr Gaunt.'

'God . . . what time is it?'

'Two minutes after six o'clock, Mr Gaunt.'

She was always so precise, what made her so valued. He reached up, took the tea from her and gulped.

Now that he was awake, she switched on the light. Its brightness bathed him. He had slept only in his singlet and pants. She gazed at him with rather frank interest. He couldn't see why. He was skeletally thin, his facial features were drawn tight over his bones and his legs and arms were like fencing posts, but his shoulders were strong. Perhaps her interest in his white body, on which the sun was never permitted to shine, came from the absence of a man in her life. He would not have cared to list in priority the three features of her existence. Gloria, as he knew it, had her job, her self-appointed role of caring for Frederick Gaunt, and a spaniel, with the name C hung on a disc from its collar. Gaunt might come first or last, and did not ask. The tea cleansed his mind.

He shivered. New regulations demanded money be saved – of course it should be: without money saved there would not be the resources to pay for bloody pamphlets on glossy paper, *The* goddam *Secret Intelligence Service in 2010* – the central heating came on at seven, no longer at five. He held his spindly arms across his chest, not for modesty but for warmth. 'What's in?'

'Wilco's signal and her passports. Nothing after that.' Then the stern schoolma'am reminder: 'Everybody has to sleep, Mr Gaunt – not just you.'

He drank the last of the tea, then waved the mug towards his desk. 'I think I'd like those pictures up so as we get under the blighter's skin.'

Off the bed. He padded to the door, retrieved his suit trousers from the hanger and slipped into them. From his desk cupboard he took clean socks, an ironed and folded shirt, a towel and his washbag. Gloria, the blessed woman, always made sure he had a change of clothes. He collapsed the bed, the blanket inside it, and took it to the little annexe off the office. Then he was off, his waist-coat, jacket and tie on his arm, shoes in his hand, to wash, shave and ready himself for the day with a cooked breakfast in the canteen far below.

He saw the river traffic from the window and behind the capital city's waterway were the great buildings of prestige and govern-ment – any of them could be a target if the co-ordinator came this way. From the door Gaunt glanced back. She had already Sellotaped the blown-up picture – A3 size – from the Argentina passport to the wall and was tearing off strips to fasten up the photograph lifted from the Canada passport. Strictly forbidden to cover office walls with posters and images – interfered with the master plan of the contract interior designer. The faces, one bearded and one clean-shaven with heavy-framed spectacles, stared back at him, seeming to threaten him. Again, Gaunt shivered, but not with cold.

He traipsed off down the corridor to the solace of the shower and war drums sounded in his ears.

The light came slowly under heavy cloud, and he waited.

The man did not go to the Florenc coach station for long-distance travel, or the principal rail terminus, the Mazarykovo Nadrazi, where the international trains left from. He was at a stop for a local bus that would take him only as far as the edge of Prague. His intention was to move away from the city in short, stuttered steps, not to use the coach station or any of the rail termini that he assumed would be watched.

He had slept rough in the Mala Strana parkland, had not dared since his flight to find a bed in a hostel. Most of each day he had sat in the shadowed pews of St Thomas Church or St Nicholas Church or the Church of Our Lady Below the Chain, but for part of each of those days he had tramped the streets to learn.

The flight had taken him up through the hatch above the apartment's kitchen, and for a moment there he had reached down and grasped the hand of Iyad, their fists locking together. He had seen into the eyes of the bodyguard and had known that time would be bought for him – an hour, half a day, a day and a night. He would not waste the time. He had crawled, slowly, over the common wall between the buildings, scraping himself into the small space between masonry and roof tiles, and gone at snail's pace over the rafters and had heard TVs, radios and voices below him . . . and over another building's wall, and across more rafters.

The last had been the hardest. There he had had to scratch out the mortar, centuries old, that held the wall's stones, remove them silently, pray to his God that he did not make a disturbance. He had lifted a hatch, had found himself above a staircase, had dropped

173

down, replaced the hatch, gone down the steps and out into the night air. A policeman had shouted at him: language not understood, gestures clear. The alley was evacuated. Residents should be gone. Why was he so late? His God had walked with him. A woman came behind him and held a pet, a lapdog, in her arms, and the policeman was distracted. The man thought she had slipped back in to retrieve her dog. He had drifted into the darkness.

An artisan, with his work bag on his shoulder, and his head protected against the rain by a cap, broke open a chocolate bar, ate two squares and gave one to the man. They smiled at each other. They were the only two persons waiting for the first suburban bus.

He had gone to the café near the coach station. He had seen the vans parked, had stood among the watching crowd and heard the smashing destruction of the search. He had seen the café owner led away, cowed and handcuffed. The crowds stayed to witness the show, but the man had sidled away. He had been alone in a strange city with only a tourist street map, a passport and the name of the contact he must reach. He had thought the vigilance, once the apartment had been stormed and once Iyad's defence was ended, would be greatest in the first hours. He did not know if they had his face or the identity of the passport against his chest.

The chocolate made his stomach growl with hunger, but the bus came in the early thin light and the man travelled on through empty streets, past concrete tower blocks and by old factories, resumed his journey to the north and the coast.

When the torments came worst, when he could not sleep, Oskar Netzer would give up the fight. He sat on the sandbank, the first beat of the low sun on his back, and watched the strand across the channel between Baltrum and the greater island of Norderney.

For the dawning of those days when he was persecuted by memories, he dressed in the gloom of his house, kicked his feet into his boots, and searched for salvation. The torments that afflicted him had killed her, his Gertrud, as surely as if he had bent over her while she slept and smothered her with a pillow. She was dead, buried in the cemetery at Ostdorf, because of him, as if by his hand.

174

The water in the channel rippled and dazzled and sunbeams danced on the waves. On the strand beyond, uncovered and wide because the tide was out, lay an old wreck whose hull was rusty dark and had sunk into the windblown sand. Near it were the seals, bulls and cows, who had not yet produced pups. After his love of the eider ducks, Oskar revered most the seals, *Phoca vitulina*, great gentle creatures. The island still slept and the visitors had not yet come, and watching the seals at dawn gave him slight respite from the agonies of the past. The words written on the sheet of paper by his uncle, Rolf, stayed with him, as clear as they had been on the day he had heard them read in the lawyer's office – and the pain he had run from, had not escaped.

The Deposition of Rolf Hegner – the story of my guilt for which I expect to burn in hell. Those who have given me undeserved love should know the truth of me.

In 1941 I joined the Schutzstaffel. Because of the problem of fallen arches in my feet I was not sent to a combat unit, but was posted to the concentration camp at Neuengamme. I worked there as a driver. I took prisoners, many of them foreign resistance fighters from France, Holland and Scandinavia, to work on building projects outside the camp and to dig from the clay pits for the lining of canals. After the firestorm raids of the British and Americans on Hamburg, I drove prisoners to the city for clearance and for the excavation of the mass graves for citizens at Ohlsdorf cemetery.

At Neuengamme, medical experiments were carried out on Russian prisoners and on Jewish children who were inoculated with live tubercle bacilli.

On 20 April 1945, when the British military forces were near to Neuengamme, I received orders to prepare two lorries to drive to Hamburg. That day was the Führer's birthday. Late at night, the twenty children, with two Dutch persons who cared for them and two French doctors who knew of the experiments and twenty-four Russians, were brought out of their quarters and loaded on the lorries. Pedersen drove the lorry with the children, Dreimann brought the ropes, Speck guarded the children. I drove the lorry that transported the Russians. We went in convoy, with high camp officials in cars, to the school at Bullenhuser Damm in the Rothenburgsort district. The Jewish children were taken inside, then down into the cellars where there was a hook embedded in the ceiling. While the Russians, the Dutch and the French doctors were kept in the yard, the children were hanged one at a time in the cellar after being given injections of morphine while they waited their turn in an outer corridor. Trzebinski, the camp medical chief, supervised the executions. The noose was put round the children's necks by Frahm who then pulled on their legs.

After all the children were dead, their bodies were brought back to the lorries, but the Russians, Dutch and French were taken inside and hanged or shot. Before morning, all the bodies had been cremated at Neuengamme.

We were the only witnesses who lived.

After they had made investigations, the British authorities tried Trzebinski, and Thurman who had commanded the prisoner compound and Pauly who had been commandant at Neuengamme. They were executed by hanging at Hameln. Many others, myself among them, were not prosecuted but were left free to follow our lives in the aftermath of war.

I see the children today, as I write, I see them every day – I see them every night.

We did not stay to clear up the school's cellar. Where the children had been until they were called forward, we left behind clothes, shoes, toys. A little carved wood car was on the floor.

I acknowledge that I have shamed my family by my actions on the night of 20 April 1945, and have contaminated the blood strain of my relatives.

Rolf Hegner

He watched the seals roll on the sandspit and heave their bulk towards the water. They basked, they dived, and had innocence.

He had sat beside the bed in the clinic, had held his uncle's hand and comforted him. He had believed him to be a good man. His own innocence had gone inside the lawyer's office. A week afterwards he and Gertrud had fled the city where the school was and he had set up home on the island, hoping to distance himself from the torments . . . His family, his blood, his guilt, which lit a fierce fury in him.

'How long have you been here?' A harsh voice rang in Alicia's ear.

It was her aunt – her housekeeper and minder.

The refuge for Timo Rahman's wife was the summer-house among the tall oaks at the back of the house. When self-esteem fled her, when she lay on her back and he slept beside her, snoring through his open mouth, when the isolation of her life seemed to crush her, she came to the summer-house. He never did.

Everything inside the main house had been changed after he had purchased it: new kitchen, new decoration, new carpets and curtains, new furniture, all in the style that he believed was suitable. Outside, the flowerbeds had been uprooted, then turfed over: an ornamental garden would require continuous attention, would need maintenance from strangers or would become a wilderness. Only the summer-house was hers. Built of old, untreated timbers and planking nearly waterproof, it was set against the fence and the hedge – and the security wire on stanchions, the alarm sensors – and was masked by trees from the rear windows of the house. It was hers because he had no interest in it. He never sat, relaxed. He never idled, and the clock was an enemy to him.

The dawn light was behind her aunt, silhouetting her stout peasant hips and shoulders.

'I could not sleep,' Alicia said feebly.

All areas of her life had been arranged. The marriage in the mountains of Albania had been arranged by her father and his father. The timing of her two daughters' conception had been arranged by Timo and a gynaecologist in the city. The fitting out of her home in Blankenese had been arranged by Timo and her aunt. The schools for the girls had been arranged by Timo and a lawyer who lived four streets away. Her clothes were chosen by her aunt, and the food for the family meals . . . Everything arranged, everything chosen. She was decorative, expected to stay attractive and keep her waist narrow, but she was not required to make any contribution to her husband's life. Beyond the hedge, the fence and the wire were the gardens of

German women – smart, chic professionals – whose names she barely knew, whose lives she could hardly imagine, whose language she did not speak. Only in the summer-house could she find peace. The aunt had travelled with her from Albania, but the woman's loyalty was first to Timo Rahman.

'You could catch a chill out here.'

'I needed the air,' Alicia said limply.

'You want for nothing.'

'There is nothing I want.'

The aunt bored on: 'You have the love of your husband and your children.'

'I do.'

'You have a home to be in, and a bed.'

'Yes.'

'And a husband you should please.' The aunt leered.

What she knew of sex, how to 'please' and where her hands should go, had been taught her by the aunt, a demonstration with the woman's coarse hands guiding her fingers over the body flab – but what she had learned had been used to conceive the daughters, then to try for a son. When the boy-child had not come – as if it were understood between them – Timo no longer pulled her over and hoisted up her nightdress. He had no other woman, she knew that. She thought he had no more interest in *fucking* her, doing what dogs did in the village high up in the mountains, or goats or sheep. He had no need of her. She had love of a sort and children and a home, and emptiness.

She pushed herself up from the cushions on the bench, and followed her aunt back to the house. The cold fanned her skin, and thin sunlight fell on her.

Malachy stepped off the train. He had walked through the night and believed he had defeated the cameras. Instead of taking a train from Pluckley or Ashford, he had gone north to Wye, hammering out the miles on country lanes. He had taken the first service of the morning, wool hat still down and collar still up, that meandered off towards Canterbury. He had walked out of the station there, as if that was his destination, had headed for a car park, had pocketed his hat and folded his coat, then kept it under his arm, unrecognizable, when he had gone back to the ticket office. The London train staggered into the city. All that told of his night's work was the faint smell of petrol on his sweater and the scorch in his trousers where the first flames had lashed back through the broken window of the living room.

He stepped out of the carriage and was carried on by the wave of the London workforce that hit the platform. He felt no elation, no excitement, no pride – but knew he climbed the ladder. If the garage had not been empty, if the house had not been silent and all windows closed, if the stable with the restless pony had not been well distanced from the house, would he still have broken the window and splashed the contents of the canister inside against curtains, down on to carpets and lit the coil of paper?

'I don't have to answer that,' Malachy murmured to himself. 'I take what I find.'

9

Voices from the darkness of the parking bay, his and the one from the masked mouth inside the car.

'You did well, you don't have to do more.'

'You don't know what I have to do.'

'You've been as far as you can go.'

'Wrong. You cannot understand.'

'I know about you, read it in files. I have the picture of it.'

'Wrong. Paper doesn't tell it.'

'Three strikes, all well done. It's enough.'

'Wrong. Doesn't purge it.'

'The next step is too far, Malachy. It's what I'm telling you, too bloody far.'

'Wrong. Nothing's too far if you've been where I have.'

'Walk away. You've done all that was asked of you, and some. Forget it.'

The darkness of the parking bay swamped him and around him was the new quiet of the Amersham. In the afternoon he had heard the same voice, now muffled by a face covering, then by a thin adjoining wall. He had unlocked his door, closed it after him, gone fast down the steps and waited at the bottom of the stairwell. He'd heard, faint and far above him, 'You look after yourself, Millie, you take care. I'll see you.' He had waited. The heavy shoes had clipped down the steps and when the detective had stepped off the last, Malachy had stood in front of him. 'Call me, please call me,' Malachy had said, and the detective had walked by him, no response on his face, as if nothing had been said. He had gone to his car and had not looked back, and Malachy had climbed the steps, put the bolt back, turned the key and waited. Three rings late in the night, then silence, then three more rings pealing in the room.

'What is the next level?'

'The next level, pal, would put you way out of your depth. For sure, you'd sink.'

'I sank once.'

'At the next level, they kill. Last one was dumped over a cliff, went down into the sea, but he didn't drown . . . Was dead already, tortured and then dead. Late on his payments – only this isn't being late on a credit agreement for a living-room suite and getting a rap from the finance company. The repossession order is a sentence of death. Every bone in his body was broken, and that was before he went over the cliff. Scrub it out of your head.'

'When I sank I hadn't the courage to end it. They took everything from me. Any self-respect and I'd have put myself away. They didn't leave me anything.'

'I helped you, Malachy. Don't look for more.'

'A dealer feeds the pushers. A supplier feeds a dealer. Who's next up the ladder?'

'We know who the corpse over the cliff defaulted on. Know who killed him, having tortured him. I know, my inspector knows, my superintendent knows.'

'Who feeds the supplier?'

'We know the name, but we don't know where to look for evidence. What I said, forget it. It's big league, beyond your reach. Be satisfied.'

'I'm going up your pyramid. Who sold to George Wright?'

'Tell me, old friend, what is it you need to lose?'

'Disgust, what you can't imagine, shame. All of them queuing up to belt me . . .'

'Just self-pity, like a jerk-off.'

'You weren't there – you only read it in the file.'

'Then tell me, Malachy, what it is you need to get?'

'Ability to live, to walk, to laugh. Something of that. You started me, put the ladder there. Don't take it from me. Please, I'm asking you – who sells to the supplier? It's not to do with Millie Johnson, it's for myself . . . please.'

From deep in the car there was a long, hissed sigh. A ballpoint clicked. He heard the scribbled writing. A sheet was torn off a pad.

Through the open top of the window a gloved hand passed the scrap of paper. He took it. A thin torchbeam shone on the scrap. He read a name and an address. Then the gloved hand snatched back the paper and the torchbeam was cut, replaced by the flash of a cigarette lighter and a little guttering flame.

'It's big boys' league. The importer sells to the supplier. Malachy, you watch yourself. Don't do anything if you haven't looked it over good and proper. Take time.'

'Thank you.'

'Was it that bad, what was done to you?'

'It was bad.'

14 January 2004

When the sun was up, past eight, Dogsy limped to the lorry. Fran, his friend, who was going to ride shotgun, reached down from the back to give him a hand up. Dogsy milked the moment, all his weight on his right boot and none on his bandaged left foot, and let out a little groan, not stifled, as he came on board.

He settled at the tail end of the bench, opposite Fran. Inside the lorry, under the canvas, it would get to be rotten hot on the journey, but by the tailgate there would be air. He stretched out his left foot. Fran made a play of kicking it and Dogsy gave him a finger. The dust swirled, and the convoy moved off from Bravo.

It was because of personal hygiene that Dogsy had a seat on the lorry, and a bandaged left foot. The previous night, the stink of his boots had caused enough aggravation for them to be chucked out of the room where 2 Section of Salamanca platoon slept. In the morning, when they'd dressed for the lift operation, he'd gone in his socks, cursing, to retrieve them, and had stepped on a feckin' scorpion. Little bugger had a bloody great sting in its tail. Dogsy had missed the lift: the corporal medic had bandaged him, and he had the ride back to Battalion and a look-over from the medical officer.

They had armour, Warriors, in front and behind for fire power. No chopper available. The lorry whined for power and the personnel carrier behind them gave a sort of comfort. It was a feckin' awful road back to Battalion – a sniper alley, and RPG-missile alley, a

182

buried-bomb-at-the-end-of-a-control-wire alley. But the heat, feckin'
awful, calmed him.

It was the smell, worse than his feckin' boots would have been. He
looked inside the lorry. 'You know what, Fran? One of them's shat
himself.'

'Which one?'

He looked up the line of men, five of them, on the bench opposite,
beyond Fran. Each had his ankles roped to the bench stanchions,
wrists manacled behind them, and each was blindfolded with sticking
tape. How would Dogsy decide which of them had fouled himself? He
leaned forward so that he could check the men on his bench. Four more
men with ropes, manacles and tape blindfolds – and another. At the
lorry's bulkhead, up against the driver's cab, without restraints, was
an officer.

'Hey, Fran, is that him?' he whispered.

'What you say, Dogsy? You got to shout. What?'

He did. 'Is that the Rupert?' he yelled.

'That's him.'

'The Rupert that Baz said was feckin' yellow?'

'Bottled out. That's him, Dogsy.'

'How could a guy do that, Fran – an officer?'

'Couldn't hack it. The section had a good fight, used up juice like
no tomorrow, did slots, but the Rupert didn't stay around to see it.'

'What'll they do to him?'

'God knows . . . Who cares? I don't, you shouldn't.'

He stared up the swaying length of the lorry. They had been shout-
ing questions, yelling answers. The officer's head shook against the
bulkhead and he did not seem to feel pain, as if he was in deep sleep,
and his body moved with the lorry's lurch when the wheels hit
potholes . . . Poor bastard. Not that, to Fran, Dogsy would have
uttered sympathy for the man called a coward. He looked away, back
at the nose of the following Warrior.

Polly did lunch with Ludvik. She had booked the table at the restaurant over the Vltava from the embassy. It would not come cheap but
would be on expenses, authorized by Justin Braithwaite. 'I want to
take you out and show you my thanks, up close and personal, for the

co-operation and professionalism at Kostecna,' she'd said, when she'd rung him – and, like an afterthought, 'Oh, by the by, something that's been hanging around on my desk for weeks. I'm sure it's not important, but I've a phone number. I need to know whose it is, what they do. Got a pencil?' She'd let him order – grilled carp and salad, after local soup, and fine beer. She'd waited, made small-talk, rolled her eyes at him and played at being fascinated by what he said.

During the salad, he'd let his knee nudge her thigh. When she'd struggled to fillet the carp, he had leaned across the table, head close, hands near hers, to work the flesh expertly off the bone. Too much looking earnestly into the eyes around which she'd smeared the makeup. Thought he was in with a chance, didn't he? Thought the afternoon might end up at his apartment or hers, hadn't he? Then coffee, strong. It was what she had done with Dominic, end up at his flat, when she'd had a day off and the Foreign and Commonwealth wouldn't miss him, and they'd taken a bottle with them to bed . . . but that was all long gone.

She left it late, then slid in the question. 'That number, any luck?'

First, she was told what she knew – wasn't bloody stupid: the number was at Ostrava, near the Polish border.

'Oh, did you find whose it was? The office dumped me with it last month.'

She was given a name. She had her pencil out of her bag and scribbled what she was told on the back of a torn-open envelope, which she thought was an indication of the matter's minimal importance. Gaunt's favourite mantra was about trust: don't. His second favourite was about sharing intelligence with an ally: never, if it can be avoided. If it could not be avoided it should be economical in the extreme. He reached across the table, almost shyly, but far enough for his fingertips to brush against her hand, holding the envelope.

She smiled, in what she thought was a warm, caring way, then shrugged. 'Don't know why the office wanted it . . . God, some of the work I get loaded with is dross. Anyway, what does he do in Ostrava?'

The man with that telephone number ran a factory producing furniture for export to Germany and was a subsidiary of a larger conglomerate.

'Riveting stuff. You'd have thought, in this day and age, that my people had better things to do with their time. Whose conglomerate?'

The furniture factory was a small part of the empire owned by Timo Rahman . . .

'Never heard of him.'

'A multi-millionaire from Hamburg, an Albanian.'

'OK, OK, we don't have to overwhelm my people – that'll do for them. I'll get a commendation for it . . . Tell me, is carp better grilled, like ours, or fried, or just put in the oven? What would your mother do?'

She paid, insisted. The bill would just about wipe away Justin Braithwaite's entertainment allowance for the week. Short rations, there'd be, in the Service's annexe.

On the pavement, his hand touched hers, then slipped into the crook of her arm.

'That was really nice, and we'll do it again,' Polly said. 'I'd have loved to spend the afternoon in a couple of churches, with you to guide me, but that's for another day. Must get back. See you soon, I hope.'

'Gloria, have you ever been to Hamburg?' he shouted.

'Twice, Mr Gaunt, just the twice. I liked it, rather a civilized city.'

He had his hands together as if in prayer, fingers under his nostrils and thumbs against his mouth. Gloria would have come to the door behind him, would be leaning against the jamb. She would allow his thought processes, without interruption, to stutter out, as if that were part of her duties.

'Perhaps "civilized", yes. Quality prostitutes, quality bankers, quality scenic views. Bravo, Hamburg. But it's where it all started, isn't it? While we were faffing over Baghdad, pushed by those bloody politicians, the eye was off the ball – our eye, the German eye and the American eye. Saddam's legacy – don't you know, Gloria? – was to be the fox that led the trail away from the den, where the vixen was and the bloody cubs.'

'Quite apposite, Mr Gaunt,' she said drily, but she would never be impertinent. 'You should use that allusion in a report.'

'Eye off the ball and not seeing the supreme target. In Hamburg.'

'It wasn't just you, Mr Gaunt. There was an AQ desk.'

'Everybody's eye off the ball. While we were wetting ourselves waiting for the next download of satellite imagery from some God-forsaken heap of sand in Iraq, the threat was incubated in Hamburg. What was the name of that wretched place?'

'Harburg, across the Elbe river.'

'And the name of that wretched street?'

'Marienstrasse, Mr Gaunt.'

'And the spores are still in the bloody pavements of your "civilized" city. It's where they were, where that horrendous plot was hatched, nine/eleven, where war was declared, the ultimate attack – and we knew nothing. Now, little Wilco sends her signal ... A man resists torture – and his interrogators were well trained – to protect a notepad on which a telephone number was written. I'm getting there, Gloria. The telephone number is that of a factory that exports furniture. To where? To bloody "civilized" Hamburg. *Hamburg* again.'

'Do you not think, Mr Gaunt, that you should rest for an hour or two?'

'God, and wouldn't it be easy if we had some proper equipment to turn on them – a squadron of tanks, a battery of artillery, a brigade of paratroops I can deploy against them? Then I'm laughing. But this is a city that is "civilized". Hamburg is where they plot, plan, then launch from. Once a month I go to a lecture where an academic tells me I have to get into the mind of an enemy. How? I am white-skinned, middle-aged, middle-class, a little Englander. I have no chance ...'

'Should I make more coffee?'

'... no bloody chance.' He waved at the pictures she had Sellotaped to the wall. 'Half my age, without possessions, with faith, without conscience, with the ability to justify strapping bloody "martyrs' belts" round foot-soldiers' stomachs. Only a fool suggests I can understand him.'

'You're digging this weekend. That will be good for you.'

'So wise, Gloria, always so wise. You filed it, remember, the commentary from *Moskovsky Komsomolets* at the time of that obscenity of the school siege: "Why are they always ahead of us? Why are they winning? Because they are at war, and we are just at work. It is time to realize that we, too, are at war." I believe I quote correctly.'

'Don't you think, Mr Gaunt, you ought to have another coffee?'

'I'd like, thank you, a gallon of coffee.' He intoned, ' "They are at war, and we are just at work." And I'd like some tanks on Hamburg's streets.'

At a minor Customs post, north of the Czech town of Liberec and south of the Polish town of Zgorzelec, two officials slept and one staggered sleepily from the hut as the old saloon car, headlights bright, approached. Because of the telex from Prague received at the hut two days before, the solitary Customs man gestured with his hand for the car to slow. It stopped under a high light. He motioned to the driver to wind down his window and the rock music blasted out – what his own kids played. There were five inside, two girls and three youths. The telex had said that Arabs should be checked, but had listed no name; nor had a photograph been faxed to the post. He asked for the passports. Two of the boys, flaxen-haired, languidly offered him their papers – Polish. The girls, one red-head and the other with a mauve streak, had Czech documentation. The fifth passport was from the back of the car. A man, early thirties maybe older and maybe younger, was sandwiched between the girls and gave him the German passport. He shone his torch into the interior, let the beam light on darker skin. He held the opened pages under the high light. German citizenship. Date of birth, 1974. Place of birth listed as Colombo in Sri Lanka . . . Not an Arab. Sourly, he gave the passport back through the window. Somebody's daughters, from Liberec, Jablonec or Ceská Lipa, out for the night – without modesty but no doubt with condoms – with Polish boys and an Asian. Could have been his girls. These were new freedoms.

He stamped back to the hut. It had not said on the telex that an Arab might have hitched a lift, joined a car filled with youngsters, to cross the frontier. The Customs official had no reason to be suspicious of the German passport-holder crushed between the girls in the back of the car. Nor did he have reason to suspect that, when the car reached Zgorzelec, and parked at the back of the discothèque hall, the man would sidle into the night, away from the booming noise, and head for the railway station. He poured himself some soup from his flask and returned to his magazine.

'You have to believe it, Father, he will come.' The Bear had said it to him.

'What did the television say?' Timo asked him. 'Tell me again.'

'A siege in the Old Quarter of Prague. A man of the Russian *mafiya* finally killed by the police. Lies, of course.'

'But not a lie that one was killed.'

'One only, the television said. The lies were that he was Russian, a member of the *mafiya*. Father, they would lie on that.'

'If one was dead, which of them would it be?'

'Not the principal. Father, he will come.' The great paw of the Bear had settled on Timo's shoulder, and had squeezed reassurance.

'Call Enver. He should send the mouseboy here.'

He sat now with Alicia in the gymnasium of the school in Blankenese, sensing her nervousness. He could acknowledge that, through all the hours since he had met the young man from the warehouse in the Hammerbrook district – *Regret cargo load 1824 has not been forwarded* – he had given her little attention, his mind clouded by the import of what he had been told. If he had not had the confidence of the Bear to stiffen him, Timo would not have been at the school that evening.

For good work in year nine and year seven, imitation parchment scrolls were to be presented to the best students. His girls were among them. They, with the rest of the favoured students of their classes, were at the front. He and Alicia sat with the comfort and wealth of the élite of Blankenese's community. She had worried about what she should wear, what jewellery she should display, what cosmetics, what shoes were suitable. Before the Bear had spoken to him, he had ignored her concerns. Afterwards, he had gone through the wardrobes of dresses with her, had unlocked the safe with her jewellery and chosen for her, and the shoes, and he had pointed to

188

the lipstick she should use. Timo Rahman was the *pate* of Hamburg, but he needed a man of brutish strength and limited intellect to soften nagging anxiety.

Their younger girl stepped forward, climbed the steps to the stage, had her hand shaken, was given the scroll, and Timo jagged a glance sideways and saw love for her daughter light Alicia's eyes – but the woman, the wife of the *pate* of the city, did not know whether she should clap, whether she should cheer. They were peasants of the mountains. He did what no other father, whose son or daughter had gone forward, had done. Timo stood. His arms were above his head and his hands thundered together in applause. He pulled Alicia to her feet. At that moment he cared not a fuck what other parents, the best of Blankenese, thought of them.

Last summer, with Alicia, the girls, the Bear and Alicia's aunt, he had flown to Tirana and then they had travelled in a fleet of Mercedes limousines along the rutted, broken roads to the north, guarded by the guns of his clan. On the fourth day of the vacation at the villa he had built above Shkodra, he had sent the women and girls to visit Alicia's family in their village. Watched only by the Bear, he had negotiated with those men who had travelled to meet him. Matters of mutual co-operation. Intense men, they had stared around them with naked disapproval at the lavish trappings of the villa, had demanded prayer breaks, but had come with proposals. They had talked of transportation and safe addresses, the movement of weapons and the production of international travel documents: areas where he was strong and they were weak, or where he was weak and they were stronger. They had left, driven away by his people, before the return of the women and girls. Four days later, when his wife, her aunt and his daughters had travelled to see the site of his newest villa, where the foundations were already dug, the men had returned. The talk had been of money, what he would be paid and what would be demanded of him. At the end of that second day, Timo Rahman had shaken their hands and seen the fire in their eyes. By the shaking of hands he had pledged his word with the strength of the *Canun*, written down centuries before by Lek Dukagjeni, and their guarantee was on the word of their faith. He had gone into a world that was a clouded sky to him – right or wrong, with sense or idiocy – and he had made the deal. Now a man came – the Bear promised him. His elder girl went up the steps.

He stood again, pulled Alicia up. They were peasants from the mountains. He had come to Hamburg with holes in his shoes, tears in the knees of his trousers and money to sustain him for a week. Alicia wriggled free of his grip, and sat, her face flushed red with embarrassment. He saw the sneers, the little titters of amusement his enthusiasm made, and clapped harder.

A dosser stood under the street-light at the junction of Bevin Close and the main road, a woollen cap pulled down on his forehead and his coat collar up. Only a little of his face was visible to Davey, orange-coloured from the light, but what he could see of it was unshaven. The light caught his eyes, flashed on them. The dosser stared up the length of Bevin Close and his attention seemed to be far down it, where the cul-de-sac opened out and gave room for vehicles to turn, to the semi-detached houses where Ricky lived.

Davey was careful, which was what Ricky paid him to be. He had been in the garage alongside his house to check the alarm on the car, then to satisfy himself that the sensors covering the garage interior were blinking red and alive. He was paid well to be careful of Ricky's security. When Davey turned from the garage, the dosser still stood there.

Then the man moved.

A little frown of surprise flicked at Davey's forehead.

No longer at the junction of the main road and the cul-de-sac, the dosser now walked in a slow, rolling stride down the pavement on the opposite side to his garage and came into Bevin Close. Didn't stop, didn't look around him, went on as if he knew where to go. Davey heard the shout from inside: his meal was on the table. He called back that he would be a moment, not long. He was now on the step and there was the scent of cooked food from the kitchen, but he hesitated.

The voice bit behind him: 'Come on, Davey, or it'll be cold.'

'Be a second, just a second.'

He saw the dosser stop in front of a door and peer past the gate and up the little pathway, as if he looked for a number, then briskly head on. He was supposed to know of everything that moved on Bevin Close. It was his work to maintain a constant watch for Crime Squad surveillance and the Criminal Intelligence Service's bugs. He knew every delivery van that called regularly, and the faces of relations who came often to visit. There had never before been a dosser in the cul-de-sac. If it had not been for his blood link to Ricky Capel, Davey would have been small-time – perhaps a thief and dreaming of one big pay-out job, perhaps a mini-cab driver doing eighty hours a week. One day, and he had no idea of how far away it was, he would be able to buy an apartment or a little villa on the Spanish coast, with a patio and a pool. Or, one day, if he was not always careful, he would be in the Central Criminal Court hearing a judge slag him off and send him down. The dosser had slowed, was outside number eight, Ricky's place, and seemed to stare inside. Joanne – God, he didn't know why – never pulled the curtains after dark.

'You coming or not?'

'Just a moment.'

He went out through his own gate and started to stride to the corner junction. He looked both ways, raked over what was parked there, and saw nothing that alarmed him. Then he swung back and headed down Bevin Close. He recognized all the cars parked on the kerb, either side of those numbers that did not have garages. The figure of the dosser was lit by the brightness spilling out from the window. He was confused, could admit it. Benji and Charlie had the brains, did the thinking, but they all depended on Davey's nose for danger. A dosser had no call to be in the cul-de-sac. If the dosser was some fancy caper from the Crime Squad or the Criminal Intelligence Service he would have back-up in a van or a car close by, and there was no vehicle that fitted on the main road or in Bevin Close. So what the hell was he doing there?

The shout carried in the evening to him. 'You please yourself. It's in the oven, I'm starting.'

He yelled, not over his shoulder but ahead: 'Hey, you. What's the game? What do you want?'

The dosser didn't turn. If he'd been Crime Squad or Intelligence, he would now – challenged – be lifting his arm or ducking his head sideways and speaking urgently into his wrist microphone or the one on his collar. But the dosser just stared ahead at the window where the curtains weren't drawn.

'Hey, I'm talking to you – what you doing?'

No movement, no motion. Davey started to run. He could see the torn dank clothes of the dosser. He was panting, didn't do much running. He'd used to box in Peckham, super middle-weight, but that was way back. No call for him to run once he'd joined up with Ricky Capel. He came up behind the dosser, and the smells of the man were in his nose, but he hadn't turned – like it didn't matter that Davey had come down, fast, the length of the close and had yelled at him. That he was Ricky's man, his enforcer, was known through Lewisham, Peckham, Camberwell and Catford: in a pub he was bought drinks, in the betting shop he was allowed without fuss to the queue's front, in the street people moved out of his way. Davey was never ignored. He had stature as Ricky Capel's minder. He came up behind the dosser.

'Don't you bloody listen? I was speaking to you. What's your business?'

The shoulders, sagging, stayed in his face. Davey was a short-fuse man. The nearest place where dossers hung out, where they begged or slept or drank, was the underpass at Elephant and Castle, but that was up past Rotherhithe and over the Old Kent Road, not here. He grabbed the shoulder. No resistance. The stink seemed to billow over him. Davey boiled. He had the man's coat in his fist and swung his body round to face him. There was no fight in the man, but no fear. Davey was used to fear, inflicting it. Used to men cowering from him, cringing away.

'Who are you? What you doing?'

Not a quiver from the lips. Davey did not know whether it was dumb insolence or dumb stupidity. If the dosser had shown the fear then he might have frogmarched him up the length of Bevin Close and kicked his arse back on to the main road's pavement, and watched him go, then gone inside to get the supper out of the oven. The eyes stared back into his. Was the man mental? One of those Care in the Community people? Didn't seem that way to Davey. No madness in the eyes.

'You were lucky I was free – I'm not often free.'

'And again I regret my lateness, unavoidable business.'

He thought the bruise on her cheek had come from a hard blow.

'So, what is it that couldn't wait? I mean, I'm out with Joanne.'

'I had a call from Timo, from my uncle.'

'So?'

'Timo Rahman requests your company in Hamburg – to discuss a matter of mutual interest.'

'When?'

'Within two days or three, that is what my uncle requests.'

'I don't think I can do that. I've a heavy diary. Maybe in a week or two.'

He leaned forward. The wife watched him. She would have known that Enver Rahman, associate of her husband, ran brothels in north Haringey, Soho and behind King's Cross. She would have realized that he had noted the bruise on her face. She watched him and he thought she loathed him. Enver took the mouseboy's hand, opened it, laid it against his own palm. The hand snapped shut on the gold chain. It had been on the bed – the clasp had broken open while the girl had grunted and faked.

'Maybe I can rework my diary. I've never been to Germany.'

'I will book the tickets and I will accompany you. The day after tomorrow.'

Ricky Capel's fist was clenched tight. 'Yes, I can do that. It will be good to meet your uncle.'

'My uncle will hope that he has not inconvenienced your diary, Ricky. He will be most grateful to you. My apologies, Mrs Capel, for disturbing the enjoyment of your evening. I will ring you, Ricky, with the flight.' He gave a last subservient smile, that of a lesser man, and worked his way out through the tables and past the drinkers. Outside, he tipped the barman another of his twenty-pound notes for watching the car, and drove away.

Late, near to midnight, the *Anneliese Royal* docked. A poor catch. Hardly enough in the fish room, boxed in ice, to pay for the engine's diesel, and little enough for his son and for the boy's wage. For himself, there would be no money.

Skilfully, Harry nudged the beam trawler alongside the floodlit quay. Beyond the harbour the bars of the east-coast port town were chucking out. When his boat was unloaded and he walked towards the gate, if he met other skippers he would be asked how his catch had gone. For an answer he would shrug and shake his head. If the *Anneliese Royal* had been bought with a bank loan or a mortgage, had not been given to him, he would have gone to the wall with what the catch paid him. He would have been another swamped by the quotas, the lack of fish, the cost of diesel and the wages bill. But Ricky Capel had given him the trawler and often enough there were packages to be hooked up from buoys off the German and Dutch coasts, and Harry Rogers survived as a fraud. The ropes were made fast and the boy had started to put the few boxes on the conveyor-belt.

Harry said to Billy, 'Can't see any point hanging about this dump, not with the weather turning. No sense being here. I fancy home, going down west, till the storms are blown out.'

'You been in a war, Chief?'

'I'm fine, thank you.'

'I don't wish to interfere, but you don't look all right, Chief.'

'Very fine – never been better.'

'Have you been robbed?'

There was, and Malachy recognized it, genuine concern in her voice. It was an effort for him but he turned to the woman driver, took the change and the ticket that she dropped into the tray. Through the glass that protected her he saw the way she squinted at him.

He grimaced, which hurt his chin. 'I don't have anything to steal.'

'You should get them washed, those cuts.' She engaged the gears. 'Right now, get yourself a seat. On the night bus we go like the wind.'

He clung to the pole, steadied himself as she pulled away from the stop, then lurched for the nearest seat. He heard her voice behind him: 'Him what done that to you, did he get pain?'

'Not yet.'

She giggled raucously, then accelerated, and Malachy slumped down. The bus raced through empty streets, took him home to the

Amersham. Bruised and bloodied, he felt the first welling of respect for himself, after so long. Like he had climbed a ladder or scaled the terraced wall of the pyramid. He was too tired, too battered, to know how Ricky Capel would 'get pain', but he promised it.

IO

He sat on the floor. Round him were the sheets of paper torn off his notepad, and on the sheets were pencil lines, and he did it as he had been taught. The lines on the paper were maps, as he remembered them, of the main road and the junction, the length of Bevin Close and the street behind it where the gardens shared the common fence with those of the cul-de-sac, and of the house, number eight. He searched deep in his memory for exact recall of everything he had seen under the street-lights.

He heard the tap on the wall.

The house had surprised him. He had expected that Lewisham's roads would open – without warning – into a closed suburb of high walls, high gates, with mansions set behind them, the equivalent of the supplier's place in the country. What he had found, its ordinariness, had wrecked his concentration: he had spent too long down the cul-de-sac after going into its mouth. It was clever, having a place so unremarkable, which could only be reached by going into the mouth and down the throat of Bevin Close.

The tap came louder on the wall behind him, and its persistence grew.

That very ordinariness helped him. Over London, over the country, there were three-bedroomed semi-detached homes, all built to a common design. He knew it by heart – as an officer, he had had one. His rank at Chicksands was assigned homes of that status in Alamein Drive – into a hall with a living room off it, then another door opposite the staircase into a dining room, a kitchen at the end of the hall; up the stairs and four doors, to two double bedrooms, a single and a bathroom; a garden at the back. In Alamein Drive, Roz had kept the second double bedroom empty and ready for the once-a-year visit of her parents, and he had used the single bedroom as an office bolt-hole. When he had been dragged along by the hair and the shoulder of his overcoat, in Bevin Close, he had seen a woman at the window of number eight – she had hung on to a child, as if to prevent him coming out and joining in the beating and kicking.

The tapping was firmer, more demanding.

The man from next door had shouted, 'Don't be a bloody fool, Ricky.' He had been called 'Dad'. At the cost of a cut lip, welts on his face and a knee in the testicles, Malachy reckoned he had learned much. Fair exchange. He knew the design of the house, knew that family lived alongside it, knew that the entrance to the close was watched. He tidied the pages of his maps.

He locked the door behind him and stood for a moment on the walkway, then heard the distorted sound of the tapping, and rang the bell beside the grille gate.

Malachy followed Millie Johnson into her flat. She walked unsteadily ahead of him, leaning hard on the medical stick, but she waved him away when he went to take her arm. She was smaller than when he had last seen her, smaller than she had been in the hospital bed when she'd had the fierce bruising and the tubes in her. She sat in her chair and her small eyes pierced him. She was pale, frail, and the arm in which the pin had been put was held in a sling. Would she like tea? Yes, she would. Did she have biscuits? She did: Dawn had shopped for her. He went into the kitchen, boiled the kettle, made the tea and did a tray of cups and saucers, milk, sugar and a plate of digestives. The woman had changed his life. He paused, in the kitchen, with the tray. The widow of the bus driver had changed his life, utterly, by going alone to an evening of bingo for pensioners. Without her . . .

'Hurry up. I can't abide stewed tea. It needs to be fresh out of the pot.'

'Of course, Millie.'

He carried the tray to her. She watched, hawk-eyed, as he dripped in the milk, put a spoon and a half of sugar in her cup, and poured the tea. He'd get no praise for his care. He laid a biscuit on her saucer – and waited. She sipped the tea, nibbled the biscuit and irritably brushed crumbs from her lap. He broke the quiet: 'You're looking well, Millie. Very good.'

She challenged, her gaze beading at him: 'What have you been doing with yourself?'

'Not much.'

She mimicked him, 'Oh, "not much". What's with your face?'

'Walked into a lamp post.'

'Try again.'

'Must have been dreaming, didn't see the door.'

'Do better.'

'Tripped on a paving-stone, fell in the gutter.'

'Is that the best you can do?'

'Something like that.'

'You think Dawn doesn't talk to me? Dawn talks. Who did it?'

'Did what, Millie?'

He saw the shrewdness of the old eyes. If he shifted in the chair, they followed him. If he ducked his head, they lifted. If he threw it back, they were with him. They were aged, but the eyes were keen.

'Bless you, for what you've done.'

'Millie, I've done nothing.'

Still the eyes tracked him. 'You lie there in the bed, in the hospital. People come, you don't want them. They fuss over you. All you do is hope they will go and leave you. When they've left you, then you can hate. I'm not good with words, Malachy . . . You hate because of what was done to you, but you are helpless . . . You see them. They have contempt for you because you are old. You cannot fight them. You hold on to the bag, all that is left for you. You cannot stand. You are down. There is nothing in your purse but they have your bag. You hate them, and those who sent them. A priest came to me, a simpering fool. What did I feel? I told him I felt *hate*. I had his lecture: "We are all God's children, my dear. Hate belittles us. We must learn to forgive." Couldn't wait to see the back of him. I hated them. What I wanted, in that bed, seeing their faces, was that they be hurt . . .'

'You shouldn't talk because it will tire you.'

'Rubbish. Dawn told me what's happened on the Amersham. It made me laugh. I did not say it to Dawn, but I knew it. After the laughter, in the quiet, I realized it . . . I am attacked and then these things happen. I had not given myself such importance. Thank you.'

202

'I don't think, Millie, I'll be here much longer,' Malachy said, and his voice was a whisper.

'Thank you for what you did.' The eyes, misting, struck at his. 'Please, kiss me.'

He came off his chair, knelt by her and kissed Millie Johnson's forehead. He owed her so much, more than she could have known. Then, he stood, poured her a second cup of tea and left her.

'Tony, got a moment?'

Tony Johnson, detective sergeant, had a moment, had an hour, had all day.

'Yes, Guv, how can I help?'

His chief inspector was eleven years younger than Tony, was on a fast-track career path and was part of the new world: 'Guv' was old, where Tony came from. He saw the man wince.

'Yes, well . . . Do you do Enver Rahman? Is he one of yours?'

'One of mine, like having shit on your heel.'

'Tell me.'

'He's twenty-seven, runs tarts, has a fair part of vice in north London and the West End tied down. He's scum, but clever with it. Lives in the King's Cross area, nothing permanent. Pride and joy is a Ferrari Spider. I suppose that would be worth dousing in paint-stripper.' He saw the detective inspector's mouth pucker with annoyance; no bloody sense of humour, never was for any of them that had been on the command course. 'He brings in girls from eastern Europe, and he gets muscle from Lunar House. His goons would hang about the queues at the immigration centre and look for the likely ones. Has he been arrested? No – and frankly, we've never been close to it. The girls are taught that we're all corrupt, that if they come to us the first thing we'll do is shop them to their pimps, and to Enver Rahman. They're more frightened of us than of their own . . . And let's say that one was prepared to shop him on a vice charge – what's to happen to her? Are we coming up with a witness-protection package for life? Because that's what she'll need. We are not. If she goes home to Ukraine, she's vulnerable to a knife slash or worse, and her father and mother. If she stays here and we're not doing twenty-four/seven guard – which we won't be – she wouldn't know where to hide. That's why we're not close to locking him away . . . And he has connections. What we've heard, his uncle is the godfather of Hamburg. A sparrow doesn't fart in Hamburg without his uncle's permission. Am I of help to you, Guv?'

'An airline ticket, Heathrow–Hamburg return but open dated, was bought this morning for Ricky Capel.'

Choice lying was an art form for Tony Johnson. 'Don't think I know that name. Ricky Capel? No.'

'Capel's on the computer trigger stuff for organized crime. His name came up from the airline booking. Runs drugs in south-east London. Interesting thing is that two tickets were bought, same destination, one for Capel and the other in the name of Enver Rahman.'

'Is Capel low-life, Guv?'

'Would think himself bigger than he is, vain little swine . . . But it's interesting that he should travel to the city where Enver Rahman has an uncle. Big-time, the uncle, you say?'

'About as big as they get, Guv. It's what I heard. Are we going to send?'

'Be wonderful, wouldn't it? With our resources the way they are? No chance. Thanks for your time, Tony.'

'No problem, Guv.'

He went on pushing paper, moving pages on his screen. It would be hours before he could slip away into the dusk and find a callbox.

'I hear what you say, Mr Kitchen, and will do my best to oblige. First things first, you've given me no proof of identity. I regret that a rent book from a London borough's housing department is not sufficient. Not that I'm suggesting anything, but I assume they can be bought for the price of a moderate lunch. No, Mr Kitchen, I'm afraid I'll require something more reliable.'

As senior partner in the company, as a solicitor of thirty years' experience, he took few short-cuts. None on that morning. The man had been on the doorstep of their offices when he had arrived. Eight thirty, and the man had actually been sitting on the bottom step with his feet trailing on to the pavement. Everything about him – except his shoes – was shabby. He'd sensed trouble, had decided to handle the man's business himself . . . Had also sensed a matter of intriguing interest, which seldom came into his office in Bedford.

'My problem, Mr Kitchen, is that the solicitor who handled your affairs is now in South Africa, and his secretary who met you is now married and has moved away. So, please, further proof of identity is needed.'

On his screen were copies of terse communications. He had telephoned down to the basement archive and there was indeed a box there, in the name of Captain Malachy Kitchen, Army Intelligence Corps, of Alamein Drive at Chicksands. He had suggested a call be made to the base but there had been a violent shake of the head opposite him. His firm did wills and conveyancing for many of the officers there: this man hardly seemed one of them. Old clothes on his back, new scars and bruises on his face. Only the shoes showed a military man's care.

'When is it you were last a visitor here?'

He was told, a month more than two years back, but not an exact date to match against the screen's correspondence.

'I'm sorry, Mr Kitchen, but that is too vague. Anything else?'

The man sat straighter, pulled down the zip of his anorak, pushed away the neck of his pullover, opened the upper buttons of his shirt and reached down. The twin tags came out in his hand, held by an aged leather bootlace. They were held up for him to examine. He craned forward, read, wrote down the religion, blood group and number, and when the tag with the number was turned, he could see the name. They were returned to their resting-place against the man's chest. The smell was stifled once the anorak was zipped again.

'That'll do nicely, Mr Kitchen. I'll have the box sent up.'

Ten minutes later the senior partner escorted his client to the main door, wished him well and watched him walk away. For a man so obviously facing acute difficulties in his life, there was a quite cheerful roll in his gait. Back at his desk he cast a quick glance at the box. A will, still there. A building-society savings book, still there. A marriage certificate, still there. Only the passport had been taken. He wondered what the client had run from, and where he was going now with his passport. He had not liked to ask – but if he had, he doubted that he would have been answered.

They turned into the drive, past the broken gates, and Davey braked. Charlie thought that the gates, electronically controlled, would have been flattened by the first fire appliance to reach the house. All of them in the car, Charlie realized – and it was as true of himself as the others – were strung up tight, like a bow string pulled back. Davey had reckoned they shouldn't be there, not so soon: Ricky had rubbished him. In the car, Benji had tried to raise the journey to Hamburg, where it would lead and why he was called for: Ricky had shut him down. Himself, Charlie was concerned about the cash-flow implications of the fire: Ricky had said he should wait and watch. Ricky wore the big gold chain at his throat, that Joanne had given him, and Charlie knew it had been lost and that Joanne had been belted for asking about it. Ricky fingered it obsessively. Not a bundle of laughs between them as they had driven down from London and into the countryside, not even enough laughs to wrap in a handkerchief. They went past a fence and a horse that had been grazing saw the car and seemed to scream and run. Then they turned a corner in the drive and the house was in front of them.

'Bloody hell,' Charlie murmured, a little gasp.

Ricky and Davey lived in the semi-detached houses of Bevin Close. Benji was in a brick terrace by Loampit Vale. Charlie's place was detached, joined to his neighbour by their garages, nearer to Ladywell Road. They had four houses that were typical of Lewisham in south-east London. This had been a big pile, *had* been. A wooden stable block, but the wind must have been coming from behind it, and it hadn't caught. A double garage, with the doors up, was untouched. In front of the building was a mountain of debris, some of which Charlie could make out as furniture, some of which was too charred for recognition. He could make out easy chairs where the material had burned off to leave the wood and springs, a tabletop without legs, wardrobe doors, frames without pictures, the shell of a TV and the front door, but most of the heap had no shape. And parked beside the burned mess, like it was the only place to park, was a scarlet vintage Jaguar.

Beside him in the back, he heard Ricky hiss through his teeth.

The roof in the central part of the house was off. Some of the beams were in place, others had gone, a few sagged. All the windows were out, like black tooth gaps in a mouth. It was desolation, and quiet. All of them peered forward through the windscreen. Sort of made Charlie shudder, everything at bloody peace except for the wrecked house – like it had been a target, picked out and chosen. His father had been a builder, odd jobs, a bit of roofing, a bit of plumbing, a bit of whatever – when he wasn't doing scams with old folks' benefit books – and Charlie had helped him out before he'd joined up with Ricky. He didn't know much about building, but he could see that this pile was beyond repair. It would be a bulldozer job. A site to be cleared, not just scaffolding and work for a year. George Wright had been done over, done proper. He saw the other car, by the side of what had been the house, and there was a man in a suit, and George. He nudged Ricky and pointed. They stayed put, sat in their car.

The man had a clipboard and a pencil. At that distance the sound of the voices did not travel, didn't need to. The man from the insurance was with George and he had a dour look. He finished scribbling on his clipboard and shrugged, like he was only explaining the reality of the situation confronting him. George was shaking and animated. He gripped the man's sleeve, dropped it, and had his hands at his head, like that was despair. All bastards, weren't they, insurance men? Then George had his head up, gazed at the trees, and the bloody crows – black sods – sat there and honked at the show, and the man hadn't shaken George's hand or had anything good to say and was going for his car. George was left, in a pair of suit trousers and a shirt that had been white before it was stained by the fire's smoke, alone with the crows. The car came towards them but Davey didn't shift off the drive, and it had to go on to the lawn where the first cut had just been done and the lines were good and straight and it left the tyre treads – didn't matter . . . Bigger problems for George than his grass.

They went forward.

Ricky said, 'We sort this out, and now. Then there's no misunderstandings.'

He seemed not to see them as they came out of the car, and not to hear them as they stamped on the tarmacadam past the mountain and the open doorway, the kitchen windows that had been smashed, and came to the corner of the house. Behind him were apple trees but the gale from the fire had singed the blossom off them. Ricky was ahead, with Davey trailing him by a couple of paces, and Benji and Charlie hung back because this was not about to be their style of business.

'Sorry to see this, George,' Ricky said briskly. 'What'd you do, leave the chipper on?'

Christ, Charlie thought, his man could play cold. George Wright had spun on his heel. On his face: end of tether, edge of control.

'What the fuck do you want?'

'That's not nice, George. I come down all polite like a friend, all sympathy. Didn't come down for abuse. Came to find out what the situation was. You got a difficulty with that?'

'The *situation*, right. The situation is that the insurance wasn't jacked up in the last five years and it's way under. Got that? My Melanie, she's gone to her mother, she's broke down, and Hannah's with her and worse. I had a load of stuff in the house, and the safe went like an oven. The stuff's cooked – got that? So, thank you for your bloody consideration, but I am fucked. So, *please*, drive back where you came from. Have you got that?'

'That is not helpful, George.'

'What is bloody *helpful*? I'd like to hear it.'

Charlie could hear the softness of Ricky's voice, and could hear the rising crescendo of George Wright's anger. Davey, behind Ricky, had his hands together behind his back – where they always were when he minded Ricky – but his fists were white-knuckled, clenched.

'I tell you what's helpful, George. You had, from me, stuff on trust. I give to you and you supply, and then you pay me. Now you tell me that the stuff is burned, and I ask myself, "How is George going to pay me what he owes me?" About a hundred grand, yes? Charlie's the one with the head for figures. Maybe a bit over a hundred thousand that's owed me. What would be helpful is knowing when you're going to pay me – today, tomorrow, or by the end of the week.'

208

'Whistle for it, Ricky.'

'Not helpful.'

'I got nothing left. Whistle down your arse for it.'

Ricky's voice was ever softer, his chuckle ever more shrill. 'You're a joker, George. You do a good turn, George. "I got nothing left" – that's funny, George. No building-society book? No deposit account? A little place down on the Algarve that you can raise a mortgage on? Very funny, George. By the end of the week, and that's really generous. What you say, George?'

'Fuck off's what I say.'

Ricky moved sideways. Charlie recognized the manoeuvre. Davey now had a clear sight of George Wright. Charlie knew what would happen, had seen it before.

Ricky said, 'You know how it is, George, if I'm too generous then word of it gets round. People who owe me money hear I'm a soft touch. I get promises for payment, next month or next year, because it's said that Ricky Capel's easy to blow over. "Can't pay this month because the missus has a headache." Might be "Can't pay next month because the family's going on holiday." Could be "Can't pay this year because the price on the street's down." Or, if the word gets round, "Can't pay ever because the chipper caught fire." George, I won't have that word get round, but that's your problem.'

'What I said, get lost, get off my property. I got nothing.'

Charlie knew where it was going and could not argue with the reason for it. Maybe there was a little gesture against his thigh from Ricky, or maybe Davey just read him. If ever the authority of Ricky Capel was challenged successfully then he was dead in the water. And not only Ricky, all of them. All gone, if the word went out that Ricky was the soft touch. Charlie didn't do violence, or Benji, but Davey did. Davey closed on George Wright. He lost sight of the fat little man with the bald head and the sweat on it, lost the sight of him behind Davey's shoulders.

George Wright was felled. Davey stood over him, and the heavy steel-toecapped shoe pressed down on a sprawled-out shin.

Ricky said, 'Problem with a place like this, George, the problem with all the muck around – planks, furniture, beams, everything – is that you could fall over. You could fall over and break your leg. Be easy. Of course, if you said – after you'd broken your leg – that you hadn't tripped up on the muck, if you said different, then you'd have to wonder where you'd hide, and where your Melanie and your Hannah would hide, come to think of it . . . I'm very generous, by the end of the week.'

'Fuck off.'

A blur of movement, almost too fast for Charlie to follow. The shoe went up. He saw the flash of the steel on the toecap. It stamped down on the suit trousers halfway up the shin.

The scream ripped at Charlie, but Ricky didn't flinch.

The foot and ankle below the shin were bent at an idiot angle from the knee.

Ricky was walking away and Davey followed him. It was two months since Charlie had eaten a meal with George Wright in a little bistro in Blackheath and the guy had been good company. It was a week since Benji had done the last drop-off to George Wright. He hadn't spoken up for him, and Benji beside him had not.

'Not yet, you will be . . . bastard, Ricky Capel . . . you will be . . . Your turn, see if it isn't coming . . . You know fuck all of nothing, but you will, when it's your turn . . . What do you think's happening? You got any idea? Big man, you know everything – wait till it's your turn and see what you know . . . I want to be there, watch it, when it's your turn . . .'

'Come on, guys,' Ricky said.

He was walking past Charlie, standing and rooted. Charlie caught Ricky's arm, held him.

George Wright, from the ground, yelled, 'Want to hear it, then, want to? Bloody funny, Ricky Capel, about a chip fire. I was a target! It was petrol – petrol through the window. The target was me. Three kids on the Amersham estate were found hung upside down off a roof – did you hear that? Fucking didn't, did you? You know nothing. They pushed. Next it's the dealer. The dealer sold to the kids on the Amersham. He was tied up to a lamp post, and now he's gone. You don't know where the Amersham is? Too low for you, Ricky Capel . . . I sold to that dealer. It's a line. Me to the dealer, the dealer to the pusher kids. I had petrol chucked in my home. Does the line go the other way? Think about it, Ricky bloody Capel. Look over your shoulder.'

Ricky pulled himself clear of Charlie.

'Mad, isn't he? Crazy man. He'll come up with it, he'll pay.' The big smile breezed on his face. 'May have to go on sticks to the bank, but he'll pay.'

It was a joke between Charlie and Benji that Davey was plank thick. He could always see when something major exercised Davey's brain. Nothing of a flywheel, like a slow set of cogs turning without oil to help. Always frowned, always blinked, always seemed to rub the side of his face hard, before spewing it.

Davey said, 'Couldn't think of it, Ricky, what the stink was. The dosser down the close, outside your house. The dosser that was there, and his stink.'

Ricky was at the car. 'What you trying to say?'

Davey blurted it: 'The stink, it was petrol. On his coat, he had the stink of petrol.'

'Forget it,' Ricky said, and dropped into the car.

Charlie didn't. And he hardly listened as they drove through the Kent countryside back towards Lewisham, and Ricky retold stories of his grandfather's war fought alongside the father of Timo Rahman whom he was flying to meet the next day, in Hamburg.

'I want to move her there. I really urge you to sanction Polly Wilkins going to Hamburg, as a matter of urgency.'

The assistant deputy director sat, so Gaunt paced. If the ADD had stood, Gaunt would have taken a chair. Contrariness was a trusted weapon. His stride across the carpeted office was fast, intended to create an atmosphere of crisis. To wrongfoot the man was his aim. The supine beggar would buckle, he knew it.

'I can't say I'm happy . . .'

'It's what's necessary.'

'. . . and Fenwick in Berlin, he won't be happy.'

'I'm up to speed and Polly Wilkins is.'

'It's his territory, that's what Fenwick will say.'

Gaunt rapped his response: 'Rather than satisfying Fenwick's turf aspirations, it would be better to put in place, under my control, an officer who has the feel of him.'

No name, but two faces. Last thing before coming to the assistant deputy director, on high, he had sat in his desk chair and had tilted it back and made the request of Gloria that she describe the faces. She was expert at the task, and he believed he saw better into a man's soul when his eyes were closed and he listened as she portrayed him, the quarry: so much better, so much greater insight, than when he stared at a two-dimensional photograph. She had said, 'The hair is thick, dark and worn long, but it is not unkempt and is cared-for. In the centre the hair curls back, and I don't believe that is accidental, more of a style. There is a high forehead, clean and without the skin cracks of anxiety, that pushes up on either side where the hair recedes. The forehead is that of an intelligent man, not of a brute. The eyes are big. They are open, they do not evade; there are rings under them but that is from tiredness . . . more than rings, almost bags. I like the eyes. They persuade, but do not threaten. They have a confidence. Yes, you would trust the eyes. The nose is prominent, straight and without blemishes. It is not the nose of a fighting man, has not been broken, fractured or lost alignment. I discard the moustache and the beard. They are from the passports used for the first stage of his journey, not from the second stage. If they have been shaven off, he cannot have regrown that degree of facial hair. The mouth, with or without a beard and moustache, is distinctive – distinctive because it is unique to him. Two aspects – his smile, we'll start with that. Few men smile for a passport picture. He does in each case. It is a good smile, one of honesty. I like his smile and I warm to him, open and frank, showing no deviousness. The second aspect is the teeth. The teeth are dreadful, but clean. The upper bite comes down over the lower teeth and is overfilled and prominent. Big incisors that are packed too close, so they bulge. I venture, he never met an orthodontist – sorry, Mr Gaunt. His ears are not flappers but are close back against his hair, those of my dog when it is listening, keen and alert. He is not big-boned, and from the set of him I would hazard that he is slightly built . . . If I had to pick on one point, I'd say that most of our guests, given wall space, have a deep-rooted suspicion of the camera, but this man is not frightened of it . . . Put another way, there's nothing in the face that demonstrates the stresses of anxiety.' He had heard Gloria out, then had buttoned his waistcoat, lifted his tie, shrugged into his jacket and taken the elevator up to where the Gods rested.

'You promised me the moon last time. All bottled up in Prague.'

'And did not deliver because of Czech incompetence.'

'Hamburg would be different enough to override Fenwick's irritation?'

'I think so.'

'*Think?* Is that all you have for me to bite on?'

'I believe so. That we are this far forward is due to Polly Wilkins's efforts. She deserves the chance ...' He stopped, gazed without mercy into the assistant deputy director's face, then resumed pacing. 'After what was done to her she most emphatically deserves the chance.'

'Sanctioned.'

'A good decision.'

Not a time to hang about. Gaunt had what he had come for. He was heading for the door, anxious to be away before riders were attached. He heard the bleat at his back.

'He's dangerous, isn't he? Our man who's on the run – dangerous, yes?'

'Exceptionally so.'

'Murderous little bastard.'

The mischief caught him as he went into the outer office. Gaunt said, 'Perhaps, but rather a nice face, don't you know?'

She packed.

'Don't I get told where you're going?'

Ronnie was watching from the door. It was her apartment and Polly was the guest imposed on the girl from the visa section. Polly would not have said that she was going to Hamburg, but could have said she was going to Germany and left it vague. She did not answer but went on folding blouses and skirts, laying them over the shoes at the bottom and her smalls – didn't really have an idea of what she needed, whether the spring came warm up there or whether it would be perishing cold. The sharing arrangement had been intended as temporary, while a one-bedroom apartment for herself was redecorated, but then a refurbishment budget had gone dry and time had slipped on. It wasn't satisfactory for an officer in the Service, however junior, to share but having her own room was good enough and she'd given up nagging the man at the embassy who allocated premises. She was precious little use to Ronnie, a lonely woman. Too early at work and too late back to offer company.

'Well, how long are you going to be away?'

She didn't know how long she would be away, and didn't answer, just went on filling the case. She could share the apartment but not her life.

The bridling voice whipped her. 'Don't mind me. I'm not important. I'm not need-to-know. You have a good time, wherever. I'll say this, you look like the cat that found the cream. You just come back when it's finished, whenever.'

A last pair of jeans and a sweater went in. No photographs in leather frames, nothing personal. 'The cat that found the cream'? Probably. Not very fair to show it because there was little enough cream in Ronnie's existence in the visa section. While she was packing the bag Polly had thought she walked tall for the first time since the collapse of the unit in London. Two years' work there, hard and slogging study. Satellite photos of every corner of Iraq's deserts pored over. Defectors' statements gutted, analysed, each word weighed. Businessmen from every corner of that wretched region who travelled to Baghdad had been met in hotel bars, had money shoved at them, and been pestered for descriptions of factories and chemical plants. Phone calls and emails intercepted and transcribed. All to answer the great question: were there, in Iraq, programmes for the manufacture of weapons of mass destruction? Papers written. In Service tradition it was taught: *Capability + Intent = Threat*. Had Iraq the capability or the intent to justify the wolf cry of realistic threat? Caution expressed, caveats and hesitations. Papers returned with red-ink scratchings obliterating the cautions that were embedded in the Service's work practices. Papers resubmitted with honesty seeping out from them. Caveats and hesitations removed. What they wrote, by Service tradition, was supposed to exude 'provenance'. But provenance had died, and the team – scattered to the winds – she assumed cursed themselves now for bending at the knee, for allowing valued practices – $C+I=T$ – to be steamrollered and crushed.

214

She could remember the day when politicians, jutting their chins, had spoken of 'irrefutable proof' of the WMD programmes as justification for the tanks rolling in the sands: she had stood behind Frederick Gaunt's shoulder, had watched the television and heard his silence, and had known it would burst. So quiet when it had done, but a violence in his words she had never heard before. 'They wanted the fucking war. We gave them the fucking war – and our reward will be to be fucked by them.' The inquest, then the cull of the casualties of failure to find the weapons. Polly Wilkins had been categorized as NBA by the investigators – No Blame Attached – and sent to Prague, but the message had been clear to her: all of the unit was contaminated by that failure. She was scarred by the inquest, poisoned by the failure. She checked her bag for her passport, ticket and euros. She heaved it off the bed, grimaced, and went to call a taxi for the airport. Because she was the chosen one, elation gripped her.

In the city of Dresden, on their first visit to Germany, an elderly American couple waited for one of a line of public telephones in the square to come free.

That afternoon they had toured the opera house and the Kreuzkirche, then crossed the Augustusbrücke to trawl the galleries of old masters' works in the Zwinger houses. Next they would visit the Hofkirche in the Theaterplatz. They needed a telephone to ring their hotel to confirm a booking for the morning, car and driver, to travel out of the city to the Pillnitz Palace and take them later to Meissen where they would buy porcelain for shipment to Chicago.

They stood, Dwight and Janet, behind a young man. He had dialled, and now he waited for an answer. Always the difficulty at such a time, which phone to target. Which caller would take the least time? They had chosen to stand behind this young man, slight and with bowed shoulders. He spoke. They could not hear him. But even if he had raised his voice they would have been too polite to listen – and, anyway, their knowledge of German was scant. She had her thumb to keep the guidebook open at the page for the Hofkirche and together they matched the view of its towering spire across the Theaterplatz with the photograph.

In front of them, the man hooked the phone back, turned, smiled politely and gestured that the booth was now available. Such a charming-looking young man ... Her husband would not have done it – Dwight had the shyness that age brought – but Janet was bolder. Would he, please, show them how to operate the payphone? She gave him their hotel-room card with the number they needed, and coins. He did it for them, waited until the call was connected with Reception, then passed the receiver to her. And he was gone.

It made them both feel good, as they crossed the Theaterplatz, to have met a young man so considerate.

'Where do you think, Dwight, that guy was from?'

'Couldn't say, could have been from anywhere.'

The office worker was brought by the Bear to Timo Rahman.

In the life of the *pate* no deals were too small, none was unworthy of his attention. He had come from the yard where he owned the fleet of haulage lorries that carried loads across Europe, legal and contraband, and had arrived at a site on the Elbe side of St Pauli where the old building had been flattened. Bulldozers worked there and shifted aside the mess of concrete, wire and rubble. He had a share, thirty-three and a third per cent, in the hotel to be built on what was now a hole. Dust swirled round him and he wore an orange hard hat jauntily. He would move on from there to the fruit, vegetable and flower market at the Hauptbahnhof where money was paid him for the right to set up a stall. The haulage business brought him tens of thousands of euros a year; the hotel would earn him millions on completion; the stalls were only worth hundreds. Attention to details, whether big or small, was the cornerstone of Timo Rahman's life.

He stood with an architect and the site manager and watched the crawling machines eat at the debris, and he saw the Bear bring the boy. The boy, a cousin's son, would have owned only one suit, and one pair of shoes fit for an office worker, and he walked with great care through the dust clouds, and maybe his shoes would be scratched and certainly his suit trousers would be saturated with the floating dirt. Timo Rahman broke away from the site manager and the architect.

The boy reached him, stood in his presence and the nerves showed.

Timo Rahman stared out at the bulldozers. It was not for him to show anxiety or any great interest in a messenger who was only the son of a cousin. The demand for news of the lost cargo had screamed at him in the night, had been with him in the days. His casualness was expert as he made the boy wait, then turned to him.

'Again it is you. What matter of home furnishing is there for my interest?'

The boy stuttered, could not be heard.

'Speak up, boy. Shout.'

The boy sucked the dust and air into his throat, coughed, then shouted, 'My manager in the shipping section ordered me to report to you. He has received a telephone message concerning a cargo from Ostrava, in the Czech Republic.'

'I know where my factory is. And you have no reason to fear me.'

'He instructs me to tell you that a part of cargo load 1824 is *en route* to Hamburg. The time of delivery to the warehouse is uncertain, but it will be within two days.'

'Thank you for bringing such a small matter to my attention. Sometimes you are in the showroom and sometimes in the office, and you should be a credit to the company you serve. I think your suit is damaged by coming to this place. Replace it.'

He took a note from his wallet, of sufficient value to purchase a clerk's suit and a pair of shoes in any clothing shop on the Steindamm, folded it carefully and slipped it to the boy. His generosity would be remembered rather than the message haltingly delivered. He told the boy with firmness that he should be careful when going back across the site, and dismissed him. Long ago Timo Rahman, who was the *pate* of Hamburg, had learned that a wall of fear protected him, but that kindness generated absolute loyalty among his people. He turned to the Bear.

'He comes . . . He has evaded them. Already he has proven himself to be a man of quality. If it were known that I assisted him then the wrath – anger and fury – of the world is turned against me. Why do I do these things? They would spit in my eye and break my bones if it were known what help I shall give. Why? I am a little man,

217

I am a peasant from the mountains of Albania. I am sneered at, but not to my face. Those who know of my origins despise me . . . The time will come. My time.'

He thought the Bear understood not a word that he said, but the man's head nodded vigorous agreement. He rejoined the architect and the site manager, wiped the dust from his forehead, listened to them, studied their plans, and a quarter of an hour later was on his way to the Hauptbahnhof to talk with the traders at their stalls. He thought little of the hotel that would sit where there was now a hole. What filled his mind was the image of a seashore where a boat would come, and the enormity of what would follow.

The ferry carried Oskar Netzer back to paradise. One day in every two months he took the boat to the main-land, to Nessmersiel, and from there a bus brought him to Norden. In the town he shopped. As a pensioner he travelled free on the ferry and what he bought in Norden was cheaper than in the island's supermarkets. The tide was far out and the mudflats crept to the limits of the channel used by the ferry. He stood on the back deck and watched the mainland shore, all he hated, diminish.

The wind came hard off the mud, from the northwest.

They had travelled together, he and Gertrud, on that same ferry-boat five years before. She could have gone by ambulance to the hospital in Norden. Oskar had refused that. He had taken her. They had stood together, her leaning on his arm for support and the blanket round her to keep the chill from her, where he stood now – where he always stood on the boat. And a week later, he had brought her back, and when the crane had lowered the coffin on to the quay at Baltrum, the crew had taken off their caps in respect for her, and he had held the horse's bridle that pulled the cart carrying her to the cemetery at Ostdorf. Sometimes, and that day he did, he wept as he stood alone at the back of the ferry; his jaw quivered and his cheeks were wet with tears.

When the ferry swung to starboard for the approach to the island's harbour, he saw the seals on their sandspit close to the wreck. It pleased him, lightened the blackness of the mood that sat on him each time he took the ferry. Beyond the seals and the wreck, out in the North Sea, was a darkening skyline that merged into the horizon.

11

No goodbyes, no farewells, he switched off the lights and locked the door.

Malachy dropped the keys of flat thirteen, level three, block nine, into the hatch beside the barricaded door of the housing offices.

Its use for him was finished and he was gone from the Amersham into the night.

<h1 style="text-align:center">II</h1>

Music blared from high loudspeakers, pounded at Malachy Kitchen.

He stepped from the train that had brought him from Cologne. The Hauptbahnhof of Hamburg echoed with Beethoven. Something of it lifted him and he stepped out along the platform, carried by the swell of passengers, as if a little of his purpose was regained – he knew what he would attempt to achieve in that city, but not why. The Amersham was behind him and after ten hours of travel from Waterloo International to Brussels, from Brussels to Cologne, from Cologne to Hamburg, the estate had already faded in his mind. He no longer felt its pulsebeat. He stepped on to the escalator and was carried up to the concourse. He heard announcements in a mass of languages, the arrivals and departures of trains from and to all of Europe. His stride was bolder than at any time since he had come down the tail ramp, exhausted and sweating, in the heat's blast off the Hercules aircraft that had done the corkscrew descent on to the runway at Basra. But the road had been long, so damn long, into what was unknown ... It was as if he clutched at the pride so that he should not lose hold of it.

The concourse was scrubbed clean, and high above it, like a cathedral's arched roof, was the great shape of glass and iron. He held tight in his hand, the black plastic sack containing all the clothes he owned that were not on his back, and among the smells of the quick food stalls was the whiff of the petrol still. embedded in the heavy coat. He saw police with guns and unarmed men in uniform with the flash of the Bahnwacht on their sleeves. He crossed the concourse and saw nothing that threatened him. He walked to the exit for taxis and in front of him were stalls of cleaned vegetables, piled fruit and cheerful flowers; above them, the wind tickled the multi-colours of the awnings. At the tourist kiosk Malachy asked in halting German, learned at Chicksands, for a tourist map of the city and was told where he could find a cheap room near to the Hauptbahnhof. The smartly dressed girl behind the kiosk counter curled her lip in disdain at his appearance, and drew a line on the map down a street – that was where the inexpensive rooms were.

For politeness, he said, 'It's a fine station – and I enjoyed the music.'

'The music is not for your enjoyment,' she responded curtly.

'I don't understand. Why, then, is it played?'

'Psychologists told us to – narcotics addicts hate classical music broadcast loud. It's why they are not here. The music makes the station free of them. We have in Hamburg a big drugs problem, and you should be careful in the city, most careful where accommodation is inexpensive . . . We are cursed by immigrants and the crime levels they bring, most particularly the Albanians. Enjoy your visit.'

He went out into a brittle midday sunlight. The wind trapped his hair and scoured his face. Beyond the stalls, when he reached the edge of the big, wide square that burst with traffic, he paused, opened the map and took his bearings.

He had come to destroy a man, but did not know how and would have been hard put to articulate why – except that breaking the man was the only road sign posted to him as a way back for his pride.

After he had crossed the square and had started out down a wide street, he understood why the woman in the tourist kiosk had curled her lip when he had insisted on a cheap room. So little money had been given him that he must husband it. She had sent him to where rooms were inexpensive, on the Steindamm. He passed shops that sold sex videos and sex gear, and by cafés where Algerians, Moroccans, Tunisians or Afghans lounged on plastic chairs, and by doorways where hookers – young and old, heavy-hipped and skeletal thin – waited, smoked and eyed him. He saw the sign for rooms to rent. He stopped.

A woman, African, stared at him. Her chest bulged in a halter-top and her thighs were bare below the short, tight skirt. She sucked at her cigarette, then blew the smoke at him but the wind snatched it away. He smiled, but shook his head. The recruits in Basic Training had talked sex – talked sex, described sex, gloried in sex. Had sat around the TV while the videos played sex, had boasted sex. Malachy Kitchen's first sex had been with a girl from a farm, in a barn, on the edge of the Devon village where his parents had moved to. Second sex had been with a corporal's wife, and he'd washed for a week afterwards, had scrubbed himself and prayed there wouldn't be a rash to show for it. Third sex had been with a girl at the end of a ball at the Royal Military Academy: he hadn't known her name, had been half-cut and it had been under a tree across the grass from the Old Building. Fourth sex had been with Roz. He gestured, he hoped politely, to the prostitute from Africa that he wanted to pass by her and she moved aside with reluctance. He went inside and there was a man at the counter, small, wiry, with plastered hair, and he asked in the correct German, as taught him, for a room.

'For one hour or for two hours?'

He shook his head.

'For a half-day?'

He said he wanted a room to stay in, and sleep in – alone.

'For how many nights?'

Malachy was about to say that he did not know, but that seemed inadequate. For three nights. He was given a price. No haggling, no dispute. The key was handed to him, and then, as an afterthought, a residents' book was opened on the counter and a pen pushed forward. He thought of giving the name Ricky Capel, and the address Bevin Close. He shook his head, heaved the black plastic sack on to his shoulder and started to climb the stairs. On the first landing, in one of the rooms that would have been hired for an hour or two he heard a bed's springs whine. On the second landing a man came by him still pulling up his zip. He was wondering how long it would be before the African girl took a client to the first or second floor. He went on up.

The room allocated to Malachy was bare but for a bed, a basin and a faded print of a mountain scene. He crossed a worn rug over linoleum and dropped his sack.

He was there because of what had been said to him, and said of him – none of it yet wiped.

222

'Is it a crisis? That's what I'm asking.'

'Way outside my loop of experience. What I can tell you, he's not a mark on him.'

'I've got a gunshot wound, a P1 category, and a road-traffic accident casualty – and a Jock with a scorpion sting. Where in that does Kitchen figure?'

'For God's sake,' Fergal said, 'I'm the adjutant. You're the MO. You want my judgement – pretty far down, propping up the heap, I'd say . . . From what they said at Bravo, maybe a bit lower than propping it up.'

The medical officer was bent over the trolley. The gunshot victim was dosed with morphine. It was an ugly wound, but a challenge for him. He had to stabilize the man before he could be shipped out by helicopter. Not much else he could do. What struck him, as he probed to get the worst of the detritus from the wound – fragments of the bullet, fragments of the camouflage trouser material – was the consummate bravery of the young guy. Not a whimper, not a scream, not a shout. Trust in his watering eyes . . . A damn good soldier. And alongside him, flat out on the second trolley and waiting patiently for his turn, was the casualty from the road-traffic accident. Oh, God – and there was the I Corps captain, who stood remote from them in the doorway and had not spoken since Fergal had brought him to the aid post.

'What's the latest on that bloody chopper – or are the blue jobs on a day off?'

The adjutant peered over his shoulder. *'You wouldn't think so much stuff could get in there . . . Extraordinary. They had a dust storm back at Brigade, but the RAF are up now. The chopper's ETA is just down from thirty minutes. Is that going to be time enough?'*

The medical officer growled, *'Have to be, won't it? For both of them.'*

As a captain, the MO had the qualifications of a general-duties doctor. He had trained at medical school in London and had then thought that any future was better than an inner-city practice so he'd joined the army and been posted to the Scottish regiment. The work gave him swagger and was not demanding. Back in the UK, at the regiment's barracks, he spent his time patching up injuries from *training and sports. In Iraq, his duties varied between extremes: from gunshot wounds to the complicated childbirth problems of local women. He was accepted: his skills were admired from Sunray down to the youngest soldier, and he revelled in it.*

With minute tweezers he lifted clear threads of cotton cloth matted in the blood. He stood to his full height. 'Not much more I can do.'

'There's a surgical team on the chopper,' the adjutant said.

He asked his orderly to cover the gunshot wound, then peeled off the gloves and went to the basin. Disinfectant soap and water. He sluiced his hands together, and when he looked up he saw the man, Mal Kitchen, still in the doorway, still silent. He turned to Fergal. 'What's the story about him?'

'Varnished or unvarnished?'

'Plain bloody truth will be good enough.'

The adjutant hesitated. 'It's all hearsay, of course.'

'Don't fuck me about, what's being said?' He dried his hands with vigour and went to the second trolley,' the road-traffic accident. He was worried now – this patient might be a more serious casualty than the gunshot wound. He boomed, 'Spit it out.'

While he worked, the medical officer listened.

'It's pretty unpleasant . . . Here goes. He went on patrol yesterday, familiarization with the ground before a lift this morning. He was in place to assist with interrogation and screening of prisoners. The patrol was hit. Two or three rifle positions and an RPG was fired. He was somewhere near the back of the stick when it started. What I'm hearing from Bravo's people is that Kitchen did a runner.'

'You are joking? What – just flipped out and left them?'

'There, and then not there. Gone. The corporal thinks he's been hit. Goes back – puts the whole section at risk, but Jocks don't leave a man who's down – and retraces the ground covered in the ambush site. He's nowhere to be found. Hits the panic button. Then they find his helmet in the street – and his flak-jacket. Bravo's gearing up for a major search-and-rescue operation, loading the Warriors, the full works. Then he's found. He's walking back to Bravo, but without his weapon. Two questions, natural enough. What happened? Where's his weapon? No answer. Not a word out of him. Up at Bravo, they say he's yellow.'

'*Christ Almighty – you serious?*'

'*Personally, I couldn't stand him. So, does he classify as a medical case?*'

'*Well, he doesn't get to slide under white sheets, if that's what you mean. I don't call him a patient. This is a patient.*' His fingers moved with extreme gentleness over the ribcage of the casualty. He yearned to hear the thudding of an approaching helicopter's rotors. Sandwiched, long ago, into courses on the treatment of gunshot wounds, shrapnel injuries and débridement infection caused by clothing fibres and lead particles, there had been a bare hour on the recognition of what the lecturer had called '*battle shock*'. The medical officer had been with commanders and seconds-in-command, and none had taken seriously what they were told.

He looked up. Maybe anger caught him. Maybe the growing pallor on the casualty's face frightened him. Maybe the helicopter would be delayed too long. He shouted at the man in the doorway: '*Don't just bloody stand there like a spare part. Move yourself. Do something. There's a mop. Orderly, give him a mop and bucket. Give him a broom to sweep with. Clean the place.*'

When the time came, when the two Jocks on their trolleys were wheeled out from the aid post, the man – Kitchen – still, with mechanical movements, swabbed the floor with the mop and squeezed it out into the bucket.

Later, the medical officer walked briskly back with the adjutant, his pistol bouncing against his thigh, and said, '*I'm not taking responsibility for him. Sunray'll have to see him. He's not mine. Yellow's not a colour I fancy. Kitchen's nothing to do with me.*'

Benji met Charlie and together they sipped coffee.

'So, he's up and away, Ricky is.'

'Did he tell you, Benji, what for?'

'Told me, big surprise, nothing.'

'You happy, Benji, with nothing?'

'I tell you why it's nothing – because he doesn't know nothing. He didn't tell me why he was going to Hamburg because he didn't know. I'm straight with you. He got the call and he jumped – and I don't like it. The Albanians are bad news. Does he listen? Does he

225

hell . . . You heard me, I've told him. I told him two years back and a year back and six months back that he shouldn't be in bed with those people. Does he listen?'

'You told him, Benji, and I heard.'

'Doesn't listen to us, but listens to them. I take him to the airport. I think he's going to talk plans. He talks about his brat's football. Not till we're there, going through the tunnel into the airport, does he start chattering about the big guy he's going to meet. What worries me, they'll eat him.'

'Worry you bad, Benji?'

'They don't share, the Albanians, they don't do equals. All co-operation until they're ready. They get inside you, a worm in your gut, and the worm bloody kills you when they're ready. Everybody had a share of Soho and King's Cross till they were ready. Now nobody's in Soho or King's Cross except them. Right now, he thinks he's the big number and Timo Rahman wants to share with him.'

'You thinking of bugging out, Benji?'

'Be great. I got enough put away, you have – Davey has . . . Where to? Nobody bugs out. Sort of on a rope, aren't we? And the rope's got a bloody knot on your ankle and mine. That shit-face, little Enver, he's at the airport door to meet us. He's out of the car and the shit-face takes his bag, like he's Ricky's bloody porter, and they're off and gone. I'd trust the shit-face as far as I could kick him, wouldn't let him carry my bag. You just get that feeling, don't you, when it's all going to finish in grief?'

'You heard, Benji, what Davey said. Petrol.'

'On the dosser's clothes in Bevin Close, the stink of petrol. I heard what Davey said. And petrol done George Wright's place . . . I don't know what's happening – used to, but I don't now. He went off all trusting, Ricky did, with his bag carried for him, and what I'm thinking about is the claws stuck in him – and I didn't tell him, and I never do and you don't – and grief.'

'No, Mr Capel, he is not in the hotel. I am sorry. I have paged him and he is not in the restaurants or in the bar. You heard yourself the paging announcement for Mr Enver Rahman, and he has not come. He is not here.'

He sagged. He gazed at the tall, leggy woman behind the desk, who wore the hotel's uniform, its logo sewn over a shallow breast. Nothing that had happened was what he had expected. No answers when he had pumped on the flight as to what business he would be doing with Timo Rahman; questions brushed aside like he was a kid and talking too much and would find out when elders, betters, decided. No chauffeur at the airport to meet them, but Enver had gone to Avis who had held a car for them. No explanations as they had driven into the city. The hotel was a tower of glass and concrete, not in the city centre, and they'd come past gardens to get there; the sort of hotel that did conferences, twenty-six floors of it. He'd checked in. Enver had said that he had phone calls to make and they'd meet up later, had to do the arrangements. No suite for him, no flowers, no bowl of fruit: just an ordinary room. He'd kicked his shoes off and lain on the bed because the one easy chair was dead hard, and he'd flicked the zapper and the channels were all German except one that was American news. Who gave a fuck for American news? Not Ricky Capel . . . And he'd waited . . . and waited some more . . . had waited for the phone to ring and it had not. Maybe he'd dozed off on the bed. Then he'd woken, had worked the phone buttons and called down, had asked to be connected to the room of Enver Rahman, and a dumb cow had told him there was no gentleman of that name resident in the hotel, and she'd checked, and she'd repeated it. It was like he'd been dumped. He'd just assumed that Enver was booking in after he'd gone to the elevator. It wasn't *LIFT* respect. The disrespect was on the plane, was a hire car, was a hotel that was shit, was him being abandoned and Enver bugging out. What wound up Ricky Capel tightest was disrespect. He believed nothing, nobody.

He strode away from the desk, went to the swing doors, pushed them open violently, didn't care that they battered into the back of a man manoeuvring his bags inside, and walked out into the fore-court. He could see where Enver had parked the green VW Passat that had been his lift from the airport. There was a BMW 5 series, black, where the Passat had been. He strode back inside and anger pounded in his head . . . All disrespect. There was a family now at the desk, in tracksuits: that sort of hotel, short breaks, cut rate, for bloody families. He pushed past them and imposed himself in front of her.

He demanded that she look for any message left him. She left the desk and walked elegantly away, but slowly – he reckoned that deliberate, like she thought he was shit. He turned and saw the faces of the family, kids and adults, all staring sourly at him, like they thought the same of him as she did. She returned, a folded sheet of notepaper between her fingers. He snatched it.

No smile on her face, but she pissed on him. 'You can read German, Mr Capel?'

He felt the blood run in his face.

'Would you like me to translate for you, Mr Capel?'

He nodded.

'It says, "Ricky, you will be collected later. Have a good stay in Hamburg, Enver." That is all.'

'What's it mean, *later*?' He was Ricky Capel. He was big. He ran an area of south-east London. He was—He blurted, 'What does that mean?'

The skinny bitch said, 'I think, Mr Capel, it means that you will be collected later.'

He stood on a great dyke and gazed out at the sea. The Bear had stayed in the car, on the road on the land side of the barrier built to hold back flood tides. Timo Rahman knew about the life throb of cities and the demands of men for the titillation of the shows provided by his clubs and the requirement of the young for heroin, cocaine and pills, which he sold, but he knew nothing of the coast and its wildness.

The tang of the salt was in his nose, and the wind ripped at his hair and tugged his coat tight against his chest and flapped it away from his legs, and there was the spit of rain in it. He stared out over the white crests of the waves and watched seabirds ride on them in the shelter of inlets. He had looked at the motoring-book map in the car, had searched for a place on the coast where there were fewest roads, had seen the line of islands and had made his decision. It would be here that the man would be brought, then shipped to the island and taken on board the trawler. Because he had no knowledge of the sea, it seemed to Timo Rahman to be a simple matter.

If he braced himself against the wind's power, held his hand across his forehead to divert the rain and squinted, he could make out the faint line that was the island's shore facing him. It was remote, isolated. Always Timo Rahman went with the instinct that his gut gave him . . . From his car, before they had driven along the road behind the dyke, he had watched the ferry go, with fewer passengers on it than he had fingers on his hands.

He had seen what he needed to see. He turned away. Beyond the road and the Mercedes, a solitary tractor ploughed a field of dark earth, and further back, shielded by trees, was a farm with brick outbuildings, and on that horizon, inland, were the towering wind turbines that turned briskly. Mud splattered his trousers at the ankles and smeared his shoes as he went down the dyke's slope, and reached the Bear.

He asked if there had been a call but the Bear shook his head.

Timo Rahman said quietly, 'He will come, I have no doubt of it, and it is from here that we will send him on.'

Malachy left them his key and went out into the afternoon light. Time to kill till darkness. He cut down towards the Hafen City of modern-built apartments on reclaimed land, then left behind the two big church spires, like markers for him, and found the pavement that led him west along the Elbe. He would walk the whole way. Walking was best for soaking up the atmosphere of a city never visited before: time spent walking, his mentor at Chicksands had said, was never time wasted. He had no plan, only the determination that he would manufacture one when the evening came, when he was in place. He walked well, with brisk purpose, and his only stop was at the Landungsbrücken where he parsimoniously pecked coins from his pocket and bought himself a burger and an ice-cream. There was no weapon for self-defence or attack in his pocket, but he was without fear: nothing worse could be done to him than had been.

He was home for lunch. One night in every three weeks on his roster, Tony Johnson did a thirty-hour shift, worked through the night, then came home for a meal and sleep. He was dead beat.

'You actually did that – God, I can't believe it.'

He had no secrets from her. While she cooked, he had sat at the table, with the coffee mug in his hands, which shook, and told her what he had done.

'You bought his ticket, you gave him money, you sent him to Hamburg? I find it hard to credit.'

He hung his head, then lifted the mug, both hands, and slurped the coffee.

'Have you any idea of what you've done? To him?'

In his reply, exhausted and rambling, he tried to explain why he had done it. It was hard for him to be rational, coherent. He spoke of the man and the files that the National Criminal Intelligence Service computers had trawled up for him. He told of the devastation to a man's self-respect, personal esteem. A man on the floor who wanted to drag himself up and stand again.

'But you gave him Capel's name. You sent him after Capel. Almighty God – he could be killed – killed and dumped, killed and disappeared. Tony, have you no conscience?'

The struggle to describe the smile and the light in the eyes, then slamming down the mug, splashing the cloth on the table. Recalling the battering of the questions. Where to in Hamburg? To meet whom? Spilling out the answers that Intelligence had produced – and the name of Timo Rahman.

'I know that name. You could rot in hell, Tony.'

His explanation, yelled, that he had lost control of the man. It was what the man *needed*, what the man *demanded*. He was now only the vehicle for the journey. His wife stood by the cooker and saucepans bubbled behind her. Her arms were folded tight across her chest, and her face was set, stern. The question was inevitable.

'Your man, Malachy Kitchen, would he know when to back off? Where he's gone, would he have the nous to recognize the impossible and step back?'

No answer necessary, but he shook his head.

She beat on the wall with her stick, hammered at it. Behind Millie Johnson, in her little kitchen, the kettle whistled, and beside the hob was the teapot with the bags in it and a plate on which she had placed biscuits – the sort she thought he liked.

Her impatience was curbed only when her bell rang.

She struggled from her chair, used the stick to move towards the door and unlocked it. On the far side of the barred gate was the social worker, not him. Because she felt it, there must have been – like a murmur of it – disappointment on her face. Twice that day, and twice the day before, she had beaten on the wall and hoped he would come.

'Only me, Millie,' Ivanhoe Manners said. He pulled a face, his teeth flashed, and he shrugged. 'Second best, am I?'

'Did he go?'

'Dropped the keys in – no note, nothing – left the place clean like he was never there. Gone, as if he was finished with us. What I came to say, you have new folk next door from tomorrow. A mother and her daughter, from Sudan. I thought you should know . . . Did he not say goodbye to you?'

She said gruffly, 'You'd better go and make the tea, and you can have a biscuit.'

She slumped back in her chair. She heard the rattle of the cups, then the kettle's whistle was cut and water poured.

'I'll let it stand a minute,' he called to her. 'Did you learn anything about him?'

'He didn't tell me – told me nothing – but he'd been a soldier. I tell you, believe me, he was a soldier.'

'Nothing about where he was going?'

She looked out of her window, down over the plaza and up to the blocks and flat roofs of the Amersham. She felt frail and the pain was in her arm. She felt aged and alone, and she remembered what Dawn had said to her about the High Fly Boys and about the dealer at the lamp post. His kiss was on her forehead.

She said tartly, 'I have one and a half sugars . . . Going to do? What soldiers do, I imagine, find somewhere to go and fight.'

He played chess. Victory was assured because Frederick Gaunt competed against himself.

The train thrashed north at speed and the roll of the carriage on the track bumped his knees against those of the man opposite. Other passengers beavered over work files or peered at the screens of their laptops, but Gaunt had his chess, and the man who obstructed his leg room and had joined the train at Rugby had his newspaper. After each move, Gaunt rotated the pocket set. He could not have brought work files or a laptop with him: in these times, it was damn near a capital offence to lose either on public transport.

There was a grunt across the table but Gaunt was not sure if it had been obscenity or blasphemy. He pondered the moves of the little plastic figures on his board and thought of the futility with which he wasted his journey time: did it matter if a blue bishop was lost or a red knight?

Perhaps . . .

Perhaps it mattered greatly . . .

Perhaps it mattered more than his mind could articulate.

He studied the positioning of his kings and queens, bishops and knights, the pawns. Was Wilco a pawn? Most certainly the minder who had died in Prague, burned, had been a pawn. Was Timo Rahman a knight? Was the co-ordinator, who had escaped them, a bishop? Was the city where he lived, worked, the queen that must be protected? He began to move the pieces. Pawns were lost, removed. A knight fell. A bishop moved against a queen . . . Not a bloody game. Quite deliberately, he kicked out his leg and his toecap caught the ankle of the man opposite. He smiled sweetly.

When he played against himself, he always won – but it was not a bloody game when Polly Wilkins, the pawn, was on the board, and not a bloody game if the queen could not be protected by the bishop's move. He was quiet, hunched, and his eyes did not leave the board and the plastic pieces. He felt cold, as if he were intimidated. She was not the only pawn: the bishop, too, had them and would sacrifice them, the sleepers.

He did not know the codename that had been given him. He worked in the Fast Friar food outlet in the conurbation of Hounslow to the west of London. It was nineteen months since he had last been to the mosque. Then he had been told what he should study and that he should not return there for worship. Neither did he know that his true name and the address of the Fast Friar, where he scrubbed the cooking surfaces and cleaned out the frying vats, were spoken of in caves in the mountain landscapes of the tribal areas of Pakistan and in safe-houses in a town of eastern Yemen; and that they were in the mind of a man who travelled ever closer. He was a few days short of his twenty-first birthday. He lived with his parents and two sisters a bus ride from the Fast Friar, and nineteen months before he had, as instructed, taken down from his bedroom wall the posters celebrating the *jihad* in Iraq and pictures of *mujahidin* fighters in Chechnya. He was on no list – as he would have been had he continued to attend the mosque – of potential activists compiled by the Security Service or the Special Branch or the Anti-terrorist Unit of Scotland Yard. In nineteen months he had not seen the imam who had recruited him, but he harboured in the depths of his mind the promise made and the instruction given him. His family, second-generation immigrants from Karachi, had no access to his mind. The promise made him was that *one day* – at a time not known – a man would come to him, would seek him out, would use him. The instruction given him was that he should spend every waking hour, when he was not at the Fast Friar, down the A4 road at Heathrow airport. He had gained, because of his dedication, a near encyclopedic knowledge of the perimeters and their wire defences, the patterns of the patrols, and dead ground on the flight paths for landings and take-offs, and his friends who worked inside never realized they were gutted for information. He did not go to the mosque, did not worship with his family, but his concept of faith burned bright in him and what he would do for his God. A man would come *one day* to his home or to the Fast Friar and would lead him to the side, beyond the earshot of his family or his employer, and would quote from the Book, 2:25: 'And give good news to those who believe and do good deeds . . .' And he would answer: '. . . that they will have gardens in which rivers flow.' It would happen, and every-thing he knew of the airport would be told.

The door to Eternal Paradise would be opened to receive him.

Polly listened – had little choice – as she climbed the stairs and followed the woman.

'You'll enjoy it here, of course you will. Such a lovely building, so impressive. Dates back a hundred and sixty years. We're so fortunate to be here but – I'm being frank – after all the downsizing, we five

Brits, and I'm not counting the locally employed staff, we rather rattle around here. It's so good to have a visitor and an excuse to open a bit more up.'

She was at 8a Harvestehuder Weg, the seat of the British Consulate in Hamburg. The taxi had dropped her outside a white stucco-fronted building that was indeed magnificent, opulent. The woman escorted her to the top floor where there would be a door reinforced with steel plate and behind it a room available to the Service.

'A shipping magnate built it, then sold it on to a Chilean family who were in the saltpetre trade, but they went under in the great Stock Exchange crash of 'twenty-nine. In 1930 everything inside was auctioned off – quite extraordinary, among the items under the hammer were three hundred pairs of antlers and, would you believe?, four and a half thousand bottles of wine of best vintage going back nearly forty years. Then it was headquarters for an SS Gruppenführer. Very convenient, because Kaufmann, who was top Nazi for the city, was just a few doors down, where the Americans are now. It missed all the bombing – a providential wind blew the Pathfinder marker flares away from this district. The annexe was built by concentration-camp inmates from Neuengamme. Anyway we came, got our feet under the table, and have been here ever since. We're very lucky.'

She knew she was escorted by a junior member of staff because the consul-general would not want to be within spitting distance of an officer from the Service. Her own ambassador down in Prague, if they met in a corridor, always found papers to put his head into or a window to look out of for fear of contamination. They were at the door and the woman gave her the keys. Polly unlocked it. A darkened room, and a musty smell, confronted her, like a mausoleum. She saw a table, an armchair and a straight chair, a rack of communications equipment, and the familiar red telephone that would give secure speech contact to London, to Gaunt, and a camp-bed with blankets folded on it. There was a shower in one corner, a small partitioned unit beside it with access to a lavatory, and a small cooker over a fridge on the other side of the shower. She could make herself at home, she thought, maybe take a holiday on Harvestehuder Weg.

'I hope you'll be all right. Just sing out if there's anything you need. We usually gather for sherry with the CG at about five on

Fridays, in the salon, what was the ballroom – if you're still here, you'd be very welcome.'

Polly said that she had just a few 'bits and bobs' to sort out and didn't know how long that would take, whether she would be finished by Friday or not. Alone, the door shut behind her, she rang the number of the organized-crime section of the Hamburg police, her starting point, and wondered if he was here yet, in the city, the man she was tasked to hunt for.

'It is Sami . . .'

He heard the silence, then a gasp, then a hiss of shock, then something clattered in his ear as if she had dropped a cup or a plate that she carried, then the silence. The first time he had rung, from the Hauptbahnhof, the phone had not been picked up. He had walked for many hours, first doing great circles round the square in front of the station, ever increasing, then taken the S-Bahn through the docks area and over the river. He had left it at the Wilhelmsburg stop. There, he had rung again, and the coin had dropped when the phone was answered, and the crisp voice had answered, 'Yes, this is Else. Who is that?' He had given the name she would know, from five years before. He imagined her standing with the phone at her ear, eyes wide, mouth gaping.

'We should meet.'

A pause of many seconds, then a choke, then, 'I don't know if . . .'

The voice – each cadence the same as he had known it – faded. She was, in his adolescent and adult life, the only woman he had loved. In all the years since he had been in Hamburg, he had remembered the telephone number of the apartment high in the concrete block. At first, when he had left, the memory of her had been in his mind each day and each night, but the years had tripped on and the memory had slipped to once a week, but was always there. Of course, if a recruit given to him to mould to the state of grace, readied to wear a martyr's belt, had made such a contact with old life and old love, he would have castigated him, rejected him and exorcized him from what he planned. But she was Else Borchardt, and he had come back to her city: she was his weakness.

'No – everything is possible. We should meet.'

'Where are you? I don't think . . .'

'I am close. I will come.'

He put down the phone. The wind thrashed around him. Cigarette packets, empty and discarded, scattered in front of its force. He thought the wind came over the flat lands from Bremerhaven and Buxtehude to the west, or from Luneburg to the south. When it reached the blocks of Wilhelmsburg, the concrete towers, it eddied in their shelter or was funnelled between them. He had many names. His given name at birth in the Egyptian city of Alexandria was but the first. To those he served, he was Abu Khaled. On the passports he had used on his journey, each carried a different name. For the German documentation shown at the crossing between Liberec and Zgorzelec, with his place of birth listed as Colombo in Sri Lanka, he was Mahela Zoysa. In Hamburg, eighteen months as a student, he was Sami to his lecturers, his friends and his lover. She was sharp in his mind: five years after he had slipped from her bed, gone into a dawn and left her asleep, everything of her face and body was clear to him.

It was where they had lived. He passed an arcade of shops with nameplates in Arabic or Turkish characters, and from them they had bought their food. He stopped to watch the football game on a dirt surface enclosed with mesh wire, where he had played and she had watched him. He walked on. Ahead was the statue. Made from weather-darkened bronze, the figure showed a diving 'keeper – what he did on the dirt surface behind the wire – horizontal but with a groping arm and a ball that hugged the fingertips. Nothing had changed in Wilhelmsburg in the five years since he had gone. She would not have changed.

He came to the doorway.

The blocks were where the city put immigrants and students and those without work, far from its wealth, distanced from its prosperity by the Elbe river. She had said, 'I don't know if . . .' on the phone, and had said, 'I don't think . . .' He could not believe that Else Borchardt's love for him was lost, but he hesitated in front of the bank of names and bells, and he scanned the list but did not find her name. Within, perhaps, two minutes, a child elbowed past him and rang a bell and there was the click of the closed door being unlatched.

He followed the child inside. She was on the twelfth floor of fourteen. He took the stairs. At each landing, as the breath spurted in his lungs, the certainty that had brought him to Wilhelmsburg diminished, a fraction of confidence at each flight; but he pressed on. When he came to the door on the twelfth floor, when his finger hovered over the bell button, he saw that the name typed on paper in the slot beside it was not Borchardt. It was five years since he had closed that door on his back, quietly so that she should not wake. He killed the doubts, pressed the button, kept his finger on it and heard the bell ring out.

She stood in front of him.

He saw no welcome, but fear.

She was heavier than the image of her he had carried in his mind, thicker at the hips, and her waist sagged on the belt of her jeans. There were lines at her mouth and eyes where there had been none, and she wore lipstick that before she had despised. Her hair hung loose and was not kept tight against her scalp by the scarlet bandanna of protest she had always worn. He had thought, climbing the stairs, that she would gasp, then melt, then hold out her arms to grasp him, as she had always done, but the arms were across her chest and folded tight over her blouse, not the T-shirt of Guevara's face that she had worn each and every day. Past her shoulder an electric fire burned and in front of it was a rack on which a baby's clothes dried. He looked above the fire and saw the print of a watercolour view, popular, of the castle at Heidelberg, and the same print had been in a corridor off the entrance to the college where he had been enrolled and where she had studied to be a teacher, and which all of them had regarded with derision. Five years back, there had been in that place above the fire, a poster to commemorate the sacrifices of the Palestinian people. Everything he saw, he thought was betrayal.

There was a chest beside the fire.

A framed photograph was on the chest.

In the photograph she stood with her baby and a uniformed man – Caucasian white – was beside her, an arm round her shoulder.

She said, 'We have been married for three years. He is from Krakow, but now he has citizenship. He is a good man and a good father. It was a long time ago, Sami.'

237

'What does he do?' The question had an innocence.

'He is on the Bahn-Wacht – sometimes he works at the Hauptbahnhof, sometimes on the U-Bahn, sometimes at the Dammtor. In two years he hopes to join the city's police, it is his ambition . . . It was too long ago, Sami. We change. It was the old life, we were young – everything is changed. You went, I cried for a week. I thought you would come back, I promised myself that you would come back . . . Then the planes hit the towers, and everything changed.'

His voice was a whisper: 'Did you ever speak of it?'

'Of who we knew? No. Whom we met? No . . . But I changed my life and hid what had been.' She looked into his face. 'Did you change, Sami, move on? Or do you still belong to the struggle? Have you left them or are you a part of them?'

He should not have come, and he knew it. It played in his mind. The man from Krakow returned in the evening from his work shift, pulled off his tie, loosened his uniform tunic, waited for food to be set before him, had his baby sit on his knee and asked if she had had a good day. And he had ambition to be a policeman. How better to achieve ambition? She would tell him that a man, from her past, had arrived at the door without warning and who he was and who his associates had been at the college. And he would telephone to the police or the BfV – and ambition would be realized for an immigrant from Krakow . . . and he knew also that his weakness must be covered.

The baby had begun to cry and she turned to go to it.

He stepped inside the room and reached out.

She recoiled when his fingers found her neck. He remembered the softness of the skin, where his fingers had played patterns. Then she had snuggled closer to him, had slipped undone the belt of her jeans and lifted up the T-shirt with the face of Guevara. He tightened his fingers and no scream came from her throat, just a choke. He pressed harder. When she no longer struggled, when she was limp and he supported her weight, he dragged her into the bedroom. He left her on the bed, beside the cot where the baby cried.

At the door, before he quietly, carefully, closed it, as he had five years before, he paused and used the back of his hand to smear away the wetness from his face.

★   ★   ★

He had trekked up the long hill of the Elbchaussee, had left the river behind him. Malachy came to Blankenese and by the station he found a board with a street map. Nothing written down, everything remembered. He searched for the name and found a side turning that was scarcely visible on the map. But the dusk had not yet come, and he walked in the opposite direction towards parkland, away from the side turning, sat on a bench and waited for darkness.

239

I2

Hours had passed. The rain had come on heavier, then eased, but the wind was fierce. The rain had penetrated the material of his heavy coat and the wind pushed the damp deeper. But in the park, where he sat on the bench and shivered and the cold caught at his bones, night had fallen. Malachy stood up, then stepped out.

Why? That there was no clear reason for the actions he had taken, merely a higher step on the ladder, seemed of small importance to him. He had little conception of what it would mean to his life if he teetered on the top rung . . . but he did not believe he could escape it. A kaleidoscope of images sped in his mind, the faces of those who had been kind, generous to him: old Cloughie at school, Adam Barnett, war studies tutor at the military academy, Brian Arnold, his guide into Intelligence at Chicksands . . . All would now have rooted for him. Then he heard the sneers, jibes, cruelty of those who had denied him . . . Best foot forward, Malachy, and fast, before courage was lost.

He left the park and walked up into the village of Blankenese. There would have been communities like this one in Surrey, Berkshire and Cheshire. He passed the dim-lit windows of shops for antique furniture, imported clothes and food, and restaurants with candles at the tables and laughter, rows of parked Mercedes and BMW high-performance cars. He went through the village, and thought that prosperity oozed from it and comfort. He reached across a low, newly painted white wicket fence and grabbed a handful of earth from a hoed bed, then bent and smeared it on his shoes. He pulled his wool hat lower on his forehead and lifted the collar of his overcoat higher. He paused at a crossroads, took bearings from the signs, then headed on. He was hungry, thirsty, chilled, but the combination made his senses keen.

Alert, he saw the camera.

The stanchion to hold it was on a high street-light on the main road inland from the village. Branches from a tree wove a trellis of obstructions round the post at a level lower than the camera and the light. Its position surprised him, not right for monitoring traffic in a road leading out of a village centre. A hundred metres past the light, the camera, was the side road leading off to the right. He went towards the camera, under it, and its lens would only have caught the dark mass of his coat and hat, not registered his face. Opposite the side road was a narrow entrance into a garden. A hedge had been clipped around the doorway, which was recessed in the beech leaves that the winter had not stripped. He was in shadow when he crouched on the step, and he tucked his dirt-stained shoes under himself; a man or woman with a dog would have been beside him before he was noticed. He could see up the side road, and there were distant lights behind trees and hedges, above fences and walls. He settled.

He did not know yet which was Timo Rahman's home. He did not know where Timo Rahman would meet Ricky Capel. Where else to be, what else to do? He could not have gone to every hotel in Hamburg, stood at the reception desks and asked if Ricky Capel, importer of narcotics to the United Kingdom, stayed there. This was the only place to begin his vigil.

Cars sped along the main road but their lights did not find him. He was protected by the hedge and the shadows. The cold racked him. He huddled.

It happened very quickly, as his head was clouded with thoughts, all useless.

A car coming down the main road, big headlights powering in front of it. A car coming up the road and braking hard, indicators winking for a turn to the right. The Mercedes was stationary and the approaching lights speared through its windscreen.

He saw the face, the smooth skin that was almost juvenile. The face had been above him. The headlights of the oncoming car lit the eyes. The Mercedes swung into the side road.

Malachy watched the track of its lights, then saw it turn in, and lost it.

He pushed himself up – his hips and knees ached – then walked forward.

The gates closed behind the car.

Ricky looked around him. The security lights showed him the house, their beams spilling out on to lawns and beds of shrub; it was a big pad, impressive, but not a mansion, not like some of the places they had passed on the drive here. The driver had not spoken a word that Ricky had understood. At the reception desk, the skinny bitch who had rung up to his room and called him down had led him to the swing doors, pointed to the parking area and the Mercedes and told him it had been sent to collect him. Half a day and half an evening he had been stuck in his bloody hotel room, and at the end of it there was no Timo Rahman to meet him personally, and to apologize that he had been left for nine hours to kick his heels; just a driver he couldn't understand, who had gripped his hand, shaken it and half crushed his fist.

He was not one to hang about: first, he'd find out where the little shit-face was, where Enver, who had dumped him, had gone, and why; second, he'd get the business done, whatever; third, he'd ask for the arrangements to be made for his flight home in the morning. He waited in the car for the driver to open the door for him, and waited . . . The bastard didn't: he was at the front door, beckoning him to follow, like he was dirt. His temper was high and the blood pounded in him, as it had all through the hours in the hotel room – disrespect was shown him.

The front door was open. He saw a short, squat little beggar, slacks and an open-necked shirt, in the hall. He had never met Timo Rahman but instinctively knew him. All the deals with the Hamburg end for the shipment of packages had been handled by Enver, the nephew. All the loads of immigrants brought in on the lorries he'd brokered had been dealt with by Enver. He felt uncertain, rare for him, and alone – awkward because he wore a suit and a tie. The man in the hall, Timo Rahman, flexed his hands in front of his groin, then slid them behind his back. Ricky had the message, and didn't like it. He chucked the car door open, climbed out, slammed it shut, stamped across the gravel and came to the step. He looked into Timo

Rahman's eyes – Ricky wasn't tall, but he was taller than the man. Ricky backed off from no one. But he saw the eyes. The hall lights shone in them. Ricky wiped from his mind what he was going to say about the shit-face, Enver.

His shoulders were grasped, he smelt the lotion, he was kissed on each cheek and the lips – cold as bloody death – brushed his skin.

In accented English. 'You are welcome, Ricky Capel.'

'Good to be here, Mr Rahman.'

'And your journey was satisfactory?'

'No problems, Mr Rahman.'

'I am grateful you were able to find time in your busy life to visit me.'

'A pleasure, Mr Rahman.'

The eyes never left Ricky's. Years back, when he was a kid and when Mikey wasn't away, they had gone as a family, with the girls, to the zoo up in London, and they'd taken in the reptile house, and there had been snakes, most of them curled up and asleep, but a cobra had had its head up, had hissed and shown its fangs at the glass, and its eyes had watched them. He couldn't hold Timo Rahman's gaze and he was looking down at the carpet and saw that his feet shuffled, like he had nerves. His arm was gripped at the elbow.

'I want to show you something that is precious to me, Ricky.'

'Anything, Mr Rahman.'

He was led across the hall and up a wide staircase. At the landing he heard TVs playing behind two closed doors. A door into a bedroom was opened for him.

On through the bedroom, into a dressing room where a wall was lined with a wardrobe. He didn't understand.

'Look, Ricky Capel.'

The pudgy finger pointed.

It was the picture his grandfather had. Black-and-white, the same. Different frame, plastic and cheap, but the same handwriting scrawled across it. A mountain background, a cave with a narrow entrance, five men tooled up and standing in a line. A fire with a cooking tin on it, and three men sitting cross-legged with the smoke blowing against them. There was his grandfather, and the tall guy whose funeral his grandfather had trekked north to attend, and the one that his grandfather called Mehmet.

'We got that,' he said.

'My father, your grandfather and Major Anstruther, comrades.'

'He's dead, Anstruther is. Grandfather went to his funeral. We got that same picture.'

'Comrades, Ricky Capel. They fought together, fought for each other. Each of them would have died that the others would live. Joined by blood, all men of value. Heroes, fighters, brothers. So, Ricky Capel, your family and mine are bound together in loyalty to them.'

'We do business, yes.'

'In the mountains, in the snow of winter, they lay together to give warmth that one of them should not freeze. In combat they gave covering fire that one of them should not be a target. Your grandfather and my father, they bound our families in loyalty. It is more than business – their blood ran together, as does ours.'

It was a quiet, gentle voice and Ricky had to strain to hear it. He looked, mesmerized, at the photograph. Sharon, his mum, said the picture spooked her. Mikey, his dad, dismissed it as sad, but said old men needed a memory to hang on to. Percy, his grandfather, never talked about the war and what he'd done, lost up there in those bloody mountains.

'I suppose so, yes.'

'They were men of honour. Whatever the one asked, the other would give. They lived together, they killed together.'

'I see what you mean, Mr Rahman.'

'Do you have, Ricky Capel, your grandfather's loyalty?'

'I hope so. I . . .' He checked himself. 'Of course I do.'

He was led from the dressing room, from the bedroom and down the stairs into a dining room of heavy, gloomy furniture – wouldn't have entertained any of it – where two places were laid. Wasn't offered a drink, was told they would eat and then work at their business.

The night had closed on him and the storm had grown. Oskar Netzer reckoned it now at force eight, and worsening. He had laboured into the dusk. Only when the drill bit had nicked the finger steadying the

244

screw, and drawn blood, had he decided he could no longer continue strengthening the viewing platform. It was not for visitors that he sought to repair it but for himself. A part of paradise for this old and troubled man was to be on its deck and gaze down at the small waterscape, and see the eiders. It would be bad that night, but the forecasts for the next week that were pinned up by the harbour told of worse to come. As he blundered back along the sand path through the dunes and the scrub, he prided himself that he knew every step of the way from the viewing platform to the cemetery at Ostdorf where the nearest street-lights were.

When he reached them he stood in their pool, leaned on the closed gate and told Gertrud what he had been doing, and how he had let the drill's bit cut into his finger. He thought he heard her voice: 'You are an old fool, Oskar, nothing but an old fool.' Then he went on home, and the wind sang in the wires, and he thought of what he would eat for his meal, and of his book that he would read afterwards . . . But the meal and the book soon slipped because he worried more about the fierceness of the storm gathering out in the North Sea. The worst of the gales were always in the days and nights before Easter.

He passed the harbour, brightly lit, and saw the Baltrum ferry moored, and every boat the islanders owned seemed to be corralled in the shelter of the groyne, finding safety from the sea – and a new worry surged: would the wind take tiles off his roof? So much to worry about, so little peace.

'You people are wrong, Freddie, about as mistaken as it is possible to be.'

He was not the first and most certainly would not be the last. Gaunt had taken the train north to this provincial university to hear heresies and listen to unpalatable opinions.

'Osama has been made, by you and the Agency, into an icon – it was a grievous error at your doors to have done so.'

The man across the Formica-topped table from him was of around his age but that was the only similarity between them. Gaunt was groomed, wore his three-piece suit with a quiet tie and had a polka-dot handkerchief sprouting from the breast pocket. His shoes were highly polished and he'd burnished them in the last minutes of the journey with the cloth from his briefcase. The professor wore scratched sandals over loud socks, shapeless cord trousers held up by sagging braces, a check shirt frayed at wrists and collar, topped with a stained self-knotted bow-tie, his white hair sprang from the sides of his scalp and made a halo round his head.

'First you set him on a pedestal and gave him an undeserved value, then you compounded the fault by failing to topple him. You lifted Osama to a position where he became the equal to the heads of government of your coalition. I have told your colleagues, so many times, of that error, and their response has been to wring their hands and whine that it is the demand of their masters. You should have stood up, been counted, refused to travel on that road.'

As chair of Islamic studies at the university, the professor had a rightful place of merit in academic circles, but to the Service he was more valuable. Living, working outside the bubble of the Service at Vauxhall Bridge Cross and the Whitehall ministries across the river, he offered opinions that grated with the normal well-oiled meshings of government's gears. At a time of crisis, it was predictable that Frederick Gaunt would have used up precious hours and gone north.

'So, you believe a man is coming, perhaps with a destination of the United Kingdom. You show me a photograph. He looks pleasant enough. You have gauged his importance by the fact that another was prepared to give his life and meet death in agonizing circumstances; a life sacrificed that a more valued person, whom you believe to be of the rank of coordinator, should have time to make good his escape. You ask me to penetrate the co-ordinator's mind. First, forget Osama bin Laden, who – I venture – is irrelevant now, other than as a carved, painted totem.'

They sat in the far corner of the canteen in the students' union building. They ate. Gaunt picked at a stale salad of tomato, chives and lettuce, and had a bottle of gassy water. The professor had had a mountain of chips with wrinkled sausages floating on a brown sauce lake, and drank from a can of Chardonnay. A few minutes before, when a pair of girls had come close with their trays, Gaunt had imperiously waved them away.

'We live in a top-down society. Decisions are made at the top and passed down, but the top demands that authority is guarded most jealously . . . It is impossible for Osama to ape that act. I assume he is in a cave, on the snowline of a mountain, worrying more about his rheumatism and kidney problems than the progress of your co-ordinator. In that cave, with four or five men as company and security, he would probably not know the name of the co-ordinator, would not have met him, would not know the target in Europe – or in the United Kingdom – that your man will strike against. There can hardly be a courier column beating a trail through the mountains to the cave. I don't see the tracks used by wild goats being tramped flat by men with messages in their minds or taped between the cheeks of their arses. Every satellite the Agency can launch has lenses aimed at that trifling mountain range. There are operations in the detailed stages of planning on every continent of our earth. If Osama did top-down, he would need a highway for the couriers and the cameras would find them, heavy bombs would fall on the cliff face, wherever it is, and seal the mouth of the cave, leaving him to death by suffocation. I said he was the icon you have made, no more than that. An inspiration, an example, but not a decision-taker. You have created that inspiration and that example, and you pay for it in the dedication it has created for the new men.'

A flashed glance. Gaunt looked at the face of his watch. In his mind was the time of the evening's last train to London.

'The new men want only from Osama that inspiration and example – not just for themselves but, more importantly, for their foot-soldiers. They need those who will wear the martyr's belts, those who yearn for entry to Paradise. The new men are already hardened and they have learned from the stupidities of the first generation of Osama's supporters. Your co-ordinator, Freddie, will use a telephone of any sort only with extreme caution. He will not carry a laptop with plans, localities, biographies stored in the hard disk. Lessons have been learned. The new men are more careful, therefore more deadly . . . Must you leave, so soon?'

Gaunt pushed back his chair, and stood. He asked his first question since the professor had launched his monologue. 'The new man, where is his weakness?'

247

The last chip was swallowed, and a belch stifled with the dregs of the Chardonnay. 'He is human. However much he attempts to suppress weakness it must, in time, manifest itself. I suggest you quarter the field of arrogance. A man who lives such a life will have supreme self-confidence. If confidence tips to arrogance you have weakness – whether you identify the arrogance and can exploit it, well, that is your profession. I venture the suggestion that you consult with colleagues in Cairo – that pleasant face has, to me, the mark of Egyptian nationality, merely a suggestion and humbly given . . . A thought to travel with, Freddie. You like to call it the War on Terror, but your mentality is still that of a policeman: gathering evidence to arrest, convict, imprison. Too ponderous, too cumber-some, and he will skip round you. Victory in war comes from the destruction of your enemy. Eradicate from your mind the due process of law – kill him.'

Gaunt strode away. At the far distant double doors of the canteen he turned to wave a final farewell, but the professor was bent over his plate, working a finger round it. Gaunt ran down corridors and out into the night, and hurried to the car park where his taxi waited. He had learned, from his long journey north, that he had cause to be afraid of the havoc a new man, bred in hate, could achieve. He saw the face that smiled from passport photographs but could not travel into the depths of those eyes.

Nothing had altered. Everything was as he remembered it when he had been Sami, student of mechanical engineering, lover of Else Borchardt, friend of heroes.

He had taken the S-Bahn on from Wilhelmsburg, route S31, which terminated at Neugraben, as far as the stop for Harburg *Rathaus*. He had walked past the *Rathaus*, through the shopping area and past the new building that housed the social club for Muslim men who were far from their ethnic homes. He had paused outside the police station where posters requested information on missing women and required help in murder investigations. He had noted one that showed photographs of three men he did not know who were identified as hunted terrorists. When he had been here – with Muhammad, Said and Ramzi – he had walked past the police station every day, and officers coming to their cars had ignored him, had never second-glanced any of them.

Another narrow street to cross, and he reached Marienstrasse. Still he would be within the view of any officer or detective who stood in the police station and looked out through its wide plate-glass windows.

It was as if he came back to where – carrying the name of Sami – he had been born again. The café was on the corner. He had drunk coffee there with Muhammad, who had flown into the north tower, and with Ziad, whose aircraft had crashed in the fields of Pennsylvania, and with Marwan who had piloted the jet-liner against the south tower, and with Said, who was the logistics man and provided passports and money, and with Ramzi. All were dead or in the hands of the Americans, except Said who was hunted in the mountains of Pakistan. When he had had the name Sami, all of them had drunk coffee with him in the café on the corner, and there they had talked about the nothingness of football, about their courses at the college in Harburg, and then they had gone up the street where the women had cooked for them.

He walked that pavement. The darkness fell around him but he moved sharply between the light pools thrown down on him.

It was as if he made a pilgrim's journey.

Being there strengthened him.

On the opposite side of the street was number fifty-four. Curtains were not drawn to mask the ground-floor room. He saw two young men in the room of the age to be students as he had been, but they had blond hair and one was crouched over a computer screen. The other stood in the centre of the room, as if without purpose, and smoked a cigarette. Else had been there with him. When she had talked love to him and had promised that she would embrace Islam, when she had gone to the tutorials for women at the al-Quds mosque and had given up the T-shirt of Guevara for a headscarf, she had been in that room with him. Of course, the plan for the taking of aircraft had not been spoken of in his presence or in hers, but he had been in that room when wills were witnessed and he had seen the tickets for the flights to the United States. He went on up Marienstrasse's gentle incline. The laughter of that room rang in

249

him, and he seemed to regain the sense of brotherhood. Before he had known Else Borchardt and had lived in her apartment in the tower block at Wilhelmsburg, he had slept on the floor of number fifty-four, and he had known he was with great men, with the finest.

He thought it fuelled his courage, being here.

Out in the back kitchen of the apartment, standing with his back to the window that overlooked the yard, Heydar had told the student, Sami, in a voice pitched so low that he had strained to hear him, that he should be a warrior of *jihad* and glory in his work. He had been dismissed from that kitchen, sent away. Five years before, without hugged farewells but with a ticket for Sana'a in the Yemen, he had gone out through that door, on to the pavement and had walked away. He had gone back to Wilhelmsburg, had slept part of the night with the woman he loved and had not woken her, had left her. He had heard it said that Heydar Zammar, with the pebble glasses, the uncut beard and the voice of icy quietness, was now in a Syrian gaol and would have been tortured but had not broken. If he had, the name of Sami, sleeper of al-Qaeda, would have been on the Internet images of the Americans' most-wanted fugitives.

He remembered all of them. He must be worthy of them.

He passed the café halfway up Marienstrasse, which they did not use, then saw the window on the street beside him of the shop where shoes could be repaired – Marwan had been there with his most comfortable pair for new heels and the room at number fifty-four had cascaded with laughter that he had the shoes repaired and did not buy new ones. He would have worn those shoes, with the new heels from that shop, when he had taken the aircraft against the south tower.

The pilgrimage was done. The smallest doubt was lost. He thought himself ready to resume his journey to a destination where foot-soldiers slept, and waited for him.

He had no knowledge of the codename by which others, so few of them, identified him.

He lived in a students' hall of residence in the east of the capital city and it was a five-minute walk for him to go from his bedsit room to the minor college under the administrative umbrella of the

University of London. He was enrolled to study advanced computer sciences, and if he finished his course with a half-respectable degree he would be qualified for work in any of the myriad departments of the civil service where statistics were analysed. *If* . . . He was twenty years old, now approaching the end of his second year. His parents and extended family lived in the West Midlands, were originally from the Pakistani city of Rawalpindi. His father drove a taxi in Dudley, one of his brothers was unemployed and another was a waiter in a curry house. To his father, mother and brothers, and to a network of aunts, uncles, nephews, nieces and cousins, he was an object of pride for having won a place to gain a university qualification. His father's one complaint concerning his son was the lapsing of his devotion to the faith.

As an eighteen-year-old living at home he had regularly attended the local mosque. In London he did not. It was the one blot on his father's enjoyment of his son's success. Instead of going to a mosque, their student son – when he was not at compulsory lectures or engaged in specific coursework in front of his screen – roamed the trains and stations of the capital's underground system. He knew the depths of stations, knew the junctions where carriages packed tight with commuters passed each other, knew the signalling cables' locations, knew where the main power wires were laid, knew the times when platforms were most densely filled. He was a wraith-like figure, unseen and unnoticed, who gained new knowledge from every journey he made. The sole frustration in his life was the direct order made to him that he should not fill a hard disk or a three-and-a-half inch floppy with what he learned.

Everything was stored in his mind. He did not know if he would finish his course before a man came and sought him out, perhaps in the hall of residence, perhaps as he walked to the college, perhaps in the library or the corridors. A man would come and would say: 'Those who have disbelieved and died in disbelief, the earth full of gold would not be accepted from any of them if one offered it as a ransom.' And he would look into the eyes of the man and he would answer, perhaps with a faltering voice: 'They will have a painful punishment, and they will have no helpers.' The words from the Book, 3:91, were as crisp in his mind – what would be said to him and what he would reply – as any of the detail of the London Underground network.

He had dedicated himself to his faith and knew the man would come.

'There has been no liaison, Miss Wilkins. There has been no contact between your Service and ours. There has been no introduction from your consulate, Miss Wilkins . . . Should I escort you from the premises?'

'I don't think that would help either of us.'

She could play, when she judged it right, feminine and gamine. Little-girl-lost was an act at which Polly was adept – also, she did tough well.

'There are procedures laid down.'

'And times when procedures should be bypassed,' she said brusquely. She was dressed in the one black executive trouser suit she had travelled with. The blouse under the jacket was buttoned at the throat. She had brushed the styling out of her hair.

'Explain to me, Miss Wilkins, why I should ignore the liaison procedures.'

'For mutual advantage.'

Bizarre, she thought it, their conversation and sparring. She spoke to him in fluent German and he replied to her in fluent English, as if both put down a small marker of superiority. From the moment she had been escorted into the office of assistant deputy commander Johan Konig, she had known that begging favours would fail. She had come to police headquarters by taxi with the confidence to send away the driver, not ask him to wait for her in the eventuality of rejection. At the desk, late in the evening, she had spoken with the bark of authority and had claimed an appointment with the senior official specializing in organized crime, a name gained in her telephone call from Harvestehuder Weg. He, of course, was long gone. Then, to a junior sent down to the reception area, she had played magician and uttered the name to which there would be a reaction: *Timo Rahman*. Her skill was in avoiding obstruction. She had been led to the third floor of the A wing of the building, and had met Konig.

'What is the "mutual advantage" on offer to me?'

'That depends on the help given to me. Imagine a set of scales.'

'Scales must be balanced, Miss Wilkins, if they are to perform satisfactorily.'

'You share with me on matters affecting Timo Rahman, and I will share with you.'

'But, Miss Wilkins, I am a police officer and you are an intelligence agent. In the matter of Timo Rahman, I do not think our paths cross.'

She sought to jolt him. 'Then your thinking is wrong.'

His head jerked up and his eyes flashed away from the desk. None of its surface was visible under the mass of files, papers, bank statements and photographs that littered it. She liked him well enough . . . He seemed to her so tired, bagged eyes that wavered in their attention and slouched shoulders. She understood the loneliness of the zealot. His accent told her he was a Berliner, the strewn papers told her he was reading his way into the life of a target. The clock on the wall showed a few minutes to ten o'clock – the end of a day, the building quiet, but for the skeleton night staff. Dedication had kept him – as if he was hand-cuffed – at his desk. No photograph of a family was set in a frame on the desk, the window-ledge or bookcase, or on the cavernous safe against a wall.

'My intention is to put Timo Rahman, the *pate* of Hamburg, through the courts and into the Fuhlsbüttel gaol for so long that he is a senile invalid when released, and to have sequestered from his investments sufficient monies to render him a pauper.'

'I'll help you.'

'He believes himself an untouchable in this city.'

'Then we'll touch him. I'd like to read his files, and I'd like to see his home.'

'What do we share?'

'We link him with human trafficking.'

'Of whores, yes – but he distances himself from the basic dirt of involvement.'

She threw her card, the big play that Gaunt always preached against except at a time of last resort. 'No, Johan, not tarts for the pavements, but human trafficking in politicals. We are into an area

253

that will not be shared with your authorities, only between ourselves. Mutual advantage. Timo Rahman is on uncharted territory. He is moving a political.'

A grim, dry response. 'For this co-operation I could be hung up from a meat hook. We will go, Miss Wilkins, to the suburb of Blankenese – because, against all the laws of good sense, I trust you.'

The Bear served her husband and his guest at the table. Alicia had cooked for them and had eaten in the kitchen with her girls and her aunt. The girls were now upstairs in their rooms, and the aunt had washed up the plates that the Bear had brought out. Now the crockery was stacked clumsily in the rack on the draining-board and the aunt sat by the stove in the kitchen to read an old magazine from home.

In her home, Alicia felt herself a prisoner – with prisoner's rights.

On the left side of her gaol-home was the family that owned outright the second largest holiday travel agency in the city; on the right side the family had the controlling interest in a company selling building materials. Alicia knew the wives by sight, occasionally spoke to them on tiptoe over the garden fence at the back and across the footpath that separated the properties, and the wire and the sensors, sometimes met them at the Blankenese shops when she was with her aunt, saw them at the school gate when she was driven by the Bear to drop or collect the girls. She had no link with the wives who were her neighbours; she was shy and nervous of them. From what little she knew of them, they were smart, sleek and careless with their wealth – everything she was not.

She thought her aunt too engrossed in the old magazine to notice what she did.

Alicia was stifled in the kitchen, hurt by the thought of her neighbours' wives, who were a part of their husbands' lives, and she slipped towards the kitchen door. By the door, on a unit, was a small television set – not showing a noisy game show but the silent black-and-white image of the drive where the Bear had parked the Mercedes. Above the set, screwed to the wall, was the console board of pressure buttons that each had a single red light, bright and constant. She pressed two buttons, to nullify the beams covering the back garden. She turned the door key. She was halfway outside, and the chill of the night was on her face, the suffocation of the kitchen's heat and her sense of rejection lessened, when the voice grated behind her: 'Where are you going?'

'Out,' she said. 'To walk.'

'You'll catch your death.'

Who would notice? If she caught a chill that sent her to bed, who would care? She said meekly, 'I will be a few minutes.'

She closed the door after her.

Alicia headed for her summer-house, her refuge. She could never leave, could never go home. Not one man or woman in her family, back at the village in the mountains north of Shkodra, would welcome her or risk the inevitability of the blood feud – the *hakmarrje* – with the Rahman clan. She had no existence away from the house in Blankenese, and was as much a prisoner there as the women who worked on their backs in the brothels owned by her husband on the Reeperbahn or the Steindamm. She skirted the light thrown on to the lawn from the dining-room window, saw her husband and his guest standing but bent as if they studied papers, and the Bear with them. She reached the summer-house, her place of safety.

Settling among the cushions on the bench, nestled in the darkness, Alicia shivered and clasped her arms round her for warmth. An owl called, broke the night's silence.

From where she sat Alicia could see the men in the dining room.

He had found the path. Its entrypoint off the side road was some thirty yards along the thick-growing hedge from the closed steel-shuttered gates. Malachy groped down it in darkness, and thought it an old right-of-way track now used by dog-walkers. He was sand-wiched between the two fences: he held out his hands and felt the rough wood of the planks on either side. He came to the end of the Rahman garden. The property behind it had a security light on a high wall that flooded a lawn. He stopped, reached up and wrapped his fist over the top of the Rahman fence, above his head. His hand grip tracked along the top of the fence till it reached the obstruction of a concrete post, where he judged the fence to be strongest and most able to take his weight.

He breathed in, deep into his chest. He had no plan but felt calm. Malachy steadied himself.

He heaved himself up. The fence rocked but held against the post. He struggled but finally he had worked his knee on to the sharpness of the plank tops. He saw the light that spilled from a ground-floor room on to the grass, and more light that came through a blind's slats at the end of the house. In a room on the first floor a child gazed out as she undressed. In the ground-floor room, his view of it broken by branches, he saw the shapes of three men with their backs to him. He balanced, wavering on his perch as the wood gouged into his knees. He found what he expected to find. They ran from a hidden stanchion off the upper part of the post: layers of barbed wire. Below the upper strand, with the needle-sharp points, was a smooth length that was narrow but tautened: a tumbler wire.

Brian Arnold had talked about them. On a quiet afternoon at Chicksands, Brian Arnold liked to reminisce about old Cold War days. Behind his back, most of the young officers and sergeants would make mock yawns, dab their hands over their mouths and offer any excuse to quit his presence. Malachy had not: he had sucked in the anecdotes. The Inner-German border stretching from the Baltic to the Czech frontier, six hundred miles of it, had been fenced with barbed wire and with the tumbler strands that activated sirens. If the fugitive, usually a kid with a dream of the greener grass of capitalism, had hiked from Leipzig, Halle or Dresden, and had circumvented the trip-wires, minefields, dogs and guards, he reached the final fence with barbed wire to snag him and the tumblers to bring the border troops, who shot to kill. The way Brian Arnold told it – from the memory of a young Intelligence Corps officer based at Helmstedt – the tumblers had cost young men their lives.

He crouched with the heels of his shoes on the top of the fence, coiled himself – swayed and prayed that he would not fall – balanced, kicked and launched. As he fell, his shoe brushed the top strand, the barbed wire, but did not snag. His heavy coat billowed out when he was in free fall, then he thudded down and the branches of a bush arrowed into him. The breath was knocked out of him. He stayed still for a full minute until his breathing softened, his nose and face in earth and old leaves. He moved forward on his stomach, wove his way through the bushes.

Away to his left was the dark silhouette of a summer-house, in front of him the house with the half-lit lawn. He assumed there would be security beams, but there were woods at the back and he assumed also that foxes lived there and would roam to hunt, and predatory cats: security beams, safe to bet on it, would be set to catch the waist of a walking man to give foxes and cats free passage at a lower level. Malachy crawled from the shrub bed.

He went on his stomach, hugging shadows, pressing himself low, as if he was a slug.

As a focus point, Malachy took halfway between the window with the slat blinds and the window from which light poured. Down on his stomach he could no longer see the men, but as he came closer he heard low, indistinct voices. There was winter-dead creeper, maybe a clematis, climbing by the window where the curtains were open and when he'd reached the wall he edged towards it, eased up off his stomach and on to his knees, then stood and flattened himself against the brickwork. He heard the voice he remembered: 'I say so, Dad . . . Get rid of him, Davey.' Then his ears had been ringing from the impact of the kick. 'We don't want people like that in our close – and I'm surprised you let him get this far.' The voice was a murmur to him.

'What's it called?'

'Baltrum.' A quiet growl marked the difference of a second voice. 'It is called Baltrum. I think it suitable.'

'You got co-ordinates for it, what the skipper'll need?'

'Yes . . . Are you cold, Ricky? It is cold, yes?'

The curtains were snatched at and drawn across the window. Light died on the grass, and the voices were lost. But, Malachy had only the frail outline of a plan, not thought through but made on the hoof. No rope, no binding tape, no plastic toy and no canister. He slid away. Past the slatted window was a lock-up shed, and he thought it would be where a lawnmower was kept, shut away for the winter, and where there would be fuel for it. He reached the shed door and his fingers found a smooth hasp, no rust or weakness on it, and a heavy padlock. There was the summer-house. Oil, rags – would they be in a summer-house? No plan. It was only reconnaissance. He needed control. Control was calm. There was the darkened summer-house as a place for a lie-up, a sangar from which to watch the building. For a moment, hand on the padlock he had felt a winnow of disappointment, but it was now wiped. He crawled on his belly round the edge of the grass then came to the decking ledge in front of the summer-house. His chest, his belly, his groin and his knees went up two steps and his fingers found the opened door.

He was inside.

He could watch from here, learn of the movement of the house. The house, the home of Timo Rahman who was the godfather of the city of Hamburg, was the last step of his journey. He crawled on old dried wood and . . . There were short pants of terror. His movement across the floor made a rumbling creak on the boards and the pitch of the breathing grew more frantic. He had been long enough in the darkness to see in the gloom. The pants came from the outline of a body, the head softened by a mass of hair. A girl or a woman . . . She was whispering to him but Malachy did not understand the words. If she screamed . . . Yes, Malachy, yes – what? If she screamed, if she brought the men from the house, if she screamed and he had to jump at the wires strung from the stanchions – what? He had never, in violence, touched a woman. If she screamed . . . What price his journey, what price his crusade? The voice had gone, replaced by a whimper of tears. A hand caught Malachy's shoulder. He went to tear it clear and realized in that moment that its grip did not threaten him. He felt the hand, a jewelled ring and a smooth ring. It held his, but not to restrain him. The woman sobbed softly and he loosed his hand from hers. He backed away, scraping his body across the boards.

Outside, at the back of the summer-house, he chose his exit route. He reckoned he could jump from the roof of the building, could clear the wires that were linked to the stanchions. No other way. He clawed his way up, then slithered on the sloped roof and old leaves cascaded down. She did not scream. A woman had wept, had held his hand, and Malachy's thoughts blurred. Too soon, he jumped. Too soon because he should have allowed time to regain concentration. He scrambled to gain leverage and his shoes kicked air but he was short of the fence and the barbs held him. His fingers, grappling, caught the tumbler wire. His body swung. Brian Arnold had described it: the fugitive on the wire, the alarms screaming, the guards coming and the scrape of an automatic rifle being cocked. The wire held his coat, and he felt panic – so long since the last time, but as bad. He heard a door behind him snap open and the scream.

The aunt hitched her skirt, shouted over her shoulder and ran.

The light on the console by the door winked angrily on red.

She thought her shout loud enough, from the kitchen, to be heard in the dining room, that it would bring the Bear lumbering, but fast, after her. She knew every button on the console and charged towards the sector of the fencing where the wire had been tripped. With a rolling stride, from her stiffened old joints, she crossed the lawn and as she came to the summer-house she saw, behind its low, sloped roof, the figure of a man struggling to free himself.

She yelled again to the Bear.

She was a tough woman, past sixty, but muscled. An upbringing in a mountain village bringing water from wells, heaving stones to make fields' walls, walking to a distant road where a bus sometimes came, enduring the harsh conditions of childbirth, burying a husband, had given her strength. Her years in Blankenese, watching over her niece, had not dulled her determination. She had no fear. At the wire, shoes flailed on a level with her head.

She reached up, caught a shoe, lost it, then held the ankle. For a moment she clung to it, then it was torn away. She caught the hem of the long coat.

The heel of a shoe banged against her forehead, dazed her. A toecap caught her mouth, split her lip, and she spat away the broken tooth cap. She clung to the coat. She heard the voice of the Bear. Her fingers clawed into the coat, and the man inside it writhed – and then he was gone.

She had the coat, which sagged down and swamped her. It was a blanket on her head. As she threw it off, the aunt saw the body – a sharp moment – astride the fence and then he jumped. She stamped in fury, frustration.

★   ★   ★

The assistant deputy commander broke the fall, and the breath squealed out of him.

Polly grabbed the man's arm and pulled him up, her grip loose from blood spilling out. She heard Konig, cursing, follow her up the path between the fences.

Slithering, stumbling, they reached the side road.

The man she held started to struggle as if his own fall, on to Konig, had first winded him but now he fought for his life. Not in time. The arm she held at the elbow was dragged back and she heard the metallic click of handcuffs closing, then the belt of a fist into the man's head. They careered down the side-street and towards the lights of the main road.

Konig gasped, 'There's a firearm, legally held, in the house. If we're found we're fucked – no questions – we're dead.'

'Don't you carry a weapon?'

'What? Use it in defence of a thief, an intruder? Grow up, child.'

'A thief?'

'An idiot.'

They passed the gate and lights now shone down on the garden and the front of the house and she heard the confused yells behind the steel plates and the thickened hedge. Between them, they pulled the man, each holding one of his arms and he was limp. His shoes scraped on the pavement. What had happened coursed in Polly Wilkins's mind.

Konig had parked his unmarked car at the main road. He had pointed out to her the camera half hidden by branches, on his orders in place for three days, and had murmured wryly that it was 'for statistics of traffic analysis, and in no way contravening the Human Rights of Timo Rahman by intrusion', had explained that to go to an investigating judge for authorization would have risked involvement with a corrupt official. They had been in front of the house, walking briskly, when they had heard the first shrill shout. They had found the path between the fences and been drawn down it towards the yelling and screaming. When the struggle was at the far side of the fence they had stopped. He had come over, clothes ripping, had been on top of the fence, outlined against the night, then had dropped on to Konig. What she recalled most clearly of the man as she had

260

lifted him was the smell of old, stale dirt. They reached the main road, turned the corner, and behind them heard the scrape of the gates opening. Doors zapped as they ran to the car. They pitched the man on to the floor space between the seats, and Polly went in after him. From the car's roof light, she saw the man's face, then Konig's door slammed shut and they accelerated away.

She grinned. 'Not much of a return for all the drama, Johan. Your catch looks and stinks like a damn vagrant.'

Dazed and numbed – as he had been once before – Malachy lay prone, not in a gutter but on the carpet of a car's floor.

Against his face, holding down his head, was the smooth, warm, stockinged ankle of the woman. He did not know what havoc he had left behind him or what chaos lay ahead.

13

'My name is Malachy David Kitchen, and my date of birth is—'

'We know your date of birth.'

'—and my date of birth is the twenty-fifth of May, 1973.'

'And your blood group is O positive, and your religion is Church of England. I think we have covered that ground.'

They had taken his wristwatch, shoe laces and belt. The German swung the dog tags in circles. He sat hunched on the mattress, rubber sheeting around thin foam, on the concrete bench that was the cell's bed. The German was propped against the concrete slab, the table, beside the lavatory, and the woman leaned against the closed door and held the passport lifted from his hip pocket.

'My name is Malachy David Kitchen, and my date of birth is the twenty-fifth of May 1973.'

She said, 'And your passport lists your occupation as government service.'

The German said, 'Your military number is 525 329. It is late, I want my bed, and you should tell me why you were at the house of Timo Rahman.'

She yawned. 'What government service requires a man with British military identification to be at the home of Timo Rahman?'

'My name is Malachy David Kitchen and my DOB is the twenty-fifth of May, '73.'

The tags swung faster, their shapes blurred in front of him. His passport was now closed, held behind her back. His scratches from the barbed wire were not cleaned and they made little stabs of pain on his palms and thighs.

He did not know their names because he had not been told them but he could assume the man was senior. They had taken him fast out of the car and had dragged him up the steps of a monstrous glass and concrete building. Police had hurried out of the protected reception area and had shown acute deference to the man, but had been waved away. He had been taken down two flights of stairs, along a corridor, then pitched headlong into a cell. They had followed him inside and the man had kicked the door shut behind him. He had half fallen to the bed, then had settled on the mattress. The storm of questions had begun. Over and over again, a repeated litany. *When* had he come to Germany? *What* was his business in Hamburg? *Why* had he broken into the grounds of the residence of Timo Rahman? He had taken as his focus point the barred ceiling light.

'It's a simple enough question, Malachy.' She could not suppress another yawn. 'Come on, don't mess with us, not at a quarter past three. Why were you there?'

The German had come close to him, knelt in front of him and swung the tags. 'What "government service" brings a British citizen to the home of the *pate* of organized crime in Hamburg, when that citizen has military identification but is dressed like a derelict and stinks of sleeping on the streets? What?'

'My name is Malachy Kitchen, my—'

'Oh, for Christ's sake! Don't you know how to help yourself?' Her shoes thudded on the cell floor in theatrical exasperation.

'—date of birth is the twenty-fifth of May, 1973.'

'You are in debt to us,' the German grated. 'If we had not been there to help you, they would have killed you. Killed you and dumped you where your body would never be found.'

'Who sent you, Malachy?'

'Who put you against Timo Rahman?'

At the light on the ceiling, a fly came close to the bulb. For minutes it had circled the brightness, and he had watched it. His mentor at Chicksands, Brian Arnold, used to talk – if an audience could be found – on resistance to interrogation, and the stories were of time spent at Gough Barracks, County Armagh, and the experts he spoke of were not the relays of questioners from Special Branch but the men from the 'bandit country' of Crossmaglen, Forkhill and Newtown Hamilton. The best of the prisoners took a point on the ceiling, a wall or the tiled cell floor, and locked their eyes on it.

Sometimes a hundred questions and not one answer. He'd learned well over coffee in Brian Arnold's room.

'My name is Malachy Kitchen . . .'

She said she was dead on her feet.

'. . . and my date of birth is the twenty-fifth of May, 1973.'

The German pushed himself up off the cell floor, strode to the door, swung it back and allowed the woman through. It was heaved shut and the lock fastened.

Why was he there? Why had he levered himself on to the top of the fence and jumped down clear of the wire at the home of Timo Rahman? Why had he climbed, in desperation, higher on the ladder? Images surged into his mind, like a nightmare. Worse than the insults had been the cloying kindness, the bloody syrup stuff, the understanding.

16 January 2004

'You've been very helpful, Mal, most co-operative, and I don't want you to think that your silence at most of the questions I've put to you in any way jeopardizes your position in the army. Your inability to answer is quite predictable and you show the well-known symptoms of post-traumatic stress disorder. We are not in the Stone Age, so we don't give elbow room to expressions such as "cowardice", or to "lack of moral fibre". We accept – it's taken us psychiatrists long enough to get there, and we've walked a hard road – that PTSD is a medical condition. Now, and this is very important to your peace of mind, there is only a remote possibility that you could face a court-martial and a charge of desertion or dereliction of duty. A slight and remote possibility but I'll do my damnedest to see it doesn't happen. My report will say this is as clear a case of PTSD as I have come across. Is there anything you'd like to ask me?'

In civilian life, the psychiatrist worked for a health trust on the south coast of England, but for more than thirty years he had been a member of the Territorial Army. God alone knew now how his regular patients, back home, were surviving his six-month absence. In the medical unit attached to the division's headquarters outside Basra, he had the rank of colonel and headed the Battleshock Recovery Team, a small empire of a lieutenant, who was less than half his age, and two orderlies who typed and doubled as nurses. In the sprawling hospital in the seaside town, his caseload was overwhelming; in Iraq it was minimal. When a general or a brigadier came to inspect the BRT he'd sometimes joke that he felt like travelling round the combat units and touting for trade, but patients came infrequently.

'Nothing to ask me? Well, that's not unusual. You've had a hard time and probably suffered some pretty cruel cuts but that's because of soldiers' ignorance of mental disturbance. It's all behind you. My promise is that we're going to get you right, get you back on track. You're not the first, and you won't be the last, but we're going to deal with it. You are not abnormal. Most importantly, Mal, you're not a failure. I emphasize it. Not an outcast or a pariah. You've had an horrendous experience but with time and care, and with the love of your family, you're going to come through it . . . I'm going to ask you to wait outside a few minutes while I draw up some papers that need your signature, and when that's done I'll call you back in. I urge you to remember very clearly what I've said – not a pariah or an outcast, but a patient with post-traumatic stress syndrome, not a failure.'

He watched the captain stand and go, a stilted step, towards the door . . . Fascinating. In the last month he'd had an RAF corporal who had been spooked by night guard duty on the airstrip perimeter, and a lance-corporal chef from the Catering Corps who had been pressed into service for patrol and had frozen; two months before him there had been a clerk from Logistics who had sat on a Portakabin roof and refused to come down claiming that local cleaners, heavily vetted, intended to kill him . . . This fellow was the real thing, what the textbooks described.

'Right, let's get some notes down, Donald.'

His duty orderly settled at the computer, and the psychiatrist dictated a skeleton analysis.

'"From field reports, the patient seems to have suffered initially from convertive collapse, with consequent loss of limb movement. Brackets, I do not believe we are dealing with a malingerer or a faker of symptoms, close brackets. This became dissociative collapse, loss of contact with his environment and inability to relate to it." Take a paragraph. Donald, what did you make of him?'

'I'd be going with what they said at Bravo, Colonel. Sounds to me like he just flipped his bottle.'

'Hardly a medical statement. No, he's most interesting because he's a classic case. Could even be a paper in it, might get to be a lecture subject – no names, of course. Next paragraph. "From outside the family of the regiment he was serving with, so beyond the 'buddy' network. Probably, worth checking, poorly trained for being alongside an active-service unit. Asked whether his home domestic relationship was satisfactory, patient flushed and made no reply – all three make PTSD a top starter." I'm actually quite excited. People back home would kill to get their hands on him. We're rather lucky.'

'Boot him out, won't they? Don't mind me saying it, Colonel, but where's he going to go? Who'll have him, with this lot in his knapsack? You soft-soaped him, sir, but he's on the outside, long-term.'

'Getting science into your skull, Donald, is a labour of Sisyphus.'

'Beg pardon?'

'He had to roll a stone up a hill – Homeric legend, father of Odysseus – and each time he reached the top it rolled back down and he had to start again. Next paragraph. "Patient's silence during consultation is compatible with a current state of dissociative fugue. Brackets. Only basic self-care maintained, but refusal to acknowledge familiar locations and life structures. Close brackets." What you have to understand, Donald, is that cowardice is no longer a word in our lexicon. In the modern environment, PTSD explains everything.'

'The guys with him won't buy that, Colonel. You dressing it up won't change it, with respect. To them, he's just a coward. No escape from that reputation, being called a coward.'

'You'd tax the patience of a saint, Donald. More's the pity, I won't have enough time with him – going to damn well try, though. Paragraph. "Treatment of patient is handicapped by the delay in his movement from a forward area to my Battleshock Recovery Team unit. Valuable time has been lost, with consequent onset of acute stress reaction. The – capitals, PIE, close capitals – principle has been negated. Proximity, Immediacy, Expectancy cannot now apply. In a more ideal world than provided by combat in Iraq, the patient should have talked his actions through with a qualified expert at the location, within hours of it happening, and should then have been assured he

266

would be subject to fast recovery from a 'one-off' behavioural incident." That's about it.'

'But the PIE principle didn't happen, sir, did it?'

'It did not.'

'Which is why, Colonel, he's shafted. He's labelled a coward, and big-time he'll believe what's written on that label.'

It was the moment when he realized the flimsy nature of the plywood walls and the lightweight door that divided his consulting room from the waiting area beyond. He cursed softly and felt a little moment of shame.

'Perhaps, Donald, you could get those consent forms out. Make some coffee, then get him back in.'

Ricky had asked, 'What you got? A dozen passengers for the boat?'

Timo had said, 'One.'

'No, not the boat, one boat. What I asked was, how many passengers is it carrying? Twelve?'

'One passenger.'

They had been at the table, now cleared by the Bear, and the map was unfolded to its full size and lay spread across the mats.

Ricky had laughed in surprise. 'What? One passenger? The boat comes all that way for one body?'

'I see nothing to laugh for. The boat comes now for one passenger. The purpose of the boat's journey is not to fish. It is to carry back across the sea the one passenger.'

Because he was bent over the table, because his eyes were set on the island marked on the map, Ricky had not seen the piercing brightness of the eyes of Timo Rahman or the narrowed lips that signified his annoyance. 'You know what it costs, Mr Rahman, to put that boat to sea? A bloody fortune. It costs . . .'

A hand had slipped on to his shoulder and fingers had squeezed tighter into the flesh and the bones, and the voice had been silkily smooth: 'You bring the boat now, Ricky, for one passenger. Not next month or next week but *now*. That is very easy for you to understand, yes? And you will remember the many favours I have shown you, yes?'

'Yes, Mr Rahman.'

267

And the hand had loosened but had left behind it the pain of the pressure on the nerves, and there had been the first shout from the kitchen, and the chaos had followed.

Ricky Capel, far from home, had sat for close on two hours in the dining room. Had not spoken, had not moved, had not known what the fuck had happened. He had heard the yelled commands and questions, the staccato orders given down the telephone in a language he knew not a word of. He had sat motionless with the map in front of him. Twice the Bear had come through the dining room, like Ricky wasn't there, with a Luger pistol in his hand. Now, from the kitchen, among the savagery of voices, a woman sobbed.

In the door was Timo Rahman. He hurled a heavy coat across the room – an overcoat, brown and with a fleck in the material. It hit the table and slithered half its length. The coat was in front of Ricky. 'You know that coat?'

'Not mine.' Ricky giggled, not from mischief or cheek but fear.

The voice was soft. 'I asked, Ricky, do you know that coat?'

'No – no, I don't.' The smell of the coat was under his nose, and made the fear acute. 'How could I?'

Timo Rahman's arms were folded across his chest, seemed to make him stronger, more powerful. Looming behind him was the brute of the man who had driven him to the house, who had served him at the table, who was always close, who still held the pistol. Rahman said, a gentle sing-song pitch, 'From England, Ricky, you come to my house as my guest. At my house, Ricky, you are given my hospitality. We agree?'

'Yes, I agree.'

'I say to you, Ricky, and you should believe me, that never has a thief or an intruder come to my house since my family and I moved to Blankenese. Any thief or intruder would prefer to attack the home of the police chief of Hamburg than risk my anger and retribution. You come, and my house is attacked, and this coat is left on my garden fence.'

'Never seen it before, Mr Rahman, never.'

On the coat, faint but recognizable, was the smell of petrol.

'My housekeeper had hold of his coat, but he slipped from it and went over the fence – and you have never seen it before?'

'It's what I said, Mr Rahman.'

'And the label of the coat is from Britain. I think Harris tweed is from Britain, and in the lining under a hole in the pocket, in two pieces, is a train ticket, Victoria to Folkestone, and they are in Britain. Ricky, what should I think?'

'Don't know, can't help you – I never saw that coat before, honest.' His voice was shrill. 'That's the truth.'

'As your grandfather would have told you, Ricky, in Albania we live by a code of *besa*. It is the word of honour. No Albanian would dare to break it. It is the guarantee of honesty. Can you imagine what would happen to a man whose guarantee of honesty and truthfulness is found to fail?'

'I think I can,' Ricky said, breathy. 'Yes.'

'And you do not know who wore the coat?'

He seemed to see, from the doorway of his home in Bevin Close, the short-arm jab that dropped the man at Davey's feet, seemed to see the bundle of the man on the pavement made larger by the size and thickness of the brown overcoat. Seemed to hear Davey: *Some bloody vagrant scum, Ricky*. Seemed to feel the recoil in his shoe when he had kicked the face above the overcoat's upturned collar . . . seemed to hear, clear, Davey: *On his coat, he had the stink of petrol*. Seemed to see George Wright's place, burned, and heard what George Wright, his leg fractured, had yelled about kids on the Amersham estate and a dealer, and a line from bottom to top: *I want to be there, watch it, when it's your turn*. He hadn't Davey at his back, and he hadn't Benji and Charlie at his shoulder . . . Had no one to tell him what sort of crazy idiot, a mad dog, went after pushers and a dealer, a supplier and an importer, and turned up at the place of an untouchable who ran a city. If he had stood, his legs would have been weak and his knees would have shaken. Anyone knew, Ricky Capel knew, what Albanians would do to enforce a contract. Himself, he had Merks on hire, from shit-face Enver, with baseball bats to kill a man who was late with payment, had seen them used on a man strapped to a chair.

'I swear it. I never seen that coat, not on anyone . . . First thing, I'll do the boat, like you said. I'll get it over here.'

★　★　★

269

With their second bottle of Slovenian wine, their favourite, which they had carried off the ferry, the couple from Düsseldorf discussed their ill luck. Both had taken a week away from work to travel to their holiday home on the island of Baltrum.

The man, a chemist, said, 'The forecast is foul. You have to book vacation days away. Of course it is chance, but you are entitled to look for breaks in weather even before Easter. I spoke to Jurgen at the shop, and he says it is only storms that we can expect. I tell you, the day we go home, it will change.'

She, the principal of a school for infants, said, 'You can't go on the roof, clear the gutters and check the tiles in this wind. You cannot paint the window-frames and the doors, which need it, in the rain. I cannot air the bedding and the rugs. It's hopeless.'

It had been the intention of the chemist and his teacher wife to open up their home and let the fresh air waft through it after its winter closure; each spring it was necessary to add a fresh layer of paint to the outside woodwork.

She drank, then grimaced. 'Have you seen *him*?'

His face, already sour from the prediction of the weather, cracked in annoyance. 'Sadly, he has survived the winter. I have not seen him, but have heard him. He came back through the rain after dark. The door slammed. That is how I know he is there.'

They tried hard, both of them, to ignore their neighbour, who was one of the few twelve-months-a-year residents on the island. It was four years since they had bought the perfect home to escape from the pressure-cooker life of the city. The first summer there they had brought with them their grandchildren, two small, lively kids, who had kicked a football on their little patch of grass at the back and each time the ball had crossed the wire fence dividing their property from their neighbour's garden there had been increasing rudeness when the chemist had asked permission to retrieve it. The children had been reduced to tears and had not come during another summer.

He said, 'I wonder what he does all those months when we are not here, who he insults.'

She said, 'I think we are a recreation for him.'

'He is a man of misery, he takes happiness from it.'

'Death, when it finds him, will be a blessed relief – for us.'

They laughed grimly, chiming a cackle together. The second summer they had left a note on Oskar Netzer's door inviting him to join them for a drink that evening. He had come, had filled their bijou furnished living room with the odour of a body long unwashed, and they had shown him the architect's plans drawn up in Düsseldorf for an extension of a garden room topped by a third bedroom and a shower cubicle. He had refused the drink, then had refused to endorse the plan – they had thought it commensurate with every environmental and aesthetic consideration. He had rubbished the architect's drawings. Through the rest of that summer, the following winter and into the third summer, their neighbour had fought the plan in Baltrum's *Rathaus* committees: its size, its materials, its concept. Last summer they had consigned the plan to the rubbish bin, had given up on the project. Last year when they had been at their house, if he came out into his garden they went inside. They had nothing to say to him, and he made no secret of his opinion that they were intruders and unwelcome – but his death would come, and their liberation.

He said, 'I cannot imagine a life so detached from reality. They say that even when his wife was alive he was no different.'

She said, 'That woman, she must have suffered. It is not possible she could have been the same.'

'You never see newspapers outside the house for the rubbish, you never hear a radio. There is no television. He must know nothing of the world he inhabits.'

'Would not know about the economy, its downturn? The unemployment . . .'

'Would not care, isolated here.'

'Would not know about the war, in Iraq? Not know about the terrorists . . .'

'Ignorance – stubborn, obstinate, hate-filled ignorance. So pathetic, to be at the autumn of life and to realize, deep in your heart, that you will do nothing in your last days that is valuable, nothing that is respected.'

A memory for both of them, when they had packed up the house at the end of the last summer and loaded the trolley to wheel it to the ferry, had been the lowering and gloom-laden face of Oskar Netzer

271

behind a grimy window. At home in Düsseldorf, each time they spoke of their neighbour, anger grew, and they had to stifle it or accept that he hurt their love of the island and their small home.

He poured the last of the wine from the second bottle into his wife's glass. 'You are right, my love. He would reject any action that made him loved, respected.'

She drank, then cackled in laughter and the drink spurted from her lips. 'Sorry, sorry . . . His ducks will love him. The bloody ducks will mourn him when he's dead, no one else.'

The wind hit their windows and the rain ran on them, and the curtains fluttered, and next door to them – unloved – their neighbour slept.

'You can take him. Please, get him out of here.'

'Don't know that I want him.'

'Remove him, Miss Wilkins.'

'If you say so.'

She had sent her signal, encrypted on the laptop. Coffee had kept her awake while she'd typed. She followed Johan Konig out of the side room and back into his office.

'Squeeze it from him, why he was at the Rahman house.'

'Without your help?'

'If I hold him I have to charge him and put him before a court. It is not a road I wish to follow.'

'Understood.'

He passed her the plastic bag, then turned his back on her. For a moment she looked around the bare room, which, she had decided, displayed a man's aloneness and a life without emotion. She fastened on the one item that showed humanity – a photograph of a hippopotamus in a muddied river with a white bird on its back. In her imagination, she delved into Konig's past. Perhaps a holiday in east Africa with a wife or a partner, and that was a favourite picture. Maybe the wife or partner had now left him or had died. She reckoned it involved a sadness. She betrayed herself, her eyes lingered too long on it.

'It is the better to understand them,' Konig said.

'What do you mean?'

'The better to understand them in Berlin, now in Hamburg.'

She said quietly, 'I assumed it was something personal.'

'God, no . . . The better to understand the men who control organized crime, to understand Rahman. The hippopotamus is the society in which we live, and the bird is the godfather. The egret, the bird, is not the enemy of the hippopotamus. Instead it fulfils a need of that great creature by picking off its back the parasites that will damage its skin. It is a symbiotic relationship – the hippopotamus provides sustenance for the bird, the bird returns gratitude by cleaning the hippopotamus's back. They need each other. Society wants drugs, prostitutes and sex shows, and the godfather gives it. He does not leech the blood of society, he merely provides a service that is demanded. That is why the picture is there, to remind me of reality.'

'What is the relationship between the bird, the godfather and terror cells?'

He pressed a small button on the leg of his desk. 'Again, symbiosis. The bird goes wherever there are parasites. Parasites are money. The terror cells have money, safe-houses and conduits for weapons. If there is benefit from co-operation you will find the egret there. Do not imagine, Miss Wilkins, that Timo Rahman steps back on the dictates of conscience or morality when there are parasites to feed off. The picture tells me much.'

She grimaced. 'I suppose so.'

'Take him.'

She held the plastic bag. 'Yes, I will.'

A man stood in the outer door, blinking in the bright light and she recognized him as the one who had brought the relays of coffee since they had emerged from the basement cell block.

'May I offer you advice? The power of Timo Rahman in this city stretches far, wide. He has a network of clan leaders, who control the foot-soldiers. All of them will, by now, be out searching for an Englishman who dared to violate "sacred" territory, Rahman's home. Keep him safe, Miss Wilkins, or he will be hurt, severely, and so will you, if you are with him. I warn you, and you should listen to me.'

'That's a cheerful message to start the day.'

273

The night-duty man led her away along the corridor. They went down three floors in an elevator. Down more flights of stairs. She realized then that none of the big battalions marched with her. She had no weapon and no back-up to call on. The cell door was unlocked. He lay on the bed.

She threw the plastic bag at his head and it cannoned into his face. His eyes burst open.

'Come on,' she snapped. 'My options were shifting you out or learning more about the hygiene habits of hippopotami – I chose you. Move yourself.'

He looked up at her, eyes glazed with bewilderment, and shook himself.

From the bag, he took the belt and slotted it into his trousers. He laced his shoes, put the watch on his wrist and hung the tags at his throat. Then she took him out into the last of the night's darkness.

His train had been delayed, a points failure on the track south of Lincoln, and the taxi queue at the station had been endless. By the time he returned to his office, the bells behind Big Ben's clock face were chiming midnight. Gaunt found the signal. Because it rambled and was strewn with typescript errors, he thought his precious Polly suffered acute exhaustion. Most of the others of her age who had desks scattered through the building popularly known as Ceaușescu Towers – but not Wilco – would have gone to their beds and then, after toast and coffee, have composed a report without errors of syntax, punctuation, spelling. She had responded, and he blessed her, to her understanding of urgency.

The signal, and he had read it four times before he unfolded the camp-bed and shook out the blankets, was a masterclass in confusion – yet there was clarity.

A clear enough link, he believed, now existed between a fugitive escaping from Prague, a coordinator, and a considerable player in Hamburg's community of organized crime, a high-value target.

The lights switched off, his jacket and waistcoat, shirt, tie and suit trousers over the hanger on the back of the door, his shoes neatly laid at its foot, he stretched himself out on the bed, and spread a blanket over him. God, was this not business that should

274

be consigned to the young? Work tossed in his mind, and in his hand – gripped tight – was the sheet of paper that described a man rescued from the security fence around that HVT's property. A name, a date of birth, a six-digit service number, a blood group, an occupation of government service, a tongue that stayed silent and a British-issued passport.

Confusion, because he did not know whether Polly Wilkins had blundered on something of importance or was distracted by an irrelevance.

And no way of telling, not till dawn, not before the banks of government computers in the outposts of the ministries across the Thames sprang to life. God, was he not too old for all of it? He saw them sometimes, rarely more than often, the men and women who had taken the retirement carriage clock or the decanter and glasses set, and had handed in their swipe-card IDs for entry to the main doors of Vauxhall Bridge Cross. All had gone out, at the end of a Friday afternoon, last day of the month, bowed with tiredness and clutching their gift of appreciation. Every one of those whom he met, on a pavement or by chance in a restaurant, seemed reborn. They were like those come-lately Christians, oozing confidence and brimming health. 'You know the best-kept secret inside that bloody place, Freddie? There's a life outside. Never knew it till I got there – outside. Haven't ever felt better. Don't mind me, Freddie, but you look a bit washed through. When are you chucking it in, Freddie? My only regret, should have done it years back.' It frightened him, alone on the bed with the quiet of the building hugging him, that he should be gone from the place, yesterday's man, with work unfinished. 'That bloody place' was Freddie Gaunt's home . . . He was drifting towards a fitful sleep . . . And the enemies he hunted were his life-blood – but he could not guess where they were, could not identify them because they wore no damned uniform.

He did not know where his name was written down, what alias was used, and how many had access to it.

He travelled to work each day in his uncle's transit van, with his uncle's logo on the side, sitting with his tools and his uncle's sons. He was far from his immediate family: his parents, brothers and sisters lived in the port city of Karachi where his father and brothers broke up the steel hulls of unwanted ships for scrap metal. He had wanted more and his ambitions had led him to join his mother's brother in London. Ambition had not been fulfilled. At the age of twenty-three, he was not a laboratory scientist, not an engineer, not a scholar, but a plumber's mate. The resentment had flourished sufficiently to take him to a mosque in south London where an imam talked at Friday prayers about injustice. There was the injustice that permitted white society to walk over the aspirations of Muslim youth in his new homeland, the injustice shown to worshippers of Islam in Saudi, Afghanistan, Chechnya and Palestine. He no longer harboured resentment. Two years ago, less a month, he had been asked to stay behind as the faithful had slipped away from the prayers, and the imam had spoken to him in a hushed tone. Would he serve? Would he wait until he was called? Did he have the strength of his faith? Was patience a virtue of his? He went now to a new mosque, in the west of the city, where an imam preached religion but did not speak of the war zones where Muslim brothers fought for the privilege of martyrdom.

He was brighter at work, did not complain about rising and dressing before the dawn's light lifted over the capital. Each morning and each evening he crossed the City of London on his way to and from work. Some days the crowded Transit van was stopped by the armed police officers at their road-blocks, but their route was always the same and they had become known. More often now they were waved through and drove away from the men with protective vests and machine-guns without being quizzed and the van's contents searched. The same applied at his place of work, where he wore an identification tag hung from a neck chain, and there also the security guards were familiar to them.

Five days a week, the van was parked in a designated bay deep in the basement of the great tower that was Canary Wharf. In those two years he had learned by heart the hidden ducts that carried the air-conditioning systems, water supplies and sewage outlets in the building that dominated the skyline and could be seen from many miles away. He thought it a symbol of the power that had denied him the opportunity to fulfil his ambitions. Each working day, he saw the surge in and out of the many thousands who had blocked him, and did not know of him. One day, he had been told, a man would seek him out, would speak to him: 'God will say, "How many days did you stay on the earth?" ' He would answer, and the words were always in his mind: 'They will say, "We stayed a day or part of a day." ' It no longer troubled him that his response, from the Book, 23:112–113, gave him the answer of the unbelievers on the Day of Judgement.

He had been promised that one day the man would come, and he believed the promise.

His primary job was to drive the forklift vehicle that moved the flat-packs of self-assembly furniture from the lorries that came from the factory at Ostrava in the Czech Republic. His secondary job was to be first at the warehouse to unlock the side gates of the yard and the main building where the offices were, flush on the street, and in the evening he was the last to leave, and fastened and checked the doors, windows and main gate.

The forklift driver walked along the street, briskly because he was late on his schedule, and saw a man on the step outside the offices' door, hunched, low and in the shadow. Few matters concerning the warehouse surprised the driver. He worked for a company owned by Timo Rahman, and knew a little of the complexities of his employer's business. He understood that, in the affairs of Timo Rahman, men came without warning and without introduction to the warehouse, and that questions were not asked and explanations were not offered. He passed the man and, because the head was bowed, did not see the face. He went on to the corner, turned into the narrow driveway that separated the warehouse and offices from the next premises. He loosed the padlock on the yard gates. Cursorily he checked the vans, then opened, with the keys entrusted to him, the back door of the offices.

Because he had been delayed that morning by the police cordon and was behind with his routine, he hurried to the toilets – men's and women's. His first task of each day was to wash them, clean the hand basins and sluice the floors. Then, he should have— The bell at the office door pealed. He left the toilets, his mop and bucket, and hurried past the unlit offices of Administration, Sales and Accounts, and unbolted – top and bottom – the street door. The man glanced over his shoulder, scanned the street, then pushed past him.

'I'm late, I'm sorry.'

The man who had waited on the doorstep shrugged.

The forklift driver babbled, 'I was delayed this morning . . .'

It was many months since he had been late opening the yard and offices. He thought the man had not slept that night – his eyes were baggy and lines cut his face at the side of them. The man leaned against the corridor wall and his shoulder was against a photograph of a dining-room table and chairs set after they had been assembled from a flat-pack.

'. . . I could not leave home. You know Hamburg, I suppose. Yes? I live at Wilhelmsburg. Police, so many police, there. I have to prove my residence to the police before I can leave, show my papers, but there is a long queue ahead of me. Not in my block; but the one next to it, a woman was killed.'

The head turned and tired eyes raked his face. As an Albanian he was trusted, and sometimes Timo Rahman – when he came to the warehouse – would drop a hand on his shoulder and tighten it there. Then he glowed with pride. He thought, for what he did, he was well paid, but the wage given him allowed him to live only in a Wilhelmsburg tower block. The reaction of the man encouraged the forklift driver to go further with his explanation of lateness.

'My wife knows everything. She says the woman was murdered in her apartment by strangulation. It is not her husband – he was at work. It is not a thief. The people of the towers in Wilhelmsburg, they have nothing to steal. My wife made coffee for the police when they came yesterday. They said what they think. She was killed, most probably, by a boyfriend she entertained in secrecy. They will go back in her history because always there is a trace of a friend, they told her. They are confident that, very soon, they will have the identity of the friend. It is good. A man who kills a woman close to her baby, he is a beast. He is contemptible.' He apologized again for his lateness, and asked what he could do.

Did he have a number for the residence of Timo Rahman?

278

'I have, but I am instructed to call it only on matters of great importance.'

He should ring the number.

'What am I to say?' He felt a tremor of nervousness at the thought of ringing the residence of Timo Rahman before dawn. 'Would you not wait till the manager comes, in less than two hours?'

He should ring the number now. He should say that a Traveller has come.

'A Traveller, yes.' The man's eyes were locked on him. 'I will say to Timo Rahman that a Traveller has come.'

'Who is he?'

His wife, Alicia, mother of his children, stared back dumbly at him.

'What is his name?'

The children, the girls, had come to the bedroom door, had huddled there and had shaken in fear, and he had dismissed them.

'Does he come often?'

Timo Rahman did not believe that Ricky Capel, the mouseboy, would have dared lie to him. Nobody lied to him. If Ricky Capel said he did not know the man who had broken into their garden, then he was believed. It was inconceivable that Ricky Capel – in his power – should lie to him.

'You were in the summer-house. You give me no explanation why, in the darkness, you were in the summer-house. When he is seen, the man is on the wire behind the summer-house. Why was he there?'

His wife, Alicia, was on the bed, curled, shrivelled, against the pillows. She had pulled her knees close up to her chest, and he could see her shins and thighs. Anger swarmed through him.

'Is my wife, to whom I have given everything she could want, a whore?'

Her arms were round her head and her body shook with her tears.

'Does my wife go to the summer-house in the evening to be fucked? Do you lie on the cushions and open your legs wide to take him? Is that what my wife does?'

She seemed to wait for him to strike her.

'You are in the summer-house, and he is there. What else should I think?'

She flinched, was back against the cushions, could not escape further from him.

'Do you not understand the shame you have brought on me, on my children?'

There was a light knock on the door.

'I will clean you. The dirt on your skin will be taken off, where his body was against your body. I promise it – I will clean you.'

He left her. Outside the door, Timo Rahman turned the key in the lock. The Bear was impassive, as if he knew of no crisis gripping the family. He had made his promise: he would clean her. He was told of the telephone message sent from the warehouse of his company that sold self-assembly furniture, and as he strode away from the bedroom door, he showed no sign of the hurt that wounded him – deeper than a knife had, more painfully than a bullet had.

He believed that his wife, his children's mother, was a whore.

Malachy saw the dawn come up.

She'd said, 'I am reliably told you are a man with a price on your head. So, to keep that pretty head on your shoulders, you keep it down. What you've seen already is good enough for me and should be for you. Play the silent wallflower in the corner, if you want to, but understand that, right now, computers are spilling out your life story. When I come back, with your biography, I want you here, no more silly buggers, with explanations.'

First light caught the beds of flowers, with colours laid in tight-set banks, and above them were canopies of spring blossom. She had clasped her hands together, made a stirrup for his shoe, taken his weight, then heaved him up so that he could straddle the top of the fence separating the empty car park of the conference centre from the botanical garden and she had waved him off towards dense shrubs. Her questions in the car on the drive through the city had gone unanswered. He had been shaken awake in the car, a few minutes after he had given her the name and street where the hotel was. Then they had gone slowly down Steindamm and had seen men hurry out through the doors carrying the clothes he had left there and the bag. They had shouldered past two girls looking for the last trade of the night, and one had had a mobile at his face. He had not been able to answer the spray of questions because to have done so would mean reliving the pain of his disgrace. He could not, yet, confront it. The low point, down in a gutter of slime and shit, was deep-set agony – since he had taken the train to London, months before, he had not known a friendship tight enough for him to confide in. A dog did not go, after so hard a kicking, back in search of love.

She'd called after him, as he'd sloped towards deeper shadows, 'Did you hear me? I want some talk out of you, no more of wasting my bloody time.'

Hidden from the main path by the bushes, he sat on a bench and the wind flaked blossom petals down on him. They lingered on his hair, face and shoulders. He doubted he could fight her any more.

Last thing, as he'd gone for cover, she'd yelled, 'When I'm back, I'll have you stripped as bare as the day you were born, believe it. I'll be getting more than your blood group, religion and your damn number. Try me.'

14

'It's quite a read, your life, isn't it?' She gazed at him, her mouth set. The eyes behind the spectacles were big and seemed to bore into him. Malachy looked away from her.

'And that's only the digest that I've been sent. I suppose when the whole lot of it spews up it gets worse.'

'I don't look for sympathy,' he muttered.

'Wouldn't have thought, where you're coming from, there were too many barrowloads of pity. Can you talk about it? I'm not a shrink, don't know about couch therapy.'

She'd found him in a squared-off sunken area on the edge of the Japanese garden. A feeble fountain trilled a spray down into a stone-banked pool and its drops mingled with the rain. The blossom snow covered his shoulders and the cobbles round his feet, and had begun to form a covering on her hair. They were together on a bench and the wind was in the trees, but they were protected from it by the high shrubs that encircled them. He felt a sharp spasm of anger.

'I don't go scavenging for a shoulder to cry on. For a simple reason, I don't give explanations for what happened, for what I did. I don't know what happened.'

'That's a good enough line. In your boots I'd stick with it.'

'Hear me again . . . I don't know what happened – everybody else does, but not me.'

'They called you a coward.' She seemed to roll the word on her tongue, as if it were strange to her, not a word she had used before. Beyond her experience. But she said it with a boldness, *coward*, like it was of no importance to her if he were hurt by the word. 'My boss has dug it up. Seems there were other descriptions of you, but all end up in the same locker, "coward". Were they correct in their assessment?'

'I don't know. That's not just soap and water to wash it out. It's what I'm tagged with . . . but I don't know. Why, Miss Wilkins, do you not just go and find something else to do?'

Her face, which had been cold, chilled further. Her voice had edge: 'I am trying to make a decision that involves you. Do I spend time with you? Do I dump you and walk away? My work is on a short fuse of opportunity and I am loath to waste the few opportunities available to me in semantic bloody sparring with you. I work at VBX and—'

Malachy said, 'I know what's at Vauxhall Bridge Cross, haven't been there but people from the place came to us.'

She flared, 'Learn, please, not to damn well interrupt me. I am wet through, tired and hungry and . . . I am tasked, for reasons that have sod-all to do with you, to investigate Timo Rahman, godfather, brothel-owner and people-trafficker. What do I find? I find, on hour one, a guy in dosser's gear hanging on Rahman's security fence with the dogs of hell trying to pull him off it, and the dosser is a former Brit officer whom I then learn has enough disgrace on his back to bury him. This guy is now a fox, no cover to run to, with the hounds baying and bloody horns toot-ing . . . What's extraordinary about the fox, he's put his head over the wall and gone into the hounds' kennelyard. That is either death-wish stupidity or courage based on purpose. Are you going to help me make my decision?'

'If it were easy . . .'

'Don't wriggle, get honest. For God's sake, look at me.' Her arm snaked out, her wet hand snatched at his chin, her fingers caught the flesh and her nails pressed on his jawbone. She twisted his face towards hers. He blinked, but did not try to break her grip. 'Are you worth any of my time or not? Two sorts of bravery that I can think of *Physical* – blokes jumping out of aeroplanes, running across open ground chucking hand grenades at pill-boxes, doing boys' games stuff. Don't know, but I'd reckon that's the easy bit. Try the next one. *Moral*, standing against the flow, not crossing to the other side of the road to avoid involvement, being your own person. Going into Timo Rahman's garden is bravery, but I don't know which. Do I stay or do I dump you? I give you my word, you'll get no sympathy from me.

Tell it like it was, not all the crap about Iraq and what you were called and how far you fell, but what brought you here. Tell it straight.'

He felt the grip on his chin and jawbone slacken. Her spectacles had misted and the blossom flakes obscured her penetrating gaze. Malachy began haltingly, as if a great shyness enveloped him, to tell a story of an old lady – widow of a London Transport bus driver – who had gone to bingo alone. 'But it was not for her, it was for me. It was to be able to stand and not back away, confront and not flinch. I'm not proud.'

'Just get on with it,' she said.

He told her about a pyramid, where the vagrants were at the base, and about the High Fly Boys who were the next stratum up.

A manhunt fanned out across streets, parks, hotels, churches, clubs and pavement cafés to search for the owner of a brown fleck overcoat.

The target area was the city where a fortress had been built in the ninth century on the instructions of Ludwig the Pious, son of Charlemagne, at the junction of the Alster, Bille and Elbe rivers.

An army of men was mobilized, all of ethnic Albanian origin, and had the common factor of loyalty to the *fis*, the clan, headed by the absolute authority of Timo Rahman. Ignorant of history, driven by obedience to Timo Rahman, men were briefed by the *kryetar*, the under-bosses, and were directed to smaller squares on the city map where they should seek a prey. In charge of each *crew*, of not more than ten men, was a *chef*. That morning, the codes and disciplines of distant Albanian villages settled on the streets of Hamburg. Word passed to the smallest groups that a cheap hotel on the Steindamm had yielded up the remnants of the fugitive's clothes, and a description – taken from a terrified Tunisian at his reception desk – was given them.

The Hauptbahnhof was watched and the passengers leaving on Inter City Express trains were checked. Men stood idly by the ticket machines at U-Bahn and S-Bahn stations. They were at the check-in counters of the airport, and at the terminus for long-distance buses. It was as if a foreign virus spread in the veins of a great city.

Among the hunting packs, spread out across the length and breadth of Hamburg – from Poppenbuttel in the north and to

Maschen in the south, from Eidelstadt in the west and Mummelmannsberg in the east – there was desperate enthusiasm for success, to win the praise of the *pate*, Timo Rahman, and his gratitude.

A *kryetar* directed a *chef* to work his *crew* along the length of the park, the Planten und Blumen. That *crew*, five of them, who were all from a remote village close to the Macedonian border, made a line across the gardens, with their *chef* on the central path. They were house thieves, skilled pickpockets and pimps, and they made slow, careful progress from the park's St Pauli end. They knew nothing of the heritage or history of the city around them. Prosperity, wealth, opportunity made a flame that attracted moths. They were from the immigrant masses that had surged inside the city. Welcomed at first because they provided the menial labour force, they had later become detested when they changed the nature and culture of Hamburg.

Only Timo Rahman, the power and the untouchable, had the authority to stage a search of such magnitude, to cast a net of that width ... None knew why a man had so crossed the *pate* that hundreds hunted him. The *crew* with their *chef*, all dreaming of the reward of success, moved through the park, passed the great justice building where thieves, pickpockets and pimps were sentenced, and the walls of the remand gaol where they were held before conviction – none looked at the court or the prison. As the rain poured down on them, they hunted a man.

'You are joking, Ricky? Is this some sort of wind-up?'

He swung his legs over the side and dropped down on to the pontoon.

'I tell you where I am, Ricky ... I am inside a damn great harbour with a damn great sea wall protecting it, and we are still being blown half out of the bloody water. What you're saying, Ricky, it's not a starter.'

He held the mobile to his face and used his other hand to steady himself against the boat's side. The pontoon shuddered under his boots. The rest of them on the boat were inside the old wheel-house, scraping seventy-year-old wood to make it ready for the first coat of varnish. Harry Rogers, alone on the pontoon where only an idiot would be, shouted into the phone: 'I'm down in the west. There's no possibility of putting to sea because there's a depression settled in, and going to be there for a week. I'm working with mates on a restoration. There's storms forecast all week, not just down here. The North Sea's as bad, maybe worse. It's out of the question – sorry and all that.'

The wind bent in arcs the rigging his friends had already replaced on the beam trawler whose hull had been laid down in a yard across the harbour – now gone and replaced by holiday apartments – in 1931. He had not bought into the syndicate owning the boat because it was fully subscribed, and his ambition was bigger. One day he would have his own. Across the harbour, spray burst over the sea wall. Against the pontoon, the ropes holding the boat groaned in the swell.

'I tell you this, Ricky, for nothing. No one's out, not even the fish. Not here, not in the Approaches, not in Irish waters, absolutely not in the North Sea. Try listening to the forecast. Don't take my word – listen to the bloody shipping forecast. Where are you? Don't you have a radio there? . . . Oh, you're in Germany, oh. It'll be no different there, not on their North Sea coast – could be bloody worse, frankly.'

The rain spattered on his face. It ran from his slicked hair and down his cheeks. Because he had been inside the wheel-house when the phone had rung, he had not had his waterproofs on – but it was Ricky on the phone and he'd come running from the earshot of the other men.

'I'm not being difficult, Ricky – never have been and won't start now. I'm telling it like it is . . . Steady. Of course I know what you've done for me. Steady on, Ricky. Listen, I deal in facts . . . Well, what you want and what's on the weather forecast just happen to be two different things . . . I'm not being difficult. When was I ever?'

He had blustered his protests, in the wind and in the rain, out on the pontoon that lifted and fell under him. Harry Rogers had known that in the end, push coming to shove, he would buckle. He would bend as the rigging did in the wind.

'You're not telling me what's so important? No, of course not . . . Best I can do, Ricky, is to get up there tonight, load up, sail on the night tide . . . You'll give me the co-ordinates on the VHF? . . . Have to be good enough, won't it? . . . I don't know how long it'll be. No, I am not giving you shit, Ricky. You're looking at two-fifty nautical miles and there'll be waves over the top of us. We'll make what speed we can . . . No, I'm not saying you're shouting, Ricky . . . Been good to talk, as it always is . . . Yes, and you too, you look after yourself.'

He heard the call cut, the purr in his ear, and put the phone into his pocket. He slid back on to the old trawler's deck, went into the wheel-house and lied about 'something' having come up that required his attention at home. On the quay, as he walked into the force of the weather, he rang his son and found him in a supermarket – endured the disbelief – then called his grandson.

'If you obstruct me and refuse permission for the cameras – which you are entitled to do, citing a violation of human-rights legislation – then I make a promise to you. The affairs of your company – a travel agency, yes? – will undergo a most detailed inspection from the Revenue. It would be the type of inspection that you would find both time consuming and expensive in your accountant's fees, and it is from my experience inevitable that irregularities in your financial affairs will be exposed. Or you can choose not to obstruct me but to welcome my technicians to your home and allow them to fit cameras.'

Johan Konig sat in the back office of the travel agency's flagship premises. Back in Berlin, he had learned that the kaisers of the industrial and commercial world had a fear only of excessive attention from fiscal investigators. Nothing fazed them but the nightmare of tax people rooting in their affairs.

'I am sure you are aware that the Revenue are often clumsy in their dealings with businessmen to whom a reputation of probity is important. Carrying out computers and files when the front hall of a workplace is crowded with customers, attracting inevitable attention on the pavement, with the damage that creates, is often their way . . . I would much regret us going up that route.'

He eyed the man sitting across the desk from him and playing with a pencil. Konig would sleep that night, as he had for the previous week, in a police hostel for single men. In a month, perhaps, if time had permitted it, he would hope to find two furnished rooms in a street well back from the lake in St Georg. The man spiralling his pencil over the desk lived in a mansion in Blankenese, and probably banked in a week what a policeman of Konig's rank earned in a year. He despised such men.

'A warning. Ingratiating yourself with your neighbour might be tempting, but it would not be wise. If you were foolish enough to provide information to him concerning cameras and directional microphones that we put in place, then – and this is my second promise – you will face imprisonment for, probably, seven years. Seven years in Fuhlsbüttel gaol is a long time to reflect on a warning ignored. You tell your family what you care to but the responsibility for secrecy is yours – seven years.'

The man who owned a prosperous travel agency nodded pathetic acquiescence. He was told that a delivery van would bring the equipment and a time later in the day was fixed for it. The business was done. Konig left the premises. He could not, quite, identify the mistake made by Timo Rahman, but he believed it existed. When it had been identified it could be manipulated. Later, back at Headquarters, a surveillance request would be drafted and would go to a magistrate, and the necessary paragraph of justification would describe activities of a flasher, a potential molester of women, in a residential side-street in Blankenese, and it would go through on the nod. It surprised him, when he reached his office, that there was no message for him reporting the progress of the British intelligence officer in unravelling the fugitive's story – what he did hear, in fulsome detail, was that every *crew* of Albanian foot-soldiers scoured the city's streets for a quarry.

She did not interrupt. She sat close to him, no longer smelt his clothes or his body.

'I left him there. He was all trussed up on the lamp post and there was no chance of him breaking the knots, and he'd the tape – half a dozen times – round his face. He couldn't shout. I put the toy gun back into my pocket, picked up what was left of the rope and the tape, and went home. I didn't feel good. Felt sort of flat, sort of empty ... In my mind I'd this picture of a ladder, and I was two rungs up it, and that was still nothing. Didn't feel I'd done anything. Knew it wasn't enough. There was this guy – don't even think about it, because I'm not telling you and you won't learn about him from me. He knew the way the pyramid was built. Above the pushers is the dealer, up higher than the dealer is the supplier. The dealer didn't give me what I needed – thought I needed.'

She could watch the main path through the garden. From the bench, in the sunken area, through a gap in the surrounding bushes and through the light cloud of falling blossom, she saw them.

'I was told who supplied the estate's dealer. I went after him, went with a canister of petrol. I suppose, in terms of conscience, I could square it, but not easily. I didn't think I was an avenging angel – couldn't have said that what I did was the redemption road. The supplier was a target, and I needed a bigger and better target than a dealer.'

An older man, swarthy and short, was on the path and another walked on a thinly seeded space of grass to his right, but the older man made gestures to his left as if he directed more men who were under his command. Two joggers went past the older man but he seemed not to notice them. Swarthy, as if they were tanned from old exposure to the Mediterranean sun, and slight – the same complexions and the same build as the men who had carried clothes from the hotel doorway on Steindamm. She had told Malachy Kitchen that a price was on his head.

'The supplier had this house out in the country. Would have been worth near a million. I'm not ashamed of what I did, but I took no pleasure from it. The family weren't there. I broke a window and spilled petrol inside . . .'

She saw the older man use his arm and fingers to point into the shrub bed above the small cobbled garden with the pond, where they were, where they sat on the bench, and she heard an answering cry but did not know the language.

'I slopped the carpet and curtains with the stuff, then I threw a match on to . . .'

Polly Wilkins, officer of the Secret Intelligence Service, a well-brought-up girl whose mother had lectured her as a teenager never 'to be easy', reached up – two hands – took his face in them, felt the roughness of unshaven cheeks and gulped. 'Kiss me.'

'. . . the petrol. God, it caught, half burned my face and . . .'

'Do it, you bloody fool,' she hissed. 'Kiss me.'

She could have laughed. On his face was shock, then bewilderment, then a sort of naked terror. He had no idea why . . . She pulled him closer, her lips on his face but he screwed his mouth away.

'Not for fun, idiot. Do it like you mean it.'

He softened. Maybe he had heard, now, a heavy breath spurt behind his shoulder, maybe he had heard the snap of a dead twig under a shoe. She did it like she meant it, lips on lips. She had her eyes almost closed, as if passion gripped her, and she saw a younger man hovering in the bushes and gazing down on her. She thought he was coming closer. She screwed her tongue between the teeth.

She growled at him, 'Use your bloody hands.'

He did. Like she was precious, might break, his hands came up and caught her shoulders and he pulled her nearer him. Two rain-sodden bodies entwined and his mouth was opened wider and her tongue could roam more fully. God, and the taste of his mouth was foul. And his clothes stank . . . Polly Wilkins had not tongue-kissed a man since that pathetic creep, Dominic, had flown to Buenos Aires – had near forgotten how to. The man standing above her, with the bushes waist high around him, watched, and then there was a shout from where the main path would have been, and the rustle of his feet as he moved away. He might look back. She kept her tongue in place and let the hands hold her shoulders. When the voices were distant, low, she broke away and gasped.

'Don't get any bloody ideas.'

The colour flooded his skin under the bristle growth on his cheeks. 'No.'

'They'd have had you,' she said, with emphasis, as if the explanation was important. She rattled on, 'Did you know how badly you stink? No, you wouldn't . . . Right, where were we?'

'I fired the supplier's home, perhaps a million pounds of it.'

'You said, "but I took no pleasure from it". Right?'

'Right.'

The laughter burst in Polly. 'Didn't seem to me you took much pleasure from what's just happened.'

'I'm grateful to you.'

290

'Don't, please, bloody thank me. That I cannot take.' She stiffened, touched her hair, smoothed her skirt and eased away from him. 'Where were we? Yes, we were into assault, probably grievous bodily harm, and we've just hit arson. What's next, Malachy?'

She could have bitten the tongue that had been far into his mouth. He winced. She thought she had wounded a man already hurt and down. Damage done. She did not apologize. What she knew of Malachy Kitchen had come in a terse one-page signal from Gaunt that was bald and without humanity. It would have been easier for her to sit as judge and jury on him if he had made a callow admission of guilt or had writhed behind a catalogue of mitigation. He had said: 'I don't know what happened – everybody else does, but not me.' She'd thought he spoke the truth. She had tapped into vulnerability and she felt ashamed of her laughter.

Polly said quietly, 'You burned down the home of a supplier, but you were still short of satisfaction. What had happened to you, everything, conspired to goad you forward – as if, Malachy, you're on a treadmill. But they always go faster, don't they, treadmills? So, who is above the supplier?'

'I had a name given me. Ricky Capel of Bevin Close, that's southeast London. He was the importer.'

'Going there, that's climbing higher,' she said bleakly. 'Higher than most would have.'

'Going there got me a kicking.'

She saw, for the first time, a smile – rueful, uncertain – crack his cheeks, and she listened and believed she could comprehend the burden of shame that had driven him. She thought it past the time for laughter, and for goading him. He told the story of it with detachment, as if another man had been kicked in the face – and she could taste the stale scent of his mouth.

'I really appreciate this, Mr Rahman,' Ricky Capel babbled. 'I gave my word to my grandfather, to old Percy, that I'd come here. He's never been himself, but it was important to him that I came. They were his friends – could have been him if they hadn't shipped him out the squadron and sent him to Egypt. I'm grateful you've taken the time.'

There was a shrug and a wallet was produced. Money was passed to him, and Ricky ducked his head in thanks. He chose, from the flower-seller at the gates, two bunches of red roses, each with a half-dozen blooms. In the car he sat in the back seat and water ran from the roses' stems on to his trouser leg. He looked around him and saw the high mature trees of the cemetery and the banks of rhodo-dendrons. Couldn't say when it had last happened to him, and it was not a mood he liked, but he felt moved by the great quiet of the place. He had not been to a cemetery since his grandmother, Winifred, had been buried, and it had pissed with rain and his best suit had never been right afterwards – and he hadn't cared about her death because the old woman had loathed him. He thought this place lovely. The Bear stopped the car. Ricky climbed out, but Rahman waved for him to leave the flowers on the seat – which confused him, but he followed Rahman.

They walked to a wide space among the trees, where long grass made a cross, with a square, high-walled building at its heart. There were no markers here of individual graves, not like he'd seen on TV. Each of the grassed lengths, he reckoned, was at least a hundred yards long.

'What's this, then?'

Rahman said, sarcastic, 'It is what the friends of your grandfather did, Ricky. It is where German people are. They died from the bombs when the RAF made the firestorm. The air burned. Prisoners from a concentration camp dug the pits and there are more than forty thousand souls buried here. In one week, more than forty thousand.'

'Well – Nazis, weren't they?'

'I expect some, Ricky, were children.'

He grinned. 'Well, going to be Nazis, weren't they?' He gazed around him. Couldn't really comprehend it, not forty thousand people killed, burned up, in one week.

At the car, he was passed his roses and they walked across the aisle road and down a neat pathway. Then it was like he had seen on TV. He faced rows of white stones set in careful lines. Bloody beau-tiful, and clumps of flowers growing in little areas, no weeds, in front of each. He had never been to a place like it, and so quiet. He said what the names were, old Percy's friends, and he took one sector and Rahman another, and the driver a third part – and the stones were all so clean, like they'd been there since last week and not the best part of sixty years. It made him shiver, thinking of it – men in a plane and all that flak hitting it and the plane starting to dive, out of control, and not able to get out, and coming down from three and a half miles up. How long would that bloody take? Made him feel kind of weak. All of them, heroes, weren't they? Could he have hacked it? Yes . . . sure . . . certain . . . He was Ricky Capel. But, the shiver and the weakness had come on bad and he was swaying on his feet.

The shout came. Rahman had found them, the only ones of the crew who had been intact enough for identification. Two stones side by side. A wireless-operator's grave and a bomb-aimer's grave, and they'd both been friends of his grandfather. He never did photographs and had never owned a camera: cameras and pictures, to Ricky, were the Crime Squad and the Criminal Intelligence Service. If he went, and it was rare, to a wedding, he'd spend half the reception making bloody certain he was not in a photograph, that no camera was aimed at him . . . Would have been nice to have a picture to take back to old Percy, though. One of them had been twenty years old and one was nineteen, and there were pansies and daffodils in front of the two stones. He stood in front of them, pulled in his stomach and straightened his spine, and the rain fell on him – Rahman was on the phone, which didn't help the dignity of it. The uppers of his shoes were wet from the grass and his trousers clung to him. A full minute he stood there, and Rahman came off one call, then took another. Then, doing it for his grandfather, he laid the roses in front of each stone in remembrance of a wireless-operator and a bomb-aimer, dead in the first week of August 1943, stepped away and felt good for what he'd done.

As they walked back to the car, Ricky said, 'I expect, Mr Rahman, you're proud to be Albanian, and I'm proud to be British. You'll love your country, Mr Rahman, as I love mine. Mad, isn't it? You come to a place like this and you're proud. Daft, isn't it, how a place like this gets to you? Don't mind saying it, I love my country . . .'

★　　★　　★

293

No one, in twenty-six months, had come to seek her out.

She lived in south-east central England in a town best known for its budget-cost airport and motor-manufacturing industry: Luton, with a population of 160,000. Her home was with her parents, who had come two decades before to Britain to escape the brutal ravages of political oppression in the Libyan city of Benghazi. That she had been born a healthy, vigorous baby had been by chance, her father had often told her. Her mother had been two months pregnant with her when the thugs of the regime's secret police had come to their home and beaten each of her parents in turn, on suspicion of handing out leaflets of protest at the godless rule of Gaddafi; blows from boots and batons had been used against her mother's belly. Her father, once a teacher of philosophy at the University of Benghazi, worked in Luton on a production line, manufacturing windscreen wipers for vans and lorries.

Through childhood and her teenage years she had harboured hate for any who rejected the true faith of Islam. She had been chosen at a mosque in the town: her fervour had been recognized. A video had been shown, in a back room to a selected few, of what the imam called the declaration of a martyr widow. A Chechen woman, clothed in black and veiled, had worn the belt holding the explosives, the wiring and the trigger button, and had made a statement to the camera of her happiness at gaining the chance to strike against the Russian enemy who had murdered her young husband. She had spoken – not in a language understood in the mosque's back room – in a voice of calm, love and resolve. The film had continued with a distant street shot. A slight, small figure in black had approached a checkpoint of soldiers and when she reached them there had been the detonation, fire, smoke and chaos. At that moment, the woman in Luton had stood before the video ended, and cheered in exultation, in admiration at the blessing of martyrdom.

Now she never watched such videos and was never invited to the back room of the mosque. She worked in a crèche with children too young for school, while their mothers stood in lines and manufactured PVC windows. She was good with the children and her employers praised her dedication – and she waited. A man would come, either to her home or to the crèche, one day. He would say: 'And He sends down hail from mountains in the sky, and He strikes with it whomever He wills, and turns it from whomever He wills.' She would answer: 'The vivid flash of its lightning nearly blinds the sight.' His statement and hers were in the Book, 24:43. Five days a week she played with and amused small children, and at the end of each day she was thanked by mothers for her kindness and devotion.

When he came, she would slip away from the crèche and would do what was asked of her.

'What we cannot accept, Freddie, is a further failure.'

'Of course not.'

The meeting between Frederick Gaunt and the assistant deputy director took a familiar choreography. He paced as he talked and the ADD, Gilbert, stayed awkwardly hunched at his desk.

'Quite simply put, a new failure would be intolerable.'

'Of course.'

Rain laced on the window and the desk light failed to lift the gloom.

'It just cannot be countenanced, Freddie.'

'I'm on board. Bodies crammed in morgues, mutilated victims stacked on corridor trolleys waiting for doctors, the shock and trauma of blood on the pavements. Without reservation, I accept that a major atrocity in our cities is not acceptable. No argument.'

He saw a splash of surprise on his superior's face, then annoyance that the obvious drift of the argument had not been interpreted.

'No, no, Freddie – take that as read.' He leaned forward and jabbed his finger for emphasis at the moving target, Gaunt striding. 'I am talking – don't you follow me? – about the effect of a new failure on *us*. Difficult times we live in. It is as if we are under siege. The reputation of the Service is at stake. There are corners of Whitehall in which our efforts, first-class efforts, are derided. There are, Freddie, enemies at large and they wait for one more cock-up – forgive me – on the scale of Iraq. We are perpetually scrutinized. Surely, Freddie, you see that? If there were to be a new failure, it's *we* who would be the victims. I don't exaggerate, there would be another weeding out and we would face desperate times.'

'Oh, yes.'

There was a shrill laugh from the desk. 'You know, Freddie, for a moment I didn't think you understood the true seriousness of the danger to the integrity, dignity, of the Service. Forgive me. Have you all you need?'

'Computer time at Menwith, too low on the priority list. Do I want a galley-load of young Turks bustling around me? No. Do I want Berlin in on the act? No. Do I want a full charabanc sent from London to sit on Polly Wilkins in whom I have complete faith? No. What I want is luck, buckets of it.'

'That is hardly a satisfactory shopping list. Freddie, very frankly, are you up for this one?'

Was he? Wasn't he? He wondered briefly whether selfishness and a personal pride in his ability caused him to reject the battalions of help on offer. Word of any section's success always eddied through the building, crossed the need-to-know fences erected for internal security, and the men and women responsible for secret triumphs achieved an heroic status, and rank envy – damned if he would pass up the chance, damned if he would share.

Gaunt said airily, 'Never been more confident, Gilbert. It's falling nicely into place.'

'But you promised me, with the Prague business, you talked of a rat run that you'd interrupt—'

'Just a blip,' Gaunt said. He turned for the door, then paused. 'I anticipate we will finish this one in good shape.'

In the corridor, he found that sweat dribbled on his skin. Deer were culled by rifle shots, foxes by poison and rats by gas, birds of prey by the teeth of post traps. He mopped his forehead with his breast-pocket handkerchief, and pondered it: how would they cull old warriors who had failed to protect the Service's reputation? Dump them on the street and let them walk away up the Albert Embankment with the carriage clock or decanter or a presentation box of tools, airbrush them out of history and sweep them to retirement? God, he needed luck, sacks of it.

*   *   *

He led the way into the office block and down the corridor. Inside each room that he passed, which had the door open – Administration, Sales, Accounts – the staff snapped to their feet. He went through the swing doors and into the warehouse.

Trailing Timo Rahman was the Bear. Far behind the Bear, ignored, was the mouseboy. His feet rapped across the concrete flooring as he went down the wide aisle between towers of cardboard-wrapped flat-packs. At the aisle's far end was the door to a store room, where mops, buckets and the chemicals for cleaning toilets were kept.

He had wasted an hour at the Ohlsdorf cemetery, to humour the mouseboy, and more minutes than he had anticipated had been taken up in the search for names on stones. A little of his certainty was gone as he pushed open the store-room door – and the image of his wife danced before him, as it had all the time in the cemetery, and what she had done to him.

The man sat on the plastic seat of a chair.

He looked up.

There was a calmness about him, a presence. Timo Rahman saw it, recognized it. The man put his hand on the table, on which lay a cleaned plate and half-full plastic water-bottle and pushed himself to his feet. The face of a man short of confidence would have cracked, Timo knew, with relief, but this one did not. The man bowed his head gravely – not in deference but in a gesture of courtesy to an equal. Timo introduced himself, murmured his name, but was not given a response. Instead, the man moved the half-pace forward and kissed his cheeks. Questions were asked softly, without preamble.

When would he move on? Soon, one day or two.

Was the transport in place? Arriving, about to start its journey.

Was the transport secure? As secure as was possible.

A lesson Timo Rahman had learned over many years was that conversation, idle and unnecessary, between men of stature was beneath dignity. He said that bedding would be provided, that the location provided safety and secrecy. Nothing more.

He left the man, and the Bear closed the door. Then he saw the mouseboy's gaping eyes, and his sleeve was pulled.

'Is that him?'

297

No man snatched the sleeve of Timo Rahman's shirt. His life was myriad compartments, each sealed from the other, each carried in his mind. Behind him, the door had closed on a compartment and another replaced it. The new compartment was his wife, his home, an intruder, a lover . . . For a flashed moment there was a blurred line between the compartments. He squeezed hard on Ricky Capel's hand, held it in his tightening fist, removed it from his sleeve, then let it drop. He thought then that the mouseboy was too stupid to recognize that anger.

'It is.'

'We're bringing the boat over for that one man?'

'He, that man.'

'What is he? An Arab?'

'He is the passenger on your boat.'

'We're talking big money – he doesn't look big money.'

'I am paid to move him, as you will be.'

He started to walk away down the aisle of the warehouse, and ahead of him were the swing doors to the corridor and the offices of Administration, Sales and Accounts. Again the fingers, because the mouseboy was stupid, held him – at the wrist, where the gold-chain bracelet was.

'What I'm asking, Mr Rahman, who is he?'

'You need to know nothing of him, you have only to transport him.'

'For you, Mr Rahman, I move a gang of girls, get them to Enver, or a lorry full of Chinese, Kurds, whatever . . . but one Arab, a boat coming for one man, that's different.'

'You will do what you are paid to do.' Timo softened his voice, the better to hide his anger. 'It is not a difficulty.'

'I'll tell you why it's different. He's a scumbag, not a business-man – not anything normal that I move for you. Why's he so impor-tant that we're not taking him through Dover or Harwich? Why's he not going into Heathrow or Manchester? Why's he got a bloody boat coming just for him? An Arab, dressed like a wreck, I know why he's important.'

'It does not concern you, Ricky.'

Like a fly that flew at his ear, the pitch was more shrill. 'A packet, no problem. A packet and you've no problem with me, money on the nail. Good dealing between us. This, Mr Rahman, is out of order. You saw those headstones this morning, I saw them, laid flowers for them. It's my country. An Arab, can't go through an airport or a ferryport, has to have a boat sent to bring him – you think I'm a right fool, Mr Rahman? That scumbag's a terrorist. I don't want to know, not about shifting a terrorist.'

He pushed open the swing doors into the corridor. It was the skill of Timo Rahman, the core of his success as he believed it, that problems were anticipated and fall-back positions were in place. He swung his arm, like a friend, round the mouseboy's shoulders – could have kicked him, there, half to death – could have broken his neck with the heel of his hand.

Said quietly, 'I ask nothing of you, Ricky, that you are not at ease with. I do not pressure you, but I listen to you. We are comrades, Ricky.'

'As long as that's understood.'

'Everything is understood.'

They went out into the rain, and all the time Timo Rahman's arm was, like a friend's, round Ricky Capel's shoulders.

He thought she had waited with patience for the story to run its course. Malachy ploughed on to its end. 'I didn't have petrol. Didn't have a weapon – didn't have a plan. I was just driven forward. I went right up to the house . . .'

The yawn split her face.

'. . . and they were talking about a shipment. Drugs, I suppose.'

She stifled it, but the yawn's last heave muffled her voice. 'I think I'm there . . . I'm sorry, Malachy, for what happened to you but it's not my corner to stand in.'

'Drugs movements, they don't interest you?'

'I don't do drugs – half a hundred agencies do, but it's not why I'm here.'

'They're going to ship them out from an island – it's called Baltrum, don't know where it is. I'll find a map. They've a boat coming.'

'You go careful.'

'It's the finish of the road for me. I reckon there I can screw the man – the importer – and then I'm about through with it.'

299

'Will you have gone far enough along the road?'

'Don't know, to be honest with you, don't know whether it is.' He said weakly, 'I think it's all I have.'

'Well, I'll be getting along,' she said brusquely, and she stood and looked down at him. 'If you reckon that buggering up one shipment of heroin or cocaine is the dog's bollocks I'll not argue with you. What does that add up to? A tenth of one per cent of the capital's supply for a month? About that? You tell yourself that you've made a difference and get back to the real world, Malachy. Good luck.'

She walked away.

He watched her as she slipped to the path and the heaviness of her sodden coat seemed to bow her. She walked on the carpet of fallen blossom and through the puddles, and the wind threw back her hair. He thought the roughness of her last words was a veneer: she, too, was fragile. He sensed that, at the last, frustration had spilled through her. She had given him most of a day, had brought him out of a police cell, had snatched him away from the home of Timo Rahman, and her reward had been a mumbled location for a transfer of drugs. Peering after her, on his feet, he saw her as a diminishing figure under the prison wall at the boundary of the gardens. Yes, as vulnerable as him – and he felt her tongue and the warmth of her. *I don't do drugs.* Her time with him had been wasted, and before he finally lost sight of her, her stride had lengthened – and then she was gone.

He went to find a map that would tell him where the island was.

15

He walked and could have dropped. Without the strength and tread of his shoes, he would long ago have stopped and sunk down to a bench beside a pavement. He had a sandwich in him, sausage and chilli, and the bulk of a map bulged his hip pocket. He had gone east from the city.

Behind him were the proud places of the city, and its shamed corners – the outer and inner Alster lakes, the *Rathaus*, the New City and the Old City, the warehouse quarter and the former docks where cranes now lifted building materials for apartment blocks, over bridges and alongside canals, and through satellite communities housed in high towers, under *autobahn* routes using threatening pedestrian tunnels. But at Kirchsteinbek, with the map unfolded and his finger tracing the route, he turned south – and he thought the danger of the city receded. Ahead of him now were scattered villages, small towns and fields, drainage channels excavated geometrically across them. The map guided him.

Bare poplar trees, tops bent in the wind, made aisles for him along straight roads. He passed a modern gaol wall, set back on his left, and the light had gone down enough for the arc-lights to shine out brilliantly. The map told him that soon he would swing his course to the west. There was a memorial stone set in the grass short of the prison perimeter but his eyes were too exhausted and his attention too dulled for him to read its inscription. In the growing darkness, beyond the gaol, a track led to low buildings, and beside the road, set among the poplars, was the sign: KZ – Gedenkstatte Neuengamme, and below it was a second sign directing visitors to a museum and exhibition centre. Before the prison there had been traffic on the straight, endless road, but none after it. The buildings, what remained of a concentration camp, seemed isolated. Malachy went faster, struggled to lengthen his step, and his shoes stamped out on the road's Tarmac. He wondered who came here, and why. Were there still lessons for learning? Hallucinations delved in his mind. Did men in vertical striped pyjama suits, which hung on fleshless bodies, watch the tramp of a lone figure on the road? Did he smell the smoke that curled from a high brick chimney? Did he hear the trap of a gallows sprung, and the rattle of shots? If he could have run he would have. He did not have it in his limbs to hurry and the sights and sounds of the fantasy played in him till he was far beyond the shadows of the place.

Malachy Kitchen lived. Ghosts had died there – starved and died, fallen from exhaustion at a work site and died, had been dragged to a noose and had died, or had been forced down to kneel in a grave pit and had died. He saw no self-pity and heard no cry for mercy.

He lived.

Far away, behind his back, was the evening glow of a city with orange light bouncing off low clouds, where men searched for him.

At the end of the road was the Elbe river and a bridge. Across it was a bus shelter where two elderly ladies waited. They eyed him with acute suspicion. The stubble was on his face, his clothes hung wet on his body, his breath came in pants and he sagged down on to a seat beside them. They shifted from him as far as was possible and held their handbags tight in their gloved fists. He thought of the young woman who, to save him, had kissed his mouth, and he thought of the last young woman he had tried to kiss: she had turned away from him, flinched from him.

He asked them where the bus went. They were in their best as if they had visited family or friends. The bus went to Seevetal.

Was there a railway station at Seevetal? They showed no willingness to engage in conversation with the vagrant who shared their shelter. There was a railway station there.

Where did the trains go to from Seevetal? They sniffed in unison, as if he disgusted them – to Hamburg, Rotenburg and Bremen.

Malachy's head dropped. The tiredness came in waves across him. He thought of two young women. One had turned her face from him, one had kissed him and he dreamed . . . The sharp jab of a bony elbow woke him, and he walked behind them to board the bus. In his mind was only pain and the sight of the one young woman, his wife.

25 January 2004
'For God's sake, don't you understand anything? No way was I going to traipse down to Brize Norton. What did you think I was going to do? Hold up a bloody banner on the apron, "Welcome Home to My Hero"? Don't you know what you've done to me?'

The doorbell rang.

He might at least have shown some fight, but he played what they called him, 'a gutless bastard', and denied nothing. Just said, each and every time, that he didn't know what had happened. In denial: that was what her father had said on the phone when Roz had called him an hour ago, denying it because he couldn't face what he'd done – and her father had said he was right behind his girl for not meeting the aircraft in from Basra.

The doorbell rang again, as if this time a finger was on the button and staying there . . . It was now eight days, on the corps's calendar in the kitchen, since 'it' had happened, whatever it was, and six days since the gossip mill in Alamein Drive had produced the whisper. He'd come home the afternoon before, like a rat running, with a train warrant and a taxi from Bedford station. He'd tried to kiss her when he'd dumped his bag down – no bloody chance. Explanations were what she'd demanded, but all she'd had was the whimper that he didn't know what had happened, like that was supposed to be enough for her.

The bloody bell kept ringing.

It had all been explained to her in the secretariat, while he'd been on the train and coming home. Resignation would be best, and then a quiet departure – no future. The papers would be sent round. God, there were some hateful bitches in Alamein Drive! So she'd entertained a couple of guys – what was the big deal? Just Jerry and Algy, and maybe they'd stayed till late, or was it early? Didn't half the bitches entertain a friend when the husband was away? If he'd fought, Roz could have believed him. All that last evening, she had followed him

303

round the house and demanded to know if it were true: was he, her husband, a 'gutless bastard'? Doors slamming behind him, he'd retreated, but she'd followed. Through the kitchen, the dining room, the sitting room, out into the garden where the whole bloody world of Alamein Drive would hear her yelled question, but not the answer. She'd slept in her bed; he'd used the sitting-room sofa. She'd shopped that morning, every curtain in Alamein Drive twitching as she'd gone to the car, and twitching again when she'd come back and offloaded the plastic bags – like it was she who had done it.

'Right bloody entertaining for me, my husband called a coward. I don't suppose you thought of that.'

Maybe if he'd hit her it would have been better. He was slumped at the kitchen table and he winced each time she attacked. She spun.

She crossed the hall. Roz's dad, retired sergeant – a man who had spent the best part of his service in ditches in Ireland knowing that if a farmer's dog located him it was down to a Browning 9mm automatic to stop him being bloody tortured, then slotted, by the Provos – her dad had said on the phone that her room was all shipshape at home for her, that she should ditch the useless bastard.

The padre, who doubled as the welfare officer – and wanted everyone to call him Luke – was at the door.

She said curtly, 'Yes, Luke, good to see you. Before you ask, is it convenient? No.'

The old fart had papers in his hands, shuffled them in his fingers. 'I brought these round, and I wanted to know how he was.'

She did it mock-brightly, a little flutter in her voice. 'He's fine. Nothing wrong with him. Quite himself – why shouldn't he be? Sort of everyday thing, isn't it, being labelled as a runner, a cop-out, a coward? He's in good shape.'

'I'm very sorry.'

'I doubt you're half as sorry as me.'

'He'll have to go. No choice but to resign his commission. It's not something you can come back from. I wish it were.'

'Marked with it, yes.'

'It could be said, Mrs Kitchen, that a little too much revelry went on here in his absence. Frankly, that's what I heard from Major Arnold. He was quite distressed but thought he ought to tell me. If Mal

304

had heard about them, your visitors, then that might account for a poor performance in a combat situation.'

'He would only have heard such lies, Luke, if bloody nosy sods had passed them on. Is that right?'

Only over her dead body was the padre entering her home. Roz stood square in the doorway. A woman, nearly opposite, had found a reason to visit her wheelie dustbin. Another woman, down the drive, had come out of her home with a brush and started sweeping her path. Be a bloody shame when their entertainment ended, but she'd be gone before the next day broke. He was flushed and had a twitch at the side of his chin. He rubbed a mole there with the hand holding the papers.

'I have to say, Mrs Kitchen, that I was monumentally disappointed to hear of this. I thought Mal a first-class officer – but, we are all subject to errors of judgement when assessing colleagues. Actually, I appreciate your discomfort. It's not easy for any of us when a man falls short of expected standards. Wearing my welfare hat, I've brought his resignation form, which has already been counter-signed by the colonel, so he'll need to do that. There's an AFO 1700 that I am formally delivering – it requires this married-quarter to be vacated within ninety-three days, but better sooner rather than up to the deadline. It's a wretched shame, Mrs Kitchen – trouble is that you cannot go back on life and patch up mistakes. It goes without saying that it would be better for all concerned if Mal stayed away from the mess.'

She snatched the papers from him. 'I'll tell him.'

'Excuse me, Mrs Kitchen. What I've said to you has been one-on-one – not for repeating. I wouldn't want—'

'Wouldn't want to join the back-stabbers,' she spat at him savagely. 'No, there's enough of them already. You'd have to be in the queue. Don't lose sleep over it, Luke, because you'd be behind me in the line.'

Roz turned away.

The padre's parting shot had a worried whine in it: 'He'll need a deal of love, and some care.'

'He won't get that from me.' She kicked the door shut behind her.

He was standing three paces from her in the sitting-room doorway. So, he had learned what she thought of him. So, he had heard what was his future. Not her fault. None of it was Roz Kitchen's fault. He took the papers from her, not a word, and scrawled his signature, and *she slumped, buried her head and wept. She heard the stamp of those damn great heavy shoes on the stairs, then the sounds of him moving in the bedroom. She heard him call for a taxi to be at the main gate in an hour. She felt no love, and doubted he would find it anywhere.*

She had written her signal, interminably long but everything that she had been told, and had transmitted it. Then she had flopped on to the camp-bed.

Polly Wilkins slept, dreamless.

She was curled on the top blanket and below her the sounds of the consulate and its business went unheard.

The phone woke her. She started up, did not know where she was. Darkness had gathered in the room, the wind heaved at the tiles and the rain pounded against the one small window. She groped towards the phone, banged her shin on the desk edge and swore.

'Yes – who is it?'

'Polly?' She heard Gaunt's voice sharp in her ear.

'Yes, me.'

'Polly, I sing your praises. To that venal idiot aloft upstairs, I said this morning I had complete faith in you. He wanted Berlin on the road to Hamburg double damn fast. I declined that offer. Were you asleep?'

'Yes, afraid I was.'

'Would you say, Polly, that I was always honest with you?'

She sighed deep. 'Spit it out, Mr Gaunt.'

There was a pause. She heard the silence on the line. She wondered if he was tilted back in his chair, if he had straightened his tie first, and she waited to be punched.

'I'd say, Polly, that you fucked up . . . A bit harsh? I don't think so. Yes, that's being honest.'

'In what way did I fuck up, Mr Gaunt?' she asked, control in her voice, which suppressed her winded fury.

'Simple enough, my dear. Put with greater politeness, there's a boring old saying, "Can't see the wood for the trees." You heard a story, an extraordinary one, and then you rejected its relevance. You were told about drugs importation and said to yourself, "That's off my bailiwick," and discarded it. You could not see, in my humble opinion, the wood for the trees. Your man's laudable, but useless, obsession with the narcotics trade is the *trees* but you missed a sight of the *wood*. Hear me. A boat, a remote shoreline, a collection . . . It was laid in your lap. It was the information that I was confident enough you'd find. It was why I backed you.'

She let the air seep from her lungs and hiss between her teeth. 'Yes, Mr Gaunt, I fucked up.'

'Get there.'

'Do I have the cavalry?'

'I rather think not – better to keep it close . . . Oh, yes. What's he like, the Crusader?'

'Rather sweet.' For a moment, to the intimacy of the phone, she giggled – then cut it. 'But damaged, quite badly damaged,' she said, with sincerity.

'And capable?'

'Have to be, wouldn't he? Or he wouldn't have come this far.'

'He should be a bellwether to you – a sheep that leads and others follow, know what I mean? That island, Polly, is where you should be.'

The phone purred in her ear.

The van in the driveway had a logo of an antenna on its side and below, in printed paintwork, the slogan 'Better Satellite TV Reception Throughout Your Residence'. Two men carried boxes of equipment into the travel agent's home.

He said to his wife, 'I don't know what it's for, but they have me by the balls and if they twist it will hurt.'

'The Rahmans are only new rich, unimportant to us,' his wife said.

They stood in the hall, their children dismissed to their bedrooms, and watched the boxes taken past them, up the stairs and left on the landing. The two men came down again, went outside and returned with a collapsible ladder and tools. The loft hatch in the ceiling above the landing was opened, and they manoeuvred the boxes through the gap.

He said, 'They are from the organized-crime unit – they would make bad enemies, the worst.'

'The Rahmans are Albanians. We owe them nothing.'

Later, one of the men came down, went again to the van and returned with two galvanized buckets. The travel agent asked him why they were needed. He was told, matter-of-fact, that two roof tiles would be moved. From one hole there would be a view for the camera lens down on to the back garden of the adjacent home, from the other there would be a view of the drive at the next-door house and the front door under the porch. When rain dripped down between the shifted tiles, the buckets would catch it. He noted, and she did, that neither man had wiped his feet on the inside mat, and that the dirt from their shoes had made a track up the stair carpet. He did not complain, nor did she. Because *they have me by the balls and if they twist it will hurt*, neither dared to protest at the mess tramped into their home.

She held his arm. 'What would happen to us if Rahman knew what we have agreed to?'

'I thought of him as a businessman who had done well – but he is the target of the organized-crime unit.' Any man in the city who read, daily, the *Hamburger Abendblatt* was familiar with the blood vendettas and feuds of the Albanians and the viciousness of their response when crossed. 'I don't know what would happen to us,' he lied.

Later the men came down the stairs with their empty boxes and their ladder, and one said that if the equipment worked satisfactorily they would be back within two weeks to change the batteries. The travel agent's wife now found halting courage. What about the buckets? If it rained, and the forecast said it would, for the next several days, who would empty the buckets when they were full and overflowed? But the men shrugged in disinterest. They went out into the evening and left their trail of dirt behind them. There was the crunch of tyres on the drive. The act of betrayal of a neighbour was marked by the roar of a vacuum-cleaner on the carpets of the hall, stairs and landing, and above the replaced hatch in the roof, two lenses beamed down on the Rahman house.

The club on the Reeperbahn – across the wide street from the dour brick-built police station – was sandwiched between an Italian restaurant and a shop, now closed, that sold sex aids. The club advertised itself in neon as providing a bar, dancing girls and *kino* booths for single or multiple occupancy. Timo Rahman had acquired the club nine years before. The last conscious act of its previous owner, a Russian from the Dnieper region, had been to sign away the deeds in the belief that the transfer would save his life: with the ink not dry on the paper, he had been clubbed, then dragged out and thrown into the boot of his own car. It had been driven to the quayside by the Fish Market. As the effect of the clubbing had worn off he had kicked frantically at the tomb he was in as the car had been manhandled forward and had toppled into the oiled water. The club now provided some four per cent of the annual turnover of the Rahman empire.

'You will enjoy the show, Ricky,' he said.

He treated the mouseboy as an honoured guest. The best table, the best view of the girls on the stage, the best service. He was an attentive host. As a cosmetic blonde danced, and her implanted bosom bounced, he explained the history of the Reeperbahn street, the quarter where rope was made for the docks and the rigging of sail-powered trading ships, but the mouseboy was distant from him, seemed not to hear him and fidgeted with the stem of his glass. When the girl, naked now, finished her dance and stood full-frontal to accept the applause, he smiled with warmth.

'I am told by Enver that you have bars at home, Ricky, in London. But I think they are different from those in Hamburg. Let me show you what we offer.'

He had raised an eyebrow, the merest gesture. The manager hovered close to him and passed a padded envelope to the Bear.

'The speciality of the club, Ricky, is in the *kino* booths – explicit videos . . .' In his own tongue he murmured a question to his manager, heard out the reply and turned again to the mouseboy. 'Many customers are satisfied sufficiently to return here, perhaps each year. The one I would like to show you is being watched by a party of factory workers, from Essen, where they make toothpaste. They are always satisfied and come each March. We should see what they are enjoying.'

He led. Ricky Capel followed, and a pace behind was the Bear with the envelope.

They crossed the bar and he held back a curtain. They were in a corridor lined by doorways in which were set small glass windows. He heard the baying laughter, as his guest would have, of the factory workers from Essen.

He took his guest to the far door of the corridor, the source of the laughter.

Timo Rahman peered through the window in the door. He saw a dozen men, in jeans and casual shirts, some balding and some grey-haired, some standing and some hunched forward on chairs, all of them, as they rocked in laughter, gazing at the wide screen on the far wall. The good boy, his best nephew, Enver had said the video was high quality, and the sound.

'Here, Ricky, look and enjoy.'

Because the Bear was behind him, pressed against him, his guest was nudged forward, pushed close enough for his nose and eyes to be against the glass. Where he stood, Timo could see the screen. He saw Ricky Capel flush, his eyes widen. Around them, in the corridor, was a cacophony of laughter from the booth and the ever louder grunting from the girl on the screen. She rode her man. The man's head rolled, swayed, and he seemed to cry out but the noise of his little yell was drowned by the girl's grunts. He saw the curse slip from Ricky Capel's lips, but soundless. More of the factory workers from Essen stood and now they clapped in the rhythm of the girl's down thrusts and some, bent with laughter, grunted with her, as she did. The Bear's weight was against Ricky Capel and he could not have extricated himself from the viewing window had he tried to. On the screen, in a crescendo, she thrust down and he thrust up, and now the grunting overwhelmed the laughter and the clapping – then they both sagged. She rolled off him and there was a long, collective gasp of disappointment from the audience, like a moan. She moved from the camera's view, and the mouseboy was left on the bed and in the moment before his stiffness fled him, he reached up – a kid at a football game who has scored a goal – and punched the air. The factory workers beat their hands together above their heads as if they were on the terraces of a stadium, and the screen went black.

Timo led them back up the corridor, but he paused at the curtain. He took the envelope from the Bear and held it in front of his guest.

He let him read the address. The envelope was large enough to take a video cassette and he had written on it: *Mrs Joanne Capel, 9 Bevin Close, London SE, England.* Beside him, Ricky Capel panted and the colour had gone from his face, as if he was about to vomit.

'I think, Ricky, we do not have a problem.'

'No, Mr Rahman, we don't.'

'I think, Ricky, it is unnecessary for that envelope to go in the post.'

'Yes, Mr Rahman, I'll take him.'

'I think, Ricky, that always I knew I could depend on you.'

'That's right, Mr Rahman.' A small low voice with its character hacked from it.

They went back into the bar where another girl danced, where Timo took the envelope from the Bear and used the strength of his hands to rip it to many pieces.

'You sure about this, Dad?'

'Not happy, son, but sure on it.'

He turned the key, kick-started the diesel. The planking of the wheel-house of the *Anneliese Royal* throbbed with the motion, and the roar was in Harry Rogers's ears. Billy watched him for a moment, then turned and pushed young Paul outside. They had done better time up from the west than he'd anticipated, had hammered in the car up the motorway and there was – without anything to spare – enough of the previous tide to get them out of the east-coast harbour. He saw below him, from the side window, his son and grandson working with the ropes, one on the quayside loosening them and one furling them on the deck. Annie had said, on the step as he had left home, that just once – once in his life – he should have told his nephew, Ricky Capel, where to jump off, and she'd said, and meant it, that she'd break his back if anything happened to the boy, Paul – which was bloody daft, because if anything happened to the boy, out in those seas they were sailing into, then it was short odds it would happen to all of them.

The ropes were done and Harry edged them away from the quay, going in reverse. He throttled up power and black smoke spewed behind. When they'd climbed on board, the assistant harbourmaster had braved the wind and rain and come down from the sanctuary he shared with the coastguard and Customs people. Probably bored out of his mind because no other boat was putting to sea that night. Harry had blustered that mortgage repayments on the *Anneliese Royal* didn't wait on the weather, and had parried him with bullshit about being in place when the storm blew itself out. Good hunting, he'd been told, and the assistant harbourmaster had run for shelter.

They moved towards the end of the groyne, where the light flashed.

He could see, from the wheel-house, the big plate-glass window and could make out the small shapes of the assistant harbourmaster, the duty coastguard and the Customs woman, who was doing the night shift. They'd all have had their binoculars up, but Harry didn't see that because the rain ran rivers on the wheel-house. Ricky Capel had called him again and had given him co-ordinates for the German coast, but had sounded sort of distant and had said, 'It's not a hundred per cent, Harry. It may not happen. Just as likely you'll get a cancel from me. A good chance of a cancel, but you get moving. Don't tell the world where you're headed. If it's a cancel I'll call you on the mobile and turn you back. It'll probably be that, a cancel.' But the cancel call hadn't come.

The old boys, eighty years before, going to sea in a beam trawler under sail power and taking on a force nine or ten – fifty-knot wind speed – had had a saying: 'Grumble you may, but go you must.' He thought of them, weather hardened, and of the boat that would be his one day, which they had gone to sea in. She passed the end of the groyne, where a solitary lunatic watched his fishing-rod, and left the safety of the harbour. Waves slashed against the *Anneliese Royal*, lifted and dropped her.

'My chief waited for you, Mr Gaunt, but he's gone now. Has a dinner this evening with Home Office fat cats – I don't reckon wild horses would have pulled him off that. For my chief, a dinner with them is like a call to the Sepulchre. He asked me to hang on and see you, see how we can help. So, I'm what you've got . . . Sorry about that.'

'I'm grateful to you, Detective Sergeant. I hope I haven't mucked up your evening.'

'You haven't – and please call me Tony.'

'Fine, Tony. Could we set some ground rules? Official Secrets Act, no notes taken, conversation that didn't happen – you know the game. I don't want the party line, just want it straight, the way it is, and don't ask me why I requested this meeting. The subject of my interest is Ricky Capel.'

'Aged thirty-four, married to Joanne, one son, lives at nine Bevin Close, that's south London on the east side.'

They were in a chief superintendent's office with beech panelling, pastel slat blinds and photographs from courses of sitting and standing participants; there was a picture of the office resident in uniform and shaking the hand of the grinning prime minister. Among the photographs there were shields presented by Texan, Jordanian and Brazilian police forces – and the room was scrupulously tidy. Gaunt wondered balefully if, as a visitor, he should have removed his shoes before entering. What was a refreshing relief, the detective sergeant had pushed aside the leather-tipped blotter and the crystal ink-stand, and had planted his backside on the desk. Immaculate as always in his suit and waistcoat, with his tie over the collar button, Gaunt could recognize a worker ant. A damned tired one . . . He liked such men.

'I'm assuming there are a hundred places you'd rather be than here, and I'll try not to waste your time. What is the single most important thing about Ricky Capel?'

'That he's never been nicked.'

'He's a big player. Why has he never been arrested and charged?'

'Cunning, not educated, intelligent but clever. Doesn't overreach himself.'

'As easy as that?'

'A guy who's never been nicked, each year he gets to be more careful, cuts down on the risk factor.'

'But you target him?'

The detective sergeant snorted, almost derision. Gaunt liked that near streak of contempt for his question. It was not the right place for him to pace and intimidate, so he leaned back in the visitor's chair, swung his feet on to the desk and rested them beside the baggy flop of the policeman's jacket. He thought it would show a welcome disrespect for the high and mighty whose office it was.

'How does he walk round you?'

'Because we're in the quick-fix world. Focus groups and think-tanks rule us, and they say that targets must be met, *must* be. We have a slop of money coming in here at Criminal Intelligence, and there's budgets for Crime Squad and the organized-crime people at the Yard. Best way to justify the cash is to get results, achieve those bloody targets. What you don't do – and it's my chief's Bible – is think long-term. Resources are allocated at targets where results can be guaranteed. Then my chief can go down the Home Office, take a dinner and spiel out the statistics of success. To go after a clever, cunning bastard – Ricky Capel – takes cash, manpower, commitment, with no promise of getting the handcuffs on him. He's doing very nicely, it's what he'd tell you . . . There's all sorts of wars being fought at the moment and I reckon we're losing the lot of them. My war, people-trafficking for vice and the importation of narcotics, is going down the plug-hole and fast. Not that my chief would tell you, but we got it wrong and we're losing. Is that out of order?'

'I wouldn't say so, Tony.' He asked with effortless casualness, well practised, 'What business would take Ricky Capel to Hamburg?'

He saw the policeman's eyes flash, and the rhythm with which he slapped his heels against the front of his chief's desk was cut.

'You're well informed, Mr Gaunt.'

'Why would he be there?'

'You know about Albanians?'

Gaunt said easily, 'I cast an eye over matters Albanian from time to time.'

'The big hook-up is with Timo Rahman, godfather of that city, supplier of the heroin that Capel brings in. I don't know the route used but Rahman is the source. The link goes back a long way, right back to Capel's grandfather. I read that in the file. The grandfather, that's Percy Capel, did time in the war in Albania and worked with a gang led by Rahman's father. That's where you'd find what the link is. Percy's an old thief and lives next door to Capel . . . not that he'd give you the time of day.'

'No, I don't suppose he would.' He knew more, and it gave him little pleasure, than the policeman – could have told him about a boat supposedly coming to an island off the Frisian coast of Germany, but

314

that would have meant sharing. It was Gaunt's habit to leech blood, a one-way trade. He lifted his shoes off the table and glanced, with slight ostentation, at his watch, as if he had consumed enough of the detective's time. 'I much appreciate you staying on and meeting me.'

'What I'm saying to you, Mr Gaunt, is that Capel's supping with the devil, but for both of them it's a mistake.'

'How's that?'

'We've learned it. The Albanians suck a man dry when he thinks they're just partners, then move in and ditch him. The other side, Capel isn't in Rahman's league of skills and on anything big he would be the weak leg.'

'An interesting observation. I'll let you get on home. Been grand meeting you.'

But the man was not finished, and gushed, 'I tell you, Mr Gaunt, it pisses me off that we're losing, that Capel and his like are winning. We've the courts and the legislation and the prisons, but we're not filling them. I could take you to an estate, not much more than a mile from here, where there's addicts and pushers who sell to them, and dealers, where there's old ladies who live behind barricades and in fear. I don't suppose that's in your remit, Mr Gaunt, old ladies getting their arm broken for what's in a purse.'

It seared in Gaunt's mind. He recalled the long signal sent him by Polly Wilkins that detailed hours spent in the Planten und Blumen garden and what a man had told her. It fell into place. A man had tried to claw back his life by climbing a pyramid. He offered no sign of it, and stood.

'Very helpful you've been, Tony. A last chore for you. Please, see if there's anything in the Capel file that might equate with a rat run – you know, a round-the-houses short-cut as an importation route – any trace to a boat . . . Oh, if I ever wanted to go to that estate – probably very close to where I work – and meet a pensioner who was mugged for her purse, who would I go to see, and where?'

A slip of paper was taken from the chief's desk notepad, and the accompanying silver-coated pencil, inscribed 'To a Valued Colleague From the Police Academy, Toronto', scribbled something. Gaunt pocketed it without reading what had been written. He never showed enthusiasm for information given.

Going down in the lift and out into the evening, he realized that he had spent an hour with a policeman who was so embittered by defeat that he had pulled the marionette strings of a broken man and given the poor beggar purpose – quite bizarre, but life was ever thus. He reflected: a man with purpose in his step could always be found useful work.

He lay full length on a platform bench.

Police had come to him a half-hour before and towered over him. They'd had pistols, handcuffs, gas and batons on their belts, but he had shown them his passport and his onward train ticket. The man had grimaced contempt, the woman had sniffed, and they had left him. A train came through, pulling half a hundred, Malachy's best guess, wagons of chemicals. He was awake, had been since the police had checked him. When the wagons had rumbled away into the night, a silence fell round him and the station's life died. He had reached Rotenburg. He must wait, chilled and damp, another hour for a night service that would take him – via Bremen, Oldenburg and Emden – to the coast.

Off the coast was an island, but he did not know what he would find there, or if he would find anything.

He sat on his bed and a blanket shrouded his shoulders.

The nightmare had worked in the mind of Oskar Netzer. If he lay on his bed, he would sleep because of his age and his tiredness. If he slept he dreamed, and the nightmares chased relentlessly after him. He saw men loosen the noose round a frail neck, take down a child's corpse and put the noose on another.

The blanket gave him sparse warmth. Always at the last, the picture in his mind was of his uncle Rolf, who had helped to drive the children, their carers and guards, their doctor and the ropes to the cellar where hooks were set in the ceiling. Because that blood ran in him, he was part of the evil. He had come to the island of Baltrum, with his wife, to find peace but it escaped him. The blood in his veins was contaminated. He threw off the blanket and stood up heavily. The joints of his legs – as if he was cursed – ached at the movement, and he went to his living room. Respite, if it were to be found, would be in the bundles of planning applications that littered his table, and the drawings of a proposed new sewage works.

Only by fighting each change that came to the paradise, Baltrum, could Oskar Netzer exorcize the guilt that ran in his blood. He pored over applications and the proposal . . . Anything and any person who was new to the island and threatened it must be fought root and branch – as Lutherans had said three centuries before – without compromise. The light, from a low-wattage bulb with no shade, beamed down on him as he scanned typescripts and drawings, and was saved from sleep.

He had many names, discarded, and in the morning he would have a new one. In the morning he would be given the passport and documents for Social Security.

He had the name given him at birth – Anwar.

He had the names, for a week or a month, on the travel papers with which he criss-crossed international boundaries.

He had the name Sami, student of mechanical engineering and lover of Else Borchardt.

He had the name Mahela Zoysa, on whose Sinhalese identity he had come into Germany and which, in the morning, he would give up.

He had the name, in the Organization, of Abu Khaled but he was far from the company of colleagues. For Abu Khaled, a man had died in the top-floor rooms of an apartment – that sacrifice had been made for him.

He preferred to sit on the linoleum, with his back against a wall and a calendar above him that showed a faded picture of the fortress of Gjirokastra in Albania. He shunned comfort, preferred the floor to a chair or a mattress . . . Alone, unwatched and delving into memories he would choose the floor to rest on. The memories danced for him, changed step as if a beat altered, seemed to him to be on a loop and always returned to him as the boy, Anwar – a child of the city of Alexandria.

He had been born in 1972: that year, as he knew now, was when Palestinians had assaulted the festival of the Munich games – and had not been prepared: the planning had been inadequate. A year later, 1973, a month after his first birthday, as he knew now, Egyptian troops had stormed the Zionist defences on the Canal, but had lost and been humiliated. He was Anwar, named in deference to the president whom his father supported. He had been nine when patriots, rich with faith, had killed the Great Pharaoh, Anwar al-Sadat, and later, as a teenager and out on the breakwater beyond the yacht club and alone, he had learned to be shamed by his name. He should have enrolled at the university in 1991, but he had gone from his home in the night with a small bag, and had left no note. He had never, since the night he had gone from his father's house, sought to make contact.

His father, if not dead, would now be in his seventy-sixth year. His mother, if not dead, would be in her seventy-third. He did not know if they lived, if they knew of the life of their youngest child. Nor did he know of the careers taken by his two brothers and his sister, of their aspirations and ambitions. He did not know if the family still occupied the house with the veranda at the front and the wide balcony beyond the bedrooms at the back, whether there was still a yacht club for them to visit and the Semiramis Hotel for them to eat at . . . Did they still buy books at the Al-Ahram shop? Did they, any of them, have love for him? Did they curse him? Was his name ever mentioned in that house?

It was, he accepted it, weakness to hold memories.

In the morning he would take a new name, and the next night or the night after he would travel on. Then he would find the young men and women, whose names, addresses and coded greetings were locked in his mind.

He waited and had never challenged the promise made to him that a man would come.

He worked in a shop selling sportswear and shoes. Each day, from his home in the Manchester suburb of Wythenshawe, he travelled on three buses to get to the Trafford Park retail complex. He was twenty-two and his parents were from the old military city of Peshawar, in the North West Frontier province of Pakistan, but they were now anglicized and his father worked in a local education authority office as a clerk, his mother part-time on the counter of the local library.

318

Both had expressed surprise when at the age of seventeen, he had begun to attend Friday prayers at a mosque close to the city centre, but they had not prevented him. A year and a half later, abruptly, he had abandoned the religious training; then his parents had shown relief. What gave them the greatest pleasure was that their one child had a job with corporate training and a smart outfit to wear at work. It was where he had been told he should find employment, and he had accepted dirt wages and long hours. He had seen, last Christmas and last Easter, the masses pour into Trafford Park to saturation point – more people than had been in the Twin Towers that the martyrs had flown against. A man would come, one day, into the shop or would sit beside him on one of the three buses and say, 'And let not the hatred of others make you avoid justice.' He would answer the man: 'Be just: that is nearer to piety.' The words from the Book, 5:8, were clear in his mind and always with him.

He waited for the man to come and served in the sports shop during the day, and prayed each night in his room that he would be worthy of the trust placed in him.

Malachy felt the train slow, and as the rattle of the wheels died he heard the scream of sea birds. He reached up, unhitched the window blind, let it fly clear, and rubbed condensation off the glass.

He did not know whether he had reached, almost, the end of a journey or the start of one. Could not have said if this was where, almost, an old life ended and for him a new day started. Would not have been able to tell himself if this was the place, almost, that disgrace was finished and where he would now find the searched-for quality of respect.

His face was pressed against the cleared window.

Under the platform lights passengers, dazed from the night journey, coughed, spat and hacked their throats clear, then lugged down suitcases, parcels and rucksacks. The station was Norden. He could smell, distantly, sea air, but by the time the train jolted away and picked up speed, the rain falling from the darkness obscured the glass. When he stretched up and looked down the length of the carriage he saw only emptiness. He was alone. Through the mist now settled on the window, he saw occasional front-porch lights, an illuminated forecourt to a petrol station, a car showroom. Some of the roads were lit like daylight and some were dark – and the gulls cried louder, as if greeting him.

The last stop of the train's route – from Munich, on to Cologne, then to Rotenburg, Bremen, Oldenburg and Emden – was the harbour at Norddeich. It was flat there, exposed, and the wind ripped at flags and came in battering gusts on to the side of the carriage. The isolation, he thought, was precious to him and gave him strength. He stepped down from the carriage.

Ahead of him, tied up, was a ferry. To his left a marina of yachts nestled behind a sea wall, and to his right, crowded close, a fishing fleet. He saw the wind, the rain, hit the ferry's superstructure and rock the masts of the pleasure-craft and the small trawlers.

He walked towards the ferry and the elements almost keeled him over. He braced himself to advance. He found a man in a precariously rocking hut, who smoked an old pipe and had a coffee mug cupped in his hands as if for warmth.

Was this the boat, the ferry, for the island of Baltrum?

The man, bored and cold, shook his head.

Where was the ferry that went to the island?

The man growled, indistinct, 'Nessmersiel,' then sucked at his pipe and billowed smoke.

How could he reach Nessmersiel for the ferry?

He should go by bus.

When and where did the bus go from?

First the man shrugged. Then he took his pipe from his mouth, sipped from his mug and waved back in the direction the train had come.

Malachy thanked the man for his kindness and wished him a good day. In another world, the old one, he would have felt a spurt of anger at the slowness of the extraction of answers ... but the former life of Malachy Kitchen had ebbed. He smiled. He went out through the door where a length of string, holding it open, strained to breaking-point. Where he had been, what had happened to him, had slowed his anger, deadened it.

The wind scurried against his back as he walked past the deserted train, away from the tethered fishing fleet and the rattle of rigging on the yachts in the marina. Rain bit at his shoulders and hips and at the back of his legs. He walked well and the pains, aches and itches were behind him. He was alone, as he would have wanted to be, and his journey was nearly done, or was nearly started.

16

The bus parked beside the gangplank.

The dawn had come, and the rain had eased but not the gale.

The bus for which he had waited nearly two hours had brought Malachy, and three others, along a straight road behind the sea-defence dyke. Then, at the village of Nessmersiel, the bus had swung to the north, and the last stretch of the route had been on a road flanked by neat, darkened homes. The driver had broken clear of the village and brought them to the harbour where a squat ferry waited.

She stood a little step aside from the gangway, and had a packed rucksack high on her shoulders. She had two small stubs, tickets, in her hand and held them out. 'We get two for the price of one,' she said.

'I didn't ask you to come,' he said flatly.

'Our people always like it when field people go cheapskate. I didn't say you asked me. Next week, getting ready for the season, the full fare starts.'

'I don't want you with me.'

'Don't sulk – you look grim enough without that.'

'And I don't want your concern.'

Her eyes sparked. 'Well, I'm here, and you should get used to it.'

Malachy took a ticket from her and went up the gangway. He heard her heavy shoes tramp up after him. The other passengers from the bus, on boarding, bolted from the open deck and went inside a doorway that advertised a cafeteria service. Exhausted obstinacy led him to a part of the open deck where the rain slanted in hard, and the wind. He slumped down on a plastic-coated bench that puddled water. She followed him and tried to wriggle the rucksack off her back. He made no move to help her but then she gasped in frustration and he reached to take the weight of it.

'That's better. Well done. Join the human race.'

'I was fine on my own,' he said.

The rain made a film on her hair but when she twisted her head to face him and dumped the rucksack down, the wind caught and tousled it, broke the film and droplets sparkled. She sat beside him. She wore strong lace-up shoes and a long waxed coat that she hitched round her knees but, out on the deck, her ankles took the rain.

She snatched off her spectacles, blinked, then rummaged in a pocket for a handkerchief and wiped furiously at the lenses. She grinned. 'You display, Malachy, a quite staggering degree of self-importance. I'd like to give that a kick. I'm not with you to watch your back. Get yourself thumped and see if I care. Now, get a load of this: parallel lines run along adjacent to each other – not often, but sometimes, they move together and merge. Then, geometry or what-ever pushes the lines apart again, so that they're no longer joined but are parallel. Pretty simple, eh? Maybe everybody gets a chance to wave goodbye and maybe they don't, but for a few hours, or at most a couple of days, the lines go together, then . . . nothing's permanent. I brought us some kit.'

'What for?'

'Don't go sour again, Malachy. It spoils you.'

The eyes danced and the mouth quivered. He felt the ludicrous-ness of the sulk she'd identified. She dived her hands into the ruck-sack's neck.

She showed him dry socks and clean Union Jack boxer shorts, rolled up all-weather trousers and a rainproof top, a battery razor, a plastic bag with a toothbrush and paste, and a shirt crumpled by the weight on it. She laid them on his lap. As the boat's engine shud-dered beneath them, a man came out, waited for them to find their ticket stubs, punched them and hurried for cover. She showed him, then put back in the rucksack, a miniature radio transmitter with earphones, a Thermos and a collapsible Primus stove, big binoculars and, last, a sleeping-bag that was rolled tightly. She dug deeper, and swore with vigour.

A pistol fell from the sleeping-bag and clattered on the deck planks.

He jerked down, fast reaction – as if the tiredness was gone – and snatched it up while it still rolled by his shoes. 'If you didn't know, they're quite dangerous things.'

'It's not my area, couldn't hit a front door at three yards.'

Astonished, confused but wary. 'Is that for me?'

'Take it. Think of it as insurance. Do you know what it is?'

He held it carefully, his finger way clear of the trigger, then sucked in a breath, looked over his shoulder and saw that the deck was clear. The boat moved away from the quay. As he had been taught, Malachy took out the magazine, cleared the breech, and depressed the safety button, then pressed on the trigger, felt its resistance and heard the click of the harmless mechanism. He gazed at it. At Brigade and Battalion, he had worn a pistol at his webbing belt. On the patrol he had carried, and had lost, an assault rifle. It came at him, the memory of running hunched with the file of soldiers, like a knife thrust.

He said, 'It's a nine-millimetre PMM self-loading pistol, updated from the Makarov, twelve-round magazine, around four hundred and twenty metres per second muzzle velocity. It's—'

'Don't wave it around, just put the bloody thing in your pocket.'

He did. He thought it weighed, in his pocket, two or three times more than the plastic toy he had carried in the Amersham. He gazed at her and she seemed amused. She let the tip of her tongue jut between her teeth, and he thought she brought danger with her.

'What is the need for insurance?'

'Not the place to start. You've done the Secrets Act stuff? Believe in it?'

'I have, I think I do . . . in spite of.'

'Forget the mawkish bit. That's history. We'll start with the convergence of parallel lines. It's not original, did it at university. The right-wing Christian Democrats and the left-wing Italian Communists were edging towards a coalition government – it's nearly forty years ago. Two parallel lines of political opinion, but coming together and ultimately merging. The originator was Aldo Moro, a CD bigwig. Didn't do him much good, because extremists, from the Brigate Rosse, kidnapped and shot him. You and I, Malachy, are parallel lines but for convenience we've linked up.

What I like about you, you don't interrupt. Perhaps you're too bloody cold to bother.'

She told him, sketchily, about a man who had sent his wife a gold chain to mark his love, about a co-ordinator who had been bought time in an apartment under the roofs, about a Czech furniture factory and the link to Timo Rahman who ran organized crime in Hamburg, and she told him about an *idiot* who had broken into the grounds of the home of Timo Rahman and eavesdropped the name of an island – and she said they would, together, observe and possibly disrupt what her boss called a 'rat run' . . . and then she told him that only a serious idiot would sit in the rain in soaked clothes without protection from the wind. He took into the toilets the clothing given him.

When he returned, warmer, drier and with insurance heavy in his pocket, she was leaning against the rail at the back of the ferry, and gulls flew prettily above her. She took the clothes that Ivanhoe Manners had bought for him in a charity shop, long ago, and didn't dump them in the rubbish bin near to her but chucked them up and high, so that for a moment socks, pants and a shirt soared with the birds, then dropped into the ferry's wake.

'At least now,' she said, 'you won't stink. You did, worse than a pheasant hung too long.'

'For your consideration, Miss Wilkins, thank you,' he said evenly.

'Polly'll do . . . Too much formality might screw up the convergence of parallel lines.'

When the mainland had slipped away into the mist, while the shaking boat went slow up a channel marked by dead wood poles, they left the back, went to the side and leaned out. The wind ripped at their hair, and he stood close enough for her to feel the weight of the pistol in his pocket. They saw a sand-bank high above the surf with seals on it, then the island's shoreline.

'Don't think I need you,' he said.

'Believe what you want to.'

Oskar Netzer snarled at the man, his neighbour, 'You'll take it with you. We don't want it here.'

He had opened his front door, pushed it wide enough against the wind's force to slip through it and it had slammed behind him. Across the sagged wire fence that divided their properties, the chemist from the mainland was putting out plastic bags by the little wicket gate at the end of his front garden path; bottle necks peeped from one. Already, with the day hardly started, he had heard the clatter of the pushed mower on the aprons of grass flanking the path and down the side of their house.

The man stood up slowly, as if that made for a more defiant pose, and gazed back at him. Oskar had a canvas bag slung on his shoulder, heavy with the tools he would need for his day's work, but he held his ground and allowed the wind to whip his face. On a point of principle he burned his own rubbish, everything he could, in a brazier at the back, letting the elements take the smoke and scatter the ashes. There was a rubbish collection each week in Westdorf and the disposal of it was a constant burden on the permanent residents and was paid for by their taxes, but Oskar Netzer, self-appointed guardian of Baltrum's purity, was considered too impoverished to pay dues to the island's council.

The woman, the chemist's wife, had come to the door of their house and stared back at Oskar. He saw her annoyance, and also that her husband's chin shook at the effort to suppress his anger. He went down his own path, where weeds grew in the spaces between flagstones, and past his own beds, where more weeds flourished: he would clear those beds only when flowers came up in the summer. Then he would cut them and take them to the cemetery in Ostdorf.

He glanced down at the neatly stacked plastic bags. 'Is that all you do, make rubbish for us to clear? You should take it with you, back where you came from.'

He walked away, almost cheerfully, up the street. He heard only a hiss of breath from the chemist. Should either have sworn at him, if their annoyance had exploded, it would have made perfect the beginning of the day. But Oskar had had enough from them to be almost happy, and he strode off. He would soon be out of the abomination of close-set houses and away in the freedom of the west of the island where his ducks were, and the viewing platform he would repair. It was a relief that the rain had been blown away and he expected to be able to work a full day without interruption and alone.

326

By the time he was at the end of his street, he had forgotten them, and their rubbish.

Billy had the wheel. Harry had the chart spread on the table behind his son's back. Paul, his grandson, clung to a holding rail as if his life depended on it. The trawler crawled forward erratically, and the course set by Harry would take the *Anneliese Royal* away from the east coast of England, out through offshore gas rigs, north of the Bruine Bank. A pencil line on the chart ended south of the German Bight at an island shore. She had a maximum speed of twelve knots, but they did a mere half of that. The horizon swung between white-grey cloud and green-grey sea. It was worse because Harry's course dictated that the waves' swell came from the south-west and battered against the trawler's stern, and the pinnacle of each wave drove them, aft first, into the unyielding mass of the wave ahead. They always said, skippers with experience, that a sea coming against a boat from the stern made for hell on water. The boy had already been sick and some of his vomit had missed the bucket lashed by its handle to the back of the wheel-house.

Harry had had the course, the destination in German waters, from the radio – a frequency on the extreme of the UHF band that was rarely used and therefore was unlikely to be listened to, and Ricky had given him the co-ordinates. 'What I need to know, Harry, when are you going to be there?' He'd yelled back the answer that he didn't effing know. 'That's not co-operation, Harry, that doesn't make my life easy – you going to be there tonight?' He'd heard the distorted whine in the voice, then said he'd be there when he was there, and not an effing hour before or after. He'd smiled then, grimly, to himself and had reflected that if this weather held there would be no German craft, Customs or coastguard, out of harbour and that the sea conditions would obscure the shore radar signature of the *Anneliese Royal*. Small bloody mercy. He'd finished by cutting across Ricky's bleat to tell him that he was switching off the radio and would use it again when he was an hour or two from the rendezvous point. The sea tossed, shook and battered the trawler while his son gripped the wheel, his grandson the rail and Harry held fast to the chart table – and Ricky had said it was all to bring back to England just one man.

*   *   *

327

'So good of you to come, Mr Capel, and at such short notice. All of us on this team, we're very grateful. We sincerely appreciate your co-operation. May I call you Percy? I'd like to.'

He was a gentleman, Percy Capel knew. Hadn't met many, but there'd been enough for him to know one. He would have said that a judge at the Old Bailey was a gentleman, sent him down for five years when it could have been ten with hard labour, and there had been a whisper of a smile on his face as he'd heard the testimony of how Percy had done the entry bit. And, of course, the best gentleman had been Major Anstruther. This one, no doubt about it, was a proper gentleman.

'What we've realized, Percy, is that our records on Albania are quite pathetically thin. Files of stuff about Yugoslavia and Greece, but some very good things were done in Albania and we don't have an adequate picture of them. Time goes on, and if we don't shift ourselves the eyewitnesses, the participants, will be beyond reach. We want to talk to you about Albania and your work alongside the group led by Mehmet Rahman. Would you be up for that, Percy?'

He nodded, muttered that he'd be happy to, then saw the smile of appreciation on the gentleman's face. It had all happened fast. Him still in bed, with a cup of tea, Sharon in her housecoat doing breakfast, Mikey shaving – and the phone had rung. Sharon had screamed up the stairs that the Imperial War Museum was on the phone, and wanted Percy for his experiences – and apologies and apologies and more apologies than he could count for the lack of notice, and the liberty taken of having sent a car for him in the hope that he wasn't too busy. No, Percy Capel had not been too busy. He had been driven by a respectful chauffeur across south-east London and at the museum – beside those damn great naval guns – the gentleman had been waiting for him.

'It's what we try to do, fill holes in knowledge, and nowhere better than from the people who were on the ground. I expect you'd like some coffee, and I think we can rustle up some biscuits.'

The gentleman, all old-world courtesy, wore a three-piece suit and a puffed-out tie that was immaculate at his collar. He had a handkerchief spilling from a breast pocket, and shoes you could have seen your face in. Percy was glad he'd kept the chauffeur waiting those extra minutes while he'd rummaged for a clean white shirt and Sharon had used the stiff brush to get the dandruff off his blazer with the British Legion shield on its breast pocket.

When the coffee was in front of him – 'Two lumps, please' – and he'd had his second biscuit, he started. At his elbow, a tape-recorder turned. He didn't think they wanted crap so he told it like it was – for history and their archives – and scratched in memories that he'd long ago discarded.

He told of the old squadron, Lancasters, and how he'd been volunteered out to the Middle East so had missed the raid four weeks afterwards to Hamburg.

His new unit, flying Halifax B111 MZ971s, went up the Adriatic from the strip outside Alexandria, then turned to starboard and over the Balkans – his had had a girl in a swimsuit on the port side of the nose, with long legs, and she was shouting, 'I'm easy,' in white paint on the camouflage.

The job of the aircraft and crews was to drop agents and weapons into occupied territory.

That night, the weather people said there would be cloud cover to blank out a full moon over the target drop zone, and they'd carried a special-operations major and his sergeant, and a mountain of gear in tin cases, and he'd been in his usual place at the rear gun turret.

Never trust the bloody weather people. Clear moonlight bathed the Halifax on the approach run, not a bloody cloud for love or money, and the flak bursting, and the fire first in port outer, then in star-board inner, and the pilot had ordered them to bail out. He'd followed the gear, the major and his sergeant, but he'd been the last to go clear out through the port-side hatch in the fuselage, and then 'I'm Easy' had corkscrewed and he'd been halfway down on his parachute when she'd gone in. Bloody great bang and bloody great fire.

The major's sergeant had fallen like a stone, poor beggar, because his canopy hadn't opened.

In the days and weeks that followed, Major Anstruther had made him batman, pack-mule, explosives expert, radio-operator and killer.

They had met up with Mehmet Rahman and a gang of thugs and lived in caves. His toes still hurt from the first dose of frostbite, but it wasn't bad enough to stop him helping the major to blow a rail bridge and, later, to sabotage the shaft and winding shed of a chrome mine . . . And there was the ambush of a convoy of the 21st Mountain Corps in a valley up north of Shkodra, and his Sten gun had jammed and, beside him, the major had used up the last of his loaded magazines and thrown the last of his grenades and – if it had not been for Mehmet Rahman – they were both dead meat.

Mehmet Rahman had saved his life, and Major Anstruther's.

'They were good troops, the Mountain Corps, crack guys. Soon as we hit, they came up off the road and at us. We'd put down some of them, all yelling and hollering and shrieking. Then the major had nothing more to chuck at them and my Sten gun's jammed – bloody useless things, always getting blockages. They were all round us, coming after us, close enough to see them – damn soon and it would have been close enough to touch them. Mehmet Rahman came. Didn't have to. He was on his feet and running to us, all exposed, and his God must have watched for him, and there was bullets all round him but he didn't take a scratch. He had covering fire from his guys but he cleared a way through to us – shooting from the hip. The Germans backed off. Must have been chaos for them, the ambush and all, and they went down to what trucks and armoured stuff was still able to move and quit. Probably their priority was to get the convoy through. I reckon that's why they left their wounded, just wasn't the place to do a count. They'd have gone for two or three miles, then realized how many they'd left. We were high up, well gone, but we saw them come back. They didn't need to have bothered because there were no wounded left, only the dead.'

He was telling it like it was, and he'd never told it before. He gulped at the coffee in the bone-china cup, but a biscuit was left half eaten on the plate. The gentleman gazed into his eyes, like he knew what was to come, and the tape turned.

'Up there, we couldn't take prisoners, certainly not wounded prisoners. We couldn't – honest, believe me – do anything for the wounded. Anstruther shouted to me that I was to come away. He tried to get me behind some rocks but – shock, I suppose – I didn't move. Mehmet Rahman went among the wounded. Those that were bad, unconscious, he shot. But he had a knife. The knife was for

330

those who were hit in the legs or the shoulders or had holes in their guts, but their eyes were open. He took the eyes out first, like the knife was taking a stone out of a plumb, then he slit their throats. I still hear the screaming of some of them, those he hadn't reached. Not mercy killing, butchering them for pleasure. He did all of them, till it was all quiet. I caught the major's knee and I pointed to what Mehmet Rahman did, but the major shook his head. The major said, soft, that it was a bad war and that pretending otherwise wouldn't make it a better war. Mehmet Rahman was like a fucking – excuse me, sir – animal because he scooped those men's eyes out and cut off their heads, sawed through their pipes and their neck bones, did it so that the next in line could see what was coming to him, and did it for pleasure. Then he wiped his knife on his shirt, and we went off up the mountain and left the silence. I tell you, I never heard such silence again, not in sixty years.'

There was moisture at his eyes, and Percy Capel prodded a finger behind the lenses of his spectacles and wiped them. He was asked, the gentleman's voice silken and gentle, whether he had ever talked of this.

'What? Down the Legion? Not likely. Been part of a war crime, sir, would you? I never told my Winifred – dead and buried, bless her – nor my boy, nor . . . What's extraordinary, my grandson has met up with the Rahman family. He's in—' He stopped, but he had already launched so he groped for an explanation. 'In import and export. Buys and sells. He met up, just by chance, with Mehmet Rahman's grand-nephew, and that put him in contact – business, you know – with Mehmet Rahman's son, and they'd heard of our family name. Small world . . . My grandson asked me what I knew of Mehmet Rahman. Did I say he was a murdering swine, a bloody animal? I did not. There's truth, some of the truth, a little of the truth – that's what I chose, a little of it. I said that my family and his were joined by blood, that my life was saved by Mehmet Rahman. It's a debt, right? You can't pay off that sort of debt. It's with you all your time on earth, and with your family.'

The gentleman's face showed the vivid expression of not understanding. Percy Capel felt the obligation to explain. 'A debt like that, it owns you. Do you see that? It owns me, and my son, and my

331

grandson. It's as much my grandson's debt as mine. They do business, my grandson and Mehmet Rahman's son, and I suppose that's like paying off the debt – but I doubt my grandson sees it that way . . . Anyway, you don't want to know that.'

The frown on the gentleman's forehead had gone, as if he now understood, and Percy was nudged towards further anecdotal memories.

He talked of more demolition and more sabotage, and of a Lysander that had landed to pick up the major and himself and fly them out, and then the tape was stopped. He was told how valuable his record of events would be to historians at the Imperial War Museum.

The chauffeur drove him back to Bevin Close, and he was almost home before he realized that he had never been told the gentleman's name. He wondered then if he should have talked of Timo Rahman and Ricky, and an unpaid debt.

'Worth it?' the curator asked.

As he pocketed the tape, Frederick Gaunt smiled with warmth. 'I've never done it myself, but I can imagine it. You prise open the two sides of an encrusted oyster shell, and you find inside it a perfectly formed and lustrous pearl. Very much worth it.'

A man from Krakow who hoped to be a policeman had told detectives that his wife, strangled to death, had kept at the start of their relationship a chain of Arabic worry-beads in a drawer in their bedroom, and she had sworn to him that they were the gift of a friend, a student of mechanical engineering at Harburg – the only friend in her life before the Bahn-Wacht officer.

A lecturer at the university had recalled the name of Else Borchardt's boyfriend as Sami, but not his family name.

A child, in the Turkish language and through the help of an interpreter, had told detectives of a man who had hustled into the block after the child had pressed the bell at the outer door and his mother had activated the lock.

A clerk at the warehouse, where past student records were kept, had ferreted that previous evening and found the papers – with the photograph – of that student from seven years before.

A lecturer at the university, called by detectives from his mid-evening dinner-table, had confirmed that the photograph shown him was that of Else Borchardt's student boyfriend.

A child, roused from sleep, was shown four photographs of male students and had chosen with no hesitation the picture of Else Borchardt's boyfriend and had said that that was the man who had pushed by him when his mother had let him into the block.

A subeditor, with the front page of his newspaper about to close, had taken a call on the news desk of the *Hamburger Abendblatt* and had been alerted to receive, from Homicide, the photograph of a suspect.

A journalist had worked at his computer to key in a full-face photograph . . . and the smaller picture of a victim.

A technician had pressed the button that started the print run of the newspaper's altered front page.

A driver had brought the new editions, bound with wire for delivery to wholesale distributors, from the presses of the *Hamburger Abendblatt*, with the suspect's photograph spread across three columns of the front page, and the victim's photograph across one.

By morning, the suspect's photograph blared out at readers from Flensburg in the north, to Bremen in the south, from Lübeck in the east to Emden in the west. Above it 'Wanted for Murder' was printed in bold type, and under it was a picture of a pretty girl who had been strangled in the sight of her baby.

Carrying a plastic bag with four sealed coffee beakers, four cling-wrapped rounds of sausage sandwiches, the nut-flavoured milk-chocolate bar that was Timo Rahman's favourite and a folded newspaper, the Bear left the shop.

He sauntered towards the Mercedes, and opened the newspaper's front page.

It hit him.

He saw the photograph and the headline, and under them was the picture of a girl who had deep eyes and a smile.

It blasted him. But it was one of the Bear's skills that he could hide the shockwave caused by confusion, danger. No flicker of apprehension crossed his face, no twitch of anxiety. He could see them: Timo

333

Rahman in the front passenger seat, and the Arab immediately behind him alongside the mouseboy. The newspaper was ripped by the wind and he rolled it quickly. There was a signal, long agreed, between his master and himself. In one hand he held the newspaper and the plastic bag, and he let the fist of the other drop – apparently casually – to the seam of his trousers, below the pocket. His thumb seemed, idly, to flick his first two fingers. It was the signal that risk was around them. Only a man as cautioned in risk as Timo Rahman would have watched his driver so closely that he noticed the gesture of the thumb brushing against two fingers. The front passenger door opened.

The appearance of the Bear, huge shoulders, shambling walk and a perpetual frown of confusion, was that of a man whose body was an adult's but whose brain was that of a child. The appearance deceived. He saw Timo Rahman duck his head and make some excuse to those in the back seats, then come towards him. He was trusted with every secret of his master's life – not so the accountants, lawyers and investment brokers who surrounded Timo Rahman. Alone, the Bear had the trust.

He had been, at the end of the Hoxha regime nineteen years before, an officer of the Sigurimi, the political police of the Albanian state. Earlier than any he had worked with, he had had the intelligence to comprehend that the death of the old president would mark the start of a changed world. The morning after that death he had slipped away from his office in the town of Shkodra, had taken a bus high into the mountains and gone to the village of the Rahman *fis* and, with humility, had pledged his loyalty. For two years he had been tested as the *fis* had expanded its power in the vacuum left by Hoxha's death – by robbery, tax-collection and enforcement, the Bear had proved his worth. He had gone with Timo Rahman to Hamburg and had fought beside him as the empire was created.

They walked together, master and driver, to the back of the shop.

Out of sight of the men on the back seat of the car, he showed Timo Rahman the front page of the newspaper.

Timo Rahman scoured the page – the headline, the photograph, the picture, the report.

334

The Bear would not speak unless he was asked to, would not advise unless the request were made. He would have said that it was not wise for Timo Rahman, whatever the rewards, to associate with militants, but he had not been asked. He would not have agreed that Alicia, the wife of Timo Rahman, had met a lover in the garden's summer-house – but he had not been asked. He held his silence and waited, and then the paper was crushed in Timo Rahman's hands. He was told where he should drive to, and they walked back to the car. The face of Timo Rahman showed no mark of the crisis.

With the map spread across his knees and silence in the car, the Bear drove off the main road and away from the village shop. They took long, narrow side roads and saw tractors in fields, and cattle that had been released from winter barns. He could not see the sea because his horizon in the north was the long-grassed dyke where sheep grazed. He went on until, ahead of him, there was a tight plantation of pine trees and, to the north, the spire of a church. Level with the plantation a signpost gave the direction to the harbour, three kilometres away, of Nessmersiel. There, the plantation on one side of the road and the signpost on the other, he felt the light pressure of Timo Rahman's finger on his thigh. He braked and pulled on to the grass.

His master was first out of the car, and held the rolled newspaper.

He took the keys from the ignition, and followed, stood a half-pace behind Timo Rahman and towered over him.

The Bear did not know the language spoken, but understood its meaning.

'It is as far as we take you.'

The mouseboy, Ricky Capel, powered down his window and peered from it. 'What you mean? This is the middle of fuck-all.'

'From here you go alone, the two of you.'

The mouseboy's mouth hung open, disbelieving. 'Where the hell are we?'

'You walk to Nessmersiel, you take a small boat to the island – you wait to be collected. It is what you do.'

The mouseboy's face quivered. 'You dumping us – me? Oh, that's bloody good.'

'You go on from here together.'

The mouseboy, Ricky Capel, came out of the car and stood his full height. His chest was up against the Bear's master. 'What's this about?'

'It is about a fool. The fool is "Wanted for Murder". I do not do business with fools.'

The Bear watched and his fists were clenched. He was ready to thrust his own body between the mouse-boy's and his master. The newspaper was unfolded, the photograph was shown. He saw the man, who had no name, lean forward and look past Ricky Capel and study his own photograph. His expression was of sadness, not of surprise.

The mouseboy said, 'Then we're fucked. I don't want no part of that.'

'You should know, Ricky, that it is stupid to make enemies of those more powerful than yourself. The Americans are in love with the expression "You can run but you cannot hide". Take him, or you will make bad enemies. Do not make a bad enemy of me, or of his friends – because I will find you and they will.'

At the back of the Mercedes, Timo Rahman opened the boot. The argument, brief, was finished.

He lifted out the gear that had been checked at the warehouse in Hamburg. He laid on the grass at the side of the road, under the signpost, the case that held the short-wave radio, the heavy, weatherproofed flashlight, two sets of leggings and two heavy coats. Last, he raised the boot's flooring and extracted from it a short-barrelled machine pistol, a magazine and a small plastic pouch of loose ammunition. He gave those to the man with no name, the *fool* who was hunted. From his inside pocket he took a passport and a bulging envelope. The passport was offered to the man, the envelope to the mouseboy. Because he had collected it from the people who had printed it, the Bear knew that the passport was Slovenian and in the name of Milan Draskic – and knew that the envelope, because he had counted the notes, held seventy-five thousand American dollars. Then he went back to the front, took out the plastic bag, pocketed the chocolate, and left them with coffee and the sandwiches.

The mouseboy shook in fury. 'Not that arsehole who's the fool, it's *me*. I'm the bloody idiot for ever coming near you.'

'You can run, Ricky, but you cannot hide. Remember it.'

The Bear went back to the car and when Timo Rahman had settled into his seat, he reversed into the turning for Nessmersiel, and drove away, back where they had come from. For a long time, he could see in his mirror the two men they had abandoned by the road . . . If he had been asked, he would not have left them there because of the danger it might bring, but he had not been asked. At the last, before they were too small for him to recognize their movements, he saw them carry what they had been given into the cover of the plantation.

'Look at him. He's the sort of man we need.'

'We don't need any man – I don't need anyone.'

'That is pig-headed, Malachy, and boring.'

They had walked the length of the island's sea-shore. They had come off the ferry at the harbour on the extreme west point of Baltrum and had gone by the groynes and the packed stonework that made a barrier against the waves' surges. They had passed the knots of homes above the barrier, then struck out along the beach. With the tide far out they had been in a desert of gold-white sand, and grains of it swept across them in stinging clouds.

Polly had wondered if he would play Samaritan and offer to take the rucksack, but he had not. He had kept two paces in front of her and when she had tried to close the distance and be beside him he had lengthened his stride; she thought if she had run then so would he. Far to their left she had heard the rumble of the surf breaking, and to their right she saw the low dunes where the coarse grass was flattened by the wind's blast. The beach sand stretched to the surf and it reached as a thinning finger towards the far length of the island. Out to sea, she had not seen a single ship's silhouette against the horizon where clouds seemed to chase away the clear skies. And there had not been another living soul for distant company. At the tip of the finger, facing another island across a channel, he had turned inland. High on the beach, where the sand was softest, she had struggled under the weight of the rucksack but had kept pace with him.

337

Polly Wilkins had pride and his rejection of her presence wounded her. He had led her on to a path among the dunes and there, in gullies, they had found protection. The wind eased against the rucksack, which seemed lighter on her shoulders.

'I'll do very well without a lecture.'

'That sort of man, he's all eyes and ears.'

In the dunes, her mobile had rung. She had rummaged in pockets for it, found it, held it clamped to her ear. Gaunt. How was she? Where was she? She had shrieked against the wind that she was fine, on Baltrum, and had been told she was lucky to get the best damn holiday-place postings – and that it was about debt. About what? she had howled, louder than a crying seagull that balanced on the wind above her. Half of the call was lost on a fade-out, but she caught enough to hear that Timo Rahman had called in Ricky Capel's debt. The call was cut. They had walked on through the dunes, along a scuffed path, and each few paces she had seen his head swing right, then left, as if he soaked up an understanding of the place and memorized it.

They had dropped down into a dip, then the path bent sharply, and they had seen him – the first life since the harbour and the homes close to the sea defences. An old man was huddled against the wind, and did not have the strength to fight it, but tried to straighten the supports for a viewing platform above a shallow, weedy, stagnant pond. Maybe, she thought, the old man in combat with the wind had the same awkwardness as herself, the same bloody-minded obstinacy as Malachy Kitchen. Without help, she realized, he would fail and the platform would collapse.

'Everyone needs help. I do, you do – he does.'

'It's wrong, involving others. Involve people and they're likely to get hurt.'

'Total rubbish. If you've finished your quest for the Grail then bugger off. I haven't, and I need help.'

She saw the savagery, and heard it. 'And you won't be around after you've involved a man, and he's hurt, won't be around to pick up the pieces.'

'What do you think I've done with you, if it's not involve you?'

'I'll pick up my own pieces.'

The ethos of the Service, which they taught recruits, what was practised in field operations was the supremacy of officers over informants – milk and dump, exploit and quit. But Malachy Kitchen had told her that he was trained in intelligence-gathering, would know first hand what she had been taught and practised. The old man had his shoulder wedged against the right forward support of the pillar . . . Of course she would milk and exploit, dump and quit.

'I'm not out on a stroll, looking to get back my self-respect. My work is life and death and—' She regretted the pomposity.

He said quietly, 'Maybe there's a shop in the village up the other end and you can buy yourself a medal.'

If she had not had the rucksack on her shoulders, Polly Wilkins would have flounced away, but she hadn't that spring in her. She trudged towards the man on a tramped-down track that skirted the pond. There were ducks – heavy white ducks, who didn't seem to know it was about life and death. Her father was enthralled by birds, and her mother made sandwiches for them to take to the Chew and Blagdon reservoirs where they'd sit and watch waterfowl. As a child Polly had been dragged along too and had squinted through her father's telescope. For her sixteenth birthday they had given her a pair of pocket binoculars. There were big military-strength ones in the rucksack but she would not show them.

She moved quietly to the scrub between the track and the pond, made certain she did not disturb the ducks. She reckoned that any man who was not a fanatic or a lunatic would have been behind his front door that afternoon, not heaving, without a hope of success, at a platform's support poles. He would not have heard her against the wind but he must have seen her from the edge of his vision . . . Damn good eyes, a hawk's eyes. He stopped, took his shoulder off the pole.

As she came closer, she could see the gathering malevolence at his mouth and the suspicion in his eyes. She reached him. She saw the scarred, fleshless hands, the face creased with age and distrust, the way his overalls hung on him as if worn on a skeleton. Nothing to say. Her work was 'life and death', and for that innocents were involved. She smiled at him coolly.

339

She swung the rucksack off her shoulders and let it fall, as if it contained nothing of importance.

She went past him. Where his shoulder had been, she put hers. She heaved, gasped, and felt the support straighten two or three inches towards the vertical. She could smell him, the tang of dirt and stale sweat. How bloody long would he stay back and watch? Three inches or four . . . Her feet slipped but she dug them into the mud. There was a grunt, then the old man's body was against Polly's. Five inches or six. They pushed together. Six inches or seven. He was groping in his pocket, then nails filled his mouth, half swallowed between bloodless lips. She thought she might buckle under the weight that knifed her shoulder. The hammer slammed into the nails, taken one at a time from his mouth.

When Malachy came to them and put his weight against the support pole on the left side, she knew his name. She knew his age. She knew the name of his wife. She knew of his love for the eider ducks on the pond.

Dusk came and the platform was secure. Polly had been the leech and had sucked blood. She knew that a paradise was threatened by strangers – that if it was lost, it could never be regained.

'You should go home now, Oskar, get warm and cook yourself something hot. Mal and I will be here tonight, and we'll watch out for strangers.'

The light, through the plantation's trees, failed.

The wind sang above them and the upper branches shook. The man stood easily, then bent and took a sandwich from the bag, unwrapped it, checked its contents and wolfed it. Ricky was propped against a tree trunk and watched the man's movements in shadow. After the sandwich had been eaten, the weapon was secreted in an inner pocket, then the flashlight was thrown to him, without explanation, and he scrabbled to catch it. The man hooked the case with the radio under his arm; his posture said he would wait a moment but no longer.

'So, what are we doing?'

They had not spoken since the Mercedes had been driven away. They had gone into the depth of the trees and had each found a

340

trunk to rest against, backs to each other. Ricky had waited for him to speak, but he had not. Ricky had been reluctant to break the silence between them, as if it would show weakness. They had sat, spine to spine, through the day, had shared the quiet.

The man had an easy voice, clear but accented English, and seemed to mock: 'Does your trawler come here, Ricky, across the fields? Or do we go to your trawler?'

In Ricky Capel's world, disrespect was a crime. The punishment for that crime was handed out by Davey . . . but Davey was not here, and this was not Ricky's world. He had seen the photograph in the newspaper, a younger man but clearly recognizable, and the picture of a woman. But there was an envelope in his pocket, which contained cash, and he had been threatened. He trembled. Sitting against the tree, he had eaten two of the sandwiches left for them, but he was still hungry. What screwed his mind: the man seemed to have no fear, seemed not to care that the Mercedes had gone.

He pushed himself up, felt weak. 'Do you have a name?'

The man looked at him, pondered briefly, then again seemed to laugh at him. 'You follow football?'

'A little.' Ricky blinked, confused. 'Why?'

'In London, yes? What team?'

'My boy goes to Charlton, with his grandad. That's Charlton Athletic, at the Valley. What's that got to do—'

'What is the name of the goalkeeper?'

'He's Republic of Ireland and . . . Dean something. Christ, I can't remember his bloody name.'

'I am a goalkeeper, Ricky. Quite good, not very good . . . To you I shall be Dean. For you, Dean is my name.'

'That's just daft,' Ricky spluttered.

The mocking ended. The man said, 'If you need a name for me, it shall be Dean. What you should understand, Ricky, the less you know of me the better you are protected. I am very serious. The less you learn is the best. We go now to find a way to the island, where your boat will come.'

'Right . . .' Ricky hesitated. He pocketed the bag with the one remaining sandwich. 'Right, Dean.'

341

They left the plantation. The light was a fading smear ahead. The man led, not taking the signposted road to Nessmersiel, but headed out across fields and found a track flattened by a heavy tractor's wheels. The mud clung to Ricky's shoes – lightweight and top of the range – and spattered his trouser hems below the waterproof leggings. Gulls from the fields scattered in front of them, screaming. Once, his feet slithered away under him and he was pitched down on to his backside, but he groped himself upright and followed. The man ahead never broke his stride.

They went round a farm where security lamps were bright and saw a yard of cattle, but dogs barked and they kept clear of the buildings. They went right through a mass of wind turbines, whose great propeller blades churned circles over them, then crossed a field that had been ploughed and sown. Ricky lost his right shoe and had to grope for it in the growing darkness, then had to run to catch his man. He was panting, heaving. He was led over a barbed-wire fence and the goddamn goalkeeper didn't hold the wire down for him, and when his turn came it slashed his hands and ripped the crotch of his leggings. They crossed a tarmacadam road, then another fence, and then they climbed a steep slope of grass. Sheep, barely visible, stampeded away from them. Ricky sobbed for breath. When they reached the top, when the wind's strength slashed at them, the man stopped. He stood erect and gazed out towards a little cluster of lights beyond a black emptiness, short of the horizon's last light. Ricky felt himself shaken by the wind's force.

'That is the island, where we go.'

'Brilliant, Dean. Bloody brilliant,' Ricky gasped. 'And how do we go?'

They went down the slope, slithered and slid, and more sheep ran from them. They climbed another fence and then they were on the shoreline. Away to the left, a mile and a half or more, they saw the fierce, shining lights of a harbour, and out in that part of the empti-ness there were navigation lights, but not in front of them. Too bloody easy to go where the lights were, where a ferry boat sailed from – not a clever place to be for a man with his face plastered all over the front page of a newspaper. There was the stink of the sea, and Ricky's eyes were better now in the darkness than they had been in half-light. He could see white caps in front of them that seemed to ride into little gullies.

'How do we go? We have to find a little boat.'

'What if, Dean, we don't find a little boat?'

'We walk and we swim – but I think we will find a little boat.'

They did.

It was up on grass. It was as small as the boat, twenty years back, that Mikey might have hired for an hour down at Folkestone or Margate – if he'd been out of Wandsworth or Pentonville on a nice summer Sunday – and no way Sharon would have gone in it. The rowing boat was upturned on the grass and a frayed rope tied it to a rotted stump. Ricky thought the man had faith in luck, or faith in God, for thinking he'd find a boat. They had damn near walked into it. When they'd tipped it over, the man took the flash-light, switched it on for a few seconds at a time and ran his hands over the planking as if that way he'd find a hole in it; there were oars too.

They dragged the boat away from the grass and down on to mud. The man pulled it by the rope and Ricky pushed it. The mud clung to him. Next it would be his bloody shoes going down in the mud and bloody lost. He took them off, and his sodden socks, and shoved them into his outer pockets. At each step the mud seemed to pull him back, but he had his shoulder against the wood of the boat; funny, but Ricky Capel, who could strut in any company, found that he needed not to fail, had to show his worth to this man, was not going to be found bloody wanting. For two whole hours, with one rest time of not more than five minutes, they scraped the boat over the mud and then they reached the water. The surf came in spurts up to their knees, then ran back.

When they floated off, when the man dragged on the oars, Ricky lay in the floor of the boat and water sloshed round him. He found, under his back, a saucepan tied with string to the boat's side, and began to use it to ladle out the water. As fast as he did so, the boat filled. The water level crept up – the saucepan could not compete with it. It lapped at the top of his knees and

343

up his hips, but he kept bailing because he could not let the man see him fail.

They grounded across the channel. The moon had come up and he could see the line of a shallow hill in front of them. They stepped out, water up to their thighs, went down in a hole and crawled out.

'Well done, Ricky. That was good.'

He flushed at the praise, and a little of his exhaustion fled.

If she had asked, Malachy would have said, 'Perhaps Timo Rahman'll drop them by the ferry or have them brought over in a fast craft. They'll link up with a boat offshore, use a radio for it. The size of boat that can get across the North Sea would be too large to come in close, so it'll have to launch a dinghy and come right in to the beach, somewhere along the stretch we walked. They can use a radio for the final contact with the boat but they'll have to signal an exact spot for the dinghy, and my guess is that they'd use flashing lights to guide it in. That won't be easy – of course, I'm not a seaman and don't have exact knowledge – because of the surf that the storm's knocking up. I hope to see them when they've put the light on. It'll be when their plan is most vulnerable, but they'll know with the weather that no living soul is going to be out and watching for them, which will give them confidence. I'm not reckoning, where we are, that we can miss the light they'll use, could be tonight or could be tomorrow night – maybe right now they're lying up. We'll see that light. I want to hit them when they think they're on the last leg – they're coming down from the dunes and they're out on the beach without cover . . . I want to screw it up for Ricky Capel. You've your own target and that's your business – mine is with Ricky Capel. I want him out there in the sand and unable to get to his dinghy – for him the whole thing is failure on a mind-blowing scale. It's only a gesture, but it's what I want . . . I want to hear him scream, and then I can walk away.'

She was beside him and her sleeping-bag was already half buried in the sand that the wind pulled off the beach. He could hear the steady rhythm of her breathing. He sat hunched, and his eyes raked the shoreline and the upper points of the dunes as he watched for a light. The same sand that covered her was caking on his chest and shoulders, on his lips, cheeks and around his eyes. He would have liked to listen to his voice telling her that he would hit Ricky Capel, then walk away, but she slept and would not have heard him.

17

He sat on an upper point of the dunes, and the rain was back, and
the pledge made to Malachy was broken.

He watched and she was huddled on her side in the sleeping-bag,
eyes clamped shut, sand carpeting her hair. When the drizzle had
started, he had carefully lifted the bag's neck so that her mouth and
nose were covered; through her misted spectacles he could see that
her eyes stayed closed. The pledge, broken, had been that he would
watch till two in the morning, and then she would take her turn, and
he would sleep. He had not roused her.

He glanced regularly at her, a few seconds in each two or three
minutes, but his focus was on the sea, where a boat would come.
More likely the boat would reach them at night, guided by lights,
but he thought the weather – rain that drove up on to the dunes,
mist, low cloud that shortened the horizon – gave enough cover
for a dinghy to be launched. It was as if the few clustered houses
by the harbour where the ferry docked were detached from the
rest of the wilderness of the island. The voices he heard were those
of gulls that ducked and dived in the wind. The tide was up and
they had fewer acres of sand to feed from, so their hunt for shells
to split open was harder and more frantic. Other sounds were
from the wind's thrust in the dunes, and its singing in the low
branches of the few trees behind him. He thought she would wake
soon because her breathing was less regular than it had been
during the night.

The expanse of the beach was being steadily submerged. The tide
rolled in. In the gloom, sometimes, he saw the light of a buoy, but no
boats came past it.

She woke. Sudden movement. Wriggling in the bag and fighting
to get an arm clear, trying to see a wrist and a watch. Cursing. Head

346

lifted. Spectacles snatched off and wiped crudely on the underside of the bag. Spectacles replaced. Looking around, eyes fastening on him.

'Damn you.'

It amused Malachy to see her annoyance. 'Good morning, Miss Wilkins.'

'You promised.'

'An earthquake wouldn't have woken you.'

Her fingers were in her hair and sand flew clear. She shook her head violently. 'Damn you because you promised to wake me. If you didn't know it, that is insulting.'

He turned his eyes back to the sea. What had he seen? Nothing. What could he now see? Nothing. Why had he not woken her?

'There was nothing worth waking you for.'

'We were supposed to share the watch. You half and me half.'

'I thought you needed the sleep,' he said vaguely.

'That is what's insulting. I need the sleep and you don't? That's a cheap shot.'

He remembered Roz, remembered manufactured arguments, remembered vicious, spiky arguments coming out of a clear blue sky, remembered her ability to rouse a dispute from a half-thought-through remark. He watched the surf where the gulls danced, and saw the buoy's light.

'Right . . . You've seen nothing, so what was so important for you that you could let me sleep?'

'The chance to think.'

'Thinking about today, or thinking about your bloody past?'

Malachy felt himself stiffen, as if there was a catch in his throat. The past, *his*, was never gone from him. Worse at night when he slept, but he would not field that to Polly Wilkins as an excuse for not waking her. Bad in the day because it was the small pain that came and came again. Then he was free of it, then it was back. She would have seen his mouth stiffen. She was close to him and was kicking out of the sleeping-bag. She had a gimlet gaze on him. He did not know whether she'd intended it, but memories flooded his mind.

She said, spat, 'Your problem, you're in denial. You're hiding. My people fed me the stuff. I'm not ignorant, I know what the

347

accusation against you is, Malachy. It's a pretty bloody one ... I don't know of anything that beats it, what you were called. So, what's your answer? It's pathetic: *I don't know what happened*. Being in denial isn't good enough and hiding from it means you'll never clear it. All of this stuff, thrashing around and trying to play hero, won't clear the stigma. You have to face facts, kick some dirt in your own eyes.'

'Have you finished?'

'God – it's just that denial isn't a cure.'

'Can we move on?'

'I'm trying to help.'

'Please, don't.'

Her voice rattled in his ear above the wind and the rumble of the surf. 'Can't you understand anything? Malachy, I'm not looking to humble you – I'm not in the bloody queue that was whacking you. Denial doesn't help you. Just repeating *I don't know what happened* won't lift you. It's shit.'

She sagged back.

'Thank you. I'll do my own suffering,' he said grimly.

Her lips pursed, head down, she started to dig in the rucksack. She found what she searched for. The size of an ironed and folded handkerchief, it was layers of silver baking foil. She said quietly, as if it were important to prove herself, that she was trained and could keep her head down when she squatted and knew about burying the stuff and tinfoil masked smells, and she said she had food. She was on her hands and knees and near to him.

She touched his arm. Her hand was on his wrist.

'I think I've realized it, the truth. You really don't know what happened. Each time you say it, it's honest. You don't know, it's the truth ... I'm batting on – like some bloody shrink – about denial, but you actually don't know what happened. I can see that now. What I'm saying, Malachy, for going on like a pig, I'm sincerely sorry.'

He saw the regret on her face. He took her hand, small and cold, lifted it, brushed his lips against it and dropped it. He watched her crawl away, then disappear down into a gully, go clear of the wind, and resumed his watch on the sea, the waves and the surf. She was, he realized, the first person who believed him – and no other bastard

had. Except her, they had all rushed to judgement, vindictive or
ignorant.

27 April 2004

*He was led by the client from the hallway and into the living room,
and young Kitchen was following him.*

'Oh, that's a fine room, excellent dimensions, right for a family,'
Horace Wield enthused. He owned his high-street business outright,
did not have the clutter of partners. He liked to believe that, as an
estate agent, he provided a better service than the chains that competed
with him. It was all about reputation and building confidence with
clients, whether they were buyers or sellers. This was a seller, and his
first estimate was of an asking price of £449,000, and a bottom limit
if the going was tough of £419,000. 'So much you can do with a room
like this – have a bridge party, friends in for a football game on the
telly, a kids' session, relatives round at Christmas . . . I'm confident
that a house with a room of this size will, absolutely, not hang around,
and it's very nicely decorated. People like that – spend an arm and a
leg on the house and want to enjoy it, not have to rip the wallpaper
straight off. Very tasteful . . . Thinking of going somewhere smaller,
are we?'

They were. Their son was on the move, but they had a daughter up
north and wanted to be closer. A mass of silver-framed photographs
stood on the mantelpiece over the gas fire – small children, the daughter and her husband, and a young man standing proudly in profile,
wearing mess uniform.

'The carpets and curtains look best quality. Do I assume they'll be
staying, available to a buyer? Always good if they can be left . . . Mr
Kitchen will note that.'

Well, he'd taken a chance on that young man, and Horace Wield
had built a flourishing, trusted business on following the instinct of his
nose. When he had advertised in the local free sheet for a trainee assistant agent he had been bombarded by youths with earrings and bulky
women in trouser suits with shoulder pads, and there had been young
Kitchen, who was ten years too old to be a trainee assistant, but had a
bearing about him, and damn fine shined shoes. Had something of
sadness and something remote, distant, a presence and a good voice,

had come out of the army, wanted civilian life. Horace Wield had gone with his nose, and it was a Friday that marked the end of young Kitchen's first week. Of course, the money was rubbish for a man of his age, but he'd drilled the magic word 'prospects' into him – come Monday when he had Rotary, or Tuesday when he had golf, he would seriously consider letting young Kitchen out on his own, if the property was at the market's lower end. Truth was, he liked him, and thought a bit of polish walked with him.

When they reached the kitchen, and when they were taken up the stairs to see three bedrooms and a bathroom with walk-in shower, he had found the same cleansed perfection of the living room and the garden. A door off the hall was opened. This was a different room, an untidy space . . . a shrine.

He waffled, 'Ah, a little place where a chap can shut himself away. I suppose, a bit of a refuge. Sort of room every man should have. You're getting the details, Mr Kitchen?'

Why a shrine? There must have been four more pictures of the son in uniform, but not best dress. Helmeted and in a flak-jacket; unshaven and in fatigues; with an arm round a colleague, crouched in front of a small tank; turning to the camera and grinning and wearing full combat kit with a mosque dome and minaret tower as background – and in every picture a rifle was held in obvious readiness for use. Two of the pictures were held with drawing-pins to the shelves of books, one was on the window-ledge, another was adhesive-taped to the side of the screen. Normally, Horace Wield would not have talked so fully at a first meeting with a client. He did it for the benefit of young Kitchen, to give him a feel for the patter.

'Don't tell me – your boy's out in Iraq. That's a hell-hole.'

The boy was in the Military Police. Had done Kosovo, then been posted to Al-Amara.

'I sympathize. It must be a considerable anxiety to you both having him in that awful country.'

His wife refused to look at pictures of their son in Iraq, which was why they were in his den.

'Very brave young fellows, and a scandalous lack of support for them from too many back home. We should be right behind them. I think every last one of them is a hero – yes, a hero. We ought all to be

350

grateful for their sense of duty and courage . . . Anyway, this is a very
useful space for any member of a family and of any age – don't you
think so, Mr Kitchen?'

He looked round, and the doorway was empty. When they went
into the hall, Horace Wield assumed that his trainee assistant was in
the kitchen and measuring, or in the conservatory, noting details. A
frown twitched at his forehead: against the coatstand was the clip-
board that young Kitchen had carried. A chill draught came through
the front door, which had been left ajar.

Gaunt climbed the stairs.

As a precaution, he had emptied his wallet of all credit cards and
identification documents, and had left only enough money for the
taxi ride to this feral place and a taxi back, assuming the impossible –
that he could find one.

The driver who had brought him from the gates of Vauxhall
Bridge Cross and had dropped him in the heart of the estate had
leered at him as he took the money and said, 'You sure this is where
you want to be, sir? Sorry and all that, but we don't do waits here.'

'Quite sure, thank you.' He had seen youths loitering at a corner
where the graffiti was thick. They had hoods over their heads and
scarves across their faces, and he had seen a man with two German
shepherds, studded collars on short leashes standing impatiently
while they peed in turn on mud beside a pavement. He had lifted his
tie knot, pulled a little more of his handkerchief from the breast
pocket, swung his furled umbrella forward and stepped out for the
block's entrance. He had looked at flat roofs and wondered from
which three youths had been suspended, and at lamp posts and
wondered at which a man had been trussed.

He avoided human excreta on the stairs, and at the second level
he used his umbrella tip to ease a syringe into a corner. He came out
on to the walkway. The taxi driver had said, 'I wouldn't have any of
mine live here. They'd be better off in Bosnia . . . Good luck, sir, and
watch your back.' He went by the doorways with the locked barricades, went past a door behind which a child howled and saw the
number – where the man, Kitchen, with the cross on his shoulder,
had lived. He had spoken half an hour earlier, before leaving the

safety of VBX, to Polly and . . . Another door, another barricade. He rang the bell.

'Mrs Johnson? A very good morning to you, Mrs Johnson. Tony sent me.'

He made tea.

He smelt age and wondered if he, alone in the dotage of his retirement, would smell the same.

He was told in which cupboard he would find the biscuit tin.

He carried in the tray, poured through a strainer and was instructed on how much milk she took. He used old-world charm to relax her, complimented her on the decoration of her home, the choice of pictures and the decent simplicity of her crockery.

He said, as she held her cup and saucer, that his business was Malachy Kitchen, and saw defiance settle on her face. He hurried to assure her that he intended no harm to her former neighbour but had come to learn.

Of course, he had an image of a vigilante: a swollen beer belly and shaven head, a vocabulary of obscenities and a muscular arm chucking broken bricks at the windows of a suspected pervert's home. With reedy determination in her voice, the sparrow-sized woman contradicted the image.

She said, 'No one else ever did what he done. Nobody ever stood up to them the way he did. I thought it was because of me. I was attacked for my bag, I was put in hospital – yes, I'm rid of the sling, but the arm's not right, not yet – and what he did was after that. Not that he told me it was because of what had happened to me, one old lady who is forgotten and's lived too long. There was no boast in him, wasn't trophies he went after . . . I know it was him. When you live too long you get that sense – and there wasn't any one else on the Amersham who'd have done it. I told him to his face that I had not given myself such importance, and I asked him to kiss me, and he did. Then he was gone. I'm alone too much; and alone I think. Cheeky of me, really, to believe it was for me. There was what happened here, and then my friend – that's Dawn – saw something in the paper about the house of a big drug man being burned. The last time Malachy came, when he kissed me, he had scars on him like he'd been beaten. Only after he'd

352

gone did I know it wasn't for me. I had that conceit, but I've ditched it . . . It was about the past. Something hideous happened to him in his past, and I haven't an idea what. His past gave him strength, so much of it, and more guts than any other man on the Amersham . . . Are you going to tell me what he's done now, where he is?'

Gravely, Freddie Gaunt shook his head. He did not think she expected an answer. Her cup was as full as when he had poured it. Pieces had fallen into place; confirmations had been given.

She said, 'Each thing he did was harder than the last. Down at our Pensioners' Association they have gym machines, and there's that gear you walk on and you can make it go faster. You with me? It's like each time he did something he made the machine go quicker . . . You've come to see me, which tells me he's not given up on it, and so I'm thinking he must be running now . . .'

Running rather fast, Gaunt thought, but did not tell her.

'If you ever see him, you give him my love. Give him Millie Johnson's love, please. Don't let it go too fast, that machine.'

He heard a hiss of passion in her voice, but it subsided.

'I get tired. I'm sorry.'

He took the cups, saucers and plates back into the kitchen, returned the biscuits to the tin and washed up – as her one-time neighbour would have – leaving the crockery to dry on the draining-board. When he left, her eyes were closed and she might have been asleep. He closed the front door quietly, pulled the barricade shut and heard the click of its lock.

The boy, his grandson, screamed.

Not letting go of the wheel, Harry Rogers swung his shoulders. The plate arced up and the sandwiches flew towards the ceiling. The kid was pitched sideways and his shoulder cannoned against the rail under the windows. He saw young Paul slide down. God . . . God . . . Only a bloody sandwich that he'd asked for, and the lashed bucket was already well filled with his vomit and his legs had been weak when he'd gone down to the galley to make them. Couldn't have asked his son, not Billy, to make him sandwiches because Billy was below, nursing the engines.

'You all right?' To be heard, even in the confines of the wheel-house, Harry had to shout. The kid moaned back at him. The noises, deafening, were of the engines' race when the bows went down in a trough and the propeller blades were tilted clear of water, and the thud of waves against the hull. When the big gusts hit and tilted them, the boat groaned as if she were either stretched or crushed. 'You all right, young 'un?'

'I'm sorry . . . sorry . . .'

'You got nothing to be sorry for.'

He saw the pain on the kid's face. The face, so pale. If Annie ever knew the conditions out on the North Sea into which he had taken their grandson, she might just lift a kitchen knife against him, or she might pack up and quit. No choice. Had to have the third pair of hands, and no one else he could have trusted. Men enough in harbour who yearned for a good pay-day, who didn't care about weather, but they were not family.

The whimper came through the noise belting him. 'I'm sorry for your sandwiches.'

'You broke anything?'

'I don't think so.'

'Forget the goddamn sandwiches.'

'How long is it? Is it long?'

There was pleading in the kid's eyes. He was seventeen. Back in the old days, sail days, the trawlers like the one he coveted took kids to sea, fourteen and younger, in the same storms and paid them less in a month than they needed to buy a pair of sea boots. Harry Rogers could not tell his grandson that from this sea journey, and from two more years and from the ones already done, a chest of cash was accumulating. The alternative to the chest was gaol – for the kid, for Billy, for him. Harry thought the truth cruel. He shouted back, and tried to put a smile on his face: 'I reckon we're through the worst of it . . . How long? The rest of today and a bit of tonight.'

Then, and he didn't tell the kid, there would be the coming back and maybe more of the same.

The reference to Harry Rogers, brother of Sharon (née Rogers) Capel, had been a note buried in a long-neglected file. He was described, in a report on the extended family of Mikey Capel, as a freelance skipper with a master's ticket for taking out deep-sea trawlers.

Going deeper, digging with the computer bank available to him, Tony Johnson had tapped into back numbers of *Fishing Monthly* and had failed to find a match for Harry Rogers, but had hit gold with the weekly *Fishing News*. There, two paragraphs described the purchase in the Channel Islands of a beam trawler by Rogers, and its renaming as *Anneliese Royal*, and its registration in the Devon port of Dartmouth.

From a phone call to the harbourmaster at Dartmouth, the detective sergeant had learned that the *Anneliese Royal* was never seen in West Country waters. 'Harry lives here, and I can give you his address and number, but he works the North Sea out of the east coast . . . Not in bother, is he? He's a very good guy.' Oh, no, not in any bother – only has the bloody spooks sniffing at his backside.

He had checked with harbourmasters from Immingham to Harwich. Back on his familiar workload, human-trafficking (Vice), he had revelled in the extreme secrecy, imposed by Frederick Gaunt, and had done his checks late in the evening and early that morning before the pace of the National Criminal Intelligence Service had resurfaced. A laconic answer from Lowestoft had lifted him, the last call he made before the open-plan office area filled around him. 'The *Anneliese Royal* was here and now is not. Hold on a second, friend, and I'll give you timings from our log . . . Pretty rotten weather when she sailed, and not much sign of it changing. God knows why they went because there's no way they'll have the nets down. Rather them than me . . . Here we are. I can be quite exact. It's thirty-six hours, and about fifteen minutes, since she went. Don't get me wrong, beam trawlers rarely sink, but it won't be any sort of comfort cruise.' He had waited for the coffee trolley to come round, because that was when people went out on to the front pavement for a smoke.

He left the building and walked fast, didn't use the nearest public telephones. They'd break his legs if they knew that, without sanction and authorization, he was moonlighting for the spooks. Why did he do it, risk himself? Because he had entrapped Malachy Kitchen *and*

355

because Ricky Capel walked top of the shit-heap and believed himself untouchable. Two reasons, each good enough.

With a handkerchief over his mouth, giving muffled disguise, he spoke to a recording machine on the number given him and told what he knew, didn't give his name and rang off. He hoped he had done something to help one man and skewer another.

When he came to the platform in the faint first light, he had seen the mass of scattered feathers.

Anger churned in Oskar Netzer. He stood beside the upright poles, straightened and nailed, of the platform and in the growing brightness he saw the devastation of the killing site. The feathers were spread about an area of mud beside the pond. At the moment of the attack the ducks would have fled but now they had returned and stayed on the far side of the water. The bird had flown off, low and hugging the dunes' shallow contours, the moment he had reached the platform, and it would have carried a last scrap of the duck's breast in its talons.

The killing bird circled high and at a distance.

It would have been aware, with its keen eyesight, of him standing beside the posts. It wanted to feed, to take more of the flesh of its victim . . . Oskar saw the remaining eiders, innocent and without protection, and seemed to hear the voice of his mother as she read the letter that had been left with a lawyer by his uncle, who had driven the lorry from the camp at Neuengamme to the school at Bullenhuser Damm. He saw the killer struggling for stable flight in the wind and he listened as his mother read the story of the children being hoisted up for the ropes to be dropped round their necks. Was it in the blood? Did it run in Oskar Netzer's veins, as it did in the harrier's – an instinct of barbarity? The demons tugged at him. His uncle Rolf had not intervened, had sat in the cab of the lorry as the atrocity was done in the school's cellars . . . He would break a rule of the island's wilderness. He would turn his back on a law of Baltrum's nature park. The harrier was the cock: it fed and savaged for two; the hen would be on the nest, eggs under her warmth. Alone, a little of the madness of old times ravaged him. He strode away.

The anger, and the demons, gripped him.

He knew, to within ten metres, the location of the marsh harriers' nest.

His uncle Rolf had done *nothing* to save the innocents. He would.

He would find the nest in the reeds on the land side of the island, and he would ignore the screaming of the harriers over him and he would stamp his boot down on the carefully woven bowl of fronds – and see no beauty in it – and would break the eggs and see the yolks splatter out of them. He would do it to escape the demons, and to save the eiders.

Tugged at by the wind and spat at by the rain, he was a slight, solitary figure moving among scrub and between the low trees that were crushed and stunted by the weather. He slipped into the reed bed. Beyond its expanse was the sea's inner channel, the Steinplatte, but he would not see the mainland, which was shrouded in mist and cloud. What he found was a track made by men.

Confusion smacked his mind.

The track was not clean, but blundered across the route he took to approach the nest.

He stopped. Who was the greater enemy? The harriers that killed his ducks or strangers who broke the peace of paradise? He turned away from the direction of the nest where a hen bird sat upon eggs, and felt relief swamp him that rules and laws would stay inviolate. He began to follow the track of snapped-down reeds. None of the island's residents, he knew, would have walked through the reed beds and made a track that led towards the heart of the island from the land-side shore of Baltrum.

He walked the track.

He could recognize the prints left by rabbits, different gulls, oyster-catchers, divers and ducks, and it was not hard for Oskar Netzer to follow a trail left clumsily by two men coming in darkness. New purpose came to him, and the image of demons – of children's swinging feet – was killed. He saw the tread of a pair of boots preserved in mud and the smooth sole shapes of street shoes, and he went where they had gone. Old eyes, but sharp, identified the route two men had taken when they had come out of the reed bed and on to the sand of the lower dunes and he saw the flattened grass where they had sat, then two places where they had gone in the night into the scrub thorn. At one a handkerchief had been tugged from a pocket and hung as a marker on the scrub's barbs, and at another he spotted the fibres of a coat. He imagined them cursing, trying to force a way through, twice turning back and searching for a new way. He moved now with greater care, as if he were the harrier, and tested each footstep, as if he were the hunter. The wind sang noisily around him but Oskar's movement was silent. He froze when he heard a long, hacked cough and a man spluttering phlegm from his throat, then went closer.

First he saw the shoes.

They were shoes for a city's pavements. They were sodden wet and mud-stained and had been hung on scrub branches above a small grassed hollow that was sheltered from most of the driven rain. He thought it a futile gesture to try to dry them because the wind did not come into the hollow.

A man slept there. He was on his side, his back to Oskar, hunched, knees drawn up. He thought the man had coughed in his sleep. Beside him was a plastic bag and its neck guttered in the light wind in the hollow. He saw the firearm, a loaded machine pistol, and a metal box . . . On his way home, he had stopped at the cemetery at the edge of Ostdorf, and he had sat by the grave. He had told Gertrud of the young woman who had helped him rebuild the viewing platform, of her kindness, her interest in him and her sweetness – so different from the many who abused and sneered. He saw one of two strangers, and a machine pistol, and his eyes showed him the path taken by the second man, who had the heavy tread of strong boots.

He lost the sense of time.

He would not have known, or cared, whether he followed the boots' tread for an hour or for two hours. He had seen the weapon and moved with considered caution. It did not cross his mind that he should turn on his heel, tramp back to Westdorf and go to the little brick building where the island's policeman lived. He did not have a friend in authority on the island, did not have a friend in the world – except Gertrud. He crossed the dunes, a wraith, and every few paces he would stop, listen, then go forward with his head low and his eyes searching for the tread marks.

If he had not, for a short moment, been upright, Oskar would not have seen him.

The man was briefly visible at the top of the dunes; below him would have been the soft sand that fell away to the beach and the sea. The man bent again, as if to satisfy himself a last time, then – abruptly – began to retrace his steps. On his stomach, Oskar Netzer, nine days short of his seventieth birthday, ducked and crawled into the last of the scrub. A dozen metres from him, seen through a tangle of branches, the man stopped, took a cloth from his pocket, ripped a strip from it, and tied the strip to a branch, as if for a marker. Then he was gone. Oskar saw his face as he passed, sallow and stubble-covered: the face of a stranger who threatened paradise.

When he came out from the cover and gazed back, he saw a second cloth marker knotted to a scrub bush.

He went forward, where the man had been.

At the top of the dune, where it looked over the sand, the beach and the sea, a triangular support had been made from a length of driftwood and two dead but solid branches. The pieces of wood had been driven into the ground and lashed together with string to form a cradle. In it was as large a flashlight as Oskar had ever seen, facing the beach and the surf. He believed he had found a light that would be used after darkness to signal to the sea. He believed that the two men would come in the black of the night, using markers left to guide them, unencumbered by the weight of the light. Why? He had no idea, no interest.

With clinical ferocity, he tore apart the string that held the light in place, kicked in the glass face and the bulb, then used his hands to scoop out a hole in the sand. He dug and dug, then he buried the broken light, and the glass shards, and felt some small pleasure at having safeguarded paradise.

After they had gone, the professor went out on to the veranda and dropped heavily, exhausted from the emotion of the encounter, into his favourite chair of woven rushes. He had been shown the photographs, magnified almost to life-size, of his son, and had been told they were taken from illegal travel documents. He had been asked if he could identify them. He believed that, in their search for

359

information, the political police had visited many scores of homes – any family where a son had shown an early trace of opposition to the regime, then disappeared. He had not been able to hide his recognition and he had seen the boredom of many denials flee the two men's faces; his nostrils had scented their excitement. He had dumbly nodded his agreement. Any father would know a photograph of his son, even when he had not seen or heard of him for a decade. Was he alive? He had not been told. Where was he? A second refusal. What had he done? Their backs to him, they had headed for the door. Now he sat in his chair and thought of his son, Anwar, who was betrayed by his own father. He had heard their car speed away, and knew they would be going fast to the police head-quarters in Alexandria on Sharia Yousef. He wept and thought that his own flesh and blood had destroyed him.

As he shrugged out of his overcoat and hitched his umbrella handle on the hook, Gloria gave him the signal received, via the Cairo station, from Alexandria. He read the name, then said it out loud as if that reinforced its weight: 'Anwar Maghroub ... Well, Mr Maghroub, I think I hear the clink of handcuffs on you.'

Gaunt listened and she played him the tape from the answer-machine, then passed him the transcript she had typed.

'All tightening nicely. Please, what's in my diary this afternoon?'

'You are seeing the nurse, the annual health review, blood pressure, et cetera – I did tell you.'

'Be so kind, cancel it.'

She mimicked horror. 'The AHR is set in granite, about as compulsory as anything gets.'

He grinned, acted sheepish. 'Cancel it, thank you, with abject apologies, and plead an appointment with God.'

He began to smack his console's keys furiously. For fifteen minutes, in a document he entitled 'Rat Run', which was littered with typographical errors, he wrote the report, some material sourced from provenance and some not. He spilled down through the paragraphs: what had been told him by a pensioner widow; the story of an unpaid debt; the heresies of an expert in Islamic studies; the nightmares of a Thames House colleague at Belmarsh magistrates' court; the detail given by a harbourmaster; where Polly Wilkins was, and the hired hand she had recruited . . . After he had finished, Gloria tidied and printed it.

Carrying his report, Gaunt went to heaven by the elevator, briefed the assistant deputy director, and requested that a meeting should be called for early afternoon.

Back in his room, he lowered his blind and shut out that perfect, privileged view of the river. He loosed his laces, kicked off his shoes, swung his heels on to his desk, tilted back his chair – and reflected that a chaotic, confused investigation was now close to satisfaction, cursed himself for presumption – then cat-napped.

'Come on, what have you seen?' She knew he held back but could not fathom why.

She was cold, chilled to her bones by the wind, and the old man kept a distance from her. She had been up on the platform when he had come back. He had not joined her but had squatted down against the pole she had helped to strengthen. She had come down the rickety ladder and had sat beside him, but then he had stood and moved away from her. She had closed the distance between them, and again he had moved.

Had he walked the shoreline? He had nodded, non-committal.

Had he seen anything of interest? He had pointed down to the little patch of spread feathers, then pointed up and away into the distance, and she had identified the harrier above a reed bed.

Had he watched people out in the wilderness? He had shrugged, as if the movement of people was of no matter to him. Had he noted the presence of strangers on this part of the island? He had snorted, then looked away.

She shivered, and the motion made the words in her throat croak.

'I think, Oskar, that tonight my business in your paradise will be finished. After it is finished, I will never return . . . I am here to find strangers who have come to Baltrum . . . Oskar, I need your help in finding them.' She spoke softly, tried to find gentleness. 'Please, if you have seen strangers, where was it?'

But he showed her his back and gazed down on the ducks. She had heard of, but never met before this week, men who lived their lives as hermits, cocooned in isolation. They found a refuge beyond the need of others. She reflected. This man, living with the stink of old sweat and old dirt and old damp, ran from reality – as did Malachy Kitchen. God save her – two recluses, the one trapped on this nowhere island, and the other trapped on an inner-city sink estate. Just her bloody luck to get two of them, and need them, in a single week. She sought to honey her voice.

'Oskar, you are running. You can tell me – what from?'

He faced her, and smiled at her, as if he believed himself sane and her an idiot, and he said, 'I run from the sight of the dancing bare feet of children.'

As he walked away, he took a piece of bread from his pocket and she saw the green of mould on it. He gestured with his hand that she should not follow him and he went down the slope below the viewing platform. He was breaking the bread and throwing it forward towards the cluster of ducks. Bloody mad – or worse? *The dancing, bare feet of children* . . . What did that add up to? A paedophile? *The dancing, bare feet of children.* A man who hung around playgrounds in a city, with a bag of sweets in a pocket? She saw, damn right, a reason for running, as great a reason as hiding in a sink estate from cowardice.

Her temper snapped. She had played gentle and it had taken her to bloody nowhere.

In her fluent and best German, she barked against the wind: 'You hide, then, see if it matters to me – or bloody keep running and see if I'm bothered. Not that it would interest you, with your *problem*, but I am attempting to save lives. That's the lives of ordinary, totally innocent people, but you wouldn't care, would you? So bloody absorbed in your own foul little world, voyeuring kids . . . Watching *the dancing, bare feet of children* and, no doubt, imagining what's under their skirts and shorts. You make me, with your selfishness, sick. Hear me? Sick . . .'

He did not turn. At her attack, his shoulders seemed to crumple.

His voice was frail, uncertain: 'My uncle drove a lorry from the KZ at Neuengamme that took children to a school's cellar. Medical experiments had been performed on them and they were killed so they could not testify against the doctors. The feet that danced were

362

those of the children who were hanged in the cellar of the school . . . Leave me alone. Go away.'

She rocked, reeled.

She had nothing to say.

The cold engulfed her. She went, dismissed, and shame blistered her.

He had heard the sluicing of the water and the screams.

Now Timo Rahman heard the whimpers of his wife and the stamp down the stairs of Alicia's aunt. It could not have been otherwise.

The last night he had slept in the guest room, which was never used because no guests were invited to stay at their home. The Bear had driven the girls to school and they had gone, sullen and frightened, aware of but not understanding the crisis afflicting their parents. They would never challenge their father and neither had dared to ask why their mother was locked, a prisoner, in her bedroom.

He sat in the living room, his head and body statue still, the coat with the Harris tweed label clutched in his fists on his lap, and he waited for her aunt to come off the stairs and cross the hall, which he could see.

The Bear, who loved Alicia to the point of devotion, was in the garden and away from sight through the window. He raked leaves and perhaps wept – but it could not have been otherwise.

In the village, in the mountains where Timo Rahman had been raised, she would have been beaten to death at his own hand, then buried in a shallow, unmarked grave, and would never again have been spoken of.

Her aunt passed the door. She did not stop to show her long arms and the skin on them wet from the bath, soiled with blood. She did not hold up the brush of steel bristles that had last been used by the Bear to scrape rust from an old bucket. She went by the door, but he had seen the blood and the brush.

He knew that his wife had met a man in the summer-house of their garden – knew it because Ricky Capel would not have dared to lie to him and had denied the man was at the house

363

because of him – and knew that, for her betrayal of him, she was now cleaned.

He could hear each sound she made through the bedroom's locked door and down the stairs and across the hall and into the living room – and knew her body was now cleaned by a brush of steel bristles, the dirt scoured away so that the skin bled. It could not have been otherwise.

The man, Dean – or whatever he was supposed to call him – cleaned the gun.

Ricky said, 'I'm alive ... Why am I alive? ... Because I lied. I lied to Timo Rahman. If I hadn't lied, I'd be dead. He'd have strangled me or broken my head open with a hammer, if I hadn't lied. For giving him the truth, he wouldn't have shot me because that would be too quick and he'd have wanted to hurt me.'

His body shook in spasms and he watched as each part of the weapon was laid out on a coat and meticulously wiped. He rambled.

'A man came after me where I live – I don't know who he is and I don't know what his problem is. A guy I do business with, his home was burned down with petrol. This man came to where I live and his coat stunk of petrol – the coat was distinctive, sort you see once and not again, but you don't forget it from the once ... and I'm at Rahman's. All bloody hell breaks out, alarms and things, and there's a man legging it over the fence at the back of the garden, but his coat catches on the wire, and they'd have had him if he hadn't slipped off the coat. The coat came in the house, brought in by that bloody gorilla, and it was the same coat and it had the same stink, petrol. He asked me straight, Rahman, did I know the coat? Basically, what he's asking me, was a man in his garden because of me? Simple question. I lied, said I didn't know nothing about it. I'd have been dead if I hadn't lied. I'm thinking now – the man whose coat was lost, Rahman'll believe he'd come to meet his wife. Poor cow, but not my problem. You look after yourself, in this world, first and second and third.'

The cold ached in every joint of his body but he had lost feeling in his feet however hard he rubbed them. He did not hear his own voice.

'What's just amazing, he swallowed it. I hadn't the lie off my lips before I'd reckoned it out. Nobody lies to him, don't dare to. Get caught in a lie to him and he'd take a week to kill you. Sort of making a judgement, isn't it? Get killed in an hour or two for telling the truth . . . get killed in a week because you lied and got caught out – matter of judgement. I'm telling you because I like you, because I trust you.'

The weapon was reassembled. Ricky could not have stripped it, cleaned it, put back the parts.

'We get on that boat, get across the water, and we drop you off, then you're gone. It's like you never existed. My secret and your secret, carried to your grave and mine. I don't hear of you ever again and you don't ever meet up with me. What you do, I thought it was my concern, thought it mattered to me. Isn't – doesn't. I'm telling you, honest, when I realized what you did then I told Rahman I wasn't taking you and he twisted my bloody arm, like it was right out the socket . . . Then he showed you the picture of that girl, bawled you out for what you done to her. Me, I don't have an opinion, not any more. You see, Dean, we're friends – I like you – friends with trust. That's good, us as friends.'

The weapon was loaded, cocked and laid down. Hands slipped to Ricky's feet, peeled off the socks, squeezed the last moisture from them and started to massage his skin, the soles and the insteps, and he felt the first flicker of heat. There was wet at his eyes.

'Brilliant, Dean. That's just bloody brilliant.'

'What have I done? Something brutal. What are the consequences of it? Nothing. What am I saying, Malachy? I'm saying this bloody awful place has brought out the bitch in me.'

He lifted his arm, swung it, hooked it round her shoulder. In front of them was the beach and the surf and the horizon where the sea met the clouds.

'Don't think, Malachy, that anyone from my crowd will ever thank you. They don't do that. All except one, they're as awful as here is. I'm saying that you have to stand tall for yourself. Got me?'

She wriggled. She worked her body closer to his and he tightened his grip on her shoulder. Her hair was against his chin.

'It's what you deserve, to stand tall – whatever it was that happened. You get to a time when you've paid your dues, owe nobody anything.'

He felt the warmth of her.

'I want to be there and I want to see it – you standing tall, Malachy.'

18

The tide had turned to reveal the wide depth of the beach, and the gulls wheeled while searching for washed-up crabs and shells.

And they ate.

From the rucksack she had taken a tin of chicken in white sauce, another of rice, and one of peach slices in syrup. They passed the tins between them and scooped with their fingers at the meat, the rice and the peaches, licked the sauce and syrup off themselves. Malachy felt the sand grains clog in his throat as he swallowed, and once she coughed hard and spat to clear her mouth. At the bottom of the bag, there was a small, collapsed burner and tablets in a sachet for lighting under it, and a rack the size of a palm for fastening over it, but the wind was too great and the rain too hard for them to try to heat the chicken or the rice – and the smell would have carried on the wind, with smoke that was a signature.

He made a rhythm for himself. With the binoculars he watched the skyline, where the white caps met the cloud, tracked the lenses over the dunes to the west and to the east, followed the flight of the ducks when they dived to feed, then back to the horizon, the roll of the waves and the clouds' chase. Each time he saw her, lingered on her, he thought she took longer to lick her fingers and nails, then her palm. Her face was pale and her lips; sand crusted her cheeks and settled on her glasses. All of her animation was in her tongue, working meat scraps, fruit, rice, sauce and syrup from her hand, licking and suck-ing. She sat with her shoulder pressed against his. When he lifted the binoculars, his elbow lurched against her arm. When he dropped them on their neck strap and reached to scoop from the tins, his elbow pressed against her chest and softness beneath the weather-proof coat, but he kept to the rhythm he had constructed and watched the sea, the beach and the dunes.

The tins were emptied.

She had her boots and the over-trousers inside the zipped-down sleeping-bag and he felt, through his elbow, the shiver of her body.

Through the lenses he saw the break of the waves far out and the spray leaping above the surf, but no darker shadow of a boat coming towards land. The gulls, in soft focus, were distorted, closer to him.

She shook in little convulsions. Malachy had reason to be there, huddled in soft sand and with bent grass stems around him, all that survived in the dunes. He had a purpose and she did not – should not have been there. Hunger took him back to the tin that had contained meat and sauce. For the last traces of it, his elbow against her chest, he pressed his forefinger, grimy and coated with sand, down into the tin and scraped its sides, his nail against the bottom. The skin caught the top edge, serrated with tiny teeth from the ripping out of the lid. Blood ran. No pain, but blood from a small wound spilled on to the can's base. She took his hand in hers, lifted it.

She gazed at him. Tiredness swelled the rims of her eyes at the limits of the frames of her spectacles, and hair, damp, limp, fell over them, but the eyes had brightness and light. Blood came from his cut and smeared her hand. Not looking away from him, not breaking her gaze, she slipped his finger between her lips and closed round it.

He felt her suck, swallow, and her tongue moved on the wound.

There was, at first, sweetness, gentleness – then the tongue brushed his finger with more force and the lips held it tighter.

She said, muffled, because her mouth held his finger and her tongue took the blood from it and closed the wound, 'I can't think of anything to talk about.'

The warmth from his finger ran in his hand.

'We could, if you wanted to, talk about the weather,' she said. 'Is it going to rain much longer? I think it's getting brighter in the west, don't you? The wind's not dropping, is it? Do you want to talk about the weather?'

Her tongue licked his finger and she swallowed his blood.

'If you won't talk about the weather, you could talk about damn hypothermia – or you could do something about it.'

With her free hand she pulled down a little more of the bag's zipper, but she held his finger in her mouth, and she wriggled to the

368

side. He slipped into the bag, pushed into it the old brogue shoes and felt them run against her legs, then against the bag's bottom stitching and heaved his weight against her.

She grimaced. 'I've never done it like this before – get sand in me and I'll kill you.'

She reached behind him and dragged up as much of the zip as she could, and they were pressed together. He felt the hardness of the pistol barrel gouge at his skin and the angles of the binoculars; he took his finger from her mouth and kissed her. He held her head, and her eyes did not close – as if the moment were too vital to go unseen – and his lips found hers and he tasted her breath and his own blood. He remembered what she had said to him, on a bench in a park of spring flowers: *Do it like you mean it . . . Don't get any bloody ideas*. He had done as he was told. It had not entered his mind that she had kissed him, under the blossom and watched by the search party, from affection. She squirmed in the bag.

'God, aren't you going to help? Do I have to do it all?'

There were zips and eyelets, buttons, belts and hooks, and they writhed together to free themselves. He did not think it was love . . . but need.

'I don't have one, don't suppose you do – not to worry, not that time of the month. I can feel that bloody sand.'

The need was bred on emptiness, Malachy recognized it. The void of his life and a corresponding chasm in hers. Each of them with an unspoken loneliness burdening them. He felt her skin, its coldness, had his hands under her waterproof coat, her sweater and blouse, and his fingers moved with wonderment, as if privilege was given him, and she caught the hand where the wound had been and forced it lower. Their loneliness made it desperate. He heard the zipper of the bag torn open as he came across her. They clung to each other, and she stroked him and he buried himself in her, and then the motion calmed. She moaned. She bucked under him. It was as he had never known it before. She cried out, piercing, as the gulls did over them and he felt the ecstasy of it . . . It was for need, hers and his, and they fell apart. She had said: *Do it like you mean it*. He had, and he cradled her head. He thought it took them nowhere.

369

He crawled out of the bag. She swivelled on to her side and her back was to him. He did up the zips and buttons, reefed in his belt. He did not know of any future, only that emptiness must be filled. He lifted the binoculars, scanned and tracked.

'What can you see?'

He said, 'Only the waves and the clouds and the birds – but they'll come, I know it . . . Thank you.'

'Crazy, isn't it? You being my friend, me not being your enemy. Mad, isn't it? If you saw me where you come from, whatever place it is, I'd be your enemy – and if you'd just pitched up in Bevin Close I wouldn't be your friend. But we're here.'

The voice dripped in his ear.

'Your thing is killing people . . . What's mine? I'm not bloody proud – I do heroin from Afghanistan, and cocaine from Venezuela . . . Dean, have you been in Afghanistan? Sorry, sorry, not for me to ask. Forget that. We're friends and we don't ask, don't need to know. I often wonder what Afghanistan's like. It comes on the TV but that shows you nothing, just ruins and old tanks and kids without shoes and women who cover themselves. I tell you, straight up, I've made big money out of Afghanistan, five times the money I make out of Venezuela. I'm not hating you because you kill people, and you're not judging me for what I do.'

The voice rambled, incoherent. He let him talk. He understood most of what Ricky Capel said, and he tolerated it. He took help where he could find it, and when the usefulness of the help was finished he discarded it. He had put the fool's socks against the skin of his crotch and let them dry out against his body warmth, and then he had peeled them on to the feet he had massaged, then put the shoes back on the idiot's feet, pulled the laces tight and knotted them for him. It was critical to him to have the imbecile's help.

The voice droned.

He remembered Iyad, the true friend, who had given up his life that time could be bought, a proven fighter who never bragged. On their journey there had been long hours between them of valued silence.

'You must be thinking, Dean – natural you would – can Ricky

370

Capel keep his mouth shut? You have no worries. Back home, we got police and they don't get a sniff on me. Up where I am, and I reckon I'm big enough, we have the spies that are supposed to go after high-value targets – they got bugs and tracker sensors and cameras so bloody small you can't see them. What they haven't got is me. Why? Because I'm sharper than them. They've never had me . . . Never been charged. All of that lot queuing up, after me because I'm a high-value target, and they haven't ever been able to lay a charge against me. I was in once, three years back, and was held for forty-eight hours, and a good half of that was in the interview room. I never said nothing. Four sessions, maybe six hours each. I took an eyeline on the floor and one on the ceiling, one on the table, one on the door. I said nothing, never spoke, but had a different eyeline each time. You should have seen them, Dean, and they were going fucking spare, believe it . . . You can rely on it, I don't talk, and I don't reckon you would – it's why we're friends, can depend on each other.'

In his mind, irritated by the voice, he recalled code-names given him and addresses too sensitive to be written down, and the words of the Book that he would use and the responses that would be made.

'You want to know anything, Dean, about sensors and bugs, cameras and audio, or phones – me, I never use them – then I'm your man to ask. I got a guy, clever little sod, and I pay him well, and he's ahead of their game – better than the spies. I know everything they put against me and how to block it. Didn't have an education but I'm not stupid – you've seen that. I aim to stay safe and anyone who's my friend will stay safe. It's why we've got the boat coming. An old trawler flogging around the fishing banks and putting in to port often enough for it to be familiar, clever that. You're all right with me.'

He thought of the places he had been – while the voice nagged at him – and of the young men and the young woman, all martyrs, whom he had sent out on the road to Paradise, and their cheerfulness to him and their gratitude that they were chosen, and he had been long gone from Taba, Cairo and Riyadh when their pictures were put in newspapers with the images of what they had done.

'What I like about you, Dean, is that you show respect for me. And I'm telling you, it's two-way. I don't mean respect because I'm a big man. Most who give me respect back home, it's because they're frightened of me. Men I do business with, most of them, they give me respect because of fear. I'm not afraid of you, you're not afraid of me, but there's respect because we're equals and friends. Right now, when I get back there's a matter of respect – it's disrespect – to be sorted. That old bastard, Rahman, he didn't give me it, and he has a nephew, a flash little prick, and he's ready for a lesson in respect. Off the boat and I'll be working on it . . . I got my cousins, I got people who watch my back, and will watch it when I sort out disrespect . . .'

He suggested, softly and soothing, that it might be the right time to make the radio link with the boat, and reached out, took a cold hand and squeezed it in reassurance – because he was the equal of Ricky Capel, his friend – and felt no guilt at the deceit.

'If you didn't know it, the weather out here is foul,' Harry shouted at the microphone. The trawler shook, then cascaded into the trough. Walls of water climbed higher than the wheel-house windows, then hit a solid, ungiving mass, and the *Anneliese Royal* seemed to stop. 'About as foul as I've known it.'

For a moment she was dead in the sea and lurched to port. He clung, white-knuckled hands, to the wheel, and for endless seconds she seemed to go over, then the stabilizers dragged her upright. But at the limit of the trough a wave made a cliff face and she collided with it. He heard the boy, his grandson, cry out behind him in stark fear. Now Harry saw nothing beyond the windows as sheets of spray covered them, and rivers of the damn stuff would be sluicing on to the decks, weighing her down, and he could hear the roar of the weather and the engine's howl, and the distorted voice of Ricky Capel, and the questions coming more frantic . . . When was he going to be there? What time? Why so long? A rogue wave could come as one in ten or one in a hundred. A rogue wave could not be ridden by a trawler.

They went on through it and the wheel-house seemed to go dark, seemed as though night came, of blackened blue and green. Then they burst clear. Light where there had been darkness and the *Anneliese Royal* steadied and Harry knew he would not be pitched

372

over on to the wheel-house plank floor. He loosened his hold on the wheel, and the sweat spilled down the nape of his neck and on his throat. He looked behind him, and the boy hung in misery from the rail round the wheel-house's sides, and the door to the deck had come unfastened in the impact and hammered backwards and forwards. The sea came in and cleaned some of the boy's sickness. Harry tried to smile, to find confidence for the boy, took a hand off the wheel and gestured that his grandson should get the door closed. Maybe it would be the last time he went out of harbour for Ricky Capel, maybe . . . He depressed the switch.

'Don't know where you are, Ricky. Where I am it's force ten and gusting up to force eleven and sometimes it's cyclonic . . . Right, when are we getting there? I'm reckoning to be in the approach channel for German Bight and turning into Jade Approach at approximately twenty hundred hours local, and that'll put me off shore around twenty-two thirty – if the old girl's still holding together. It'll be a dinghy pickup, which'll be no picnic. I don't want any more radio traffic before twenty-one hundred, don't want the world to know, and I'll want a light signal from twenty-two thirty for the dinghy . . . Oh, Ricky, I'll have the guest suite ready . . . and, Ricky, I won't be hanging about, so you'll need to paddle out quick for the pickup – like I said, no picnic. Over. Out.'

'Give it to the Germans? Good God, no . . . absolutely not.'

The meeting was chaired by the assistant deputy director, Gilbert.

'Let the Germans in on the act – I can promise you – and it will be pain and tears.'

He presided at the end of the table in a room set aside for conferences on the ground floor.

'If the bloody Germans are involved, their lawyers will demand access to every slip of paper, intelligence material, that we have. No way, not to be considered.'

Sandwiches, coffee, nibbles and jugs of fruit juice were at the side, and plates, cups and glasses had been brought to the table.

'We all know the German style. It's endless court cases, appeals that'll go into the next century, and weak-kneed determination to see it through. Forget them.'

373

Behind the assistant deputy director, sitting on six straight-backed chairs, was a line of stenographers. Each was there to write up the contribution of their own man, and later it would be polished in that man's interests.

'Scrub the Germans out of it, and let us do our own thing.'

Present, four on one side of the table and facing Freddie Gaunt, were Dennis from the Security Service; Trevor of Special Branch in the Metropolitan Police; Jimmy, who was senior in the Norfolk Constabulary and would also watch over the Suffolk brief, and Bill, who did liaison between Special Forces at Hereford and Poole with Vauxhall Bridge Cross. All of them, on arrival, had chimed complaints about the short notice given them, and all had let it be known with force that they expected the inconvenience to be softened by a matter of genuine importance.

The meeting had started tetchily. The assistant deputy director had sketched through a picture of a co-ordinator, who was believed to be travelling to the United Kingdom, only *believed*, and was now probably, only *probably*, on the German island of Baltrum on the Frisian coast. The ADD had then asked: Should the German agencies be informed? Should their help be sought?

'I think I have the general drift of opinion,' Gilbert said. 'I think you have all made clear a lack of enthusiasm for that course. Any final thoughts before we close on it?'

Dennis, of the Security Service and irritable because he had walked over the bridge from Thames House, been caught in a shower and had sodden trouser ankles, said, 'They'd flood the target area with goons, pick up this man who is *probably* there and *believed* to be significant and any chance of control is lost to us. Look at the last two cases to go through their courts, in Hamburg and Mainz – enough said.'

'Yes, yes . . . I'd like Freddie, now, to tell us what he knows. The ball's in your court, Freddie.'

It would be, of course, a turf war. Each of them, opposite him, would fight a corner for primacy. He started with the story of a war being fought in distant mountains in a distant time. He saw a pencil twisting, a demonstration of impatience, in Dennis's hands.

'Please, could we have something of today, not of times before I was born?'

He spoke of Ricky Capel, drugs importer from south-east London, and of alliances that facilitated the movement of class-A narcotics into Britain, and saw boredom on the face of Trevor, the fidgeting at his cufflinks.

'I hardly think, Freddie, that we have been dragged round here for a lecture on how cocaine and heroin end up on our streets. We're supposed to be flushing out al-Qaeda operatives, not mincing round the drugs problems.'

He talked of a trawler that was, in foul weather, *somewhere* out in the North Sea, and said that he thought it would be used for a rat run across the water and back to British shores, and saw the first light of interest settle in the eyes of the Norfolk policeman, as if everything said before had been dross.

'Well, there's your answer. Seems simple enough to me, Freddie. I've excellently trained firearms officers ready to be deployed, and so have Suffolk. We're not yokels out there. We have experience, we've done the exercises. We follow the trawler, radar and all that, back over the North Sea, and we have my people – and Suffolk's – on standby along the coast. Soon as they're ashore we've got them. Open-and-shut business. Not that we need it, but do you have any more for us?'

He said that the trawler did not have a regular home port, and he could not promise where it would come into harbour, and the Special Forces liaison, Bill, seemed alerted to the opportunity. All of the others round the table wore suits, but this man had obviously reckoned his different status should be recognized by his faded cord trousers and heavy cable-knit sweater.

'With the greatest respect to our country cousins, I don't think this is up the street of Norfolk and Suffolk. This is a job for us. I'm putting my weight behind a joint team, Hereford and Poole – which keeps both of them happy – and taken to sea tonight in a coastguard cutter, or anything that's got the legs on a trawler, and an interception in international waters. It's the sort of operation that should be left to professionals, and that's us. We're discreet and dynamic . . . It's for Special Forces, my people. I really don't think there's room for debate.'

He described the island. He talked of Polly Wilkins, out on the dunes, who would give a warning when the trawler came inshore.

With some pride, Gaunt spoke of the achievement of this young woman, on her first overseas posting, and of the doors she had prised open since a fire and a death in Prague. He saw overplayed incredulity snap at Dennis's face.

'Am I hearing you right, Freddie? Are you telling us that you have, on the ground, in a situation of this importance, a rookie? A slip of a girl just off your induction course? Is that it? I'll say it to your face, Freddie, if this all goes sour, and it's down to your young woman's failure, I would not imagine – as far as government service goes – your feet'll touch the ground. You'll be out on your arse, Freddie, and damn well rightly so. It is, and I'm sorry to say it, a cavalier road you're following. Not that it's for me to criticize the actions, procedures and operational decisions of a sister organization but I reckon it hard to credit that we're going to be dependent on the skills of one young woman, a rookie, a raw recruit.'

He ploughed on, led with his chin. He had learned well, at the break-up of his old unit, that when dogs circled him he could expect no help from his own, no protection from the assistant deputy director. He anticipated the sneers and inevitable derision. But, without enthusiasm, he described Polly Wilkins's companion on the island, and his past, the information he had provided. When he drew breath a babble broke round him – after the quiet and the shock.

'Are you levelling with us? You've dragged in a bloody vagrant for back-up?'

'Am I getting this correctly? A man who is disgraced with the stain of cowardice in the field has been taken on to your pay-roll?'

'Are you short of bodies, or just a sense of priorities? What's going on here, Freddie?'

He shuffled together his papers. Everything except the photograph of Anwar Maghroub went back into his briefcase. The case was his pride and gave him the small sense of belonging to the Service, little enough of it. It had been bought for him by his wife on his first birthday after their marriage. A technician down in the basement of a former building had, for cash in hand, put the gold stamp of *EIIR* on the case's flap – worn and faded now, the edges were curled from use. He felt old, tired and useless, and each barb of their contempt had hurt a little more than the last . . . but the worse hurt was that he had not defended with resolve the efforts of Polly Wilkins and the man with her on the far-away dunes. He said, with a trifle of dignity, that he did not think he could be of further help.

'Well, that's it, then. Most grateful to you, Freddie,' the assistant deputy director intoned. 'I'm sure that the comments of colleagues were in no way meant as personal, not as reflections on your very satisfactory summary of where we are ... That's the past. Our concern now is where we should be in the future, the next few hours.'

He hardly listened. Gaunt could have written the script.

'We are the providers and you, gentlemen, are the customers, and I think – bar some small blemishes – we have provided well. It seems to me that the point at issue is whether to intercept at sea—'

'It should be at sea,' Bill, the liaison man, said. 'At sea is where my people have expertise.'

'—or whether we should go for the land option.'

'So much tidier if it's us doing it,' Jimmy, the assistant chief constable, said. 'On land and done by us or Suffolk.'

Dennis was asked, did he have a dog in this fight? He shrugged. 'Doesn't matter to us, we'd be easy with land or sea.'

Watching his Almighty, who had descended from an upper-floor firmament, Gaunt saw the lips purse and the forehead of the assistant deputy director furrow. He could predict the judgement, as if from Solomon's seat. Divide the baby, chop the little beggar in half and then there would be two parts to the corpse. Special Forces to shadow the trawler and watch for a drop-off short of the coast, with constant readiness for intervention *and* a cordon of guns from the Suffolk and Norfolk forces to be on the quayside at whatever port on the East Anglian mainland the trawler docked. It was theatre but it would be compromise. The Almighty, or Solomon, held his hands together in front of his mouth and pondered, the prayer gesture, and took the deep breath. Gaunt knew what he would say, could almost recite it.

'I believe a median solution will see us where we all want to be. I suggest that—'

'Excuse me.'

Gaunt flashed a glance at the source of the interruption, the Special Branch officer.

The assistant deputy director flicked a tongue – Gaunt thought it a snake's strike – across his lips. 'Yes, Trevor?'

Not lifting his head, speaking with a gentle Welsh accent, Trevor said, 'Excuse me, but I think you miss the essential.'

'Do we, Trevor? Well, that's a late but interesting contribution. We are all busy men, so perhaps you could enlighten us. How do we "miss the essential"? You have the floor.'

Gaunt thought it that sort of moment when men in waders stand in a wretched stream and identify the reward, a trout, and prepare to cast a fly over it . . . but a damn great cormorant comes from the clear blue sky and nicks the fish. His mood lightened and he anticipated amusement.

Trevor said, 'We are missing the essential. I tell you what is our fear in the Branch, and the same fear will be mirrored at Thames House. That fear is the "sleepers". Each time we go out on an arrest job I feel little elation. The fear is not bred by what I know, but what I don't know. I am in ignorance of the sleepers. How many? Where are they located? What are their common factors? I will answer each point. There might be ten sleepers, a hundred or a thousand, I don't know. They are located anywhere you choose to put a pin in a map, in any major city or in any provincial town. The common factors are that they swim unrecognized in our society, are normal and ordinary in every outward facet of appearance – and they hate us and all that we in this room seek to defend. I go further in explanation of us missing the essentials, with due humility. We are told that a resourceful and valued man, a co-ordinator of attacks, is seeking covert entry to Britain. Such a man does not waste his time, and hazard his freedom, if the individuals he will work with are of second or third grade. He will only travel if he believes he will meet young men or women of dedication and skill – and the purpose of his journey is to wake them. Who are they? I don't know. How do I find them? I can't. What is my assessment of their worth? A team of sleepers can inflict, guided by a strong hand, damage to us not equalled since the blitz bombing of the 1940s. We have to find them.'

He paused. Gaunt reflected that any of them round the table could have made that speech – perhaps not with such Celtic flourish – and hit the same nails . . . but none had. No chair scraped, no pencil was twirled, no fist masked a yawn. The Branch man used his hands as if he spoke of something of childlike simplicity, outstretched them. Said it, like it was obvious to an idiot.

'He takes us there. Arrest him at sea or in port and we will gain little because he will carry no laptop, won't have a convenient and uncoded address book. He leads us to this disparate cadre. The new leaders are trained in counter-interrogation methods, trained well, and I doubt he would talk even without fingernails and with his testicles wired to the mains. His is the road we follow. Lift him at sea, or on a dockside, and we would have the empty shell of a body and not his mind's contents. I suggest we permit him to land and we are with him . . . Under close and expert surveillance, we let him run.'

The silence, into which only the Welsh voice had intruded, broke.

'By God, that's high-octane stuff.'

'Exciting, fascinating, challenging – a cell block filled with little scrotes.'

'Sends a signal to whatever cave that bearded bastard's in that we're on top of him, crushing him.'

The assistant deputy director smacked the palm of his hand on the table. 'I congratulate you, Trevor. Original thinking where we were lacking – we let him run. First class. What I like, *everybody* is involved. Special Forces shadow at sea. Suffolk and Norfolk are at the landfall, creating a sanitized perimeter. The Service, Dennis, are singing off the same hymn sheet as the Branch, Trevor, and will do the clever stuff, the surveillance in co-operation. I would like to suggest, if there are no dissenters, that I should chair a daily meeting of principals – I think noon as good a time as any. We're a big family and so much the more effective when we pull together. "We let him run". Brilliant. Let's get it in place, gentlemen. Let's do the detail.'

Gaunt stood, and it seemed not to be noticed. The photograph of Anwar Maghroub lay on the table, and the women who did the shorthand had the details of Ricky Capel's life, and of the trawler that was called the *Anneliese Royal*, and of the island. He thought he had no longer a part to play. He turned to Gloria and, almost imperceptibly, raised an eyebrow, then flicked a glance at the door. He saw her smooth her skirt and drop her pad into her bag.

Around the table there was a sudden explosion of voices. A call to

379

Hereford and the alerting of the section on stand-by, done staccato, then Poole notified. A barked demand to Constabulary Headquarters for firearms officers to be pulled off all other duties – no, not Sandringham. A full muster of Thames House guys and girls, A Branch people who did surveillance and bugs, to be made ready. Special Branch teams to be put together that afternoon. Gaunt moved towards the door, Gloria alongside him. He saw, from the corner of his eye, the look on her face of suppressed fury, her man put down, then hung out to dry – unwanted. He stepped aside to let her go through the door before him.

A voice, Dennis's, piped behind him: 'When you next call your island out-station, Freddie, tell the rookie we want the departure time, nothing more. Imperative that she does not show herself – no intervention – just sits on a sandcastle a mile back.'

Then Bill, the bloody man booming as if he were on a survival run in the Brecons, 'And tell her to keep old White Feather clear – not that he sounds like a hero – right out of it.'

They went up together, and the lift was full. Neither spoke, but in the corridor he said quietly, 'They didn't want a doubter, did they? Didn't want a Thomas, a sceptic. Such excitement, such certainty . . . What happens if they bloody lose him, or never bloody find him? What happens if *we let him run* screws up. I think, with our man across the water, you get one chance, and not to take it is a criminal act, but they didn't want to hear that. And they didn't want to hear what the professor up north told me: "Eradicate from your mind the due process of law – kill him." It'll rub off, always does, the gloss of excitement, and you and I will then be behind a big high wall of sandbags. Ah, well . . . time to say it was all right when it left us. *We let him run.* I wouldn't have but my opinion was not requested. What I think we need is a good strong cup of tea, with sugar.'

Inside his office, his sanctum, he dropped his briefcase as if he had no more use of it, dialled the number, heard the ringing, then her voice, the far-away wind and the cry of gulls.

Polly sat apart from him.

The phone was now back in her pocket. When it had rung she had crawled away from him and gone down a gully where the wind couldn't reach her. She had listened to Freddie Gaunt's faint voice and thought she heard his exhaustion. She had been left with the sense of a beaten man.

His back was to her. He tracked and scanned with the binoculars over the dunes and the beach, and watched the horizon; the swing of his head behind the eyepieces was the only movement he made. She did not know what the sex in the sleeping-bag meant to her, or what it meant to him. And always the bloody wind was on her, and the bloody rain . . . She did not know. She steeled herself, came and eased down beside him, but his hands stayed on the binoculars and he did not loop his arm round her.

Polly said, 'My people have decided what they want, Malachy. I don't know how it'll fit with you but it's the way it's going to be.'

She saw that his eyes followed the waving of the coarse grass stems on the dunes.

'You are – without belittling your achievements – outside the loop. They're all grateful in London, of course. We've moved on – there's a plan in place. It does not include you. I'm sorry, Malachy, but the concept of the plan is in concrete.'

His head tilted and she could follow the lenses' aim. She saw the stark, empty beach, and thought he followed the flight of the gulls.

'We have the name of a beam trawler, when it left and which port it sailed from. We have the identity of the boat's skipper, and his link to Ricky Capel, the detail of the debt between the Capel family and the Rahman clan in Blankenese . . . More than that, we can put a face and a biography to a big player in the international game, terror- ism: he's the package to be lifted off here by the trawler. We accept that parts of the jigsaw were put in place by you, but that's history. If it sounds brutal it is not intended to – I'm just telling you how the facts play.'

The binoculars were lifted. She followed them and saw the mist haze among the furthest white splash of the waves and the grim, grey line of clouds where the horizon met the water. She had thought, before Gaunt's call, that she would go back to the swamp in the island's centre and try to make a peace with the old lunatic, the recluse who had jarred her with the story of a concentration camp and victims, and pump him for what he had seen during the day but now, after the call, she had no need of him – or of Malachy.

'Under no circumstances am I to intervene in the pickup, that is a very clear order. I watch and I report. I do not go near them and I do not alert them. I am told they should board the trawler, however many there are, and not know they are under observation. I see, at a distance, the lights and I communicate that to London. The plan drops into place, and my role in all this is complete – your role, Malachy, is already finished – and I'm on my way home. The trawler will be tracked across the North Sea, will be under surveillance, and will be allowed to drop off our target. He's to be permitted to run – in the greater interest of national security – and lead the appropriate agencies, God willing, to those he would hope to meet and work with . . . I don't wish to be cruel, Malachy, but you should feel free to go back to the ferry, get to the mainland, take a shower and eat a meal, and start again on whatever life it is you want to make for yourself. Those are my instructions.'

A shaft of sunlight, low, narrow, golden, broke the cloud and fashioned a corridor over the surge of the sea, ran to the whipped sands and the grasses and lit them. His shoulders swung and he looked to his right, away from her, to the dunes.

'Damn you, Malachy . . . I'll not forget you, or what you've done and who you are . . . Can you not say something? He's to be permitted to run, we don't intervene. I have to watch and report. Isn't it enough for you, what you've already done? Have you nothing to say, nothing for me?'

She saw his forehead knitted, his concentration on the sands and grasses that made the dunes.

He was deep in holiday-leave charts, the bane of the life of a senior officer – and waiting for him were overtime dockets – when he heard the stampede of feet in the corridor. Johan Konig saw his door snap open, no knock, of which his rank should have assured him.

A detective panted, a step inside his room, and hadn't a voice, but beckoned him.

He took his time, killed the computer page, pulled his jacket from the hook and turned his back on the picture of the egret perched on a hippopotamus. He locked the door after him. He did not scurry down the corridor. It was not, in the book of Konig, good for juniors to see a ranking officer run, but he felt a rising excitement although he had no idea of its source. The detective led him to the new communications room he had demanded for his unit. His whole team, twelve men and two women, were crowded inside and their attention was on a black-and-white monitor screen. None saw him come, and none made way for him. He elbowed his way through, pushed forward.

He saw her, a small figure. The focus was poor from the camera in the roof of the neighbouring house.

He had only seen photographs of Alicia Rahman, taken covertly for her husband's file and showing her with her children at the school gate.

He peered forward, blinked to see better. She was high on the roofing tiles of the house and her arms were looped round the width of a chimney stack. The curtains of an open window flapped below. She wore a robe, at which the wind tore, but either the buttons and the belt had not been fastened when she had come through the window and climbed or they had been ripped undone. He saw her naked body and the scars, which were vague on the picture but recognizable; long, darkened marks on her chest and on her stomach, close to the dark hair mass and on her thighs. The men and women around him – all chosen for his unit because of hardened experience – cursed what they saw.

'Goddamn animals – bastards.'

'Worse than animals, barbarians.'

'They've scraped her, flayed the skin off her.'

He turned away – he had seen enough. He tapped the shoulders of Brigitte and Heinrich, told them they would come with him and asked for a car, a van of uniformed officers, an ambulance and a fire appliance with a crane and cradle. He remembered the man on the fence, his hands bleeding from the wire and their flight up the side path, the silence of the man in the cells, and his release into the care of the agent he had trusted.

'Rahman, for all his skills, has allowed himself to be provoked into making a mistake, and the mistake will bring him down,' Konig said quietly, then swung on his heel.

'Cover yourself.' Timo Rahman cupped his hands to his mouth and shouted. 'Hide yourself.'

He heard, in the distance, sirens in the streets of Blankenese. The Bear was at the kitchen table, his head in his hands, sobbing. The aunt leaned uselessly out of the open window. He had not seen them but he imagined, beyond the thick hedge and the high gates – from the far side of the street – his neighbours gathered to grandstand and stare. What he could see was her legs – long, slim, bare and wounded – and the hair – where he and she had made two daughters – and her stomach, the raw strips on her skin where blood seeped.

Timo Rahman yelled again, 'Come down. You have to come down. Come down to the window.'

The sirens closed on him at speed. Not when he had been stabbed, not when he had been shot had he felt that sense of catastrophe surging round him, developing as fast as the sirens' approach.

'Get to the window. Get inside. It is my order.'

She stayed. Her feet scratched for a grip on the tiles and he could see the hair and her stomach and a breast hung clear of her robe, but her arms had a grip on the chimney. Not a man or a woman, since he had come to Hamburg, had refused an order of Timo Rahman. The scale of the catastrophe facing him leaped in his mind: he saw the collapse of an empire . . .

He heard the crash and wrench of metal, turned from her, and saw the front of the fire engine burst the gates. The crane on it pulled down the branches of trees and snapped them carelessly. He thought, high over him and showing her nakedness to the world, displaying what he had instructed should be done to her – to clean her – that her lips moved, but the sirens destroyed the sound.

The last time, and the shriek was desperation: 'Get back in the house. Come down. You want the world to see you, see Rahman's wife?'

The world did. And what Timo Rahman saw was the fire engine's crane rising with men and women in the cradle. A policeman's gun covered him, as the Bear and the aunt were brought out of the house

384

under escort. The cradle reached his wife, and a blanket, for modesty and warmth, was wrapped round her. A man walked towards him and swung handcuffs on their chain. He recognized him. The crane lowered the cradle. He saw the shine of the handcuffs as they closed on his wrists. With kindness, his wife was helped into the ambulance and he watched it drive away between the flattened gates ... His world was broken.

He was led to the car. He had thought, if this moment ever came – hands gripping his arms and handcuffs biting at his wrists – that the chief man among them, whom he had thought to be only a tax investigator, would wear on his face a mask of gloating satisfaction ... but there was only impassive coldness. A hand wrenched down his head so that his scalp would not hit the top of the car door, and he was pushed inside. If the man had shown triumph, a little of Timo Rahman's dignity would have survived. He sat low in the back seat and humiliation swam over him.

The consul general took the call. 'What can I do for you, Dr Konig? ... I'm sorry, that name again, please ... Miss Polly Wilkins? I don't believe I know her ... She was here? Well, I never saw her and I've never heard of her. There is, and I can emphatically state it, no one of that name at my consulate ... I see, I see. Well, Dr Konig, I suggest you contact our embassy in Berlin ... I can't imagine where the confusion arose but I regret, sincerely, that I am unable to be of assistance ... Miss Wilkins is not on my staff, is not here, and I have no idea who or where she is ... *If* she were to arrive on my doorstep, is there a message for her? ... Timo Rahman is under arrest, is that it? *If* I ever meet her, I will assuredly tell her. Good day, Dr Konig.'

He rang off. He gazed bleakly through the window and out over the lake. The thought in his mind was of betrayal, promises broken, contacts thrown to the winds. He detested the presence on his premises of what he referred to as 'the shadows people'. He thanked his God that she had gone, good riddance, from the upstairs and permanently locked room to which he had no access, and wondered where she was ... He was buzzed and warned his next appointment had arrived – and he erased her, and her business, from his mind.

★   ★   ★

385

He was drawn back, as if a rope pulled him.

Oskar circled them.

He had been at the platform through the afternoon, had cleared away the eider's carcass and had watched the birds' renewal of confidence. With death gone, they had fed and preened – but he had known that he would go back. Late, as the sun's shafts dipped and fell on the birds, and made a brilliance of their plumage, he had moved. He had thought it, as he had approached them and heard one dripping voice, a small matter that he had done already. The destruction of the light, he had felt, was of minimal importance. He had looked for a larger gesture, an act that would mitigate the shame on his family and the poison in his blood.

He saw the weapon, and the steel case, which was open and showed him the dials below an extended antenna.

Moving on his stomach, so slowly, through the scrub and never pulling when a thorn caught him, Oskar was undecided as to whether to steal the radio or the firearm from the strangers who violated his paradise. He did not know which was more vital to them, the weapon or the radio. Their backs were to him.

To take either, he must crawl from the scrub's cover. If he had either the radio or the weapon, he would go in the dusk, the darkness, to the home of the island's policeman, who thought him a malcontent, a trouble-maker – who would be confounded and would offer fulsome gratitude. He had to expose at least his arms, head and shoulders if he were to stretch far enough to snatch away the weapon or the radio.

One talked – not a tongue that Oskar Netzer knew – and the other, taller, lay close to him and was on his side, seemed not to respond and might have slept. The blackness of the evening was fast coming.

He did not feel the brittle twig blown away long before by a storm that was dry from the cover of the scrub. Oskar did not feel it against his stomach and through the thickness of his outer coat. He wriggled to go closer. He knew that from exertion his old lungs croaked for breath that rattled in his throat, and he tried to suppress the wheeze. His fingers were, perhaps, ten centimetres from the weapon, but more than twenty from the radio. With what he believed to be the

386

greatest caution he brought a knee forward, and felt a creaking pain in his joint, then squirmed forward. He saw the gap, his fingers to the weapon, shorten. He heard the twig snap.

He was going back.

Thorns caught him.

He struggled to plunge deeper into the cover.

The crescendo of gunfire burst over him, and he felt numbing shock in his arm, his shoulder, his hip.

He went deep into the thorn thicket. He heard shouting. Men blundered in the scrub but had only the small beam of a torch to guide them.

The wetness of his blood was in his hand.

He lay as if dead.

Malachy had jerked upright.

The sound had come on the wind. Three single shots, not on automatic.

When he started to move – into darkness – towards where three shots had been fired, she clung to his coat. 'It is nothing to do with us,' she hissed. 'We do not intervene.'

With both hands she held his coat, fists buried in it. He listened, heard the surf break and the whine of the wind.

387

19

He no longer pulled against her grip. He could have struck out, could have broken free. Malachy did not struggle and he could feel her fingers clenched in the sleeve of his coat. If he had thought it necessary, but he did not, he could have swiped at her face with his other hand.

He allowed her to hold him and controlled his breathing. He thought she would believe that he had given up on the struggle, unequal, against her. It was three, four minutes since they had heard three shots fired. She would not have known it but all of his studied concentration was on the memory of where the gunfire had come from. One shot would have been hard for him to make the equations of the direction but three were sufficient. In his mind, as he relaxed his arm and let it sag for her, a line was drawn to his right. He estimated that the shots had been fired at a little more than a quarter of a mile from him, and perhaps three hundred yards back from where the soft sand marked the end of the dunes and the scrub, the start of the drop to the beach. He reckoned that he lulled her.

'I'm not blaming you,' she said, a small voice against the wind. 'You have to see, Malachy, the big picture. It's beyond you now. Don't think, after what you've done and where you've been, that I'm not sympathizing. But – and I've told you – you have to let it go. The big picture is supreme.'

He knew it. There was a slackening in her fingers' grip. He thought that what she had said – no blame, her sympathy – was utterly and clearly genuine. The darkness seemed to Malachy to have come fast, sun sunk, clouds heavier, and he could see only the outline of her face, but he had felt on his skin little sharp pants of breath as she had spoken of the big picture's supremacy.

'You have to bottle it down, swallow it. Hear me . . . You've done more than anyone could have asked of you. I only know the bones of your history, Malachy, but I am telling you that no one could have done more to get back what you've lost. If you say that you don't know what happened in that shit place, in Iraq, I am believing you. Already you have the right to walk tall – God, that sounds crap. Now, forget what's personal and see the wider scape . . . You're not a fool, Malachy, you're not a selfish man.'

One of her hands now rested on his sleeve. The fingers had straightened out and were no longer deep in the material. It would have hurt him to hit her. He could make out the upper point of the dune crest behind him but the gully beside it was lost. Locked in his memory, he had the imagined line that would take him to a point – where a weapon had fired three single shots – where Ricky Capel was. He had no doubt of it: Ricky Capel was at the extremity of the line in his mind. She lifted his arm, and he let her, and her lips brushed the skin at the wrist, then she lowered his arm. He made no resistance.

She said with gentleness, 'I'm out of Prague. There was a guy but it's long ago. Do you think you could get down there, Malachy, to Prague – God, I'm doing the running. Can't you help me? – and see me there? Walk around a bit, eat a bit, sleep a bit. I'd said to myself, after tonight, that I'd go my way and you'd go yours. Doesn't have to be like that. I'm saying I'd like it, Malachy, if you came down to Prague . . .'

Maybe there was a wetness behind her spectacles, in her eyes. She had them off. He saw the dull white of her handkerchief and he sensed she wiped hard at her eyes and then her head turned away from him as if, even in darkness, she did not care to show her emotion.

He was gone, away. He had not needed to hit her.

He rolled, fast, clear of her, was on his knees, then pushed himself upright, stamped his shoes for grip and sand spat from under them. He threw the pistol behind him, towards her.

He was into the gully that cut past the crest of the dune.

He heard her. 'Damn you, you bastard! For God's sake, it's not about you. It's for hundreds of people. You bastard, Malachy Kitchen. Didn't you hear what I said? The big picture?'

Up the gully, on to a path that was narrow enough for the thorn to catch his coat, Malachy ran.

'I found nothing.'

Ricky stumbled back and down into the sheltered hollow, then tripped on his own feet. Falling, arm out, he caught at a branch and tightened his fist, then squealed because he had hold of thorns. The pencil beam of the small torch approached him.

'You got the light, Dean. Don't know what I'm looking for – but I found nothing.'

He heard a murmur but could not make out what he was told. His ears rang, still, with the blast of the weapon's discharge – like he was goddamn deaf. The beam came close, then wavered and fell on the depth of the scrub. Bloodstains were on the ground below the canopy of leaves. From blundering in the thorn-bushes, Ricky's face and arms were scratched, his coat and the waterproof trousers ripped. The gun had been fired beside his face, inches from his ears. It had been so fast. Last thing he had heard was a twig, dry, breaking, and there had been the convulsion of movement beside him, then the hammer of the gun, and he had been heaved to his feet by a hand on his collar – not able to make out the command given him. Had not known what he looked for, had found nothing. He gazed down at the blood, then the torch's beam veered away.

'Who was he? What did you see?'

No answer was given him that he could understand. What was said was a whisper to him.

'No point staying quiet – you woke the damn dead.'

His hand was grabbed. For a moment he recoiled, then realized it. The grip on his hand was iron tight. The panic was in him and he was about to lash out, because fear made fury, when he felt the smooth shape of the handle against his fingers. He clamped on it, took the weight of the radio in his hand.

'Right, you tell me, where is he?'

Again the whisper.

'Haven't you got it? I can't hear nothing.'

He stood and shivered, and the shape moved around him as if he checked the ground for anything they had left there. The light came close again, a dull, narrow beam, and it showed the crushed grass, then shone on the barrel tip of the weapon, then started to move off. Ricky had to run two, three strides to catch the man. The radio's case banged against his knee and he swore, then raised his free arm and took hold of the shoulder in front of him.

'It wasn't bloody clever – I don't do mouthing off but it was not clever to fire that bloody gun. Don't get me wrong, I'm not a frightened man, but you could have brought all hell down on us, and that is not clever. Who was it creeping up on us? Did you see him? I'm asking, and I've the right to ask, what—'

He heard, in the clamour at his ears, a hiss of breath through teeth – as if he was shushed, like he was a kid talking out of turn. They were on a path and they climbed and the beam lit a jolting patch of ground in front of each of Dean's steps and the torch was held low down. If he had not held on to Dean's shoulder he would have spilled off the path and fallen into the scrub. For a moment the beam lifted and found a strip of torn cloth and there they had to push their way, him first and Ricky following, between thorns. He had pain, but the fear was worse.

When had Ricky Capel last known fear worse than pain? Couldn't bloody remember it. He saw the face. The face was on the pavement and the street light fell on it. He thought the face followed him, the face from Bevin Close – and now it tracked him . . . Three shots fired. Blood on the ground. No body. Not a scream and not a whimper. He thought the face laughed at him. Bad fear stalked Ricky Capel, like the face did. He clung to the shoulder, hung on to it as a blind man would. Never before, not as a child had he felt bad fear . . . and he thought the man came after him, dripped blood and followed him. He strained to listen for the footfall behind him but in his ears was only the ring, the clamour, of the gunshots.

'I screwed up,' Polly said. 'I screwed up big.' She sat hunched, her chin on her knees and the phone pressed to her face. 'I can't believe it, how pathetic I was.'

The darkness enveloped her, clung round her. He'd answered her call, now Gaunt's silence echoed back at her.

'I gave him the party line. I called it the big picture. What I'm saying, Freddie, is that I thought he'd accepted it. You know, his little concerns outweighed by the needs of the masses. He didn't argue. Three shots were fired somewhere out in this bloody place – God knows where – but I'd given him the instruction. No intervention. Sit, watch and report. He listened, seemed to swallow what I gave him, then quit on me. I don't know where he is . . . Freddie, it is so damn dark here you can't see the end of your nose, and I don't know what he's going to do. I'd given him a gun – pretty damn stupid, you don't have to tell me – but he chucked it back at me, like he wouldn't be needing it. What's in his mind? I just don't know.'

She was the daughter of schoolteachers. It had been drilled into Polly Wilkins that to admit failure, own up to error, won its own rewards in heaven. Most colleagues who had shared desks with her at Vauxhall Bridge Cross, she thought, would have wormed, wriggled, from admission of failure and error. The response in her ear was a long, measured sigh – she reckoned it not of anger but the sadness of disappointment.

'I will, of course, do what I can to give due warning of any pickup. I have to say that a lift off the beach will not be fun. It's a foul evening and it's not changing . . . What's worst, Freddie, I miss him. It was sort of good having him here. What I realize, he's not missing me, just dumped me, a bloody used fag carton . . . I don't know where it's going . . . Nothing much else to say.'

'I won't be here myself, but calls to this number will be routed to the necessary people . . . Thank you, Wilco.'

He knew what she meant. Frederick Gaunt could empathize, knew what it felt to be *a bloody used fag carton* and dumped. He rang off, pressed the button that deactivated the phone's scrambler. He sensed that Gloria hovered behind him and thought her mouth would be slack with astonishment. It was, he believed, a defining moment of his adult life: *I won't be here myself*. He could have reflected on other such moments of importance that had fashioned his career and domestic existence – a loveless marriage, the bitter process of divorce, children taught to reject him, the first night of utter loneliness in an old man's bachelor apartment – the initial occasion when the WMD report had been smartly returned to his desk for reappraisal, the meeting when he had been lectured on the requirement of politicians to find meat and not scrag ends in the Iraqi desert, the summons to an office on an upper floor, the averted eyes and barked voice telling him that Albania was his new area of interest, the last session in the pub with his old team before they were scattered to the winds. He could have reflected on any of them and could have claimed each of them as a defining moment. Top of the heap, and he knew it, was telling pretty little Polly, frozen half to death on a God-awful beach, that *calls to this number will be routed through to the necessary people*.

He heard her clear her throat, a brief cough, to demand his attention.

'Did you mean that?'

He said peevishly, turning to face her, 'If I said it, Gloria, I expect that I meant it.'

Her face was wreathed in bewilderment. She stuttered, 'It's coming to an end . . . It's the last hours . . . It's what you've worked for.'

'And it is not, my dear, in my hands.'

'You owe it to Polly to be here.'

'I owe very little, not even pocket change, to anyone.'

Lines creased her forehead and mouth. 'But the threat . . . What about the threat?'

He stared into the confusion of her eyes. 'Someone else's problem now. Polly's problem, a crisis committee's problem, but I fancy not mine . . . I have, Gloria, carried the problem of the bloody threat too damn long – it's been a lifetime of carrying it. Cold War threat, Irish threat, Iraq threat, al-Qaeda threat. You name it . . . Don't you understand that the *threat* has buckled me? Every day, every night, the threat is on my shoulders. Well, not any more.'

'I never thought I'd hear it, not from you.'

He grimaced, then shrugged. He saw her turn on her low heels and she clattered out. The door was slammed, which would not have been accidental. He went to the wardrobe against the wall, slipped off his jacket, unbuttoned his waistcoat and loosened his tie. The man, Malachy Kitchen, was without corporate baggage and was not answerable to a crisis committee, or to the 'party line' peddled by Polly 'Wilco' Wilkins. Gaunt dragged his laces undone and kicked off his shoes, dropped his waistcoat on to them, unhooked the braces and let his trousers fall. He opened the wardrobe's doors and took out a hanger – which carried the name of a Singapore hotel from where he had appropriated it a dozen years before – and put his suit on it. He took another hanger, from the Inter-Continental in Helsinki, for his shirt. He remembered what the old lady had said, as he had taken tea with her, of a man who did not boast and did not go after trophies, who faced challenges, each of them harder than the last, to claw back his self-respect, and she had said, *If you ever see him, you give him my love*, and he remembered what Bill, who had the rippled muscles of Special Forces training and who arrogantly wore a shapeless cabled sweater, had demanded of Wilco: *And tell her to keep old White Feather clear – not that he sounds like a hero – right out of it.* He realized he rooted more for the man, the free spirit, than for the big picture – and it was better he was gone, and soon. From an old rucksack on the wardrobe floor, he took a shirt, trousers and sweater – all caked in dried mud – boots and a rainproof coat that had over-trousers folded into an inner pocket.

He dressed, hitched the rucksack on to his shoulder and went out through the darkened outer office, past Gloria's cleared desk – and past the phones from which Polly Wilkins's next message would be routed to the crisis folk. Gaunt had the look of a jobbing gardener on his way to an allotment plot as he made his way to the lift, and he imagined the pleasure ahead of him and did not know, or care, of chaos left behind him.

Oskar left behind him the ducks, his true friends, safe in the darkness from predators.

He crawled on the track. He had set himself a target that he must reach and the pain that had overcome the shock of numbness was alive in the three wounds on his body, but he welcomed it. If there had been no pain, only exhaustion and weakness, he would have felt a clinging urge to settle in the mud and reeds beside the pond and sleep, and if he slept he would not achieve his target . . . First he had lain in the scrub and had heard voices and crashing movement

394

around him but a thin torchlight had not pierced the depths of the thorn bushes that had been his immediate refuge. They had gone. They had blundered away, and then he had moved. Sometimes he had been on his stomach, but a few times he had been able to stand, sway, stagger, and he had known that when he was on his feet he lost more blood, and with each step the pain was more acute.

He thought the pain was his penance. He thought the blood he lost was contaminated by an old atrocity. He thought he deserved the pain for the evil done by a man whose blood he shared. He thought he had cleansed himself by breaking the light set in place by the strangers who had come and threatened paradise. Oskar had no clarity of thought because the pain destroyed it.

He had told the ducks, in a reedy, bubbling whisper, that he would not be back.

Now he did not have the strength to stand, to walk. He might have the strength, if God were with him, to crawl part of the way to his target on his knees and elbows, but first he would wriggle on his stomach and lever himself forward. He prayed that the strength, little of it left, would last him.

Above him the wind sighed and the rain spattered down and he writhed on the path, made slow, agonizing progress, and left behind a trail of poisoned blood. Ahead was a distant light, his target if his strength lasted.

He sat on the bench in the cell. His belt and shoe laces had been taken from Timo Rahman. He sat because if he had stood and paced the cell he would have had to hold up his trousers or let them slump to his ankles. A light, protected by wire mesh, beamed down at him from the ceiling.

The cell stank of old faeces, urine and vomit. It was cold, bitterly so, because the high, barred window was open to the wind and rain dripped from its aperture on to the prisoner on the bench bed.

He was offered no respect, no deference.

His lawyer had sat beside him in the interview room. He had been shown a preliminary report from a police doctor that listed his wife's injuries on half of a single sheet of paper. The lawyer, German, gross and expensive, had read the report first and Timo had seen him wince. He had known then that the man – on his payroll for nine years – would have little stomach for a fight in his defence, and had not challenged the right of Konig to put his questions . . . only three of them. Had Timo Rahman, himself, attacked his wife? If he had not, himself, attacked her, had he authorized the scraping-off of skin from her body? If he had not, himself, authorized the attack, did he know who was responsible for the assault? He had been told that his housekeeper and chauffeur were in custody and would subsequently be interviewed, and that their statements would be matched with his. He had not answered any of the three questions. If they had given him the respect that was due, he would have expected Johan Konig and the woman officer with him to demonstrate frustration, but the coldness he had seen at his home was still alive in their faces, and the contempt. His lawyer had fled the interview room after leaving him little hope of bail.

Isolation settled on him. Timo Rahman did not think of the island, or of the man he had been paid to ship across the water, or of Ricky Capel who, he now realized, had lied to him, a lie he had taken in, a lie that would destroy him. He thought of wolves.

In his mind were the wolves that came down, long ago, from the mountains. Emaciated, foul-breathed, bare to the skin at the haunches and tail from mange, and they circled a failing fire. Corralled inside the fence were goats with kids and ewes with lambs. He sat with his father beside the fire and darkness masked the high ground above the village near Shkodra. Across his knee, held tight, was a loaded single-barrel shotgun, and his father had an old German rifle, and they could hear the wolves and smell them. When the wolves were closest and the smell was bad, when they were boldest from the hunger pangs of winter, the wolves came right up against the fence and then his father would hurl at them the branch from the fire that burned brightest and they would scatter, but they would return. Always a dog wolf led.

There had been a year when the high snows had lasted into spring and beyond the time that the kids and lambs were born, and starvation had been the enemy of the wolf pack. The pack leader had not been driven back by fire. His father had shot it, as it prepared to launch at the fence, with his Gewehr 98 Mauser rifle, and it had fallen dead with a head wound. The goats and ewes, the kids and lambs had stampeded and screamed with fear. His father had gripped his arm, had pointed to the downed pack leader, face alive with excitement. Father and son, they had watched. First the wolves had fled to the darkness, then had been emboldened, had circled in the shadows and scurried forward – many targets, but his father had not fired. The wolves had torn apart the carcass of their pack leader, had fought to eat, rip, swallow, savage it. Timo, the boy, had watched power gone and when nothing was left on the ground beyond the fence – not a bone or a meat scrap, no fur, not a morsel of skin – the wolves had retreated to the night's safety.

He had never forgotten the sight and sounds of the destruction of a fallen pack leader.

That evening they would be circling. Wolves would be abroad, would be coming near to a mansion in the Blankenese suburb, would be edging closer to casinos and shops, bars and brothels in the Reeperbahn, would be marching on more casinos and more shops, more bars and more brothels in the Steindamm. He had done it himself. He, a leader of a wolf pack, had buried Germans and put Russians into the trunks of cars. Word would have spread. If it were tax evasion, or the corruption of local officials, living from the rewards of vice or sex-trade trafficking, or involvement with an Islamic group for which he was investigated, then his lawyer would have fought, tooth and claw, to win his freedom. But he was investigated for the peeling of live skin from his wife's body. Who would stand by him? Who would believe he could return to a pre-eminence of power? He saw wolves. Wolves were on a cell-block landing when he returned from exercise in the yard. Wolves moved into casinos and shops, bars and brothels. He seemed to feel the heat of wolves' breath and the smell of it – because he had believed a lie. And they edged nearer and their teeth were bared.

Timo Rahman screamed.

He was not heard. The cell's walls closed around him.

A Europol advisory landed on Tony Johnson's desk. He had his coat on and was preparing himself for the evening struggle on a commuter train when the clerk brought it to him. It already had a half-dozen

397

sets of initials on it but – what else to expect in this perfect bloody world? – it would end with him and he was to field it . . . His eyes scanned the single page, and he gasped, shook, and flicked it into his in-tray for the next morning's attention. Then he punched the air.

For a detective sergeant with a reputation, deserved, for carrying equally weighted chips on each of his shoulders and for spreading contagious gloomy defeatism wherever he walked, his stride down the corridor was emphatic with cheerful energy. That morning he had repeated his refrain at the weekly meeting of colleagues to hack at current problems that drugs and organized crime, and their effect on the great mass of the capital city's punters, were on the back-burner, ignored and victim to the swollen resources pushed at the War on Terror. At the ground-floor lobby, swiping his card, he blew a kiss at the lady on Reception, and saw the shock wobble on the face of the duty guard beside her.

He went out through the swing doors and on to the street, imagined he heard the guard's question, 'God, what's the matter with that miserable beggar?' and imagined he heard the lady's answer, 'Must be that he's got hot flushes, or he's on a bloody good promise, or it's the lottery.' What he could have told them was that a Europol advisory had reached his desk and stated that police in Hamburg had arrested the Albanian national, Timo Rahman, on charges of griev-ous bodily harm and wounding, and that officers on the case urgently requested co-operation from European colleagues on all links between Rahman and criminal organizations for immediate investi-gation while Rahman was in custody, and vulnerable . . . What he could also have told them, on the reception desk, was that he had contributed – damned if he knew the detail of how – to the life of an untouchable going into the gutter.

On the pavement he turned heads as he laughed to himself like a maniac. 'You done us proud, Malachy. I hope you've a drink in your hand because that's what you deserve. You've done us proper proud – I hope it's a damn great drink and then another.'

Malachy had rainwater in his eyes, ears, nose, had it weighing down the clothes on his back and his legs. He quartered ground, was inland from the highest dunes. He moved, alternately slow and fast. When he went slowly it was to listen, because he could see so little, and then he shook his head hard. His fingers went into his ears to gouge out the wet, but he heard only the wind's bluster and the pattering of the rain. When he went fast, he held to what he believed was the line towards the source of the gunfire and often he thought he had lost it and that his instinct failed him.

Going fast, on a track, his shoes, with their worn tread, slid from under him.

He fell, went down. The breath squeezed out of his chest and his hands flailed. When they hit the mud it was not tackiness they found, but something slicked, wet, but not like mud. Malachy felt the surface of the path, realized its smoothness – as if mud had been pressed flat by a solid weight and then the slick had been left. He could not see more than the outline of his hands but there was darkness on his palms. He believed that it was blood and that the mud had been smoothed by a man's body. He thought, where he was, a wounded man had rested, then crawled forward. But Malachy did not follow the trail, and he tried again to find his line.

He came to the pond. A little of the reflection of the water shone back at him through the reeds. He saw, as a silhouette, the shape of the viewing platform where he had put his shoulder against a support post . . . In a crash of noise, and he froze, ducks fled – splashed, beat their wings, screamed – and he could smell the body of the old man, as he had done at the platform.

Malachy had warned her that it was a crime to involve others and risk hurting them. She had involved the old man, had picked at his isolation with honey words and pleading eyes, and he had been shot and crawled towards a refuge. She had rounded on him – what did he think she had done with him, if not involve him? He had said: *I'll pick up my own pieces*. He would. She – sweet girl, warm girl with a taste of sadness – did not own him; nor did those who controlled her.

In his mind, he adjusted the line.

He came to a hollow. He found a plastic bag caught on thorns and near it a Cellophane packet that would have held a shop-bought sandwich. Maybe it was because the cloud weakened in its density and a trickle of the moon's light came through, but small shapes gleamed and then their brightness died. He picked up three discarded

399

cartridge cases. On his hands, on his knees, feeling with his fingers, he found the trail they had used and the indents in the mud.

Later, Malachy came to the first marker: a strip of cloth tied to a branch.

He wanted to stand bare-faced in front of a mirror with brilliant light shining on his skin and coming back from his eyes. He wanted, as he had not done for a year and a half, to examine that face and those eyes, to search for a truth and know himself again. He would not know himself until he had hounded down Ricky Capel on the beach ahead where the sea stampeded the waves . . . Then, not before, he would learn if he was a coward, and the word beat in his head as he went forward and looked for the next marker.

19 May 2004
The old man walking towards the sandbags at the gate was hazed by the high sun.

On sentry duty with the machine-gun, Baz had called for Sergeant McQueen to come, double bloody quick time, to Bravo's gate.

The old man came slowly on the raised road from the village, hobbled forward and used a stick in his right hand to ease his weight.

Scanning him with binoculars, Hamish McQueen had called for the major to get, soonest, from the operations bunker to the gate.

The old man was alone, wizened, and an SA 80 assault rifle dangled from his left hand and against his thigh, half hidden by his robe.

'Do I slot him, sir?' Baz asked, and his eye was against the sight of the machine-gun, his finger flexed on the trigger's guard.

'I don't think so, no.'

It was for the major, the commanding officer of Bravo company, a moment of extreme inconvenience. His place was in the bunker where his clerks had for him a mountain of paper. He watched the old man and the rifle he carried through the binoculars' growing clarity. In two hours he was due to welcome to Bravo the advance force of the infantry unit that would relieve them after their six-month tour of duty. Like a hole in his skull, he needed the distraction of an old man coming to their main gate . . . He had laid down that the relieving force would not find justification for even a damned small complaint at the state of the camp left for them. The old man carried a weapon that was not used by the ragtag fighters in his area of responsibility – they had the AK47 and its variants – but had against his leg a rifle that was exclusively used by British soldiers, the SA 80. He checked that his interpreter was behind him, saw Faisal leaning against the back of the sandbags, smoking.

The major prided himself that he was blessed with a nose for danger. For the last week he had cut back on the company's patrolling, had reduced it to force protection – guaranteeing the security of Bravo's perimeter – and had withdrawn any troop movements from the village. He had dreaded losing a Jock for nothing in the last hours of the deployment, wanted all of them on the flight home to Brize Norton. He sensed no danger.

On his belt was a service pistol, and he unclipped the holster's flap. He told Baz, the machine-gunner, to cover him, and asked that Hamish McQueen be at his side. He waved for the interpreter to follow him. He walked down the entry road to Bravo's gates, then strode briskly along the road to meet the old man.

He ducked his head, smiled, and introduced himself through his interpreter. The old man transferred the rifle ponderously to his other hand, juggled it with his stick and gave his name. He shook the major's fist with a good but bony grip, then gave him the rifle. On its stock was a reference number in white paint. He knew it. Every man in the unit bloody knew it. A lost high-velocity weapon's reference number had been dinned into the heads of every Jock, NCO and officer who had been tasked for house searches since the late-afternoon patrol of 13 January – its recovery had been an unfulfilled priority. He gave it to his sergeant for checking and making safe.

The interpreter murmured in his ear, 'The gentleman, Mahmoud al-Ajouti, has heard that the British persons are going back to their country and thought it correct this weapon be returned . . . It is his apology that it has not been done before.'

'Please tell Mr al-Ajouti that I am grateful.'

He remembered, with the clarity of yesterday and not of three months before, what he had seen that day and what he had been told, and the gist of what he had said: 'Put him somewhere in isolation where he can't infect anyone else . . . I don't know how you'd ever get

401

shot of it, being called a coward . . . *I can't imagine there's any way back.' The man had been sitting on a chair outside the command bunker, head hangdog, expressionless, silent. He had heard, from the vine, that the man had been shipped home, but his failing was talked of, still, in every mess and barrack room used by the battalion.*

'Would you ask Mr al-Ajouti in what circumstances the rifle came into his possession?'

What he was told, through the hesitant voice of the interpreter, first confused the major, then rocked him.

'The soldiers came up the street where Mr al-Ajouti lives above his place of business, a bakery shop. They knew, everybody in the street knew, that an ambush was prepared, was ready, for the next soldiers, the next patrol, to come on the street. His son, his son is called Tariq. He had brought heavy stones, football-sized stones, into the home above the shop and had a window open enough to throw them down. Mr al-Ajouti did not know of the stones and he was in the back of his home with his wife and his younger children. Tariq is the eldest of his children. He does not think blame should be given to his son, Tariq, because all of the older children in the village are encouraged by men of the Mehdi army, followers of the imam, to hate soldiers – he regrets that. A soldier stopped outside Mr al-Ajouti's shop. His son told him afterwards, that is how he knows it, the soldier was lying on the ground, and his son, that is Tariq, threw down a stone and it hit the soldier's neck, which was not protected by the edge of his helmet. The stone, the size of a football, stunned the soldier – that is, he was made unconscious. It was just after a grenade had been fired into the wall near the window where Tariq was. His son – Mr al-Ajouti, at the back, did not know this at that time – went down the stairs and opened the door of the shop. He took the rifle and took the stone back into the shop. The rifle, it was hidden under his bed, and the stones he took to the yard at the rear where they had come from, from a wall that had fallen. For sixteen weeks the rifle was under his bed, because his son was frightened of having taken it, and was frightened of giving it to the Mehdi army. Yesterday, Mr al-Ajouti's wife found the rifle. Yesterday he questioned his son. Yesterday he found the truth, is certain it is the truth, of how the rifle came to his son's room, and of how the soldier was made senseless. He begs forgiveness for his son. He

402

is ashamed for what his son did. He begs it is not spoken of in the village, his returning the rifle. If it is spoken, his life will be taken by the Mehdi army. He hopes it is enough that he has returned the rifle, that his son will not be punished. Later, children came. They took the soldier's helmet and the coat against bullets. It is the flak-jacket. Mr al-Ajouti apologizes for the action of his son. He wishes you well on your return to Britain, to your families.'

The major said curtly, 'I am grateful to Mr al-Ajouti, and I can assure him that his son will not be punished, and that the taking of the rifle will not be spoken of.'

From his hip pocket, the major took a wad of dinar notes, probably the equivalent of what was put over the counter in a village bakery in a week, and pressed them into the bone-ribbed hand. The old man bobbed his gratitude, then turned, then started out on the raised road to return to the village, his bakery shop, and his home.

The major strode towards the sandbags, the machine-gun and the gate. His words snapped from the side of his mouth: 'I think, Faisal, it is a matter that is dead, buried. If you were to speak of it you would betray the trust placed in you by the British army, and your employment would cease. Understood? Hamish, it is a business best forgotten. I think your role, and mine, in the affair concerning allegations made against Mal Kitchen, would not now sustain close examination. Yes, best forgotten.'

'Forgotten, sir, already forgotten.'

'Found on wasteground, hidden there, handed in by a local who was unable to give an exact location – that'll fit the paperwork . . . No medals for digging up the past.'

'None, sir. I'll see the word goes round, found on wasteground.'

They walked back through the gate. Bravo's major returned to his bunker and the preparations for withdrawal.

He had names but no identity. He had been Anwar Maghroub, born into affluence in a suburb of Alexandria, but the character of the child was lost.

The voice behind him beat at the back of his head. 'What I'm telling you, Dean, and true – I'll be so damn bloody pleased to be finished with this. If you'd told me, anyone had, a month ago that I'd

403

be flogging myself through this place, cold like I've never known it and hungry, I'd have told them to go jump.'

He had also been Sami, a student of engineering, with a girl and with friends who understood the rigour of sacrifice, but the personality of the pupil had gone.

'A month ago, I wouldn't have thought I could do this, go through it and still be on my feet – wouldn't have been able to, not without having a friend with me, and it's because I'm tough. It's what makes me a leader. Others come to me and know that I'll lead them. Lazy sods, all of them, and feeding off me. They feed off my brains and my energy.'

He had been Abu Khaled, conspirator and activist in the Organization, who had studied and learned the lessons of success in attack and failure in security, but that man's mind was outdated and finished with.

'Because of you, what I've learned from you, I am telling you that things are going to be different when I'm back, up and running – damn different. No passengers in my team and no bloodsuckers. Slim and lean, that's what you are, and that's what I'm going to be, and ahead of the game. In my crowd, they'll have one chance and if it's blown then they're out, out on their bloody arses. Best thing that ever happened to me was meeting up with you, and that's God's truth. I'm surrounded by passengers and suckers, but not for long. They'll scream, but I won't be listening.'

He had been Dean, goalkeeper for a team he had not heard of, who listened without response to the ramblings of an idiot, but the character, personality, mind of that fantasy had never existed.

'I've got my cousins, three of them, giving me grief. I've got old Percy, who's all disrespect, and what I know is that he loathes me. I've got Mikey and Sharon, that's my parents, and they live bloody well off my back. I've got Joanne and Wayne, he's only a kid and doesn't know better, but she's got the hump with me . . . and there's a bloody great crowd like a spider web. They all live off me . . . I'm telling you, there's changes coming. I like a lot about you, but I like most that you go alone. I reckon it's class to go alone. You and me, it's good we're together.'

He was, *now*, Milan Draskic who held a Slovenian passport and was a co-ordinator and sent to erase failures of security and to drive home success in attack, but he had not yet learned to live inside the thoughts and skin of that man, and— They had come past the five marker cloths he had left on branches. He stopped dead, and gazed forward – not at the whitecaps and the surf, not at the horizon – and the idiot cannoned into him. He saw, at the top of the dune in front of him, the three legs of his tripod, but not the flashlamp.

'What's up?'

He said, quietly, with his hand shielding his voice, that the flashlamp, as he had left it, was gone from the tripod.

'What's that mean?'

He said, his words protected from the wind, that he had built the tripod in daylight so that it would be secure, fastened the flashlamp to it and aimed its face to the sea. He had lashed it in place by daylight so that its beam would be steady when it was used. He heard the first sliver of the idiot's panic.

'Well, you didn't tie it tight enough, did you? Got to bloody find it, haven't you? Didn't allow for the bloody gale, did you?'

He sank down into the softness of the sand and felt with his hands and the grains ran through his fingers, but the flashlamp was not at the base of his tripod's stakes.

'Got to be there, hasn't it? Got to be. Can't have bloody walked off, can it?'

The idiot was beside him, on his knees, and his hands were sweeping at the sand, and the idiot squealed.

'Cut my bloody self on glass. It wasn't the wind – Christ, it wasn't – that shifted it.'

His fingers found the flashlamp, buried, and they ran over shards from its face, and touched the broken end of the bulb where it went into the socket.

The panic became more shrill. 'No light! How the fuck are they going to find us? Out in this shit-heap, how they going to get to us? What'll guide them? You fucked up, putting the light up and leaving it, fucked up big-time. No light, how they going to bring the boat in?'

He had only the pencil torch and a beam with a range of only a few metres.

'It's all round us. Don't know where. The old jerk you shot. The guy who came over the fence, and I lied about him. All round us, and

we don't know how close . . . Can't bloody see them . . . Watching
us . . . How we going to get off of here? You know it and I know it,
they're watching us and-round us . . . maybe close enough to bloody
touch us. What we going to do?'

He pulled the radio set over the sand, slipped the clasp on the
case, opened it, threw the switch, reached out and dragged the idiot
close. He felt the shaking fear – and he listened. He heard only the
set's static whine and the wind's buffeting.

'You are taking a hell of a chance, Dad. A chance with me in the
dinghy, with my boy, with the boat, with yourself. You know that,
Dad. And now you're saying they've no light. Going in with that
dinghy, it's going to be six shades of hell. I reckon it's one run, that's
all. I can't be stooging there, not in that surf. They'll have to be out
in the water, deep enough so I don't snag the outboard, and have to
be ready. How am I going to find them if there's no light? Is the
money that good? Have you thought, Dad, of just turning round and
getting on home?'

What Harry Rogers knew, as he listened to the carp of his son,
was that he required two fathoms minimum of draught under the
keel of the *Anneliese Royal*, and twelve feet of water would put
him a minimum of four hundred yards from the beach. The
dinghy would need three feet of water and it would not come
closer than a hundred yards from the beach . . . The trawler and
the dinghy would both be bucking in swell. The low clouds and
the rain's mist would screw his view of the TG15 buoy and the
Accumer Ee light and he needed both to get in near. He reckoned
he was three hours from getting far enough to the island to launch
the dinghy, and the chart in the wheel-house showed him sunken
wrecks, sunken obstructions, and supposedly cleared areas of
dumped explosives. There were gas pipes and telephone lines
under them, and if they snagged one of those bastards by going
off course, they were screwed. They were on the northern edge of
a section marked as Submarine Exercise Area, not that – in these
sea conditions – a periscope would be slotting up. The boat yawed,
fell into troughs and climbed waves, and his grandson was again
retching at the bucket.

Harry said, 'I thought about it, yes, ditching them – but that's not my way. I'll use my light, keep it on you while you're taking the dinghy in, and they'll have to shift themselves and come to you . . . That's what I told them. Can't do better . . . You want to hear me say it? I'll say it – I would not dare to ditch Ricky Capel, and that's more important than the fact that I gave my word.'

He was close enough to hear them.

Malachy thought it the perfect battleground.

He had been drawn to the right place, alone, to stand and fight, unseen by any witness. He felt a great calm, and peace, and he thought a road ended here and that he was within sight of a pyramid's summit. He rested his fingers on the dog-tags at his throat.

20

He saw the light. Riddled with cramp in his stomach, pain in his hips and knees, sand in his throat that he had to endure and not cough out, Malachy saw the light's blast out to sea. Not a brilliant light but one that was misted and confused by cloud and rain, but a clear enough beacon to those watching for it.

It was not aimed at the shore but was directed upwards and bounced back from the cloudbanks and rolled, cavorted, rocked as if its platform were unstable. He thought the trawler on which it was mounted was shaken by the violence of the swell. He realized, from the light on the cloud ceiling, that the boat edged towards the shore where the surf ran.

Near to him, separated from him by the blunt sand summit of a dune, he heard a little yell of excitement – the voice of Ricky Capel. He had felt, lying twenty paces from him, the fear of the man. The fear had been on Capel's tongue, in the whine of his voice, and it had grown because he had sensed that he was watched. As the hours had passed, Malachy had felt the man's fear tighten. He had known his own fear when he had walked, without a weapon and without a helmet or flak-jacket, down a narrow street in a village with the sun low and scorching his eyes. It had been the fear of the man that had sustained him as he had lain in the sand, among the dune's grasses. He heard, now, a sharp hiss for quiet and the excitement was stifled.

The other man had shown Malachy no sign of fear. He heard low grunts, from them both, and sensed they stood.

Far away to his left, if he raised his head, Malachy could see the scattered lights of the village, and in the near sea – if he strained and peered between the bent grasses – there were two marker buoys. In the hours he had been in place, he had learned to recognize the sequences of their flashes, one red and one green. But the light further towards the horizon, beyond the surf bursts, had greater strength. There were the lights of the village, the lights of the buoys, the light from the trawler, but the rest of the scope of Malachy's vision showed him nothing more than black darkness. He had thought the world had emptied, that only he and two men existed, and one was beyond the area of his interest.

As he watched the lights, Malachy did not recognize Polly Wilkins's big picture. Neither did he listen, any longer, to the contempt of a host of soldiers and a psychiatrist, and his wife, and a man who ran a business for buying and selling houses . . . He involved no one, was owned by no one. He flexed his muscles and readied himself. When they moved, he would follow.

He heard, above the wind, the whine, 'Don't we get moving? I knew he'd come. He's a good boy, my Harry is. Shouldn't we shift down there?'

He heard, over the rain's beat, the response: 'Not yet, too early.'

'They won't hang about for us, you know.'

'It is too soon.'

Malachy realized the authority of the second man. He was Polly Wilkins's target. The second man governed the big picture. Malachy heard the authority, spoken softly. Men, he knew it, who had authority rarely found it necessary to raise a voice, never shouted, did not whine. He thought the man, joined at the hip to Ricky Capel, was burdened.

He watched the light, its beam on the clouds, approach the beach.

He was silent, did not dare to speak. Ricky stood in the force of the wind and saw the light come closer . . . Then he shuddered, shook. He was Ricky Capel. He ran a part of south-east London. He was the big man and guys backed off from him. He was above grief, too big a man to be given disrespect. He did not snivel, did not cower.

'Yes, I hear you, Dean, and I'm saying it as well – it's not yet, it's too early to move, too soon.'

Watching the light, he shed from his mind the source of the fear that had nagged, eaten at him all the hours they had waited. A man stalked him. A man followed him. Straining into the darkness and seeing the roll of the light up and against the cloud, the thought of the man was wiped from his mind. Squinting, he saw the light beyond the dim beach expanse, and the cresting lines of the surf . . . He'd be wading into it, into the force of the waves – that was what Harry had said – into that bloody sea, in bloody darkness . . . but he was Ricky Capel, and he was a big man. The wind hammered against him and would have pitched him back if he had not held, tight, to the arm beside him.

'Should stay patient – I don't reckon we should move too soon, that's my opinion.'

The light shone out ahead of her, and was away to her right, and she made her calculation on the point of the beach it approached.

Methodically, Polly rolled the sleeping-bag and the sand in it, filled the rucksack and wriggled its straps over her shoulders.

Then she hit the combination of buttons on her mobile for a secure call, and dialled. She heard it ring out twice before an automated voice – not Freddie Gaunt's – informed her that she was being diverted. It was answered. Crisply, without preamble, she was asked to speak.

'It's out there, the light. I can't be exact, it's dark as hell, and I don't know the sea, but I estimate it about a mile offshore. Damn, damn, they've killed the light . . . It was there, was coming in. I suppose it was on long enough to alert the target group, but . . .'

There was criticism. She should not 'estimate' or 'suppose'. Facts were required of her. She swore under her breath, soundless. She could not estimate why Gaunt had done it to her, could not suppose why he had quit on her.

'There was a light offshore, on for eight minutes. At the moment it was switched off, the light was one nautical mile from the tideline.'

They wanted bullshit, they would get it. She did not know whether the light had been visible for six minutes or nine minutes; neither did she know the length of a nautical mile nor see the tideline. She imagined them round a table crowded with phones, consoles and screens, with maps dominating their room's walls, and . . . She was asked for the location of Kitchen.

'Don't know, and that is neither an estimate nor a supposition. I have not the faintest idea where he is. So as you understand, it is pitch bloody black out here, and it is peeing with rain and blowing a gale. He could be a mile away or ten yards away, and that is a fact. It is also a fact that I have not been issued with night-vision equipment.'

The cold cut through Polly, but they would not have been interested in that. She was asked what were Kitchen's intentions when he left her.

'Can't estimate and can't suppose – not a clue. I will call you on further developments. Out.'

A career gone down the drain? Perhaps. Her teeth rattled as she shivered. Perhaps . . . Did she give a damn if a career was lost? Maybe . . . She pocketed the phone. Polly wondered if she now had the status of being a flagged pin on a wall map. She scrambled down off the dune and tumbled to the start of the loose sand that the sea never reached. She was perplexed that she had not seen an answering light from away to her right on a point of high ground, did not understand that, could not reckon how the trawler would be guided in – or the men to be picked up would be floundering in water, would be battered by the surf – and was confused. She went, slowly and carefully, below the dunes and above the beach, stopped to listen, then went on, stopped again . . . It hurt so bloody much that Freddie Gaunt had quit on her.

'Makes you think, doesn't it? The last chap here – his feet where we are. Wagons out at the front with everything he and his family own, and he's looking around at all that's familiar, then he's going to the door, and going to nail it shut after him, and then he'll be joining his neighbours in flight. And the enemy is over the hill – not quite literally, but the barbarians are at the gates . . . and this is where he stood for the last time.'

It no longer rained and the wind had slackened. Frederick Gaunt knelt in the pit and the high lights glistened the mud and he scraped with his trowel at the edge of the small patch of uncovered mosaic. He did not know the man beside him, had not dug with him before. In a few minutes they would break for tea from an urn and that

411

would be welcome for warmth and would be respite from the monologue in his ear . . . The man was young, lean-faced and lean-bodied, and scraped and talked with matching intensity.

'I suppose he knew it was coming – yes, he'd have realized that his time was up. Must have wounded him to think that civilization, all of the comforts of a building like this, was going to be tossed over, and that the day of the hordes – Goths, Visigoths, Picts, you name them – had come, and the start of a Dark Age with them. He wouldn't have known it, but I think it's a law of history that new forces will inevitably overwhelm an old order.'

The site was in Wiltshire, south of Keysley Down and to the west of Berwick St Leonard. It was approached by a rutted farm track, and was lit – at fifteen minutes to midnight – by a row of generator-powered arc-lights. Negotiations with the landowner had given the diggers a clear seven days and seven nights to work on the villa, and after that the excavated ground would be covered with thick plastic sheeting, which would in turn be covered with the moved soil and sods of the field. It was the third night . . . Until that afternoon, before his meeting and his butchery at VBX, Gaunt had not thought he had the vaguest chance of joining these enthusiasts. They were mostly students, recruited from a south-coast university, but he had been allocated to the team leader, who talked.

'Inevitable that it'll all come crashing down once the decadence sets in. Our chap, who stood here in his sandals, he'd become too comfortable – had too much wealth and too much privilege – and he'd lost the hardness to fight. That's it, isn't it? His civilization, morally corrupt, could not compete with the simple brutality of the barbarian – so he ran and left his home to sixteen hundred years of ruin and pillage, then the stones of the walls were taken, soil was washed by the rain over what was left, then it was buried and eventually we pitched up. Comfort and decadence, they're killers for any society confronted by an enemy that's hungry, ruthless.'

At the extremity of the mosaic there were stone slabs and then the first signs of the *praefurnium*, the stoke hole, and in the mud that he lifted on his trowel Gaunt found a small piece of compressed black material. With near reverence he placed it in the bucket by his elbow. When they took tea he would show it to the site surveyor: a piece of charcoal that could be radio-carbon-dated, that could tell them when, to the year, a fire had been lit before the arrival of the forces of that day's axis of evil. He found the man's thesis not irritating but marginally amusing.

'What I believe frightening is that corruption is at our gates now and tonight . . . Trust me, I'm a general practitioner – know what I mean? You should see what crosses my surgery five days a week, nine hours a day . . . I promise you, I'm not a doom merchant, but we're busy losing our way. Drug addiction, teenage pregnancy, child abuse and paedophilia, debt entrapment, obesity, alcoholism, benefit dependency, ignorance and illiteracy, and every symptom of yobbery. I see it, and I practise in a little backwater, in Devizes. It's the drugs culture that's the worst – and so few seem to care . . . What seems to me to be so wretchedly stupid is that we are preaching for our failing lifestyle to be adopted by Islamic states. Such conceit.'

He stiffened. The trowel slipped from his hand. Gaunt, working at the dig site with the voices – and sometimes the laughter – of young people around him, had felt rare tranquillity. He no longer scraped for charcoal pieces or for bone scraps that had been thrown away, centuries before, on to the cut wood and open-cast coal in the *praefurnium* . . . He had believed he had escaped, and had not. What now was relevant? As if a nerve in him was pinched, he saw himself as an old warrior too tired for combat when the barbarians swarmed at the gates. A man who spoke of a society, decadent and doomed, in the corridors of Vauxhall Bridge Cross, would – Gaunt thought – be taken to the stake and burned alive as a heretic. Did a doctor from Devizes tell a truth that none dared name? It was a mandatory-death-sentence offence, in the offices of VBX, to suggest that victory was not assured.

'I hope you don't mind me prattling on . . . Do you think our time's up, like this chap's was? I wonder about it. Is all this we hear of the new fundamentalist enemy just modern-speak for barbarians at the gates? Are we now as decadent as our chap, standing here for the last time? Quite a rum thought: in sixteen hundred years, folk will be scratching at the foundations of my home and getting all excited when they've found the sewer pipe and can tell what I ate, and have a chuckle and say, "Yes, he'd have known his time was up."

413

Sorry . . . sorry, talking too much, my wife says I always do . . . What's this?'

Bare fingers wiped mud smears off a length of bone, and the arc-lights pierced sufficiently into the hole to show the minute working of the decoration at the head of what had been a hairpin – consigned to the fire rather than be an ornament in the tresses of a barbarian's woman. Gaunt, with all the warmth he could muster, congratulated the doctor on his significant find. They were called for tea. He levered himself out of the pit and carried his bucket to the tent where the urn was and sandwiches. He had thought, in a Wiltshire field, he would find sanctuary, but his mind was trapped by thoughts of Polly, and the man she had believed in, and the bright but deep eyes in the photograph of an enemy . . . and the casualties of war, then and now.

It was a supreme effort to drag himself to his feet. He was so nearly there, so close to his Grail. Oskar Netzer pulled himself up, off his stomach, off his knees and elbows, and the gate rocked on his weight and his fingers clutched at the catch holding it shut. Weakness consumed him, but the pain was long gone. When the gate swung open, a little more of his feeble strength left him and he lost his hold on the ironwork. He fell forward on to the cemetery path. He stag-gered over the loose gravel towards the stone and his wife's grave. He saw nothing ahead of him in the blackness but knew where he must go . . . and he believed he had made expiation for the wrong done by his uncle. After a few short steps, he collapsed on to the sharp stones – but he hoped to reach her resting-place and to sleep there and be with her, to tell her of his ducks, and of the men who had intruded on his paradise, and that he had loosed the evil's hold on him . . . He crawled off the path and over sodden grass, reached out and found the glass jar, the stems of flowers that had been stripped by the wind.

He clasped the stone and did not know what he had achieved – did not know who would bury him – and sleep took him.

A clock chimed. A car, with lights flashing, and with an escort in front and behind, brought Timo Rahman to the prison in the north of Hamburg at Fuhlsbüttel.

414

He was led from it to a desk where the details of his life, and the charges he faced, would be processed. The gaol's landings awoke. Word had passed. Spoons beat against metal mugs. Plates rattled against doors. His name was shouted and echoed down the block's iron staircases. He was ordered to strip for medical inspection.

He was in hurtful ignorance of the reason for the collapse of his rule, and of who was responsible.

'I can't go in any further.'

'It's bloody dangerous out there, Dad.'

'Myself, I'd do it if I could,' Harry shouted at the wheel-house door, at his son. 'I can't . . . What I'm promising, it's never again.'

'Just get her stern on, Dad, and keep her there.'

He should have been down on the deck to help his boy but dared not leave the wheel and the diesel engine's controls to young Paul, his grandson, who had retched again and was now too frail to hold the wheel steady and did not know the working of the engine. The door slammed behind him, but he yelled and did not know if he was heard.

'Don't hang about. You get there, you ground, you pick them up if they're there, but you don't wait. Their problem if they're not in place in the water – my conscience is clear that my word was kept.'

Harry reached up, worked the lever that manoeuvred the light on the wheel-house roof and hit the switch. In the flood of the beam, he could see his son and grandson heaving the dinghy off the bucking deck and on to the gunwale, resting it on the trawler's side, then – as a spray surge swamped them – pushing it over. On a wave, the dinghy – held by a straining rope – climbed higher than the gunwale, higher than them, then fell like the trough had no bottom to it. He had given his word to Ricky Capel, and his word was all the honour left to him. His son seemed to punch the shoulder of his grandson, as if to reassure the kid, who was destroyed by sickness, then launched himself over the side. Harry lost sight of him in the next pit, then saw him lifted in the dinghy, and the kid loosed hold of the rope.

He kept the light on the dinghy. He watched its progress, pathetically slow, and smoke fumes spat from the outboard. It rose and it fell. It was hard, one-handed, to hold the light on the dinghy and to keep the steering on the *Anneliese Royal* steady, to control the engine and bring the forward speed down from three knots forward to two knots. To his starboard side was the roll of the buoy light, the Accumer Ee on the chart, and to port were dulled blips of colour from the island's homes.

A prayer slipped on Harry's lips.

He held the wheel-house roof light on the dinghy and saw it shaken among the whitecaps and go towards the surf . . . Whatever it cost him, he swore that he would never again be Ricky Capel's slave.

He heard, 'About bloody time. You ready? We go, yes? We don't hang about, not now.'

The world of Malachy Kitchen was now a tiny, confined space. His whole world was a dune with blown grass and soft sand, a beach, riffling surf and a light that wavered on the leaping progress of a dinghy. He felt cleansed, as if old baggage were dropped, and no one here would label him a coward. He coiled his body and made ready to run.

They were gone.

They went in a sliding chase down loose banks of sand. Little yelps of elation from Ricky Capel, like a child at play and happy, nothing from the man who led him.

The light on the boat at sea, perhaps because she was hurled up, wafted away and beyond the dinghy, and then raked over the surf and came on to the beach from which the tide ran, and Malachy saw them, saw that Capel had the box that was the radio, and that the second man carried a machine pistol that trailed loose in his hand. Malachy stood, but the light's beam did not reach him. It swung low, searched for the dinghy and found the breaking waves, then its target. They were off the loose sand, on the beach, and they ran away to his left towards a point that the dinghy headed for.

He had the tags in his hand, and he lifted the strap over his head: they were his name, his service number, his religion and his blood group, and they were his history. In his fist, fiercely clenched, Malachy held them.

Because he knew when he would hit, he waited a few long seconds more. He could not see them, only the dinghy.

416

He thought himself his own master, and all that was his old world were the shoes on his feet and the tags in his hand. He came off the dune and the sand plunged under his feet. He fell and pushed himself back to his feet. The wind blasted against him, the rain stung at his eyes, and he ran.

Shells crunched, broke, under the tread of his shoes.

He stretched his stride.

When the boat's light came up again, off the dinghy, it caught them – Ricky Capel behind and the second man in front of him – found them near to the surf line. Neither looked back.

He pounded the beach. He careered through a lagoon of water. It was where he wished to be, a battleground that was perfect.

They were in the water. He saw them against the white sweep of the surf, and against the thunder of the breaking waves the voices were shouting, screaming.

'We're coming . . . Can't you get in bloody closer?'

'You got to come to me. I'm not bloody grounding.'

'Get in nearer.'

'Won't risk tipping her. Tip her and we're all bloody gone.'

'I can't goddamn swim.'

'If the engine goes under, we're wrecked. Come on, shift it.'

They were into the surf wall, Ricky Capel trailing. Between the cresting waves, Ricky Capel had the water at his ankles and shins, but when the waves rolled at full height the water squirmed round his waist and seemed to drive him back. Malachy heard Ricky Capel's howl that he had lost a shoe. The man ahead never turned, never reached back with a hand to steady Ricky Capel, never tried to be of help. Malachy splashed into the surf and the drive of his legs was blocked. He was lifting his knees, stamping for height over the surf, and was closing on Ricky Capel. He did not think why he was there, what he did, how Ricky Capel had become an enemy to be destroyed. The past was gone from his mind. He struggled against the wind's force, against the waves. He saw that Ricky Capel had stopped and he thought exhaustion had beaten him. Malachy seemed to hear the sob of Ricky Capel's breath. The gap had opened between the two men, as if contact had been lost, and beyond both of them – riding and falling in the water, lit by the light – was the dinghy. He took the deep gulp, swallowed air into his lungs. He closed on Ricky Capel – five more strides, then three – and the water beat against his waist. A new wave came that pitched up the dinghy, ran against the other man's chest, lurched into Ricky Capel, and charged Malachy. As he braced himself, he threw back over his shoulder the two tags, and did not twist to see them fall. He had no more use for them, or for the past, and did not hear their splash. Malachy lunged. His fists snatched at space, and spray, and then his weight hit Ricky Capel.

He came without warning, and the momentum driven by the grip of his shoes collapsed Ricky Capel. Perhaps Ricky Capel, in the two or three seconds between feeling the hammer blow against his back and being forced under the surf, tried to shout. Underwater, in darkness, Malachy gripped the thrashing body and fingers gouged at his eyes and a bare foot kicked at his shin – and the height of a wave passed and the wind surged on their faces.

The light lit them.

He saw the shock in the eyes of Ricky Capel, as if he did not understand why, then the squirm of fear as if he remembered a man on the pavement of Bevin Close. The scream was choked, and water spat from his mouth. The next wave caught them, and the fight had gone from Ricky Capel. Hands grasped at Malachy's coat, then his trousers, then his shoes, then loosed.

He stood. He felt the weight, pushed by the surf, against his ankles.

The man was at the dinghy, but had turned.

Malachy did not hear the weapon, but saw the flashes from it, and the man climbed easily up and into the dinghy. He felt a weakness in his legs and in his hips . . . and was aware of vague shouts from the dinghy, then the roar of its outboard gaining power, and felt himself sink. It did not seem important to him that the sea closed over him, then freed and lifted him, covered him, then carried him . . . so tired.

The surf was in his ears and the water caressed him, as she had done – and he heard her voice.

'Fight, damn you – don't bloody give up on me.'

He craved sleep.

★   ★   ★

418

'He can count himself lucky he was shot.'

'Myself, with my own hands, I'd have throttled him.'

'It's just a total and utter shambles and the responsibility for it, a criminal responsibility, lies with those who allowed him to be there.'

When the report had been given over the loudspeakers, when her voice had gone, they had bayed their anger – Dennis of the Security Service, Jimmy from the Norfolk police, and Bill who did liaison for the Hereford- and Poole-based teams . . . and each in turn screwed his lip to outscore the derision, the hostility, of the previous intervention, and last in the line was the Special Branch officer, Trevor.

'I think, again, the essence of the issue is missed,' he said softly. 'I'm not talking of any morsel of charity owed to a man who fell far, but of the business at hand. We spoke of a rat run. What I made of the somewhat distraught communication from the officer on location, the rat run operates. She reported that he, the only individual I have interest in, boarded the dinghy and was *en route* to the mother boat when the light was cut. The *Anneliese Royal* is at sea and we are alive, have a man to track . . . Kitchen's fate is of no concern to me, is a mere distraction, as are the reasons for the stupidity of his actions.'

A dawn had gone, and the last of the storm slipped inland. A final shower of rain plastered the beach and was blown on over the German mainland and towards the heathland of Lüneburg and the Baltic coast beyond. The sun broke through, caught the tail of the shower and threw down a rainbow. One end of the rainbow was on the island's endless flat sands and on the slackening surf as the gale died. Its colours danced on the body of a drowned man that was heaved backwards and forwards by the disappearing tide. A woman walking her dog found it, and thought, from a distance, that the cadaver was a dead seal, but when she came close she saw the eyes of a man, wide in terror, and the rainbow went on.

A man – long decamped to the mainland town of Norden – brought his wife and three teenage children to the island's cemetery at Ostdorf to lay flowers on the grave of his parents. For the adults it would be a solemn few minutes of contemplation while the children rambled among the stones. He was recovering memories of a stern disciplinarian merchant mariner, and a mother who had survived Baltrum's elements into old age, when his vigil was broken by the shriek of his younger daughter. He hurried to the girl, his mood of respect fractured. He found, wrapped against this stone, the body of a man wizened with age and the sunlight fell on darkened bloodstains.

Murmuring, so that she would not be heard by her son or by the girls, his wife said, 'You know who that is? It's old Netzer, it is Oskar Netzer. Never had a good word for a living soul, never had a friend since she died, never did a day's work . . . Never did anything useful to others. The end of a wasted life. What could have happened to him to make all that blood?'

Polly crouched in front of the washing-machine. She had emptied into it everything from the rucksack that could be soaped, rinsed, tumbled, and the sleeping-bag. Dried sand caked the linoleum. She heard the door of the apartment open and it was then kicked shut.

She called out, 'I'm back – in the kitchen.'

She stood and started to strip.

She was aware that Ronnie was in the doorway.

She peeled off layers of clothing and bent to stuff them into the machine.

A trilling voice was behind her: 'Oh, brilliant, good to see you. Had a good time? Christ, that's a serious mess, bloody hell. You been sleeping on a beach? Doesn't your lot run to hotels? Don't tell me, you didn't get any shopping done. God, Polly, what's that on your hands? Is that blood, old blood, on you? Are you all right?'

She was naked, and she had to heave against the washing-machine's door to fasten it, then hit the button.

'I'm fine. Thanks for asking, but I'm fine . . . Yes, it's blood. Not to worry, not mine.'

She watched the machine churning suds through the window in the door.

'You know what I'm going to ask.' She heard the giggle. 'Whatever it was you did – don't mind me – did you win?'

She felt the cold on her skin, not the warmth of him. She felt the salt in her throat, not the taste of him.

420

'Some people won and some people lost. But they're history, the winners and losers.'

She walked past Ronnie, across the hall and into the bathroom, and lost herself behind the shower curtain. Under a cascade of hot water, near to scalding, she scrubbed herself clean. Sand from her hair welled at the plughole and she washed the last of his old blood from her hands.

She yelled, and did not know if she was heard, 'You never really learn it, do you? Who are the winners and who are the losers?'

Harry Rogers brought the trawler into harbour – and did not know that a crisis committee had monitored his progress across the North Sea and that a pilotless drone flying from Boscombe Down had been overhead and tracking the *Anneliese Royal* with a state-of-the-art lens, and that a submarine's periscope had scanned him from close quarters as he approached the East Anglian shore.

They tied up.

They reported to the harbourmaster that a winding-gear malfunction had prevented them fishing when the storm had blown out, that they had no catch to land.

His boy, Billy, took his grandson, Paul, to a doctor's surgery in the town for a check-up on his arm and to assess the damage from continuous seasickness.

Harry stayed on board.

With a hose, a brush and a mop, he sluiced through the wheel-house and the galley, and if he lifted his head he saw the rest of the town's fleet put to sea in breezy sunshine.

For more than three hours, he was alone on the trawler with memories of a storm blowing off a German island that were alive, and dreams of owning an historic sailboat that were dead.

He locked the wheel-house, hitched his bag on to his shoulder and walked the deck to the point where the old encrusted ladder would take him up on to the quay. He swung his legs over the side and on to a slippery rung, and saw two men above him.

No bullshit, no protestations of innocence . . . Too exhausted for it, too much of his life hacked from him.

They came down the ladder, gingerly, in their city shoes and suits,

421

and he led them back to the wheel-house. He made them coffee, but that did not soften the coldness on their faces.

He had no one on board. They could search if they wanted to. He had brought back no passenger.

Harry said, 'You make a mistake in your life, and each day that follows it's harder to extricate yourself from that mistake. My mistake was Ricky Capel. I have no excuses and I look for no sympathy, and the mistake is mine. You want to know about the man with Ricky Capel on the beach, and I'll tell you what you want to know. Billy went out in the dinghy, in a hell of a sea, and part of what I'm saying is from him, but most of it is from what I saw with the light. They were in the water, big swell and surf, and coming slow towards the dinghy. I saw this guy come off the beach, and he ran into the surf, and Ricky Capel and his man never saw him. Ricky was behind. The guy smacked into Ricky Capel and he put him down. They went together, under, then just the guy came up. The man, Ricky's man, turned, would have seen the guy, fired at him. I saw the flashes and I heard the gun, and the guy went down, and I killed the light. The man got on board Billy's dinghy. Billy brought him back to us. I was turning hard. Billy came on board first, and then he had hold of the rope, took it from young Paul, and the man was going to follow him. I left the wheel, left it spinning, and I went on deck, and I got the rope off Billy, and I chucked it. He lifted the gun and I was flat in his sights. He'd have blasted me but it didn't fire, must have been too much water in it, and then there was the gap between him and us . . . I went back in the wheel-house and took the engine to power. We left him. He had the dinghy, he had an outboard with a full tank, he had the reserve, but he didn't have us. I never saw him again, God's truth, and Billy didn't, nor Paul. We took her back to sea. I can't say what happened to him, but it was foul conditions for an open dinghy. Can't say whether he drowned, made a landfall, whether he survived and is still out there, can't.'

He had been summoned to the heavenly heights of Vauxhall Bridge Cross. He had knocked and there was the answering call for him to enter, but then he was kept standing for those few seconds, while the assistant deputy director studied desk papers, that confirmed celestial authority.

'Ah – sorry, good to see you, Freddie. Your leave went well?'

'Thank you, Gilbert, yes. It was excellent.' Frederick Gaunt was damned if he would show annoyance at the casual insult, or speak of the raging cold he had acquired in a Wiltshire field. 'We had a first-class dig.'

'Glad to hear it. I'll get you up to speed. Your target, Anwar Maghroub is lost, presumed drowned, but there is, sadly, no confirmation of that and no body. To be very frank, Freddie, some have spoken of your role in this, and that of Miss Wilkins, and of the "hired hand" as adding up to a shambles, the destruction of an operation that should have brought great rewards – and would have done if that bloody Kitchen, and the reasons for his actions remain a mystery, had not interfered. I, of course, and you would have the right to expect it, have fought your corner with vigour but against considerable opposition. I think we are at a time when we require new brooms and fresh perspectives, almost a cleaning of Augean stables. You know – washing out the stables of the king of Elis, a labour of Hercules.'

'I am familiar with Greek mythology.'

'Good – different minds bringing different thinking to ongoing problems. We don't want to lose you, Freddie. We'd hate a man of your talents to throw in the towel and make an overhasty decision on early retirement, though the packages on the table are generous to a fault and offer many opportunities for the pursuit of valuable hobbies. We'd hate you to walk away. What's vacant, because of Wilson's diagnosis of diabetes, is Uruguay. It's a bit of a backwater, but that's where we are. What do you say to Montevideo, three years and perhaps an extension to four?'

If he gulped, he did not show it. If he felt a frisson of anger, he hid it.

Gaunt said, 'I'd like that very much.'

They wanted his neck on the block, wanted him gone. He would deny them the satisfaction. He saw the face across the desk flex in the irritation caused by his acceptance.

'I'd say Uruguay for three years, or four, would be most challenging . . . worthwhile.'

★   ★   ★

Gulls wheeled, screamed and dived on the bright-coloured intruder that was marooned at the base of the red stone cliffs.

An ornithologist saw it and reported to the coast-guard station on the North Sea island of Helgoland that an upturned dinghy had been washed ashore. He was able to return in time to the cliffs and watch men come by cutter and retrieve it, but he was on a day's visit and did not have time to learn what they had found. He telephoned from the mainland the next morning and heard the dinghy carried the name of a British registered trawler, and heard also that the cliffs and beaches of Helgoland had been searched, but without further result.

'No bodies have come ashore?'

None had been discovered.

'Perhaps it was taken off the deck by that storm last month.'

Perhaps it had been.

He came out of the stairwell and into the summer heat that burned off the block's concrete. A voice boomed behind him, 'How you doing, Mr Johnson? How you keeping?'

He turned, saw the big West Indian with the weightlifter's shoulders.

'Fine, Ivanhoe, just fine.'

'More important than how you're doing, keeping – how's Millie?'

'She's well, as good as to be expected, quite chirpy ... She asks after him.'

He had a handkerchief out and mopped his forehead, saw that sweat ran rivers on the social worker's face.

'She can ask but I doubt she'll see him. A new man, a changed man, and without old baggage. You, Mr Johnson, and me and her, we'd be old baggage, but he came back to the Amersham.'

'Millie heard he was here, not living on the estate but working.'

'I just seen him the once, turned up at my office door and all humble requested a job. I sent him where he wanted to go. They fixed him – a low grade because of no qualifications. I've not seen him since.'

'Where did they place him?'

The arm of Ivanhoe Manners waved expansively, generalized, in

424

the direction of the estate facilities, buildings that had survived the warfare of vandalism, where the money of the New Deal for the Community had been swallowed, where the Pensioners' Association played bingo and the Tenants' Association held meetings.

'Over there's where he is.'

'You got time to show me?'

A wide frown played on Ivanhoe Manners's forehead, as if the question perplexed him, as if an answer would embarrass him. Then he scratched at his ear, and seemed to wince as if the request hurt him . . . Tony Johnson knew the basic detail of what had happened, months before, on a German beach, but what had crossed his desk had been sanitized of intelligence material. He knew the proof of it because, with half a hundred others from the Criminal Intelligence Service and the Crime Squad and the Organized Crime Unit, he had gone down to Lewisham to see the coffin of Ricky Capel – the untouchable smart kid – put down in the earth. Not a wet eye to be seen; a parson clamouring through the service like he'd another one backed up; poor turnout and almost a carnival mood from those who'd showed. He was just home from holiday, two weeks on the Algarve, and Millie had told him that Malachy was back – ears like bloody surveillance antennae the lady possessed. He had come, almost, to wish he hadn't asked.

'I'll take you, but it's not for talking – just watching.'

'That'll do me.'

They went across a plaza, through a play area and across a road. The building where the facilities were, Tony Johnson thought, was like a damn great bunker . . . and he reckoned it bloody needed to be. Past mums pushing brats in buggies, and kids on a block's corner – maybe it was the sunshine, but he rated the numbers of the kids as smaller than usual, but that would be the sunshine because the kids were night workers.

He heard the rumble of many voices and – God's truth – laughter in the Amersham.

They were at the bunker wall. One window set in it, covered with thick wire mesh.

'You heard me, Mr Johnson? Just watching, brief, and not talking, ever. We're the past and he don't need us.'

425

'I heard you . . . See nothing, hear nothing and know nothing, that's me.'

He peered through the wire and the sounds – yelling, shouting, laughing – belted him, and Ivanhoe Manners's mouth was close to his ear.

'It's the kids he's getting on his side. Now it's basketball, earlier it might have been football, later it'll be the pool tables. See him, he's a natural. Me, I'm too old for them, and you. He's not that much younger than me, or you, but it's like he's lost years. There's more kids now, playing basketball with him, than I ever seen . . . You know what? Like now, he's always in shorts and his T-shirt has no sleeves. Why? Look there, the little pucker marks on the right thigh and shoulder. They're top credibility with the kids, bullet scars. Two bullet-holes, hardly healed over, they win respect – I didn't hear where he got them, or how . . . They don't know he was ever here, like he came out of nowhere. That enough for you?'

They walked away, left a basketball game behind a window.

Tony Johnson said, 'I'll see you around, Ivanhoe . . . Like you said, best left alone, because we're the past and of no use to him. Good to see him standing, finding himself. Look after yourself.'

He went to his car.

He knew where Malachy Kitchen had been, and the hell of that place, and the price paid . . . and he wished those who had put the man there could have stood with him, on tiptoe, and peered through a wire mesh and seen a man born again.

'The best practitioner currently working in the UK . . . quite simply
the most intelligent and accomplished'
Independent

'In a class of his own'
The Times

'One of the modern masters of the craft'
Daily Mail

'A master of the thriller set on the murky edges of modern war'

'A stylish writer'
Observer

'One of the most venerable names of the thriller genre'
Independent

'Richly imagined novels that bristle with authenticity'
Washington Post

'The dabbest hand in the industry . . . a master'
City AM

'The pace leaves you breathless . . . he is the master of the thriller
genre'
Edinburgh Evening News

Continue reading to find out more about the thrillers that have
earned Gerald Seymour the title of 'best thriller writer in the
world today' (*Telegraph*) . . .

THE CORPORAL'S WIFE

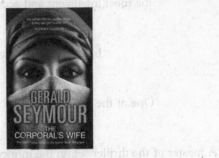

'Seymour is, quite simply, one of the finest thriller writers in England,
every bit the equal of Frederick Forsyth and Robert Harris.'
Daily Mail

A young woman determined to live her own life in an
oppressive society.

A rag-tag team of men sent to bring her out of it against all the odds.

THE CORPORAL'S WIFE is a hugely suspenseful thriller
about escaping one of the world's most explosive hostpots – Iran.
It is an epic, nail-biting story of courage and betrayal, a brilliant
glimpse into a closed society and the way the secret services
operate on both sides of the line between politics and morality.

'This is another masterly performance from an author whose
recent work turns individual spying missions into ambitious ensemble
dramas mixing action scenes and love stories with espionage.'
The Sunday Times

HODDER

THE OUTSIDERS

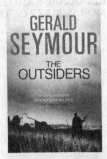

'Once again demonstrating his ability to probe the moral murkiness
of the spy trade and create an absorbingly diverse ensemble, Seymour crafts a
sophisticated, reader-teasing tale.'
The Sunday Times

MI5 officer Winnie Monks has never forgotten the death of a young
agent on her team at the hands of a former Russian Army Major-turned-gangster.
Ten years later, she hears the Major is travelling to a Spanish
villa and she asks permission to send in a surveillance unit.

There is an empty property next door, perfect to spy from – and as
a base for Winnie's darker, less official plans.

But this villa isn't deserted: the owners have invited a young British
couple to 'house sit' while they are away.

Jonno and Posie think they are embarking on a carefree holiday in the sun. But,
when the Secret Service arrives in paradise, everything changes.

'Those [Seymour] sends off into dangerous territory are, in fact, his
readers. With each book, we enter a dangerous universe, and are
totally involved with utterly plausible characters, faced with moral
choices that are rarely straightforward.'
Independent

HODDER

A DENIABLE DEATH

AN EPIC NOVEL OF HIGH COURAGE AND LOW CUNNING, OF LIFE
AND DEATH IN THE MORAL MAZE OF THE POST-9/11 WORLD.

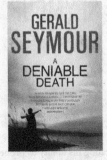

'Gerald Seymour is the grand-master of the contemporary thriller and
A DENIABLE DEATH is his greatest work yet. Gripping, revealing
and meticulously researched, this is a page-turning masterpiece that
will literally leave you breathless.'
Major Chris Hunter, bestselling author of *Extreme Risk*

YOU WATCH. YOU WAIT. THE HOURS SLIDE SLOWLY PAST.

A WHOLE DAY. THEN TWO.

YOU LIE UNDER A MERCILESS SUN IN A
MOSQUITO-INFESTED MARSH.

YOU CAN'T MOVE, LEAVE, OR RELAX.

YOUR MUSCLES ACHE FROM CLENCHING TIGHT FOR SO LONG.

IF YOU ARE DISCOVERED, YOU WILL BE TORTURED THEN KILLED.

AND HER MAJESTY'S GOVERNMENT WILL DENY ALL
KNOWLEDGE OF YOU.

'Great storytelling . . . you just have to read this novel . . . absolutely gripping.'
Eurocrime

HODDER

THE DEALER AND THE DEAD

THE ARMS DEALER BETRAYED THEM.
THE SURVIVORS WANT REVENGE.

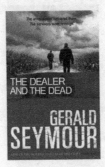

'*The Dealer and the Dead* is Seymour firing on all cylinders
and his rivals need, once again, to look to their laurels.'
Independent

In a moonlit field near the Serbian border, Croatian villagers waited for
an arms shipment that would never come. They will never forget that night,
or the slaughter that followed.

Eighteen years later, a body is discovered in a field, and with it the identity
of the arms dealer who betrayed them. Now the villagers can plot their revenge.

For Harvey Gillott, it was all a long time ago. But now the hand of the past
is reaching out across Europe, to Harvey's house in leafy England. And
it's holding a gun . . .

'The final scenes are brilliantly orchestrated . . . Without doubt, *The Dealer
and the Dead* is one of the finest thrillers to be published so far this year.'
Yorkshire Evening Post

HODDER

THE COLLABORATOR

CORRUPTION. BETRAYAL. REVENGE.

'A dense, intensely satisfying thriller from one of the modern masters
of the craft, Seymour's latest novel will remind the world just how
phenomenally accomplished a thriller writer he is.'
Daily Mail

Eddie Deacon has a new girlfriend. She's beautiful, clever and Italian.

And then she disappears.

What Eddie doesn't know is that Immacolata Borelli is the daughter of
a merciless Naples gangster. She can no longer live with her conscience and
has decided to collaborate with the police to bring down her own family.

But the Borellis will not lose their empire without a fight. They will use
or destroy anything and anyone to prevent her from talking.

Including Eddie.

'Tight writing and meticulous research . . . Seymour paints the streets
of Naples and their dark denizens with an artist's brush that lingers equally
on the grime, the glitter and the blood.'
The Times

HODDER

HARRY'S GAME

THE ICONIC THRILLER BY THE GRAND-MASTER OF THE CRAFT

THE MASTERPIECE THAT MADE HIS NAME
IN A NEW EDITION WITH FOREWORD BY ROBERT HARRIS

'Absorbing from beginning to end . . . the sort of book
that makes you lose track of time.'
New York Times

A British cabinet minister is gunned down on a London street by an IRA assassin.
In the wake of national outcry, the authorities must find the hitman. But the trail is
long cold, the killer gone to ground in Belfast, and they must resort to more unor-
thodox methods to unearth him. Ill-prepared and poorly briefed, undercover agent
Harry Brown is sent into the heart of enemy territory to infiltrate the terrorists.

But when it is a race against the clock, mistakes are made and corners cut. For
Harry Brown, alone in a city of strangers, where an intruder is the subject of immediate gossip and rumour, one false move is enough to leave him fatally isolated.

'Evokes the atmosphere and smell of the back streets of Belfast
as nothing else I have ever read.'
Frederick Forsyth

'A tough thriller, vibrant with suspense.'
Evening Standard

'Devastatingly good . . . you can smell the mean streets where the terrorists hide.'
Spectator

'First rate . . . Edge-of-the-seat reading.'
Washington Post

H
HODDER